"With attention to detail and a narrative style that draws one in, Jill Eileen Smith brings the b[...] [...] life. I find her works thoroughly [...] my highest recommendation as a [...]

Kim Vogel Sa[...]

"*Bathsheba* is a wonderful illumination of David and Bathsheba's story, ultimately one of redemption and restoration with Adonai. The historical detail drew me in as much as the vivid emotional drama, making this biblical account one that will stay with me forever."

Maureen Lang, author of *The Oak Leaves* and the Great War series

"*Bathsheba* is Jill Eileen Smith's finest work to date. It vividly portrays the devastation caused by selfish passion and betrayal, and the incredible blessing of repentance and restoration through God's grace. Readers will savor this final chapter of the Wives of King David."

Jill Stengl, award-winning author of *Wisconsin Brides*

"This well-researched and beautifully crafted story will resonate in your heart and mind long after you've read the final page. With beauty and truth, Jill Eileen Smith will take you back in time to reveal the consequences of sin coupled with the depth of God's grace and forgiveness. An excellent read with a message that transcends time."

Judith Miller, author of the Daughters of Amana series

"Jill Eileen Smith has written a beautiful, poignant tale about one of the most well-known women in the Bible. Bathsheba's story is complex and deftly handled, a fitting end to Smith's acclaimed Wives of King David series. Highly recommended."

Kathleen Fuller, author of *A Summer Secret*, *A Hand to Hold*, and *The Secrets Beneath*

BOOKS BY JILL EILEEN SMITH

THE WIVES OF KING DAVID

Michal

Abigail

Bathsheba

THE WIVES *of* KING DAVID, BOOK 3

BATHSHEBA

A NOVEL

Jill Eileen Smith

Revell

a division of Baker Publishing Group
Grand Rapids, Michigan

© 2011 by Jill Eileen Smith

Published by Revell
a division of Baker Publishing Group
P.O. Box 6287, Grand Rapids, MI 49516-6287
www.revellbooks.com

Printed in the United States of America

Library of Congress Cataloging-in-Publication Data
Smith, Jill Eileen, 1958–
    Bathsheba : a novel / Jill Eileen Smith.
      p.   cm. — (The wives of King David ; 3)
    ISBN 978-0-8007-3322-3 (pbk.)
    1. Bathsheba (Biblical figure)—Fiction. 2. David, King of Israel—Fiction. 3. Israel—Kings and rulers—Fiction. 4. Women in the Bible—Fiction. I. Title.
PS3619.M58838B37 2011
813'.6—dc22   2010043442

This is a work of historical reconstruction; the appearance of certain historical figures is therefore inevitable. All other characters, however, are products of the author's imagination, and any resemblance to actual persons, living or dead, is coincidental.

Published in association with the Books & Such Literary Agency, Wendy Lawton, Central Valley Office, P.O. Box 1227, Hilmar, CA 95324. wendy@booksandsuch.biz

11 12 13 14 15 16 17   7 6 5 4 3 2 1

To Mom and Dad:
I couldn't ask for more supportive or loving parents.

Mom,
you nurtured my love of books from the earliest days.
I can still see you with a book in one hand and a spoon
stirring whatever was on the stove in the other. You always
listened and supported even my far-fetched dreams.
Deep down, I think you're a writer at heart.

Dad,
you were always there for me, standing on the sidelines,
cheering my achievements. Your example, your faith, has
made me want to live to make you proud. I know if you
could, you would read every word I've written.
Just knowing you love me is enough.

PART I

These are the names of David's mighty men. . . . Among the Thirty were . . . Eliam son of Ahithophel the Gilonite . . . and Uriah the Hittite. There were thirty-seven in all.

2 Samuel 23:8, 24, 34, 39

Ahithophel was the king's counselor. Hushai the Arkite was the king's friend.

1 Chronicles 27:33

And one said, Is not this Bathsheba, the daughter of Eliam, the wife of Uriah the Hittite?

2 Samuel 11:3 KJV

1

Jerusalem, 994 BC

Darkness curtained the sky, hiding the stars, sheltering Bathsheba in the inner courtyard of her home. She clutched the soft linen towel to her chest, shivering, while Uriah stood with his back to her, a sentry guarding her privacy.

"Of course you must do this, but hurry, dear wife." His mischievous tone heated her blood. Suddenly the chilly spring breeze seeping from her bare feet to the rest of her robe-draped body didn't seem quite so cold.

"Yes, husband. Would you like to help?" Her tone teased him, and she took courage from his own playful manner. She had Tirzah, her maid, to pour the water over her head, but if he was in such a hurry to be with her . . .

He turned to face her, his dark eyes pools of interest. She had never suggested such a thing before. Tirzah always helped her do this. It was a woman's place, a woman's ritual. Would his strict adherence to the law of Moses let him help her? Did she want him to?

She pulled the robe tighter about her, watching him. He seemed to be assessing her question, and she knew him well enough to know he was thinking through every purification law and tradition to determine whether such a thing was proper before Adonai.

"We would defeat the purpose, Bathsheba," he said at last. "Though if Tirzah were not available to help . . . I am your husband, after all." Gentleness filled his expression, his eyes revealing how much he longed to do as she asked.

"It is a sacred moment." She looked into his face as he took a step closer. "To remind a woman she is set apart unto God, and for her husband alone." She placed a hand on his arm, seeing him warm to the thought.

"The law of Moses—it would allow for such a thing?" He rubbed a hand over his beard, the thought clearly troubling. He worked so hard to obey the law . . . If only he could relax and not take every jot, every little word, so strictly. But even after three years of marriage, she trod carefully in matters of the law lest she be party to his guilt. Guilt that was not worth the price of carelessness.

"I don't know," she said at last, stroking his cheek with her hand. "Until we do, Tirzah will help me. I will hurry." She smiled at the relief in his eyes and moved quickly to the bronze basin he had purchased for her own private use. She set the towel on the stone bench beside it, and slipped the robe from her shoulders, listening to his sigh.

"I will ask Jozadak in the morning." The lame Levite tutor Uriah paid to teach him the law would spend many hours seeking an answer to Uriah's question.

She glanced at him, his back now turned to her, the well-muscled body evident beneath a tan linen tunic. He was an intelligent, handsome man, and she marveled at his constant questions, his determination to learn the ways of her people.

"Are you ready, mistress?" Tirzah interrupted her musings, pulling her thoughts back to their purpose here. Distraction was too easy with Uriah nearby. The water in the basin sparkled with the night's chill, making her shiver again. Tirzah rested the jar on her shoulder, waiting.

Bathsheba pulled the comb from her hair, letting the length of it fall to her back, the thick tresses covering her like a cloak. She stepped into the basin and knelt, the frigid water prickling her flesh. She sucked in a quick breath as Tirzah poured the first stream of cool water over her head.

She took the hyssop from Tirzah's outstretched hand and rubbed her arms and legs, then wrapped both arms about her, bracing herself again. Tirzah lifted the water and poured a second stream over Bathsheba's head until it touched every part of her body. The shock of the cold and drenching water caused her to look up, to gaze heavenward. Her heart constricted with this gentle reminder of her need to be pure before Yahweh—something she could not do during her time of uncleanness. She bowed her head, praying her humility would grant her favor in His eyes. Would her night in Uriah's arms bring about the child they both craved?

She closed her eyes as Tirzah poured the water a third time. Shame filled her, her heart as bare before the Lord as her glistening skin. *Oh, Adonai, I am in need of You, a sinner at birth, unable to keep Your perfect law. Wash me and I will be clean, whiter than snow.*

The words, once a memorized tradition she had learned to quote by rote as a girl in her father's house, had become personal in recent months. A sense of unworthiness filled her, a stark reminder that her uncleanness must be atoned for.

She let the last of the water drain into the basin and lifted shaky hands toward the heavens, tears mingling with the moisture dripping from her hair. *Forgive me, Adonai.* She knew a sacrifice must be given to know true forgiveness, but her heart longed for it just the same. Perhaps it would be enough to acquire God's favor this night.

She stepped out of the bath and snatched the towel from the bench, drying her skin along with her tears. Slipping her arms through the sleeves of her robe again, she hurried into Uriah's outstretched arms.

❧

Bathsheba rose from the bed, careful not to awaken Uriah. He shifted at her movement, and she stilled, looking down on his contented form. His chest rose and fell in a slow rhythmic pattern, his breath even and soft. The dark hairs of his neck curled beneath his night tunic and met the edges of his beard. She felt a blush fill her cheeks as she lingered, remembering, longing to keep him with her. But they had only two more nights together before he left again for many months. On the third night he would sleep in another room, refusing any intimate touch in preparation for war. Something she could never understand and could not bring herself to accept. The days spent marching to the place of battle should give him plenty of time to become pure. Why did he have to start before he even left her side?

She sighed, felt along the wall for the clay lamp where it sat in its niche in the wall, then grasped it with one hand and slipped from the room. She padded softly through the dark halls toward the cooking room, where embers were banked in the clay oven, sufficient to spark a flame and light her lamp. She moved to the jar of oil and replenished the bowl to keep the light from going out. The lamp illumined the room where the servants would soon set the bread to baking and prepare the foods Uriah would take to break his morning fast. He always rose before dawn, ate quickly, then hurried to the tent where the ark stood, in time for the first trumpet's sound. One more way he showed his devotion to Adonai. Or perhaps he thought somehow his actions would win the Lord's favor . . .

Banishing the thought, she sat on the end of a long wooden bench and rested her elbows on the smooth table, trying to stifle a yawn to no avail. She never slept well before Uriah left for war, and she couldn't decide if it was missing him that troubled her most or the fear of losing him to an enemy arrow. She searched her mind, wishing she could stop the fear, but exhaustion kept the worry always on the fringes, clinging when she wished she could release it like chaff blown away with the wind.

What was wrong with her?

"Trouble sleeping again?" Tirzah appeared at the threshold of the cooking room, her own lamp in hand, her hair disheveled in a tangled mess. She stepped closer and took a seat at Bathsheba's side. She placed a hand on Bathsheba's shoulder, patting it softly.

Tears pricked Bathsheba's eyes. Exhaustion made her emotional, something Uriah seemed at a loss to handle. So she'd taken to hiding her feelings from him when she could. He was good at drawing them out of her when the mood was right, when he felt especially considerate.

"Worried again?" Tirzah stood and retrieved a flask of wine, pouring some into a clay cup. She handed it to Bathsheba and sat beside her. "Drink."

Bathsheba obeyed as she used to do when Tirzah had cared for her as a child, though the woman had not been all that old herself at the time her father bought her to tend his motherless child. She swiped her eyes. "Yes. I can't seem to help myself."

Tirzah smoothed her rumpled hair, then leaned an elbow against the table. "I think it's time for you to be honest, mistress."

Bathsheba's stomach fluttered, the sensation strongly resembling dread. "Honest? You think I would lie to you about something?"

"I think you would lie to yourself. To your husband. Me, you would avoid." She smiled, the lamplight casting strange shapes over her round face.

Bathsheba turned away, not liking the direction the conversation had taken. "I have nothing to lie about." She scanned the walls and ceiling of the room, listening to the scratching sound of field mice somewhere in the shadowed corners. Despite their efforts to keep the food high and away and the room swept, the creatures always managed to find some reason to invade the house. She lifted her feet beneath the bench on instinct, shuddering.

"I think . . ." Tirzah paused as if weighing whether she should continue. "I think you are lonely, perhaps even angry." She held Bathsheba's gaze for a suspended moment.

"If I am lonely, it is only because he's gone more than he's home, and I have no child to take his place. Any woman would feel the same." She took another sip from the cup, feeling the warmth of the wine move through her.

"There are things you could do to fill his absence. The poor always need attending and there are garments to be made. Perhaps your Aunt Talia could advise you?" Tirzah leaned

14

away from her, placing both hands on her knees. "She might have something for you to do."

"My aunt can't keep my bed warm at night. I don't sleep well when Uriah is away." Tirzah's compassionate look made Bathsheba regret her sharp tone. "I'm sorry. I didn't mean to snap." She toyed with her cup, then finished the last of the wine. "My aunt also has Chava's child—soon to be children—to help care for. And Rei just married a wife and they live with Aunt Talia. It is easy for her to feel worthy with so much to keep her occupied."

"You feel unworthy, mistress? Whatever for?" Tirzah moved close to Bathsheba again, the lamp between them.

Bathsheba shifted, the familiar shame filling her, adding to the emotion she could not hold in check. "A married woman without a child—there is no value in such a person. What worth is my life, my marriage, if I cannot give Uriah an heir to carry on the Hittite line? I should be helping to build his house, not live as an ornament within it." She glanced toward the door to the cooking room and lowered her voice, though the hour was too early for other servants to be about. "I fear he may take another wife if I don't conceive soon. He has his honor."

Tirzah gave a disgusted grunt but quickly looked about her as though afraid the walls had ears. "The master is as much to blame as you, mistress. If you count up the months he is gone, they would amount to more than half of every year. How can he give you a son in such conditions? You know this." She muttered something under her breath.

"What did you say?" Bathsheba leaned closer. "Tell me."

"I would rather not repeat the word I used, mistress." She looked chagrined, and Bathsheba smiled. "Men are all alike.

They put the blame on the woman when they ought to know better."

Bathsheba couldn't stop a soft laugh. "In this I will agree. But you know men would not begin to take the blame for such a thing." She set the cup on the table. "Uriah is attentive . . . when he is here." She couldn't help defending him, despite her irritation. He was a good man, a loyal husband. A bit overbearing where the law was concerned sometimes, but nothing she couldn't live with. He was honorable to the core, and she respected him for it.

Besides, it did no good to complain about war or to wish Uriah worked a trade instead of commanding a company of men always ready to do the king's bidding. She couldn't change Uriah or the king or the ever-present need to do battle with Israel's enemies. What she wouldn't give for a solid year of peace. But that wasn't likely to come any time soon if her father and Uriah were to be believed.

Tirzah yawned. "After the master leaves for the field, we will visit your aunt. Regardless of what you say, perhaps she can help." She patted Bathsheba's arm. "I'm going back to my pallet. Try to rest."

Bathsheba nodded, comforted by the servant's ability to take over and make sense of any situation. She watched Tirzah walk away, the fear of loneliness not quite so tangible now. If she could have been completely honest with Tirzah, she would have admitted that it was indeed the loneliness that worried her the most. She didn't want to end up a widow with no one to love her. Uriah did love her, didn't he? But his loyalty to her was not undivided. When the king called, he always answered.

2

The sun had clearly risen, the city fully awakened now as Uriah stepped into his courtyard, the memory of worship before the ark still fresh. He enjoyed the reading of the law, the reminder of all that God required of a man. The purification rites he accepted easily as well, but the daily sacrifices . . . He would never understand how the God of the Hebrews could accept the blood of a ram to pay for the sins of a man. If the man sinned, he ought to pay for his own sins.

Still . . . were his sins keeping the God of the Hebrews from granting his wife a child? Was he paying for them in the loss of his first wife and now the barrenness of his second? Or was Bathsheba's barrenness her own fault? The thought troubled him whenever the call to war drew near and her emotions grew frayed. Her tears made him weak, helpless, with no way to comfort her. He had offered plenty of prayers and petitions on her behalf. What more could a man do?

He crossed the court and entered the house, expecting to be met by his manservant, Anittas. But it was Bathsheba who sat on the couch opposite the door, watching him. He paused as she stood and moved closer. When she drew near enough to touch, he took both of her hands in his.

"You don't usually greet me like this." He gave her a smile, hoping to coax one from her in return. She offered him a weak response, her strained expression snuffing the effort.

"I had hoped to spend time with you today." Her soft voice sounded uncertain, though the words were not spoken as a question. "We could go for a walk to the Gihon Spring. The brook is so lovely, and I thought . . ." She looked up, her gaze earnest, transparent. "I need you," she whispered.

His heart stirred as it always did when she looked at him that way. She was beautiful beyond imagination. Not even the king's wives could compare. But Joab, the army commander, had called a meeting of the Thirty to commence before the sun rose full in the sky. He glanced at the shadows along the wall.

"There is not enough time. I'm expected at the palace soon."

Her face took on an expression he couldn't quite define. "Is there time then to visit the market? I hear a caravan from Damascus has just arrived. We wouldn't have to buy anything." She looked at him then, her eyes hopeful.

"What purpose is there in going to market if you have nothing to purchase?" Surely a day's work was enough to keep a woman occupied without needless sightseeing.

"For the pleasure of seeing new things from far away." She quirked her head, a frown wreathing her face as though she thought he had no sense whatsoever.

He studied her for a brief moment, then glanced at the shadows again. "We'll have to hurry."

Her smile deepened and a sense of relief filled her gaze. "Let me get my cloak."

While her servant helped her into her cloak and sandals, Uriah walked to the back of the house in search of Anittas. "There you are." The old servant had been with him since he was a child, faithful through the deaths of his parents and his first wife. The man had understood Uriah's need to keep Bathsheba safe, lest Uriah suffer yet another loss.

"Master Uriah. How was your visit to the tabernacle today?" Anittas tucked a clay tablet and thin stylus into a leather pouch at his side, then adjusted the cloak more securely about his neck.

"The visits are always the same, Anittas. You know this."

The man was shorter and stockier than Uriah, his thick arms strong despite his age, which was not quite as old as Uriah's father would have been, but old enough for Uriah to think of him as such. Bathsheba would be in good hands when he left for war.

"I am headed to your storehouse to give you an accounting before you leave," Anittas said as the two walked together toward the front of the house. "Is there something else you need me to do today, master?"

Uriah stopped before they neared the courtyard where Bathsheba waited. Anittas turned to look at him.

"I am worried about my wife, Anittas. I fear her moods when I leave for war are growing worse with each passing year."

"She needs a child."

"Would that she had one." Didn't God give life? Perhaps a blood sacrifice would help. "In the meantime, I want you to make sure she has plenty to do while I am away. Don't allow her time to sulk."

"I'll do my best, my lord, but the servants cannot replace you. She grieves when you are gone."

Anittas's words stung. Did the man blame him for the work he did? "I cannot stay home from war just to please my wife."

"Of course not, my lord. We will do all in our power to keep Mistress Bathsheba content." Anittas glanced toward the courtyard and Uriah followed his gaze. Bathsheba stood in the arch of the door, her profile stunning even beneath the folds of her clothing. He sucked in a breath. The woman was unaware of her ability to tempt a man. How had he managed to wed such a magnificent creature?

"There is nothing else. I trust you to oversee my household while I am away." Uriah gave Anittas a dismissive nod, then took long strides toward the courtyard.

Bathsheba smiled at Uriah's approach. He took hold of her elbow when he reached her side and gently turned her toward the street. "Come." He released his hold as they stepped onto the cobbled pavement and walked one step ahead of her. When they moved to a wider road, he slowed, motioning for her to catch up to him. He intertwined their fingers, then moved forward, his pace rushed.

They walked in silence, past the homes of their neighbors, until they reached the area of the merchants. The scents of camels and animal dung mixed with the aromas of exotic spices and honeyed sweetmeats. Bright-colored tapestries, ivory, copper, precious stones, silver-coined headdresses, and striped shawls and scarves filled overcrowded stalls. Nearby merchants haggled with the caravan master for the best prices for their wares.

Bathsheba let Uriah lead her to the side of the throng, taking in the strange markings and garments of the Damascus travelers. The men's hair and beards were short, their mustaches trimmed, unlike the Hebrews who did not shave the corners of their hair or beards. Interest piqued, she longed to move closer, but Uriah's hand at the small of her back propelled her down a side alley where the crowds were thin. He took her hand again and tugged her forward. She attempted to speak but could not concentrate on anything besides keeping up with him, making sure her feet did not stumble.

"My lord, please," she finally managed when he stopped at a bend in the road and had turned her to go back the way they had come. "Can we not stop to look at what the merchants have brought?" She wanted a moment with him to enjoy the sights together, but he seemed on a mission to get through the whole ordeal in quick progression.

He looked at her and then glanced at the sky. "I told you we didn't have much time, my love." He bent closer and cupped her cheek with his hand. "I'm sorry, but we have to head back soon."

She nodded, not trusting her voice, not willing for him to see anything but pleasure in her gaze. Apparently satisfied, he took her hand again and moved them through the crowd. They reached the camels still piled high with wares, where a Bedouin was in the process of unloading one of the packs from the animal's side. A jewel-bedecked woman, in sweeping robes of black and red and yellow, moved beside the man, the fringe of her sleeves swaying as she lifted a leather pouch from his hands. She pulled a string of multicolored scarves from the bag and draped them across her arm, the fine linen appearing as soft as the petals of a flower.

Bathsheba slowed and Uriah caught her eye. He faced the woman. "How much?" He fingered a delicate scarf, and Bathsheba feared the threads would catch on his roughened hands. The blues and reds in varying shades were beautiful.

"Three shekels."

"Too much." Uriah released his hold and took a step forward. "It is worth half a shekel, no more."

The woman touched his arm. "The pattern is a work of art."

Bathsheba's breath held as he eyed the woman. "One shekel."

The woman's mouth quirked, but her sharp eyes held his. "Two."

"One and a half."

"Done." She pulled the scarf from the others and placed it in his hands. He turned and draped it over Bathsheba's head, smiling, then paid the woman and hurried on.

She nearly tripped trying to keep up. When they were past the merchants' stalls, his pace increased, and she half ran, half walked until they reached the safety of their courtyard.

He glanced at the sky as though fearful he would be late, then bent to kiss her cheek. "I must go." He turned and walked quickly away.

"Back so soon, mistress?"

Tirzah's welcome voice soothed Bathsheba's frustration. What had she expected? She knew he could not, would not, miss a military strategy meeting called by his captain, especially this close to war. Never mind that the men could strategize on the field all they wanted, once they arrived. Why did Joab have to take up her husband's time when she had so little of it left?

Tears blurred her vision. She grasped the scarf to dry them, then looked more carefully at the fabric her husband had spontaneously purchased for her.

"It's beautiful," Tirzah said, coming up alongside her. "Tell me what it was like. Were the goods from Damascus so different from what we have here?" She guided Bathsheba to the bench and retrieved the water jar to wash her feet.

Bathsheba sat obediently and pulled the scarf from her head, examining the fine work and the intricate leaf design, so small and delicate. She'd missed it from where she'd stood while Uriah bargained for the piece. The work must have taken much time to produce, many patient hours of stitching. Perhaps she could learn to duplicate such work.

"Your thoughts are far away." Tirzah lifted her foot and undid the dusty sandal.

Bathsheba looked at her maid, breathing deeply, trying to suppress her jagged emotions. "There isn't much to tell. Uriah rushed me through the stalls. We only stopped long enough to purchase this." She ran her fingers over the scarf again. "I had to almost run to keep up with him."

"You resent him rushing you."

Tirzah read her thoughts too easily. Sometimes the thought annoyed her. But the truth was hard to ignore. "I resent Joab for demanding so much of him. I resent the king for sending his men to war. I resent Uriah for always going." She glanced around her, relieved when she saw no other servants milling about.

"Perhaps this war will end quickly." Tirzah used a soft cloth and bit of soap to wash the dirt from between Bathsheba's toes.

Bathsheba jerked and pulled back, wriggling her foot, both liking and disliking the ticklish sensation. "Be careful."

"Sorry." Tirzah smiled. She was twelve years older than Bathsheba, a pleasant-looking woman despite uneven teeth and a slightly crooked nose. Her dark hair was piled high beneath a plain, light brown cloth, and her sturdy hands had seen much use. "You can hardly blame the king for declaring war on the Ammonites—not after what they did to his messengers, his own son among them."

"I know. I understand the need. I just hate that Uriah has to be part of it all. Why can't someone else go?"

She was pouting now and she knew it. If she were in the king's place, she would have done the same thing. The audacity of the king of Ammon! King David had meant only to console the man after the death of his father, and the foreign king had disdained David's messengers, cutting their beards in half and chopping their garments off at the buttocks. The tale had gone out throughout the kingdom and was still gossiped about in the streets.

"Can you imagine how those men felt?" Tirzah asked. "They say Amnon, the king's heir, is still angry that his father did not act sooner." Tirzah rinsed Bathsheba's foot and dried it with a soft piece of linen, then reached for the other foot.

"I think the king is to be commended for giving the Ammonites the chance to repent and make amends." If her husband, father, and grandfather were to be believed, King David hadn't fully decided on war until he'd heard the Ammonites had gathered mercenary armies for battle against Israel. He'd offered King Hanun the chance to apologize. "Though I can see why Amnon would be angry. He must have been humiliated."

"They all were." Tirzah scrubbed Bathsheba's other foot, the tickling sensation again making Bathsheba jump.

"Are you trying to irritate me?" She scowled at her maid.

"Of course not, mistress." But the twinkle in her eye made Bathsheba deepen her scowl. "Come now, mistress. You need cheering up a little." She smiled again, her actions more careful this time. Bathsheba cautiously relaxed. "You really cannot blame the prince. His father should be grooming him as his heir, but everyone knows the king favors Absalom. They say Amnon only took the assignment to gain his father's favor. Then look what happened." Tirzah dried Bathsheba's foot and strained the water through a cloth to pour back into the jar. Water in Israel was too precious to waste.

Bathsheba looked up at the palace walls that rose above her, a stone's throw behind their house. What made a father, a king, favor one son over the other? Did King David prefer the son because he loved the mother? Did he love Absalom's mother? Court gossip said no. The king's affections rested mostly with Abigail, but her son, Chileab, was not fit to be king, and her second child had been a girl. Perhaps this third one, soon due to be delivered, would bring another son. Would that change the favor of Absalom in the king's eyes?

"I think it would be hard to be a son of a king." Bathsheba couldn't tear her gaze from the gleaming white stones of the king's home.

"Or his wife," Tirzah added as she moved to drape the cloth over a low rail to dry. "You are fortunate your grandfather did not have his way in this, mistress. You could have been married to the king and forced to share him, or to Amnon and forced to deal with his hurt and anger. It's a sad woman who must share the love of a man, particularly a king."

Bathsheba met Tirzah's gaze. "If Father would not give me to Rei because of our age difference, he would never have agreed to Amnon. We are more than four years apart."

"Your grandfather would not have cared. In royal circles, age does not matter." Tirzah offered Bathsheba a hand and helped her to her feet.

"I imagine you are right." Though a part of her wondered.

Would a king's wife have any less time with her husband than Bathsheba had with hers? Loneliness could be found in warriors' homes as well as in kings' palaces.

She released a pent-up breath and walked from the court-yard to the open door, fingering the scarf Uriah had given her. "Find me some fabric. I want to see if I can duplicate these stitches."

3

Uriah took his place among the Thirty beside Bathsheba's father Eliam, a step below the raised benches reserved for the king's advisors. Joab and Abishai, the king's nephews and chief army commanders; Hushai the Archite; and Bathsheba's grandfather Ahithophel were among the king's chief counselors, along with the oldest of King David's sons. Only Amnon, heir apparent to the throne, was missing.

"Amnon's beard should have filled in by now," Eliam said to the man beside him. "He should be here, supporting the troops."

"I hear tell the king tried to get him to come, but he refused," the man responded.

"That's not what I heard," another said. "I heard the king told the prince to stay away as long as he likes."

"Why would he do that? His presence here would unite us, and he might know something useful." Eliam stiffened, his tone brittle.

"Joab has already gotten anything useful out of the man. We don't need him here."

The first man's words pricked the hair on Uriah's neck. He leaned across Eliam to confront him. "We need him here to remind us of what the Ammonites deserve. They will pay in blood for what they did to the prince's honor, to the king, and to Israel."

The blast of a trumpet silenced a follow-up remark, but Uriah leaned back, satisfied at the shocked look on the man's face. Uriah stood and bowed low with the rest of the Thirty as the king followed his flag bearers and took his seat on his gilded dais, surrounded by guards. The king's ornate throne stood in his audience chamber, but in this military planning room, a raised golden seat held him in highest honor over all—something his men were quick to remember. Joab and Abishai made sure of it.

David's guard Benaiah stood to the side of the king, arms folded, his sword strapped to his side, the king's approval evident in the golden insignia given to the Thirty showing brightly on his dark cloak. Uriah touched his own pendant and sat straighter, proud of the king's approval, pleased with his own military prowess. He would be honored to guard the king as Benaiah did—a silent sentinel of protection, an imposing figure. Perhaps in time . . . He looked now to the king, who sat rigid in his seat, hands gripping the arms of his chair.

"The Ammonites have been among those whom the Lord has told us not to provoke or harass because their land has been given to Lot's descendants as an inheritance from Yahweh." The room fell silent at the king's words. "Keeping this law has always been my intent, as you well know, and why I secured an alliance of peace with Nahash, king of Ammon.

"But as it happens, Ammon is the one doing the provoking. I'm sure you are all aware of the news, but in case any of you had your heads in the sand or were too busy to pay attention, Jehoshaphat son of Ahilud will read the message received from the men I sent to console Hanun, king of the Ammonites, on the death of his father, Nahash." David nodded to Jehoshaphat, then folded his arms across his chest, the sleeves of his royal cloak hanging below the golden belt at his waist.

Jehoshaphat stood and removed a clay tablet from the folds of soft lambskin. A short, stocky man with thick hair and brows that nearly touched as he squinted, he pulled the tablet closer to read. He cleared his throat.

> My lord King David, greetings. From your servant Amnon, son of David, from the city of Jericho.

Uriah leaned closer, his gaze on the king, not wishing to miss his reaction. The king's response often told them how best to proceed, the look in his eyes their instant command.

> The nine men you sent with me are also here. We did as you requested and went to give our condolences in your name to the king, Hanun of the Ammonites. Hanun allowed us into his presence, but rather than receive us with the honor due to your name, my lord, his nobles soured his mind against us. They said to Hanun, "Do you think David is honoring your father by sending men to you to express sympathy? Hasn't David sent them to you to explore the city and spy it out and overthrow it?"
>
> So Hanun listened to his men and seized us in front of the entire court. We would have fought back save for the sharp blade held to our throats. Against our wills, to our utter humiliation, Hanun's men shaved off half of each man's beard, then cut off our garments at the buttocks and made us walk out of his palace and through the streets to the city gate, exposing us most thoroughly. Now show us what we should do, for your men are greatly humiliated, and Hanun's actions should not go unpunished.

Jehoshaphat sat down, and silence fell over the group, broken only by the men's heated breath. All eyes were on the king. Uriah felt a fire burn in his belly, imagining again what he would do to Hanun given the chance. He watched the king's face darken, his eyes smoldering embers.

The king straightened, hands grabbing the arms of his seat once again, his gaze hard, piercing. He spat onto the tiles at his feet, then stood. "I immediately sent messengers to keep the men at Jericho until their beards grew back. They returned several days ago and gave me a full report, confirming Amnon's words." He looked over the group of trusted men, his intent clear. "Hanun has become dung in my nostrils this day, and he will rue the day he ever heard the name of David, king of Israel." He looked at Joab, whose eager eyes blazed fire. "The army is ready?"

"Ready to leave at your command, my lord."

The king sat again and looked from Joab to his counselors. "What else should we know?"

Ahithophel raised a hand and David acknowledged him. "There is word that Hanun has hired the Syrians of Beth Rehob and the Syrians of Zoba—twenty thousand foot soldiers. And one thousand men from the king of Maacah, and twelve thousand men from Ish-Tob for reinforcements. He has heard of your anger and is preparing to engage us."

"Let them come," Joab said. "We have defeated every enemy up until now. The Ammonites and the Syrians will also bow to us, or they will fare worse than the men of Moab." A cheer went up from the captains and the thirty mighty men, but quickly dissipated at a wave of the king's hand.

He turned to Jehoshaphat, who held an ink-dipped reed in his hand above a scroll, recording David's every word. "Send a message to Hanun, king of Ammon. Greet him in my name and say, 'You have become a stench in my nostrils.'" His gaze lifted, taking in the room with a sweeping glance, coming to rest again on Joab. "We leave in three days."

❦

David strode the halls from the military room to his audience chamber, his blood still pumping hot and fast. Hanun would pay for his abuse, his insolence. Hanun's father, Nahash, would have been mortified if he knew what had happened, and David still felt a hint of sorrow that the son was nothing like the father. Peace would have been far better than yet another war. Perhaps he was getting too old to fight, though many of his warriors were not much younger.

He stopped at the entrance to the chamber, waiting for his trumpeters and flag bearers to announce his coming. Hurried footsteps came from behind, and he turned to watch as Benaiah and his guards intercepted whoever it was.

"I must speak with the king at once." David recognized the voice of Hannah, the women's overseer. Her alarmed tone jolted him from thoughts of the Ammonites. He moved through his bevy of guards.

"What is it, Hannah?"

She bowed low at the waist, then quickly raised her head. "My lord, you must come at once. I'm afraid we are losing your wife Abigail."

Her words rocked him, and he planted his scepter more firmly on the ground, steadying himself. He couldn't lose Abigail. The shock of the thought brought a rush of memory. He had nearly lost her with Chileab's birth.

"How can this be? Is her time upon her then?" Why wasn't he told sooner?

Hannah nodded her graying head, turning slightly away from him as if motioning for him to follow. "Please, my lord. Her pains came upon her suddenly this morning. I'm afraid it is not going well with her. The babe has come, but Abigail is very weak."

"The babe has come—that is a good thing." Chileab had taken days to come forth. Surely Hannah exaggerated. But by the look in her eyes, David dismissed the thought. "Take me to her."

His strides matched the rapid pounding of his heart, his mind berating him with every step. He couldn't be losing her. She had assured him after Anna's birth that it would be safe to allow for more children. Chileab had been the only exception, and even from his birth she had recovered, in time. He should not have listened to her. Should never have promised to keep from taking more wives. More wives would have given him sons while preserving the life of the one wife he held most dear.

Abigail.

He stopped at the threshold of her apartment, following Hannah's lead. Benaiah halted one step behind him. The door was slightly ajar, and David placed one hand on the carved cedarwood to push it open, but the cries coming from inside the room arrested his movement.

"Don't go, Abigail. Your children need you. The king needs you."

David shoved the door open and strode forward. Servants hovered nearby, and the palace physician stood, using a pestle to mix herbs in a small clay bowl. The man poured the concoction into a silver cup, and the midwife lifted Abigail's head to help her drink. Michal sat in a corner, holding a newborn infant in her arms.

"My lord," the physician said softly, then backed away, allowing David the space at Abigail's side.

But he didn't want an audience. He wanted time alone with his favored wife. Time to hold her, to coax her to live. "Is there anything more to be done for her?" he asked the physician. At the man's shake of his head, David glanced at Benaiah. "Clear the room."

His command was met with soft gasps coming from several of the women. This was not what they expected, but the servants hurried to obey him.

Michal rose slowly from her seat, carrying Abigail's child. She paused near him as though expecting him to say something, to acknowledge her somehow, but he could not bring himself to speak to her. Not while Abigail seemed to be nearing her last breath.

Ignoring her, he glanced at Benaiah, who moved to escort Michal from the room. The guard stepped outside the door to prevent anyone else from entering and interrupting.

Relieved to at last be alone with Abigail, David stepped forward and knelt at her side, taking her limp hand in his, his heart thudding slow and thick as though he were dying with her. He drew a breath. Another. Swallowed hard against the grit in his throat.

"Abigail. Beloved. Don't leave me. I need you." He bent close to her ear and kissed her damp cheek, then fingered the sweat-soaked tendrils of her hair. "Oh, beloved . . . please."

She stirred, her eyes flickering open, their dark hues now glazed, feverish. But a soft smile lifted the edges of her cracked, dry mouth. "David." She whispered his name like a caress, making his heart constrict further. "You have another daughter, my lord." She closed her eyes as she spoke, and he sensed the effort to speak had cost her dearly. Her breathing came in slow, uneven paces.

"I'm sure our daughter is beautiful, beloved. Like her mother." He drew in a ragged breath, fighting the urge to break down and weep. He stroked her hand instead, kissing each finger. He placed a hand on her brow, her cheeks, then reached for a cloth and dipped it into a bowl of water. He wrung it out and placed it over her forehead, each movement careful, accompanied by silent, pleading prayers.

Please, Adonai, don't take my Abigail.

"Do you remember when I promised not to take more wives, and the night I said I wished I'd married only you?" When she didn't respond, he hurried on, needing to speak whether she could hear him or not. "I meant what I said, beloved. But our life together isn't over. Our daughter needs you to raise her to be a woman who loves Yahweh like you do. As you've taught Anna and Chileab to do . . ." He choked on a sob. "I can't do this without you."

His throat grew dense with unshed tears, and he closed his eyes, willing himself some semblance of control. *Please, Adonai, please let her live. I need her.*

"Abigail . . . what can I do? How can I help you grow strong again?" He swallowed, tasting bile. Absently, then purposely, he caressed her cheek. "Chileab has grown into a fine son, not nearly as spoiled or self-centered as his brothers. It is because of you, beloved. You alone."

Her eyes flickered at his soft pleading, her brow furrowed, as though something troubled her. She looked at him again.

This time the glazed look had cleared. "Michal will teach our daughters, my lord. Michal loves Yahweh too." She drew a shallow breath, wincing at some pain David could not see.

"You're hurting. Let me call the physician back in." He stroked her face again with gentle fingers, tears falling unbidden, dampening his cheeks.

She smiled, a look of peace settling over her, making his gut clench in fear.

"Abigail?"

But her only response was to hold his gaze with a look of love so strong he thought the strength of it would rip his heart in two. And then she was gone. Her eyes glazed over in the unmistakable mask of death.

Grief ripped through him with the force of a mighty wind. Groans burst from his throat, and a high-pitched wail escaped his lips, piercing the silence. The door opened, and the guards and servants he had previously banished flooded the apartment. Keening sounds came from the women, matching his bitter cry.

Abigail! Oh, Adonai, why did You take her? Why now? I need her!

But he knew the questions would go unanswered, the reasons for death as varied as the reasons for life. He studied her now, every line of her face peaceful, carefree—a feeling she'd often longed for. One he could never fully give her.

His fingers closed over hers, but he recoiled at the lifelessness of her once busy hands. Never again would she stitch tunics and robes for him or for their children. She'd gained such pleasure from the task.

The women moved about him like bees, buzzing, wailing, gathering spices and water to prepare Abigail's body for the grave. He would bury her in his own royal tomb already set aside and waiting for him in the city, not in some cave too far for him to notice or visit.

He could not bring her back, that was certain. But he could honor the love they'd shared. He pressed his hand one last time to her cool, colorless cheek, then stood and turned to leave.

Michal met him as he reached the door. "Forgive me, my lord, I am very sorry for your loss. But before you leave, would you like to see Abigail's daughter?"

David stared at Michal, seeing the tears shimmering in her eyes, the sleeping bundle in her arms, noting the protective way she held the child to her barren breast. *Michal will teach our daughters, my lord. Michal loves Yahweh too.* Since Michal had made her peace with David and with Adonai, Abigail had come to appreciate her rival, befriending her when his other wives continued to disdain her. Something David had often found both unusual and amazing, given Abigail's previous struggle with jealousy.

Abigail would want Michal to raise the child for him, though any number of lesser wives or concubines could do the job with more energy. Michal was starting to show her age in the lines across her forehead and mouth, no longer the beautiful young love of his youth. She had often begged him to give her a child, but still her arms were empty, her womb barren. Another way in which he had failed to please a wife he once loved. To give her Abigail's child . . . it was the least he could do.

Not trusting his voice, he nodded at Michal. She undid the child's wrapping to reveal a round face with creamy tan skin and eyes that were dark, like her mother's. He blinked hard, then looked again at his daughter, Abigail's daughter.

"She will be like her mother," he said finally.

He touched a finger to the child's cheek, but he did not ask to hold her. He should take her and bless her as he had done for Anna, despite the fact that she wasn't a boy. But the grief of Abigail's loss was too raw, and he suddenly needed to get away, to find solitude and peace.

He looked into Michal's expectant gaze and offered her what he hoped was a convincing smile. "Will you raise her for me?" At her look of complete surprise, he added, "Abigail would want you to. You shared a love for Adonai and—" His voice caught. "Will you?"

"Yes, my lord. I would be honored." He started to move away from her toward the door, but her words stopped him. "What will you name her, my lord?"

He paused, uncertain, then looked into Michal's tender gaze. "Abigail. After her mother." He whirled about and walked away to grieve in peace.

4

Bathsheba tore off an end of the brown wheat bread and dipped it into the stew, scooping a chunk of lamb and red lentils onto the small piece. Uriah had already eaten and retired to the sitting room to go over the day's accounting with Anittas. Sometimes he would share a meal with her, but his preparations for battle had him hurried and preoccupied.

She chewed slowly, forcing the food down despite her lack of appetite, dreading his leaving but half wishing he had already gone. Would it hurt him to slow down a bit, to give her an extra measure of his time? But he had already spent the morning rushing her through the market and now doubled his efforts to make up for the loss. There was much to do in advance, though the servants managed to keep things well under control during his absences.

She took a few more bites of the stew. Unable to finish, she nodded to a servant to remove the dishes. She lingered a moment in the eating area, fluffing a pillow at the end of the couch, glancing down at the leather case holding her lyre. Not even the thought of her music cheered her with war so imminent. Later, perhaps. She stood and moved about the room, straightening the cushions and lighting lamps. Dusk cast its gray light over the orange, yellow, and blue wall hangings, and the sounds of servants' laughter drifted to her from the cooking rooms, where the women ate now that she and Uriah had taken their fill. A sense of deep loneliness crept over her at the sound. She should have joined them. At the very least she should have asked Tirzah to sit with her.

A loud blast of the trumpet nearly made her drop the small torch. Another blast jolted her. She blew out the torch, grabbed a clay lamp, and rushed to the sitting room. A loud banging on the front door accompanied the third blast. Uriah jumped up and hurried to the door.

"Master Uriah, you are commanded to appear in the courtyard of the palace at once to accompany the king to his tomb to bury his wife Abigail."

Bathsheba stood behind Uriah, noting the royal insignia—the lion of the tribe of Judah—emblazoned on the cloaks of two royal guards. Their words rocked her. Abigail was dead? How could that be?

"When did this happen?" Uriah addressed the men as he snatched his sandals from the basket by the door. He bent to tie them as Anittas handed him his soldier's tunic.

"This afternoon. The lady Abigail died giving birth to a daughter. The women have prepared her body for burial, and the king wishes to bury his wife in his own tomb. The Thirty are commanded to attend." The guards whirled about and marched out of the courtyard.

Uriah pulled the tunic over his head and fastened his captain's robe over it, tying the belt securely. Anittas retrieved Uriah's helmet and handed it to him.

"May I come, my lord?" Bathsheba asked. Other women

would accompany the throng, professional mourners among them.

He turned and met her gaze, his dark brows drawn low beneath the leather headgear. He looked as though he would deny her request, then seemed to think better of it and nodded. "Bring your maid with you." He looked at Anittas. "You may accompany them." He bent to kiss her cheek, then marched through the door.

Darkness settled swiftly over the city as Bathsheba donned her sandals and grabbed her cloak. Anittas led, and Tirzah followed Bathsheba through the courtyard into Jerusalem's narrow streets. High-pitched wailing sounds came from the direction of the palace, growing louder as they drew near. Bathsheba kept close to Anittas amidst the crowds. Torches lit the night as they maneuvered their way to the palace steps.

Inside the king's gate, the thirty mighty men stood in precise rows at the head of the procession. She spotted Uriah and her father, Eliam, toward the back of the group. Behind them, six slaves lifted the bier, holding the lifeless body of the king's favorite wife. Bathsheba stood on tiptoe, trying to get a better glimpse, but even with the many torches she could see little. Directly behind the bier, surrounded by guards, courtiers, flag bearers, and trumpeters, stood the king himself.

Anittas led them to the gate, where they could join the procession once it cleared the area and moved into the streets toward the south end of the city. Abigail would be buried in the caves near the city wall—tombs intended for King David and his heirs.

Bathsheba pulled her cloak tighter against her neck, tucking the scarf so the wind wouldn't lift it from her face. Trumpets blared, and the mighty men began a slow, steady march.

Loud and bitter wailing split the air once the sound of the trumpets faded.

Bathsheba's gaze drifted from the bier to the king. He drew closer, and though his men surrounded him, she could see him better as they approached the iron gates. His crown still sat atop his head, but his robes were sackcloth and ashes coated his hair. Tears dampened his cheeks.

"Abigail, oh, Abigail, my love. How can I live without you?"

His words, so impassioned, struck a chord in Bathsheba's heart. How he had loved this woman! She leaned in, hoping for a better glimpse, to convey with a look how she ached for him, but Anittas's hand on her arm held her back. One of David's guards looked in her direction, making her take a step backward, shame heating her face. How foolish to think she could somehow get near enough to comfort the king! What was she thinking?

She ducked her head, listening to the king's continued cries. She waited for the rest of the procession—the wives and children of the king—to pass. At last, Anittas and Tirzah led her along with the rest of the crowd to fall in behind, to take the long walk to the tombs.

The wails rose and fell like an uncertain wind. Bathsheba found it impossible to lift her voice with the throng, unable to push sound past the lump in her throat. Would Uriah mourn for her as the king mourned for Abigail? She gave her head a slight shake. Of course he would. Perhaps not as openly or with such a public display, but he would surely mourn her loss if she died.

Tirzah moved to her side as more people pressed in behind her. They were close to the wives and daughters of the king, behind her grandfather and his fellow counselors. Cool night air swirled beneath her robes, chilling her, but the weather would soon grow warm with summer heat. Uriah could be gone many months even into fall, without even one visit home. The thought depressed her.

"The caves shouldn't be too much farther, mistress," Tirzah said, bending close to her ear. Soft murmurs of the people behind her grew silent moments later as Tirzah's prediction came true.

Men moved forward, holding the torches aloft to illuminate the entire periphery surrounding the caves. Ripples of stillness settled over the crowd at the screeching sound of the heavy stone being moved from the entrance. Bathsheba looked toward the king, who stood close to the bier looking down on his beloved wife. His face crumpled and he covered it with both hands, turning away from the crowd.

"Abigail!" His pitiful cry was soft, a moan coming from deep within him, but it carried to where Bathsheba stood.

Tears filled her eyes at his pain, and again she had the sudden longing to comfort him. She looked to his wives. Would none of them step forward to place a hand on his arm, to pull him to them? Were they glad one of their rivals would no longer vie for his affection? She shuddered, grateful once more to have only Uriah.

A moment passed as the king lifted his tear-streaked face and hands to the heavens. "Praise be to Your name, Adonai, for You are good. As she loved You in life, so may You welcome her in death. I will go to her one day, but she will not return to me."

The king stepped away from the bier as a young man approached and lifted a crippled hand to touch the edge of the bier. A little girl held on to the young man's robe. Abigail's children, Chileab and Anna.

"Ima!" The little girl clung to her brother's leg. "I want Ima!" David scooped her up and held her sobbing against his chest. Her piercing wails mingled with Chileab's deep groans.

"Oh, Mama! If only you had lived to see your children's children."

King David placed an arm across the shoulders of his son and drew him into a three-way embrace, a family set apart, publicly sharing their private grief. Onlookers watched, weeping as well, and Bathsheba joined them, the tears falling freely. She brushed them away in time to see the six slaves carry Abigail's body into the cave. Moments later they returned, rolled the stone over the entrance, and placed the king's seal between the stone and the cave wall, preventing anyone from intruding on his wife's resting place.

More weeping, softer now, moved among the crowd. Still holding his daughter and supported by his son, the king strode forward, leading the throng, his eyes moist, his pain palpable. Guards and advisors, other wives, children, and mighty men came behind. He came so close to Bathsheba as he passed, she could almost touch him. A little gasp escaped her lips before she could suppress it. But he didn't appear to notice anything about her or anyone else in the crowd, his eyes blinded as they were by his tears.

A touch on her arm made her jump. She saw Anittas nod and motion her to follow. She stepped in behind the procession for the long trek home.

⌇⌇

David moved on leaden feet to his audience chamber, the marble and cedar halls echoing the footsteps of his retinue as they led the way. Noise filtered to him from the crowds of men standing in the anteroom waiting to speak with him, to reserve some judgment on their behalf, but it could not pull him from the melancholy that dogged his every step, his very breath. Tomorrow the army would head to war, and Joab expected him to join them—something he could not bring himself to do no matter how many arguments he'd heard to the contrary.

He stopped as the trumpeters announced his arrival at court, glancing at Benaiah, ever faithful at his side.

"I am in no mood to pass judgment today. Send those waiting in the outer rooms to their homes. Bid them return next week." He straightened the belt at his waist and lifted his scepter.

Benaiah nodded. "It will be as you say, my lord." He bowed and stepped away to give David's pronouncement to the guards he commanded, then stepped back to David's side. "Are you certain then about your decision to remain in Jerusalem?"

David vaguely heard the familiar announcement of his name to the court as the flag bearers moved forward. He looked at his trusted bodyguard. "I'm certain."

Benaiah acknowledged his statement with a slight tilt of his head, then fell in line behind David as he moved to take his seat at court. The cushioned purple fabric welcomed him, and he sank onto the familiar ornate throne. Abigail had designed the green leaf pattern along the edges of the cushions, which matched the color and design on the sleeves of his royal robes.

Abigail, whose arms would never hold him close again. Had they laid her to rest only two days before?

He suppressed a deep sigh, looking over the mix of counselors and army commanders. His sons had taken their places in gilded chairs along one side of the room while his counselors and scribes sat along the other. All had risen and bowed low as he entered the room. They looked to him now with expectant faces, probably wondering if the rumors were true. Soon they would know.

He spoke to Benaiah, his voice low. "Summon my commanders."

A moment later, Joab and Abishai hurried forward, bending low, each touching a knee to the tile floor.

"Rise." He extended the scepter as each man stood. "Is the army ready to leave for war?"

"Everything is ready, my lord," Joab said, his back rigid, shoulders flung back. He wore the garments of Israel's general, the gold threads of his black robe thick along the arms and across the chest, the wings of eagles stitched along his shoulder blades. "The troops march at dawn."

"Good. I have great confidence in you, Joab." David smiled at his nephew. "I am sending you out to deal with the Ammonites. Defeat them for me, for Israel."

Joab's dark, beady eyes probed David's gaze, failing to show the proper bowed head and mute nod of acceptance. "You won't change your mind?"

"Not this time."

Soft murmurs filled the room, and Joab's posture grew more rigid. "Surely you know the men expect you to lead. The Ammonites humiliated your ambassadors. Your honor is at stake."

"And I expect you to uphold that honor. But I will not be going."

"My lord, is that truly wise?" Ahithophel stood, not waiting to be acknowledged, sending a wave of irritation through

David. Joab's questioning he'd grown used to, even tolerated, because in all his years as king, he'd never been quite able to keep Joab's attitudes or actions in check. But the man was an invaluable asset, a general unequaled. Not even Saul's cousin Abner had measured up to Joab's cunning. But Ahithophel, though like an angel of God sometimes, had grown wearying of late, always questioning David's intentions. He, of all people, should understand the loss of a wife.

"Wise or not, Ahithophel, I'm not going. I would be no good to my men or anyone else right now."

"The war would take your mind off your wife." Ahithophel pressed his point, garnering David's scowl. He returned to his seat. "Forgive me, my lord."

"Your counselor has a point, Uncle. The war will give you something to do besides sit around and feel sorry for yourself." Joab's tone held challenge.

David bristled, angry now. "I am not required to explain myself to you, Nephew, or to listen to faulty advice. Do remember it is I who am king." One hand tightened on the arm of the chair, the other gripped his scepter. "I trust you and Abishai can handle the army in my stead."

"These armies are large, my lord. What if they prove too strong for us?" Abishai spoke now, his expression showing he clearly wanted David to change his mind.

"It is not like you have never fought a war without me." David pushed his back against the throne, the threat of a headache forming along his temples. "My decision is made. Do not question me further." He looked from his generals to his counselors. When no one responded, he stood. "I will expect regular reports. If the battle grows to be too much

46

for you, then I will reconsider. In the meantime, strengthen your hands for battle. Don't let me find out it is weak-kneed women I have sent to do warriors' work."

Not waiting for a response, he stepped down from the throne and strode from the room without a backward glance.

5

Bathsheba lay on the raised bed she normally shared with Uriah, attempting sleep that would not come. Moonlight bathed the room in shadow, the windows shuttered against the night's cool breeze. Tomorrow Uriah would march to war with the armies of Israel. Who knew when they would see each other again?

She pulled the sheet closer to her neck, her body yearning to feel Uriah's arms about her, longing to be held one more night against his chest. But he would sleep instead on a pallet in the sitting room, away from her, away from love. War was uppermost in his mind. Did he think of her lying so close by, needing him?

She sniffed, jabbing at the tears dampening the pillow beneath her head. Uriah wasn't to blame in this. War was the enemy, this constant need to defend Israel's borders, to take the land God had promised to them. If the Ammonites hadn't been such fools, they wouldn't be in this mess.

She flipped over to face the wall, readjusting the covers, frustrated with her train of thought. Anger would not help her sleep. She had best get used to being alone from now on.

The door creaked softly as she finally settled into the wool mattress. She rose up on one elbow. Uriah stood in the doorway, looking down at her. He closed the door and stepped into the room.

Bathsheba sat up, letting the sheet fall away from her. She searched his face in the soft moonlight, unable to clearly see his expression. What was he doing here?

"Is something wrong, my lord?" She rose from the bed, her thin night tunic draping in folds to her ankles. She placed a hand on his arm and lifted her face closer to his.

"Nothing is wrong." His voice was husky. She knew that look. He bent to place a gentle kiss on her lips.

She clung to him, wrapping her arms about his neck. His kiss deepened, but a moment later he pulled back, pushing her away. "I'm sorry." He turned his back to her, then whirled around again to face her. "I shouldn't have come."

His rejection stung. She stepped away from him until her legs hit the bed. She hugged her arms to her chest, her mouth still feeling the sensation of his kiss. "We are married. It's not wrong for you to be here." She lifted a shaky hand toward him, unable to keep the pleading from her tone. "Please don't go. I need you." It was a risk to say such a thing. But why else had he come here if his need wasn't as great as hers?

He rubbed his beard, looking miserable, studying her as if by doing so he could decide what to do. When he did not move toward her, she let her hand fall to her side. He tilted his head back, lifting his gaze toward the ceiling. At last he faced her again. "During the funeral, I couldn't stop thinking of you, of fearing I could lose you."

"You're not going to lose me."

"You don't know that."

Was he thinking of his first wife who had died like Abigail?

49

They stood still, their gazes connected, unable to break free. "I could lose you in war," she said after a lengthy silence. "Only God knows when our time will come to enter Sheol."

He dipped his head in a slight nod, the lines around his dark eyes softening. "I only know I don't want it to be tonight. I want to spend my last night with you."

Her heart warmed to his honesty. "The law doesn't say you have to keep yourself from women so soon. And it allows for purification if such a thing were to happen." She gave him a coy smile and opened her arms, beckoning him forward.

His mouth curved slightly at the edges, but his serious expression made her heart throb. He was so close yet so far. So needing her yet so anxious to obey every hint of the law, every whim of the king's commands. Could he not give in to his own desires even once? How much did he love her?

"Please, my lord." She moved closer to him, knowing she wore her heart in her eyes. Her breath touched his face. If he rejected her now, she would be devastated. But at least she would know.

A soft groan escaped his lips as he drew her near to him. "Dear wife, you will be my undoing." He pulled her closer into his arms, nearly crushing her against him, his lips claiming hers.

She returned his kiss, her heart soaring at his familiar touch. "Do you love me?" she whispered against him as he placed her among the cushions.

His mouth lifted from hers, his gaze soft, tender. "My sweet Bathsheba, was there ever any doubt?"

His kiss silenced her answer.

❦

50

Bathsheba climbed to the roof of her house after Uriah left the next morning, her gaze fixed on the roofs of her neighbors, trying to catch a glimpse of the army as it marched through Jerusalem's streets to the fields and hill country of Ammon. Uriah had frowned on her desire to join the women and children lining the streets to sing songs and wave palm fronds. Anittas and Tirzah would have seen to her safety, but his protectiveness bade her stay. No need to cause him extra worry.

But oh, to glimpse him again, to see the sparkle in his eyes when he looked at her—a sparkle she saw so rarely. She shook her head at the thought. Uriah would not give way to emotion in front of his men. But at least he had left her resting in the security of his love. Why else would he have broken his own code of conduct to be with her if not for love? He was right, of course. There was never any doubt. She'd been a fool to think otherwise.

She walked closer to the parapet, the wind whipping the scarf against her cheeks, sticking it to her mouth. As she pulled it away, the fringe caught between the rings on her fingers, and she turned about, gently tugging the threads from her hand. She glanced up toward the king's palace as she always did whenever she ventured outside, expecting to find it empty. But her breath caught at the sight of the king leaning against the parapet of the palace roof, resplendent in his royal robes.

Her hands stilled and her heart thudded. How close he seemed, yet their roofs separated them, and he wasn't looking in her direction. She tugged harder on the caught fringe of her scarf, finally wrenching it free of her hand, and quickly pulled the scarf more securely across her cheeks and nose, covering all but her eyes. If perchance he did look her way . . . Uriah would be pleased if the king could not see her face.

She should turn, pretend she didn't see him there, but even from a distance, his presence was intoxicating. She watched him, fascinated, remembering the grieving husband of a few nights before. Her grandfather seemed disgusted with the king's desire to remain in Jerusalem, but surely even a king should be allowed time to grieve.

Irritation spiked within her. War! Did a man have to be ruled by the constant need to fight? Let the enemy be hanged. A man had more important things to do. Like care for his family.

Heat filled her face at the realization she'd been staring at the king. She took a step backward and turned to look toward the street again, but stopped cold as her eye caught sudden movement. She glanced in his direction again, afraid to lift her face to his, but equally afraid not to. She was not mistaken. He'd seen her standing there, and his gaze now traveled the length of her, though his expression revealed nothing, as though what he saw posed no interest to him.

But his dark eyes held her spellbound even with the space of the roof between them, and as he walked closer to come in line just above the edge of her roof, she could not stop herself from moving toward him in response. She knelt, bowing her face to the roof's floor when she could go no farther, and he stood directly above her.

"Rise," he said, his voice at once commanding and gentle.

She slowly stood but kept her gaze downcast.

"Look at me, please." She obeyed. He was leaning over the roof in an obvious attempt to communicate more freely, but when she looked up, he straightened, his expression appreciative. "You are very beautiful."

She glanced down and sucked in a quick breath. Her scarf had come loose when she bowed low, revealing her face! Why had she not expected such a thing and taken precautions against it? She grabbed the edge of the fabric and flipped it over her shoulder, covering her mouth and leaving only her eyes visible.

"Please, don't cover yourself." A boyish smile filled his handsome face, making her heart flutter. What betrayal was this? She loved Uriah! Dare she not do as he asked?

"I am a married woman, my lord. It is proper that I obey my husband, who prefers I cover myself in public." She lowered her gaze, though she longed to search his face, to feast on the complexity of his expressions, which seemed to move from commanding to vulnerable in an instant.

"Of course, you are right to obey your husband. Tell me, who is the man who is so blessed to have such a beautiful woman for his wife?" His voice carried clearly to her on the breeze, while the sounds of the retreating army and singing women faded in the distance.

She glanced about her, but no servants from her household had joined her on the roof. She chanced another look at him. He rested both hands on the parapet, and his gaze was fixed solely on her. His boyish smile turned somber when their eyes met, and she knew she was safe with him. He would honor her as well as her husband.

"My husband is Uriah the Hittite, and my father is Eliam, son of Ahithophel your counselor, my lord." The words came out breathy against the fabric, and beads of sweat formed along her upper lip. The warmth of the spring breeze surprised her, making her wish she could remove the head covering altogether.

"Ahithophel's granddaughter? I'm surprised that old fox didn't offer you to me long ago." His dark eyes softened, and his look felt like an intimate touch. "He would not have been refused."

"You honor me, my lord." Her cheeks blazed beneath her veil. "But I believe you are mistaken."

His glance moved from his roof to hers as though he were gauging the distance between them and planning to close the gap somehow. She took a step back, half afraid her words had angered him.

"Don't go." His urgent tone halted her movement. "I only wish our roofs weren't quite so far apart—I do not wish to shout to be heard." He looked sideways then back at her again. "Or be heard by our neighbors."

She nodded, moving as close as the roof would allow, then backed up again so as not to have to strain her neck looking up.

"I would jump down, but then I would have to explain to your servants why I couldn't climb back up again." He laughed, and the sound reminded her of the music she'd once heard him sing. "But tell me before you must go—how am I mistaken?"

She gave a furtive glance behind and beside her, then slowly removed the scarf from her face, convincing herself she wouldn't have to speak as loudly with the covering removed. His appreciative smile warmed her heart in a way she wasn't sure she should feel, but she pushed the thought aside. He was the king, after all. A friend to her grandfather. She had nothing to fear.

"About four years ago, before my marriage to Uriah, my grandfather tried to arrange a marriage with me to you. But you were not interested in taking other wives because of your promise to your wife Abigail." At the shadow that crossed his face, she winced. "I'm sorry for your loss, my lord." Why did she not learn to think before she spoke?

"Thank you. Go on."

She swallowed, aware of his intense interest. "There is not much more to tell. Grandfather wanted to see if a match could be made between us or with someone of royal blood, but Father had it in mind to reward Uriah for saving his life in battle. So I married Uriah three years ago."

She looked up. The muscles worked in his jaw, but he did not say anything for a long moment. She took up the end of the scarf and draped it across her neck, leaving her face partially exposed. She should go whether he wanted her to or not. Surely the king had more important things to do than to stand here talking to her!

"What is your name?" His question held little emotion, as though he were a scribe recording an entry in a book.

"Bathsheba, my lord." She dipped her head, fearing he would dismiss her, almost wishing he would.

"Bathsheba. Seventh daughter. You have many sisters then?"

She looked up, startled. "No, my lord. I am the only daughter of my father and my mother." Dare she tell him more? He leaned both elbows on the parapet as though he had no intention of letting her go soon. "Bathsheba also means 'daughter of the oath.' My father almost lost both my mother and me in childbirth. My father prayed and asked God to spare at least one of us. If He did so, my father promised to serve Him faithfully, to be the best soldier that ever lived. Adonai chose to spare me, and so my father kept his oath and named me accordingly." She loosened the scarf as she spoke and rested against the edge of the parapet.

He shifted to the side, angling his head toward her. "I am the youngest of eight sons, though you probably already know that."

"You are fortunate to have such a large family." She hadn't meant for her tone to come out so wistful, and she looked away, embarrassed.

"If my wives are to be believed, it is you who are the fortunate one, to be the only wife of one man."

She lifted her head but met only sincerity in his smile. "Uriah is a good man." Her thoughts jumbled in her head. Thoughts of Uriah filled her with shame. He would not understand her desire to talk with this man, even if he was the king. She didn't understand it herself, but she sensed she should not be here, should not continue a conversation that could only grow more intimate.

Was the king attracted to her? The thought made her pause as she self-consciously pulled the veil across her mouth again. It couldn't be. The king had many wives to choose from, some far more beautiful than she. And he could have any woman in the kingdom.

A strange regret filled her at that thought. Was it she who was attracted to him? Confusion crept in, filling her with uncertainty.

She slipped away from the parapet and bowed low. She had to get away. She could not think straight with him looking at her like that. She straightened. "If it pleases my lord, I must go." She did not meet his gaze despite the now erratic thumping of her heart that bade her do so. "Will you please excuse me, my lord?"

The rustle of movement above her told her he had stood as well. "Of course. I am sorry to have kept you from your work." His sincere tone coaxed her gaze upward again, and his smile made her insides quiver. He dipped his head as though he were any normal man and not the king who held their fate—her fate—in his hands. "It was a pleasure to meet you, Bathsheba." Her name on his tongue felt like an intimate touch.

She shivered and backed away, fearing the feelings his nearness suddenly evoked. "Thank you, my lord. The pleasure was mine as well." She waited, hesitant. Was it proper to just turn her back and hurry down the steps away from a king?

"You may go," he said, though he did not look pleased with the prospect.

She ignored whatever desire he might be feeling, wondering at her earlier thought a few days before to comfort him on his loss of Abigail. Now the thought held too much power, and his presence too much sway over her feelings. To speak with him again would be to court trouble. His pull was too strong, his presence too commanding, his person too appealing.

She backed farther from him, her heart beating hard, matching the way her breath came in short little spurts. When she reached the stairs, she at last broke eye contact and hurried down the steps, not sure whether she was running from the king or to the safety of her home. But she was certain she would never outrun the attraction that had passed between them, or the loneliness she would find away from Uriah's protective arms.

~6~

David walked in an aimless circle along the perimeter of his palace, pausing every now and then at the parapet to gaze out over the city. Sunset had long past, and night sounds had drifted to stillness over most of Jerusalem. Lamplight flickered from below, and the voices of his closest neighbors drifted to him, their words indistinguishable. He hadn't been to his roof in three months, avoiding the desire to look in the direction of the woman he'd met the day his men left for war. To speak with her again would not be proper or bode well if others heard of it. Tonight he finally gave in to the need to visit his pavilion, but found his restless legs would not still nor his mind clearly focus.

He moved away from the edge as a sigh escaped him, an action he seemed unable to control too often of late. If he had any sense, he would fling off the responsibilities of the kingship—if for only a night—walk down the steps to his own family courtyard, and choose a wife to join him. A woman could be a great distraction from grief and war, as he'd briefly noticed the day he'd met his neighbor's wife. But the respite had been short-lived. Abigail's death had left a deep hole in his heart, and no other woman would ever be able to take her place. Why had Adonai taken the one woman who understood him, with whom he could discuss his concerns, share his burdens—the one woman who had stolen his heart?

Depression tugged at him, and he was suddenly weary of pacing, his legs growing weightier with each footfall. He stumbled forward, then righted himself, waving away the guard who hurried closer as if to help him. He was not so old that he couldn't manage to walk across his own roof! But he knew he looked more like a drunken man than a king, so he made his way to his tent pavilion, relieved to sink into the cushions of his couch. He looked up at the sound of footsteps. The guard coming to check on him, no doubt.

"My lord king, Hushai the Archite is asking to speak with you. May he approach?" Benaiah stood at the tent's opening, surprising him.

"I thought you were taking the night off, Benaiah. Go home to your wife and children. Your king can survive without you for one evening." David ran a hand over his beard, studying his faithful guard. "And yes, send Hushai to me." He leaned his head against the cushions and briefly closed his eyes, not realizing until this moment how exhausted he felt.

"My wife was needed at a birthing, leaving an empty house." Benaiah was never one to go into lengthy explanations. He turned to leave, but David knew the man would not go home. The thought was strangely comforting. He closed his eyes again, wishing he could drift into a dreamless sleep, but knew without doubt sleep would not come.

David sat up at the sound of Hushai's approach and accepted a golden goblet of wine from a servant. "What can I do for you, Hushai?" He swirled the liquid, then held it still, looking into his reflection. The likeness was too shadowed to see much. Just as well, considering how haggard he must appear. He took a long sip, tasting the sweet bitterness, so like life.

"Must I want something from you, my lord?" Hushai shifted his bulky frame and lowered himself to a cushioned seat opposite David. He smiled, his uneven teeth showing behind a graying beard, his dark eyes holding David's own.

"Everyone wants something, my friend." David set the chalice aside, picked up one of his many lyres, and plucked a soft tune. "It is the duty of a king to give to his people. I expect nothing less."

"A true friend does not always expect a favor, my lord."

David looked up, appreciating the man's effort. Of all people, Hushai would be least likely to seek favors. "A king has very few true friends." Especially not among his wives or sons. The thought brought with it a fresh wave of irritation. He strummed a discordant note, then shifted to a haunting minor key, his head bent low to avoid eye contact with Hushai. The man probably wanted to offer David a piece of well-earned advice, whether David wanted to hear it or not.

When the last chord ended, David rested the lyre on his lap and leaned back against the cushions. Hushai sipped from his silver goblet as a manservant stepped outside the tent, leaving them alone again.

"Even you have a reason for coming here, Hushai—even if all you happen to want is my company." He gave a short laugh. "Though of late, I'm not sure why anyone cares."

Hushai clasped both hands around his goblet, then appeared to change his mind and set the cup aside, folding his hands over his ample middle. "I remember when you first came to Hebron, when Judah first anointed you king over them. You were at the brink of achieving all God had promised you. It was a heady moment."

David crossed his ankles, remembering. Those days had been fraught with strife and civil war, but in certain ways they were simpler. Melancholy accompanied that thought, and he shifted uncomfortably. "Your point?"

Hushai did not look the least concerned by David's discomfort, settling more thoroughly against the cushions as though he planned on a long visit. "But there were difficult moments too, with Chileab's injury and the lady Abigail." Hushai paused, giving David a pointed look.

David fought the urge to squirm under his friend's scrutiny. Hushai was the one person who knew what David had done in sending Abigail away and what he had sacrificed to make it right again.

"You promised Abigail something, my lord, and I have watched you keep that promise."

He raised a brow and offered Hushai a wry smile. "That promise was not as hard to keep as you might think." Fewer women to vie for his attention, to beg favors for their spoiled sons. Fewer women to annoy him with their unceasing demands. Fewer women to please.

Hushai chuckled, uncrossing his arms to rest both hands on his knees. "In truth, no, I didn't think you could keep such a vow, especially when half the tribes in Israel brought their daughters to parade before you. I thought you'd give in and choose at least a few of them. To keep peace, of course."

David smiled, meaning it this time. "Of course." He'd managed to keep peace without the added wives, but he often wondered what the disappointment of those men had cost him in loyalty. A king was never without enemies.

"So what are you trying to say, Hushai?" He enjoyed his

friend, but this subject wearied him. "I kept my promise to Abigail and now she's dead. Why Adonai allowed her to be taken when I have other wives I could have suggested He consider first, I have no idea. Why take the one woman who mattered most to me? Even Michal with her newfound faith in Yahweh doesn't stir me to seek Adonai like Abigail did." He drew his hands together and studied them, palms up. How calloused his fingers, yet when he thought on it, he could still feel the silky smoothness of Abigail's skin beneath their tips. "What am I supposed to do without her, Hushai?"

He hadn't expected to voice the question or for its weight to carry so much emotion, though it had been playing in his head for months like an incessant wedding drum. Somehow, speaking it aloud made the grief seem slightly less sharp. He drew in a slow breath and let it out, his gaze fixed on Hushai.

"I am deeply sorry for your loss, David." His friend rarely used his given name, and it surprised and pleased him. "I admire you for keeping your promise to Abigail, but she is gone now. You are not bound to that promise."

"The law still tells kings not to take many wives." He'd grappled with the thought more times than he could count. He'd grown weary of his own internal arguments.

"Yes, but how many is 'many'? Do the wives you have now please you? Can one of them replace what you had with Abigail? Are you willing to see if that is possible?" The questions came like silent arrows to his heart, as though his friend had somehow peered past his outward show of kingly facade and read the depths of his soul.

David forced his body from the cushions and walked to the tent's opening, his gaze taking in the blackness of the cloudy night. "There are none who come close to Abigail, and you know it, Hushai. So why do you torment me with such questions? Why do you add to my frustration?" He ran a hand through his hair, suddenly wishing he was not so easily swayed by a woman's beauty or her charmed words. Such weakness. He blew out a breath and turned back into the pavilion, sinking again among the soft cushions. "What would you have me do? Just tell me." He had run out of answers, excuses, and reasons. Let someone else make the judgments for a change.

"Take another wife."

The words hung in the silence. Crickets sounded somewhere in the distance, their mating calls matching the steady beat of his heart.

"Take another wife. Just like that?"

"Your promise to Abigail is ended, my lord. Let us search among the women of Jerusalem. We won't have to leave the city to find someone." Hushai's eyes sparkled as if he already had someone in mind.

"What of the law? Wasn't it you who was always quick to remind me of it?" He held Hushai's intense gaze, seeing the light flicker but a moment in his dark eyes.

"You would not need to take many more, my lord. Just one—to replace Abigail." Hushai lifted a shoulder in a slight shrug. "You need a woman whose heart can hold yours like hers did. Unless, like I said, you can replace Abigail with one you already have?"

Could he? He couldn't say he had actually explored such a thought. He'd grown weary of their complaints and too used to their fake charms.

"You had something once with Michal."

David looked away, not liking the direction of the conversation. "Michal may have changed, Hushai, but our love was never what it should have been. I do not have the energy to revisit those memories."

Hushai shifted his bulk, leaning forward, both elbows on his knees. "Then take another wife."

"You seem mighty sure of yourself." David lifted the goblet from the table and took a long, slow drink. Did he honestly want another wife? But what was one more among so many, especially if he was only filling Abigail's place? He slugged down the rest in one gulp, then wiped his mouth with the back of his hand. Nothing, no one, could take Abigail's place.

"I've had some fathers approach me. I've seen some of your choices." Hushai smiled, his look mischievous.

"You have, have you?" He could not shake the melancholy thoughts but smiled anyway, holding his friend's gaze. "Perhaps you should let me have a look at these choices then."

Why did the thought actually interest him? Was he mad? Probably. But Hushai was right in another sense. There was no longer a reason to keep his house from growing stronger. Adding another wife would mean more sons, and spoiled or not, more sons would strengthen his kingdom.

Thoughts of the law flitted through his mind, but Hushai had a point there too. Many meant more than one. How many was too many? As long as they didn't turn his heart away from Yahweh, the number shouldn't matter. Nothing, no one, could shake his devotion to Adonai.

"Bring me your choices, Hushai." He called for the servant to refill his cup and bid Hushai goodnight, his heart lighter than it had been in months.

7

Bathsheba stood in the cooking room as servants moved around her, cleaning the remnants of the morning meal to begin preparations for the New Moon feast later that evening. Despite Uriah's absence, Bathsheba made certain the laws, purifications, sacrifices, and festivals were kept, knowing her husband would request an update and an accounting when he returned. She had already sent the invitations to her grandfather, Aunt Talia, Chava and her husband Matthias, and Rei and his new wife Jarah. All had agreed to join her for the feast that followed the sacrifices at Gibeon. The journey to the high place and back would take time, and she was restless to be off.

Yearning for her family tugged at her. Chava had been absent from their weekly visits at the marketplace, still sick with her second pregnancy, but it was not Chava's face she missed. If Bathsheba was honest with herself, it was a glimpse of the king she longed for most. Her pulse quickened at the thought, bringing with it a troubling sense of guilt.

She moved from the cooking area toward the front of the house, pausing at her room to snatch her cloak and head scarf. Loneliness was the only explanation for the way her mind kept replaying their conversation of months before. If Uriah had never gone to battle, she would not have been on the roof at that moment or even spoken one word to the king. That her gaze had traveled nearly every day since to the spot where he'd stood was a testament to the fact that she missed her husband. Would the war never end?

She forced her mind back to examining the servants' handiwork as she carried her cloak and scarf to the sitting room. The door to the courtyard stood ajar, letting the warm breeze filter through the house. Summer's heat had grown oppressive in the past month, but shutting up the house was no better than letting the warmth seep inside. Bathsheba hated the closed-in feeling.

In the courtyard, a middle-aged female servant stood beating dust from a rug with a heavy wooden paddle. Tirzah lifted her head from where she stood polishing tables and lamps.

"Gather your cloak and come with me." Bathsheba pulled her sandals from a basket by the door and sat on a low couch to tie them in place.

Tirzah tucked the linen dust cloth into her belt and hurried to her quarters. She returned as Bathsheba finished tying her other sandal.

"Leaving so soon, my lady?" Anittas's frame blocked her path to the courtyard, his thick arms folded over his sturdy chest. Her constant protector, Uriah had urged Anittas to keep her safe.

"I promised my aunt I would stop by and spend some time with her before we head to Gibeon."

"The master would have a servant accompany you." He moved aside, but as she took a step forward, he followed her.

She stopped, turning to face him. "Tirzah is servant enough. I will be fine, Anittas."

"Yes, mistress. Perhaps Shimron should go with you."

"My cousin Rei will go with us to Gibeon. You have nothing to fear." Uriah's insistence that a male servant always accompany her had grown annoying. She covered her face well enough, and there was nothing about her dress to reveal what she looked like. In this Uriah was too much like her father, never giving her space to breathe, always hovering as though he feared someone would snatch her from beneath his watch or she would fly away like a bird. Ridiculous!

But Anittas would never agree with her assessment. She sighed, pulled the scarf over her head and across her face, and met the servant's concerned gaze. "We will be well. Don't worry so." She patted his arm, trying to appear grateful for his fatherly concern, but was smothered by his guardedness. "My grandfather wouldn't let anything happen to me, and he will also be joining us."

Anittas nodded, apparently appeased. She stepped into the courtyard, Tirzah close behind. "If you send Shimron regardless, tell him to keep his distance." She heard Anittas chuckle as she and Tirzah moved into the street.

"Why do you have the same conversation with him every time we go somewhere? You know he will send Shimron or another servant whether you want him to or not." Tirzah tucked a basket she carried beneath one arm and came up beside Bathsheba.

"He shouldn't worry so. And there is always the chance that one of these times he will listen to me and not feel like he has to watch my every step. He's worse than a mother hen." They passed the houses of their neighbors, where women sat grinding grain in their courtyards and young children played nearby. There was little place for them to run in the city except for the semi-crowded streets.

"He is doing his best to obey the master's orders, mistress. You can hardly fault a servant for being about his master's work."

They rounded a corner to a busier street, the main thoroughfare that led to the king's palace. Curiosity tugged her attention to the imposing palace gates, but she saw nothing but polished limestone and guards standing watch. She turned away, a sense of disquiet settling within her, disappointment making her uncomfortable. What did she expect—the king to be standing in the gate waiting for a glimpse of her as she passed by? Now who was being ridiculous?

She hurried along, her sandals slapping the paved stones, taking the path toward the street of merchants. A donkey-led cart clattered behind them, and they moved quickly to the side of the road to let it pass.

"Does something trouble you, mistress?" Tirzah's soft voice in her ear made her look away. She swallowed and wrapped the scarf tighter across her face, glad for the covering to hide her expression from passersby.

"Nothing troubles me. I am only anxious to see my aunt." She could never tell her servant her traitorous thoughts, despite the woman's ability to keep her mouth from spilling over into gossip. Some things shouldn't be shared, and her desire to see the king was chief among them. The very thought sounded worse than it was. She wasn't looking for a replacement for Uriah. She only wanted someone to talk to, and he had been so captivating.

She gave herself a mental shake. No good would come of such thoughts.

Another cart rattled toward the merchants' stalls the next street over. A baaing goat galloped after the cart and a young boy chased it, shouting. Bathsheba motioned for Tirzah to follow and kept walking.

They continued in silence until they reached a house much smaller than the one she shared with Uriah. She entered the familiar courtyard and ducked her head under the arch of the open door. The weather was warm enough that Bathsheba wished she could shed her cloak, but Uriah would want her to remain covered until she was inside the house.

"Aunt Talia. Are you home?"

Voices came from one of the rooms, and a moment later her aunt and cousin Rei hurried to her. Aunt Talia embraced her before she could speak another word. Unwanted tears came unbidden then. She hadn't meant to show such emotion. She only wanted to talk to her aunt, to get some perspective on her life, to fill her loneliness.

"There, there." Aunt Talia held her at arm's length. "You come to greet me after these many months with tears? What troubles you, dear one?" She gently patted Bathsheba's cheek.

Bathsheba shook her head, her face warming under her aunt's touch. "I am fine, Aunt Talia, only missing you, missing everyone." She glanced at Rei and the heat increased.

He gave her a thoughtful, curious look. "It's good to see you, Cousin." He smiled that boyish grin she had always loved, but his expression was not boyish at all. Rei had always loved her, had wanted to marry her, and if he'd been two years older instead of two years younger, her father might have considered a match. But it was too late to consider. She was a married woman, and Rei had a new bride of his own now.

"And you as well, Rei. How are you these days?" He had

grown tall since she'd last seen him, his beard filled out, the muscles of a man beneath his tan tunic.

"I am well. I just stopped in to see if Mama needed anything from the market. I am on my way to buy some leather to cut into hinges for the doors. I have built two new rooms onto Mama's house. Jarah is expecting." His chin lifted in an obvious sense of pride.

Bathsheba's heart constricted at the news. Rei had been married less than three months and already his wife was with child? Why did Adonai deny her a similar pleasure?

She smiled despite the ache in her soul. "Best wishes to you, Cousin. When can we expect this proud day?"

"Before the barley harvest." He looked at her, then averted his gaze. "I must go if I want to make it back in time. We leave for the high place after the noon meal."

"We will be ready," Aunt Talia said, shooing Rei toward the door. "Now go."

Aunt Talia cleared her throat as Jarah appeared in the room behind him, and motioned to Bathsheba. "Come into the house, dear child."

"I will be back soon." Rei dipped his head toward Bathsheba, kissed his wife's cheek, then disappeared through the door.

"Come now, my dear." Aunt Talia took Bathsheba's arm and tugged her into the main room that doubled as a sitting and eating area. Low couches were set near a few low tables, with a lambskin draped over the stone floor. "Here, let me take your cloak." Bathsheba undid the wrap and handed it to her aunt, who laid it over a hook in the wall. She turned to Tirzah to do the same, but Tirzah shook her head.

"I'll just wait outside."

Aunt Talia smiled her understanding as Tirzah slipped back

into the courtyard. Aunt Talia looked at Jarah. "Daughter, could you get us some watered wine?" She glanced at Bathsheba. "Or tea perhaps?"

"Tea would be fine. But let me help you." She studied her cousin's wife. The girl was shorter than Chava, medium-boned and darker-skinned, sturdy like Tirzah. Her smile lit her mouth as she fluttered her arms in a dismissive gesture. "Nonsense. You and Mother must sit and catch up on things. I will join you shortly."

"She's a thoughtful girl." Bathsheba faced Aunt Talia as Jarah left the room. Her aunt was a small, stout woman with graying hair pulled back beneath a brown head scarf. Her sturdy arms had seen many a good day's work, and though widowed for several years now, she carried on, giving to those in need around her even out of her own meager means.

"She is good for Rei and a help to me in my old age." Her look held no guile, and Bathsheba sensed the comment was meant to put her at ease. They both knew how much Rei had once cared for her.

"You're hardly old, Aunt Talia. You have many good years ahead of you."

Her aunt waved the thought away. "Only God knows how long a person has on this earth." Her wistful expression told Bathsheba her aunt's thoughts had turned to her husband Shem.

"Do you miss him still?"

Aunt Talia folded her arms across her wide girth. "At times, when I am alone in this room mending, I sense someone in the chair." She pointed to the empty wooden chair across from them, the one Uncle Shem had often claimed as his. "I always look, expecting to see him, but of course he is never there."

Her chest lifted in a deep sigh. "I know he rests in Sheol, but sometimes his presence, the sense of him, is hard to forget." She glanced up as Jarah returned with a tray of seasoned flat bread and three steaming clay cups of honeyed tea. "It is good to have Rei and Jarah here to ease my loneliness."

Aunt Talia motioned for Jarah to take the seat beside her and twisted her bulk to face Bathsheba. "Now before Rei returns, tell me, what brought the emotion to your eyes? Of course, you are missing Uriah, but what else?"

Bathsheba took the cup her aunt handed to her and sipped slowly. "There is nothing else. I keep myself busy with the household duties, but the months drag on and there is no news of when the war will end. Sabba tells me that things are growing worse. The king will likely join the troops after the New Moon feast."

"Good! The king should have joined his men from the start. Perhaps the war would have ended by now if David had led them rather than leaving Joab in charge. That man may have the loyalty of the army, but the king's leadership is what they need. Besides, what good has it done for him to stay home and grieve? All he managed to do was add more wives to his household." Aunt Talia picked up a basket of mending and threaded a needle, her hands keeping time with her words.

"Sabba didn't tell me that." The king had finally broken his vow to Abigail? Such a thing made sense now that Abigail was gone. "Perhaps the king was lonely." She could understand the feeling, though the understanding did nothing to ease the guilt she felt over her interest in him.

Bathsheba took the basket from Jarah after the woman had chosen a tunic to mend, and picked up a shawl with the fringe missing in one corner. Keeping her hands busy provided a good distraction for her troubling thoughts.

"I'm sure he was lonely. No one wants to lose a spouse, child, but the king had plenty of other wives to choose from. He didn't need to add more."

"How many did he add?" Jarah's smooth voice had a slight accent Bathsheba couldn't place. Hadn't Rei mentioned meeting her outside of Jerusalem? Or perhaps she had recently moved here.

"Some say three, some say five. Ach! One would be too many! The man should have gone to war." Aunt Talia stabbed the bone needle into the soft wool fabric.

"Why should we care who the king marries?" Bathsheba's hands stilled, the question begging an answer. Why did everyone in the kingdom concern themselves with the king's private life? "Is he not entitled to happiness? Besides, Sabba says men from every tribe and even other nations are always willing to offer a daughter in marriage to the king. How can he refuse?"

"He refused just fine while Abigail lived. It is none of my business, to be sure, but it seems as though Adonai took the wrong wife." A sigh lifted her aunt's chest. "But who am I to question the Almighty? He gives and He takes away. Blessed be His name."

"Blessed be His name," Jarah and Bathsheba responded in unison.

They sat in silence stitching, while questions and uncertainty swirled in Bathsheba's head. No wonder she had not seen the king about his roof in the months since Uriah left for war. He had married more women and was undoubtedly busy getting to know them. And if the reports of the war were true and Sabba had heard correctly, the king would leave to join his troops, and perhaps then Uriah could come home. And once Uriah was home she would no longer be lonely, and her thoughts would no longer drift to a forbidden friendship she had mostly imagined.

She glanced at Jarah, whose belly was already slightly swollen with Rei's child. Seeds of envy sprouted, but just as quickly she doused them. Jarah might carry Rei's child, but did she have his love? At least she knew Uriah loved her.

But as they walked to the high place later that afternoon, it was the king's smiling face she longed to see, and she wondered if she was in love with her husband or with a figment of her imagination.

8

David stood at the curtained entrance of the tabernacle at the high place in Gibeon, surrounded by his counselors and bodyguards. The late afternoon breeze blew hot against his face, a trickle of sweat drawing a thin film along his crowned brow. The weight of the gold and jewels seemed heavier than usual as he entered the courtyard where the burnt offerings to the Lord burned continually day and night on the altar's hearth.

A bull, six lambs, and a ram rimmed the perimeter, awaiting their fate as sin offerings on the bronze altar at the center. Gibeon afforded a better place for sacrifices than Jerusalem's narrow streets. David had left Zadok, the high priest, in charge here from the moment he had brought the ark to Jerusalem. The plan had worked well, though he could never visit this place without wishing the sacrifices and worship before Adonai's ark could be united in one magnificent temple.

The blast of a ram's horn drew his attention to the priests dressed in fine linen ephods, with Zadok wearing the rich robes of Aaron's high priesthood. Zadok and his son tugged the first ram to the center. David stepped forward and placed his hands on its head, symbolically transferring his sins to the animal to act as his substitute, though he knew no animal's blood would ever be enough to cover a man's sins.

The priest slit the ram's throat in one swift motion. Moans and prayers from the hundreds of men and women spread out behind him drowned out the sound of the remaining bleating sheep.

David's heart constricted, and he knelt in the dust, bowing his face to the rocky, grass-tufted terrain. The rustling, shifting sound of the crowd met his ears. His people would have followed his example, copying his posture. As they should. But the prayers he heard whispered around him seemed distant, the words coming to his mind merely rote sayings he'd memorized long ago and repeated far too often of late. Where were the prayers that usually sprang from his own lips, the communion he'd enjoyed with Adonai since his youth? The priestly ritual, this monthly sacrifice commanded by the law of Moses, had never been a habitual task but one he embraced with delight.

What had happened to his joy?

He pushed to his feet and waited as Zadok pronounced the final blessing. The sacrifice alone did not make a man clean. He knew that. Only when the heart was engaged in confession and repentance, accepting the offering as payment for his sin, did Adonai look upon a man as clean in His eyes. David glanced at the blue expanse overhead, its wispy clouds doing little to block the heat from the relentless sun. He raised a hand to shade himself from the glare.

Am I clean before You, Lord?

The prayer went unanswered, and he turned away from the altar. He didn't feel clean, but he could name no sin in his heart either. Had he been wrong to take five new concubines?

He searched his heart as his guards paved a path to take him to the head of the crowd and return to the city. He felt nothing. No guilt. No assurance. Despite his efforts, his heart had chilled where the warmth of Abigail's love once lived. And he seemed powerless to do anything to change it. God should not have taken her from him.

He pushed ahead, picking his way over rocky ground, at last looking up at the faithful men and women who had accompanied him. He spotted Ahithophel, a familiar face he had not seen in at least a month. Catching Benaiah's ever-present attention, he motioned toward his counselor, and the crowd parted as he approached.

"Ahithophel, my friend, where have you been this past month? I have missed your wise counsel." David smiled, reached for the older man, and kissed each cheek. Ahithophel quickly bowed as David released him.

"My lord, you do me great honor." He stood as David extended his hand and helped him up. "I spent some time at my home in Giloh. I am pleased to report the grape harvest was better than expected."

"And I am happy to hear it. Come, let us walk together to the house of our God." The last stop after the sacrifices would be a visit to the tent that held the ark. "Then you may join me at my table this night. The New Moon feast is not the same without you, my friend." Though Ahithophel had a way of getting on his nerves sometimes, with his men at war, David missed his company.

"Thank you, my lord. I would be pleased to walk with you." He stepped in time with David's pace. "I have promised my granddaughter to eat the New Moon feast at her home tonight." He glanced behind him, motioning toward a woman in a striped red and blue veil, her dark eyes the only thing visible beneath its folds. Several other women accompanied her. "But I am sure she will not mind terribly if I miss it. Unless, of course, you would care to join us, my lord?"

David looked in the direction Ahithophel pointed, his gaze meeting the woman's. She appeared startled by his attention and quickly lowered her head. She had a familiar look about her, but he couldn't place where he might have seen her.

"I fear my retinue would be too large for her home, my friend. If your granddaughter would like, she may join the women's table at the banquet. Bring your whole family. I would be pleased to meet all of them then." The thought brightened his mood, a distraction from the normal routine.

"I'm afraid my son and my granddaughter's husband are away fighting the Ammonites. And my granddaughter has taken great pains to prepare the meal for myself and for my daughter's family. Begging your pardon, my lord, if I alone miss her feast, I shall be forgiven, but if we all miss, I shall be surely chastised." He chuckled, and David laughed with him.

"It is good to have you near me again, Ahithophel. Of course, I would not wish you to suffer the stinging tongue of a woman." He smiled at Ahithophel's laughter, but a part of him couldn't shake a desire to see his old friend in the company of his family. A normal family like he used to know before the trappings of kingship changed everything. "Perhaps if I were to personally extend the invitation?"

Ahithophel lifted a brow, his expression clearly doubtful. "As you wish, my lord. I'm sure my family would be most honored to be guests at your table." Ahithophel glanced behind him and motioned the young woman forward. She hurried to obey, keeping her gaze on her grandfather.

"Yes, Sabba, what do you need?"

David warmed to the intimate word and tone she used with her grandfather.

"Dear one, the king has invited our family to celebrate the New Moon feast at his table tonight. Do you have any objections?" Ahithophel glanced at David and winked as though he found the question itself humorous. What woman would defy her grandfather in front of the king? David hid a smile as he watched her, but she kept her eyes lowered and would not look in his direction.

"If the king is pleased to have us, Sabba, we would be most foolish to refuse him. Tell my lord the king the invitation is a great honor." The woman's tone was pleasant and familiar. Had he heard it before?

"You might tell him yourself," David said, surprised at his own boldness. The hum of voices around them told him he had not been overheard, but the woman still refused to so much as look at him.

She kept her eyes averted, as though every step over the rocky terrain must be carefully watched as she walked. "Thank you, my lord king. My family will be most pleased to share your table this night." She stopped and bowed low, then rose at Ahithophel's touch on her arm. Her reaction to him should not have surprised him—she was a married woman speaking to a man not her husband. What did he expect? King or not, he could not ask her to welcome the attention of a man she didn't know.

"I will look forward to it. Your grandfather can introduce you to me properly then." He shifted away from her, sensing her relief as he dismissed her, but unable to shake the interest their short interchange had provided.

He picked up his pace as Jerusalem's limestone walls came into view. He had no business letting his mind wander to a married woman. His own wives and children needed him, and though he would glimpse Ahithophel's family tonight, even briefly meet them at the feast, his focus must be where it rightfully belonged. After the feast he would spend time with his own family and bless them.

9

The king's banquet hall shimmered. Golden stands held cones of incense in the room's four corners, while others sparked with flame along the perimeter and on every table. Drinking chalices, bowls, and plates all rimmed with gold were set at each place, and food-laden platters covered fine white linen cloths. Bathsheba, Chava, Aunt Talia, and Jarah were led to seats near the front to the left of the spacious room, near enough to have a good view of the king's resplendent table.

Chava giggled, leaning close to Bathsheba. "Can you believe we're feasting with the king? I've dreamed of this all my life!" Her cousin's dramatics reminded Bathsheba of their girlhood days when Chava wanted to marry the king and Bathsheba wanted to marry for love.

Uriah's face floated before her mind's eye, growing ever dimmer with each passing day. He'd been gone since early spring, and the height of summer was now upon them. Would it never end? She was weary of war, of waiting for his return.

"Will you look at those serving plates? I've never seen so much food!" Chava caught Bathsheba's arm and tugged her to sit beside her while Aunt Talia engaged Jarah in conversation.

"Are you listening to me, Cousin? Or have I lost you to day-dreams even here?"

"I'm here." Bathsheba offered her cousin a smile, trying to pull herself from her sudden melancholy mood. "Just a little distracted. This place is beautiful!"

Chava shifted, placing a protective hand on her middle where Matthias's child lay. "Aren't those the king's wives?" She pointed unbecomingly in the direction of the table where the wives of King David sat and would soon share the meal.

"Yes, I don't think anyone else would sit so close to the king." Bathsheba leaned in, making sure not to be overheard. "They don't look too festive, do they?"

Bathsheba noted their masked hostility as she assessed each woman, recalling who they all were from overheard conversations between her father and grandfather and the few glimpses she'd had of them during festival parades. Michal was the oldest, though the lines along Ahinoam's mouth and brow and her dour expression put her age ahead of Michal's. Michal seemed the most at peace among the group, while Maacah's resentful glare made Bathsheba pause. That one could be trouble for the king or for his other wives. What had happened to make Maacah so bitter? And could these women not set aside their differences even for a feast?

Trumpets drew her attention, and Chava squeezed her arm, her excitement palpable. "There he is!" She hissed the words through clenched teeth. "What was it like meeting him? I'm so jealous!"

Bathsheba had heard Chava's questions the entire walk from the high place, from the moment her grandfather had singled her out and the king had chosen to speak with her there. Her heart had fluttered like the wings of an anxious bird at his nearness, and she wondered if he would recognize her beneath the heavy folds of her veil. When they had spoken at the beginning of spring, the day Uriah left for war, they had stood across rooftops and he might not have gotten a clear view of her. She shook her head. Of course he had, given the foolish way she had allowed her veil to fall from covering her face. But today he did not seem to recall the encounter as she did. But why should he? He had many women to look at and met many people each day at court. She was just another face to him. And that thought should not matter to her in the least.

"You have nothing to be jealous of, Chava. He simply wanted Grandfather to join him tonight, and Grandfather mentioned us. The king was just being polite. He barely spoke to me." She stood and bowed low with the rest of the room's occupants as the flag bearers preceded the king into the banquet hall. The trumpet sounded again, signaling the king had taken his seat on his gilded banquet couch.

"Nevertheless, many people would love the chance to even be in the king's presence, and you were practically close enough to touch him!" Chava placed a hand on her chest and gave a dramatic sigh.

"Matthias is going to confine you to the house if he sees you acting like a foolish, lovesick woman." Bathsheba chuckled and glanced at her aunt, who seemed equally taken with the king. Was every woman in love with him?

Her gaze shifted to the king at the thought. He was exceedingly handsome in his rich purple and green robes as he laughed at something her grandfather was saying to him. His features reminded her of a mischievous boy, his expression far lighter than it had been the night of Abigail's funeral procession, or even the day she had spoken with him from her roof. What a fascinating man!

"Matthias won't know if you don't tell him." Chava nodded to a servant, who placed choice pieces of lamb on her plate after he had already done so for Bathsheba. Fascinating or not, he was merely a symbol to her, the king of the land, not a man like other men. Despite her grandfather's original hopes, Bathsheba thought not for the first time how right her father had been to insist she marry outside of the royal household.

She nodded at something Chava said that she only half heard, shifting her gaze to the king's wives, whose snippy tones carried to her across the short distance that separated their tables. A shudder passed through her. Uriah's quiet household was far better than such a place, despite its opulence.

Chava chattered on, pulling Bathsheba's attention to her, moving from one subject to another, but Bathsheba's gaze invariably returned to watch her grandfather and the rest of the men at the king's table. The main meal came to an end too soon as servants moved about refilling wine goblets. Trays of honeyed nutmeats and pressed date cakes replaced platters of vegetables and roasted lamb.

The king took up his lyre and began to strum the strings. Bathsheba's heart warmed, a little thrill passing through her. She had long hoped to hear the king's music again, as her father and husband had so often on the battlefield. The room grew still as the king's voice rose above the chords, a determined, urgent, melodious sound.

"Let Elohim arise, may His enemies be scattered; may His foes flee before Him. As smoke is blown away by the wind, may You blow them away; as wax melts before the fire, may the wicked perish before Elohim. But may the righteous be glad and rejoice before Elohim; may they be happy and joyful. Sing to Elohim, sing praise to His name, extol Him who rides on the clouds—His name is Yahweh. Rejoice before Him."

Bathsheba leaned forward on the cushioned bench, entranced. She had never heard the king's voice so strong, yet something more . . . haunting, perhaps. She studied him in the lamplight, his crowned head bent forward, his eyes closed. His dark hair held traces of silver along the temples, but his face bore few marks of age.

Bathsheba's gaze drifted as her thoughts did the same. What was this hold the king had over them? Every man sat spellbound, every woman clearly moved. She studied him once again.

Devotion. She saw it in his face when he lifted his head above the crowd, his gaze rapt with awe and reverence. The king was so taken with Elohim that Bathsheba found herself caught up in the moment, in the worship. Her spirit soared with the music, and she realized that her own gaze had lifted heavenward, her heart yearning for the Most High. When at last the song ended, she looked at the king. He handed his lyre to a servant and turned to say something to one of his advisors.

The moment of worship was gone. The loss left her feeling strangely bereft. *Sing more.* But no one spoke the words.

The murmur of voices rose around her as men and women sampled the honeyed delicacies forgotten during the king's song. Bathsheba waved a restraining hand at her aunt as she offered her the tray of sweets. Her focus shifted to Chava, but her cousin was talking to a woman sitting on the other side of her. Bathsheba fingered the linen cloth and used it to dab her mouth, then picked up her gold-rimmed wine goblet and took a sip, her gaze drawn again to the king's table. Amnon and Absalom were engaged in what appeared to be an almost heated conversation with a third man she didn't recognize. The man was leaning forward, obviously attempting to appease them both.

"They're handsome men, like their father." Chava's voice gave her a start.

She looked at her cousin. "They have beautiful mothers, so why wouldn't they be?"

Chava shrugged. "And a handsome father." Her smile showed uneven teeth, one reason why Chava would never have married into the royal household, her lack of beauty notwithstanding.

Bathsheba laughed, hating the nervous way it sounded. "And every woman in this room has seemed to notice that fact! You included, Cousin."

Chava pushed back from the seat. "I drank too much wine and the baby knows it. If you'll excuse me." She asked a servant something and quickly followed the woman out of the room.

Bathsheba glanced at her aunt, who was caught up in conversation with Rei's wife. Feeling suddenly lost, Bathsheba watched the jugglers for a few moments, but her gaze found its way back to the king's table of its own accord.

Her heart skipped a beat as she caught him looking directly at her. Or was she mistaken? But the slight smile playing above his beard and the nod he gave her told her she was not. She told herself to look down, to lift her cup to her lips, or to glance swiftly away, but she couldn't pull her gaze from his. Her breath seemed to still inside of her. His look held recognition, making her cheeks feel like flame. She should never have come. But how did a mere woman refuse a king? Her own husband and father never could, and she was not better than they.

At last he broke eye contact, his attention snagged by one of the men sitting beside him. She longed to continue to watch the exchange. Who knew if she would ever have this chance again? Didn't he say he intended to be properly introduced to her tonight? Excitement and fear rushed through her as twin emotions. She could not refuse the king, but she dare not stay. The pull of this place, the king's very presence, took her thoughts to places they should not go, fed by her own sense of loneliness and longings she'd been forced to deny with Uriah's absence.

The heat of the lamps and the heavy scent of incense suddenly seemed more obsessive than sweet. She must go home, despite what the king wanted. She would be safe behind Uriah's thick walls with Anittas to watch over her.

She turned to her aunt. "Aunt Talia, I'm not feeling so well. I will ask a servant to take me home. Please, tell Chava to stay and enjoy the rest of the feast." She rose slowly on shaky limbs, forcing herself not to look toward the king's table again.

"Let me come with you, child." Her aunt half rose, but Bathsheba stayed her with a touch on her arm.

"No, please. I'm fine. I just need some air and to rest. It's been a long day." She sent a silent prayer heavenward that her aunt would accept her explanation. She was not up to scrutiny or to answering questions.

"You are too young to be so worn out." Aunt Talia met her gaze, her concern evident in the soft blue hues. "But if you're sure . . ."

"I'm sure." She smiled, though she knew it was far from convincing.

"I will check on you tomorrow."

"There is no need. Please, don't trouble yourself."

Her aunt looked at her hard, then slowly nodded. "Send word then to let me know you are well."

"I will." Bathsheba scooted away from the cushioned couch and turned to address a servant.

One of the king's guards approached, interrupting her. "The king's counselor Ahithophel requests his family approach the king's table to be introduced to the king." His countenance was friendly but brooked no argument.

Chava returned at that moment. "We're going to meet the king?" She grabbed Bathsheba's arm and tugged. "Come quickly. We should not keep the king waiting."

Bathsheba caught the hint of a smile on the guard's face, but she could not summon one of her own, her heart sinking. She truly did not feel well, but to refuse such a summons . . . She glanced at her aunt, who had clearly heard, concern and excitement equally evident in the look she gave Bathsheba.

Defeat settled over her. She should never have come. And now it was too late.

☙ 10 ❧

Uriah's feet ached, his head throbbed from the heat, and his muscles strained from walking for three days with barely a moment's rest. He wanted nothing more than to wash the grime from his body and rest beside his wife, to feel her soft skin, to smell the pomegranate fragrance in her hair. *Bathsheba.* It had been too long, and once his regiment had Jerusalem in their sights, he could not get the image of his wife from his mind.

He glanced up, the sky growing darker with each step now through Jerusalem's streets. The new moon hung low, the tip of its fingernail pointing west, like a sentinel guiding and guarding their way, like the gods his people had worshiped. He checked the thought, chastising himself for even imagining such a thing. The moon could not protect him. The God of the Hebrews watched over the people of Israel and the foreigners who followed His ways.

The gleaming lights of the palace approached. Up ahead, General Joab marched with his brother Abishai, leading the Thirty straight to the barracks for a quick change of clothes, then to the banquet hall where the king kept the New Moon feast. Uriah glanced down at his soiled tunic, glad he would soon be rid of it, but wished not for the first time this night that he could just go home. But duty called before rest or pleasure, and he was not about to shirk what was required of him. Bathsheba would not expect him so soon and would be feasting at her grandfather's or her aunt's home, no doubt.

At the barracks, he took full advantage of the cistern of water, rubbing dried blood from his arms, then hurried to his pallet and retrieved a clean military tunic from beneath the thin mat. Replacing his cloak and straightening the clasp with the lion's head pendant that marked him as one of the king's Thirty, he strode to the meeting place on the palace portico. Music filtered to him through the closed cedar doors, mingling with the scents of incense and the hiss of bronze lamps lighting every corner of the palace grounds.

"Are we all here?" Joab's voice with its low, steely rumble moved over the small group, silencing conversations. Uriah scanned the men, doing a mental head count.

"We're all accounted for," Eliam said. Uriah nodded his agreement.

"Good. The feast is already past, but the servants will accommodate us in the anteroom after we make our appearances and give a report to the king. Follow me." Joab made a swift turnabout and nodded to the guards to open the palace doors.

Uriah darted quick glances at the cedar-lined walls and marble pillars, then kept his gaze focused as they approached the banquet hall. The doors opened for Joab, and Jehoshaphat the recorder signaled the trumpeter and announced Joab's presence to the king. At the end of the hall, the king's table, covered in pure white linen with purple and green etchings and a golden lion's head at the center, drew Uriah's attention.

He could never enter the king's palace without feeling a certain sense of awe at the splendor and majesty emanating from King David. None of the previous kings Uriah had seen or served under had ever known such a high regard among his courtiers or his people. Somehow King David had managed to make all of Israel love him.

Of course, no king was without enemies, but Uriah sensed that David's were much fewer now than they had ever been. Especially after such a victory! And come next spring, they would return and finish off the people of Rabbah. The Ammonites would rue the day they had offended Israel.

As they approached the king's table, Joab bowed low before David. Uriah followed Joab's lead and touched his forehead to the cool tile floor. They rose as one at David's command.

"Joab, my scouts told me you were spotted coming home, but I did not expect you so soon. Tell me, how did the battle go?"

The music grew soft, the quiet strains of a single harp filling the background as voices in the room stilled. Uriah glanced at the king, who leaned against his couch, hands clasped beneath his bearded chin, his attention focused on Joab.

Half listening to Joab's recounting of the battle between Israel and both the Syrians and the Ammonites, Uriah let his gaze wander to the men seated at the king's table, wondering what such a privilege would be like. He spotted Bathsheba's grandfather, Ahithophel, and was reminded once again of the connection Bathsheba's father and grandfather had with the king, a connection he had made only since his marriage to Eliam's daughter, when he also found acceptance into David's mighty Thirty.

Ahithophel looked up from his wine cup and appeared to

notice him. He dipped his head in Uriah's direction. Uriah returned the gesture, then glanced to the left of the table where a line of men and women stood, apparently waiting to make the king's acquaintance. He'd seen the king extend the practice during the few military feasts he'd attended, but never participated in such a thing.

His gaze followed the line, stopping short near the end. Was that Bathsheba? The woman wore a thin veil across her face, but he would know his wife anywhere. How was it possible? What was she doing at the king's table at the feast of the New Moon?

His mind churned, imagining and discarding a handful of thoughts, when he saw another woman grip her arm and whisper something in her ear. He strained to see across the crowded, shadowed room. Her cousin. Further inspection revealed Bathsheba's aunt and a few male relatives. This must be Ahithophel's doing. Uriah relaxed at the thought and drew in a slow breath. To see her here intensified his longing for her.

"Thank you, Joab. I'll expect a full report tomorrow, but it appears we can expect no more trouble from our enemies until next spring." The king leaned forward, resting his palms on the table, then gestured to his right. "A table awaits you. Come, men, join in the feast, then return to your homes and rest. A rest well deserved." He smiled, then turned his attention to those waiting to meet him.

Uriah felt Eliam's hand on his arm, but the feast could wait. He nodded toward the women, then slipped from beside Eliam and made his way to the back of the room and came up near the end of the line. He maneuvered his way closer until he stood directly behind Bathsheba. He placed a gentle hand on her arm and bent close to her ear.

"Bathsheba." He whispered her name as it had played in his mind the entire walk back to Jerusalem.

She whirled about, a soft gasp escaping her lips. Had she not paid attention to Joab or noticed his arrival? "Uriah!" Her face paled beneath the soft blue veil, the flickering lamplight making her look almost ill. "I . . ." She placed a hand to her chest as though reminding herself to breathe. "I didn't expect you so soon."

"That's not exactly the reception I had hoped for." He smiled down at her, longing to pull her close and kiss her until her cheeks grew rosy again. But not here. He reached for her hand instead and squeezed her cold fingers. "Are you not happy to see me?" he whispered. He felt his stomach tighten, surprised at how much he wanted to hear a positive answer.

"Yes! Oh yes!" Her hushed voice and quick glance behind her at the moving line drew his attention away from her, and he noticed how close they were to the king's table. "I missed you so much!" She gripped his hand, and he drew closer to her, warmed at her obvious need of him, as her aunt and cousins bowed low before the king. "I'm glad you're here."

He released her hand and touched the small of her back. "As am I," he said as they passed in front of Ahithophel.

"My lord king, may I present to you my granddaughter Bathsheba and her husband, Uriah the Hittite, returned this night from the war with Ammon. I see he is anxious to see his bride." Ahithophel gave a bow, his arm stretched toward them both, but his smile seemed directed only at his granddaughter. Was that irritation hidden in the glint of his eyes?

"Uriah, welcome home. Thank you for your faithful service in the battle." The king's voice held genuine warmth, lifting Uriah's spirits.

Uriah bowed, dipped one knee to the ground, then stood. "Thank you, my lord. It is an honor to serve you."

The king nodded, meeting Uriah's gaze. He glanced at Bathsheba. "A pleasure to finally meet Ahithophel's family." He smiled but quickly turned his attention to the people waiting behind Bathsheba.

Uriah took that as his dismissal. He ushered Bathsheba past the king's table and followed the line around to the back of the hall where her aunt and cousins stood waiting.

"Oh, wasn't it wonderful to finally meet the king?" Bathsheba's cousin Chava had a grip on her husband's arm, her bright eyes clearly struck with awe. "He asked us questions and even promised Matthias to send some business his way." She turned to Matthias and planted a bold kiss on his cheek. The older man colored, his embarrassment evident, but gave his wife a good-humored smile.

"I think it's time we took you home, dearest." Matthias patted Chava's hand and tucked it beneath his arm.

Chava waved at Bathsheba as Matthias turned her toward the steps. "Wait." Chava planted her feet and faced Bathsheba. "What did he say to you? I want to hear everything." She glanced at Uriah as though only now noticing his presence. "We're glad you're safely home."

"As am I," he said, placing a hand on Bathsheba's shoulder. "I'm sure you can talk more with my wife another day. The king barely spoke to us, so there is nothing to tell." He liked Chava most of the time, and a woman in her position would have little chance of feasting with the king, so her excitement made sense. But why the king spoke more to Chava and Matthias than to Uriah, a faithful warrior who had earned the rank and right to enter the king's presence, he couldn't

94

begin to understand. The king seemed almost unwilling to look at Bathsheba, as though he had no desire at all to meet Ahithophel's granddaughter.

He hid a smile at the thought. Good. Ahithophel made no secret of the fact that he had wanted Bathsheba to marry into the king's household, but Eliam had overruled Ahithophel's desires, insisting his daughter would be happier in a home not of royal standing. Uriah often thanked the God of the Hebrews for Eliam's decision. If that meant he got less attention from the king as well, so be it. All he cared about right now was to go home and spend time with the wife he had missed these many months.

"Let's go home." He took her hand and led her through the palace halls and down the wide, columned steps.

❦

Starlight danced high above them as Uriah led Bathsheba home. She cinched her cloak closer to her neck, shivering despite the warm night and the woolen warmth. Uriah placed a protective hand at the small of her back, but he said nothing as they waved goodnight to her aunt and cousins, then turned the bend and traveled the narrow lane to their own private courtyard.

"My lord, you have returned!" Anittas, clearly pleased, met them at the edge of the court, his hand held out to take their cloaks. "We did not expect you so soon."

"So I see." Uriah looked at Bathsheba as he undid the clasp at his neck and removed his outer garment, handing it to the servant. He sat heavily on the bench along the wall, extending his feet, waiting for the man to remove his sandals.

Bathsheba stood aside, averting her gaze, surprised at

the bitter tone coming from her husband. Had she angered him somehow? She searched her mind, remembering the brief visit with the king, his obvious inattention to her, his focus on her husband—as it should be. But it was far different than the interest he had shown her that morning on the walk back from Gibeon or when they conversed across rooftops the day Uriah had left for war. Had he recognized her? What might he have said to her if Uriah had not returned when he did?

Heat moved through her middle, its flame spreading to her face. She shifted her gaze, catching Uriah's intent look. Anittas quickly washed and dried Uriah's feet and slowly stood, backing away to allow Uriah to enter the house.

Uriah waved him aside and stood in the arch of the door, watching her as Tirzah emerged to wash her feet. Tirzah slipped Bathsheba's jeweled sandal from one foot and massaged the arch before resting it in the tepid water. She lifted the other foot to repeat the action. "How was the feast?" she asked, her voice light, as though the honor of eating at the king's table were a monthly occurrence.

"The palace is beautiful, the furnishings rich, the food wonderful." She glanced over Tirzah's head and smiled at Uriah, hoping to dispel the look of mistrust. Or was it uncertainty that bathed his handsome face? He had no reason to be distressed with her. He could not know her traitorous thoughts or the betrayal hidden in her heart. A betrayal she no longer felt now that he was home, its seed rooted in loneliness she no longer need feel.

Relief washed over her at the hint of amusement she caught in the slight curve of his lips, his brows lifted as though they shared a secret meant only for her. She gave a coy look in response, hiding her smile behind her hand as she waited for Tirzah to finish washing her feet. How she had missed him!

Tirzah dried Bathsheba's feet, then draped the towel over one arm. Uriah filled the distance, taking her hand and pulling her close as Tirzah slipped from the courtyard. His lips sought hers, his kiss longing, possessive, dispelling all thoughts of the palace or the king.

"I've missed you," he said, his voice hoarse as he stroked the soft veil still covering her hair.

"And I you." She rested her head against his chest, feeling the steady beat of his heart beneath his tunic. "I'm glad you're home."

He led her into the house to their room, where he sat on the bed and pulled her down beside him. He shifted to face her, slowly stroking one finger down the length of her arm. "Why were you at the king's banquet tonight?" He searched her face, demanding truth from her.

She looked into his dark eyes, realizing once again that she should never have gone, despite her grandfather's desires or the king's wishes. "The king invited my grandfather to attend his feast, but Sabba had intended to eat with me—I had planned a feast for Aunt Talia and her family—so when the king decided he wanted Sabba's company, he invited us as well. We could not refuse the king." She averted her eyes, not wanting him to read her thoughts, fearing the transparency of her heart.

"No, of course not." His fingers found her chin and gently lifted her face to his. "I only wonder why the king cared so much for Ahithophel's family. The king is used to his counselor's company—he did not need to extend it to the rest of the household."

Bathsheba had wondered the same thing, but her only possible answers left her believing the king had taken undue interest in her. She could never tell her husband such a thing. Besides, such a thought was pure speculation. "I don't know," she said, allowing herself to hold his gaze. "I think the king was simply being generous to Sabba."

"What did you do with the food you had prepared?"

The question didn't surprise her, as Uriah expected an accounting of such things while he was away. She simply hadn't thought of how to explain it in such little time. "I told Anittas to give it to the servants and the rest to the poor. I couldn't let the feast go to waste."

He nodded, but fell silent as he often did when he contemplated something. "I cannot fault you for that. There was nothing you could have done differently. The king requested your presence. Your grandfather, your protector, concurred. There was nothing else you could do."

She let out a breath she'd been holding too long. "Thank you, my lord. I did not want to be there without you, but I didn't know what else to do."

His stiff manner softened, and he reached for her then, his suspicion replaced by the fire of longing she'd come to expect from him after he'd been gone so long. He removed the veil from her hair and slowly pulled the ivory combs from her long tresses. "You were obedient to the men in authority over you, dear one. That is all any woman can be expected to do."

His kiss silenced any response she might have uttered, his expectations that of every man she had ever known. Obedience without question to her father, her grandfather, and her husband, whether she agreed with them or not. It was her duty, what society and the law expected. But a small part of her, the part she kept hidden from everyone—even Chava and Tirzah—rebelled against such blind obedience. What if they asked her to do something wrong? Like tonight, dining with the king, unescorted by her husband. Despite the crowded room, she'd felt exposed, vulnerable, and a little afraid of her own reactions.

But she'd had no courage to refuse her grandfather or, even more so, the king. She'd been taught all her life to obey without question, and until tonight had done so without worry. Her father's and Uriah's devotion to the law had assured her they would always keep her safe, protected . . . pure. And as long as they obeyed the law, she had nothing to fear.

But as she lay in the crook of her husband's arms, listening to his even breathing, she wondered what she would do, how she would obey him, if he did something she knew was wrong and asked her to go along with him. His arm brushed her bare skin, and she shivered against him even as she enjoyed the comfort of his warmth. Uriah was not that kind of man. His strict adherence to the law would not allow him to put her in need of choosing such things.

She breathed a sigh, relief slowly calming her troubled thoughts and tattered nerves. Uriah was home and she was safe. Nothing else mattered.

~11~

Wind whipped the head scarf, threatening to pull it from her face, as Bathsheba watched the military men line up into groups to march through Jerusalem's streets to war. Her grandfather's roof afforded the best view of the area directly in front of the palace, where the king's warriors overflowed the crowded streets. She couldn't pick Uriah or her father out of the rows of men, not even when she looked for them under Judah's banner.

The din of clanking shields and male voices below her mingled with the songs of women praising their men and their king, to boost their morale as they left for war. Again.

Bathsheba lifted a hand to shade her eyes, then grasped the scarf to keep it in place, securing it more tightly with the clasp. A heavy sigh lifted her chest as her mind replayed the conversation she'd had with Uriah in the courtyard of their home earlier that week.

"I am leaving for war in three days," he'd said, standing before her in his captain's cloak, his jaw set in a firm line as though the matter were settled and nothing more need be said.

She'd studied him, an uncomfortable flutter near her heart

quickly shifting, sinking to her middle like weighted sand. "War?" The sinking feeling hardened to anger. "You just returned from the war two months ago."

"I know." He fixed her with a long look. "But the Syrians have come out to engage us again and the king is calling out the entire army to cross the Jordan to fight them. That includes me."

"Let the king fight his own foolish battles! You just returned—" She drew her words to a halt at the flash of his eyes and the direction of his gaze toward the imposing palace behind her. Her treasonous words would do them no good, and if the king had called her husband to battle, there was nothing to be done about it. Her life as the daughter of one of David's mighty men had taught her that much, and her married life had been no different from the first year until now.

"I'm sorry," she said, regretting her harsh tone, expecting his full forgiveness.

But instead of pulling her close and comforting her as he'd done so many times before, he moved back a step and crossed his arms. His gaze flicked to the palace again, as though he expected the walls to have ears or a bird to carry her comments to the king somewhere within his marble columns and cedar doors.

"I don't understand you, Bathsheba."

The heat of his glare still shamed her, warming her cheeks even now at the memory of his impassioned tone, so unlike her normally agreeable, gentle husband. Surely her comment wasn't so unusual . . . Didn't he know she was simply weary of the battles that took him from her? That she was tired of sharing him with the whims of the king?

But her attempts to justify her actions were drowned out by the memory of his words.

"You were raised to accept a father who fought many of Israel's early battles when the king was securing his place over the kingdom. You know what type of life this is, and you knew when you married me that things would be no different. Sometimes war comes often, sometimes there are years of peace. Learn to accept the inevitable, and stop making me feel like a failure because I can't give you what you want."

He had turned away from her then and stalked out of the courtyard, not returning until she had placed her lamp in its niche in the wall and pulled the bedcovers to her head. The sting of his words was like a slap to the face, something she had not felt since she had angered her father as a child.

Now three days had come and gone, with no chance to restore their relationship. Was he right? She rebelled against the thought. He could ask for time off, could take a leave from traipsing after Joab at every hint of a skirmish. Other men stayed home sometimes. The law allowed for it in certain circumstances.

Bitterness coated the tears at the back of her throat, but she swallowed them down as voices close at hand made her turn.

"There you are. I didn't expect you to already be here. I went to your house first." Her cousin Chava took the last step and paused, a hand to her middle where the child had grown large within her.

"Ah, my dear girl, you walk like your old grandfather." Ahithophel's head poked up behind Chava as the two walked across the roof to where Bathsheba had placed herself to best see the passing troops.

"One more month. This baby better not be late or I won't be

able to waddle up steps anymore." Chava huffed as she sidled up to Bathsheba, and leaned close to accept Bathsheba's kiss.

Bathsheba smiled, hoping Chava wouldn't notice the pained look in her eyes, then hurried over to kiss her grandfather, forcing her thoughts away from her fight with her husband and his disappointment with her. Chava would either agree with Uriah just to be ornery because the child made her irritable these days, or she would encourage Bathsheba's feelings of rebellion. Neither would restore her sense of peace nor improve her mood, so she sealed the thoughts up tight within her.

She looked back to the road winding like a wide thread among the buildings to the Eastern Gate. "There are so many men, Sabba. I cannot find Uriah or Father."

Her grandfather placed a hand on the shoulder of each woman and led them to the eastern edge of the parapet. Horses pawed the ground near the palace gate, drawing their attention.

"That man draped in black, riding the black steed, is the army general, Joab. I'm sure Uriah has spoken of him?" Her grandfather pointed to a man riding along the lines of soldiers, shouting something too far away to clearly hear.

She nodded but held her tongue. She had seen Joab at the feast of the New Moon when he had given a brief report to King David. His expression and posture had been respectful, but his gruff manner and what little she knew of him made her shudder. Though sometimes, when he put too many demands on her husband, she had a mind to tell him a thing or two. If she wasn't a woman and if she had it within her power . . .

"Your husband and father were among the group that went on ahead of the rest. They are already to the city gate by now."

She should have expected such news, but somehow had hoped to see Uriah one more time, even from a distance. She tucked her arms around her body, holding herself against the stiff breeze. His kiss at dawn had done nothing to restore the joy she had felt since his return from the last war with Ammon and Syria two short months ago. Instead, his pride, or perhaps his devotion to the law, had kept him focused on his task. Apparently he had forgotten all about his stinging words, but she could not—especially when he had spent the next few days in strategy meetings, with little time for her, not returning home at night until well past dark. She had lost him to battle before he had ever kissed her farewell and marched out to join his troop at dawn.

Now as the sun fully crested the horizon, bitter tears threatened again, and she could no longer hold them in check. She blinked quickly and gazed below, swiping at her eyes with the back of her hand, hoping and praying her grandfather or Chava would not see. She did not want their sympathy.

"Look, Bathsheba, there's the king. Do you see him?" Chava's excitement matched the way she had acted at the feast. Would the woman never get over her captivation with the man? He wasn't that amazing.

But just the same she turned in the direction Chava pointed. Her gaze lingered as she spotted the king's black horse, plain, not jewel-bedecked as in a parade, his garments that of any ordinary soldier, except for the thick ring of gold on the hand holding the reins. His signet ring.

"Why does the king not dress as a king?" He was a striking man even dressed as a warrior. Maybe more so.

"The king does not wish to be an easy target for our enemies. If he wears the crown, they will spot him. Our king is cunning, Bathsheba. He knows how to defeat a foe." Her grandfather stepped closer, placing a hand on her arm. "You must not fret for your husband's safety. The king knows how to lead his men. I'm only glad he joined them this time." He bent to kiss her cheek, then backed away. "You girls enjoy the view. I'm going inside."

Chava watched him leave, then faced Bathsheba. "You look like you haven't slept. Are you worried?" She gripped the parapet with one hand.

Bathsheba touched her cousin's arm. "Of course I worry. I hate war."

"You shouldn't have married a warrior then. You could have had Rei."

"My father would never have let me marry Rei, and you know it."

"Then you should have married one of the king's sons, as Sabba wanted you to."

"The king's sons are spoiled and proud and too young for me. And you forget my father had the final say." She glanced back at the king's fading form, a wistful feeling filling her heart. Irritation followed the reaction. The king was as much a warrior as her husband. Had she no control over her emotions?

"Are you saying you wish you had not obeyed your father's wishes, that you had married someone other than Uriah?" Chava faced her, and her words cut through the fog of her own thoughts. Is that what she'd been thinking since he'd upset her three days before?

"Of course not. I only hate that he's gone so much. I'm a widow, only not a widow." Suddenly she wished she could go back, could undo the things she had said and the tone she had used and hold him close to her once more. He needed her to be strong for him, and she had failed miserably.

"Things will improve when he returns. You just need to learn to accept Uriah for who he is, to stop trying to make him something he isn't. When we finally have peace in the land, he will be home so much you will get sick of him." Chava lifted her hand in a dramatic wave and rolled her eyes. "Just look at me."

Bathsheba laughed, but the joy did not reach her heart. She would have to wait until Uriah returned to make things up to him, and she had no idea how long that would take. "Come, let's go inside out of the wind."

"Yes, let's."

She followed Chava's lead, but as she did so, she took one last glance at the men now marching in time to the beat of a war drum. She watched the fading images of Joab, the king, and the few on horseback tilt proud heads forward and lead the charge.

Please, Adonai, give them quick success.

The sooner they won the war, the sooner Uriah would come home to her and she could make everything right again.

❧12❧

Bathsheba's heart kept the rhythm of the tambourine she shook in her hand. Her feet swirled in time with the beat as she joined her cousin Chava near the imposing structure of the Eastern Gate. That she'd managed to convince Tirzah and Anittas to trust her alone with Chava was nothing short of amazing. Had they sensed her need for time away from them, to be the first to watch for her husband's return?

The sound of horses' hooves and marching men nearly overpowered the songs of the women as they danced in the streets, waiting for the watcher at the gate to herald the entrance of the men into the city. Joy circled her as her colorful skirts ringed the lower half of her body. Though the two and a half months had seemed like a lifetime, Uriah was at last coming home and the Syrians had been defeated. War might at last give way to peace.

The trumpet sounded, the hoofbeats grew louder. Women scurried to the sides of the road to make way as the gates burst open. Shouts and cheers went up from the women, Bathsheba's own voice rising to greet their men. She craned her neck, hoping for a glimpse of her husband, but the crowd was too thick, the dust kicking up until its particles coated the air. When he did enter the city, he would never know her among so many women, all dressed in robes of varying shapes and colors, many veiled, with only their eyes revealing their joy.

"We should work our way back to the house or to Grandfather's roof," Chava said at her side. She had left her month-and-a-half-old son in the care of Aunt Talia to join Bathsheba here.

"They've barely finished passing under the gate." Another trumpet blast interrupted Bathsheba's words. "Look, there's the king."

A black horse led the way, the king sitting astride it straight and proud, wearing a king's robe and crown. Bathsheba's heart did a little flip at the sight, and the tambourine grew still in her hands.

Chava let out a dramatic sigh and placed a hand over her chest. "My heart, be still within me. Is he not the most handsome man you have ever seen?"

Bathsheba darted a look at her cousin, feeling warmth creep into her cheeks, but grateful to know her married cousin seemed to feel as she did. Her thoughts of attraction to the king were not traitorous. She was simply appreciating the king's handsome appearance. What woman didn't?

"Yes, cousin, the king is indeed handsome." Saying so somehow took the secrecy from her own attraction, relieving her of the nagging guilt. She could love Uriah and be attracted to the king. No one would fault her for such a thing, so why was she so hard on herself?

The snort of the king's horse caught her attention. She turned at his approach, entranced. Her breath stole after him as he slowly passed in front of them.

The Thirty marched on foot directly behind the king. She sought Uriah in the crowd, determined to keep her thoughts where they should be. Her attraction to the king was nothing—every woman in Israel loved him.

Oh, Adonai, help me to please Uriah. Uncertainty settled inside of her. Would he be happy to see her again?

She spotted him in the last line across the road from her. "There's Father and Uriah." She stood on tiptoe, pointing, her heart racing as they marched quickly past on their way to the palace. "Let's go." She clutched Chava's arm and shouldered her way through the crowd, taking a side street and hurrying to her house. "I want to get home before Uriah does."

"We're not going to follow the crowd to the palace? You don't want to hear the king's speech? Why do I take you anywhere?"

Chava rambled on, but Bathsheba ignored her chatter. When they were within a stone's throw of her home, panting and out of breath, Bathsheba slowed.

"I want to hear the king," Chava said, hands on her knees, leaning forward to draw for breath. "My son will need tending soon, and if we climb up to Grandfather's roof, we'll be able to hear some of his words."

"Matthias will be in the crowd. He will tell you."

"I want to hear him for myself. Why do you rush us away now?" Her teasing had given way to irritation, her expression scrutinizing, and Bathsheba hoped her cousin did not have the power to read into her soul.

"I want to please Uriah. Can you fault me for that?"

Chava placed a hand on her arm, her gaze softening. "If peace has truly come, Uriah will be home for a long time." Her smile turned to a half smirk. "You can please him then."

Chava straightened and continued walking, then paused. "You coming?"

Bathsheba stood torn. She wanted to hear the king's speech, but for all of the wrong reasons. If she saw him in his royal garb and listened to the timbre of his voice, she would find more excuses to admire him, feeding an attraction she did not want.

"You go. Uriah will enjoy it better if he gets to tell me everything firsthand." He would, wouldn't he? Or would he be too tired to tell her anything, and then she would be forced to ask Chava for details she could hear for herself right now? Indecision kept her rooted to the cobbled stones.

"Come on. How often do you get to hear the king speak?" Chava stepped forward and tugged her hand. "We'll leave before the crowd disperses. You'll still be home before Uriah gets there."

Would Uriah appreciate that she had come to greet him and heard the king's speech, or would he prefer she stay home and work? He enjoyed a celebration. Surely he would want her to enjoy one too.

A cheer went up from the distant crowd, jolting her attention.

"We're missing it! Are you coming or not?" Chava held Bathsheba's gaze, frustration clearly pinching her brows.

"All right." She lifted her skirts, wishing she could tuck them into her belt like men did, and ran after Chava's plump, puffing form before she could change her mind, hoping she didn't regret her decision.

❧

"The defeat of the Syrians is complete." The king's voice carried with authority from the palace steps to where Bathsheba and Chava leaned over the parapet of her grandfather's

110

Jerusalem rooftop, straining for a better view. "They will not attempt to lift a finger to help the Ammonites again."

Cheers erupted at his proclamation, and relief filled Bathsheba's heart. One less enemy to pursue.

"When the latter rains of spring come to an end, we will attack Rabbah and finish what we started with the Ammonites. We will not claim their land, only put them in submission to us, in keeping with the law. Adonai has given our enemies into our hands and restored the land He promised to our father Abraham. Blessed be His name!"

"Blessed be His name!" came the shout from the people gathered there, Bathsheba's own voice among them.

David raised his hands high over his head, quieting the crowd, and looked heavenward. "We have heard with our ears, O God; our fathers have told us what You did in their days, in days long ago. With Your hand You drove out the nations and planted our fathers; You crushed the peoples and made our fathers flourish. It was not by their sword that they won the land, nor did their arm bring them victory; it was Your right hand, Your arm, and the light of Your face, for You loved them. You are my King and my God, who decrees victories for Jacob."

Musicians took up their lutes and lyres, and the king's voice rose above the din, the melody of his song touching a deep chord within Bathsheba.

She fingered the tambourine at her side but did not lift it, afraid to break the spell of David's song. Swift yearning tugged her. How long had it been since she had strummed the strings of her lyre? In the many months when her father was off fighting David's battles, tutors had filled her head with knowledge of reading, writing, and figuring sums, a privilege her father was quick to remind her few women were offered or could afford. But her favorite lessons had always been when Rei taught her to play songs on his six-stringed lyre and would listen with rapt attention when she sang along with them, creating words of her own.

Her father never seemed to appreciate that side of her, and in order to discourage Rei's attention, he had not allowed their lessons to continue when he was home. And since Uriah had never shown much aptitude for such things or went about humming wordless tunes, she kept her desires hidden. Would he be pleased if she performed songs for him as the king did for the people? Why had she never asked him?

The music floated around her, stirring her longings. But what good was the ability to write without the freedom to purchase the quills and leather hides or the more expensive parchments? And what words would she pen if she could? Her songs would not be written in a book of remembrance for all to see.

The people below took to swaying to the rhythm. Some of the women joined hands and twirled, while others shook cymbals and tambourines until the streets fairly shook with the sound. She glanced at Chava swaying and twirling, her eyes closed, caught up with the king's words.

"Through You we push back our enemies; through Your name we trample our foes. I do not trust in my bow, my sword does not bring me victory; but You give us victory over our enemies, You put our adversaries to shame. In God we make our boast all day long, and we will praise Your name forever. Selah."

When the words finished, the king tipped his head back, laughing. Joy flew like a winged bird through the crowd, and Bathsheba's heart followed suit, lifting and soaring. She stepped back from the parapet and grabbed Chava's hands, twirling with her while the musical strains heightened and the beat of the drum moved faster and faster. When the last chord fell silent, Bathsheba fell back against the edge for support, her breath still keeping time with the absent drum.

"In honor of Adonai, in keeping with all He has done for us, bring the spoils to dedicate here to the Lord." The king's voice carried clearly to her, and Bathsheba turned to watch.

The Thirty parted the crowd while soldiers came up from different directions bearing armloads of gold, silver, bronze, precious stones, and more that was too hard for Bathsheba to distinguish. An open area below the palace steps soon filled with the spoils taken from the Syrians. When the last man had entered the grounds and deposited his allotted baggage, a lone ram's horn gave a long trumpet blast.

"Several years ago, I had it in my heart to build a temple to Adonai, but the Lord did not allow my request. He said to me through the prophet Nathan that a son born to me would one day build a temple to His name, but I would not live to see it built."

Bathsheba's heart quickened at the king's words, and sadness filled her that he would not live to see his dream come true.

"But the Lord did not restrict me from gathering materials or making plans that will be necessary for this grand structure, so I have made it my priority to do so. These riches that you see before you today are henceforth dedicated to the Lord for use in the temple my son will one day build. Zadok, please come."

The priest emerged from under the roof of the portico dressed in his priestly robes. Bathsheba listened as he prayed, asking Adonai's blessing on the riches and the future work of their hands. Something stirred deep within her as she opened her eyes to peer down on the scene. What would it be like to take part in helping to prepare for the temple, to be part of such a grand project? But what could a mere woman do?

"Adonai's blessings on you. May His mercy and peace be upon Israel."

Bathsheba watched the king turn, step away from the crowd, and enter the palace.

"Are you ready to go? My son will want to eat soon."

Chava's question brought her gaze back into focus. Guards moved in and motioned for the people to return to their homes. Uriah was probably one of the men seeing that the place was cleared before he returned to her. She'd had no reason to worry that she wouldn't be there ahead of him.

"I'm ready." She released a slow breath, letting her dreams fall where they may.

"Aren't you glad we stayed to watch?" Chava caught her arm and led the way, hurrying down the steps.

"I'm glad," she said. She bid Chava farewell and hummed the king's song all the way home.

PART II

It happened in the spring of the year, at the time when kings go out to battle, that David sent Joab and his servants with him, and all Israel; and they destroyed the people of Ammon and besieged Rabbah. But David remained at Jerusalem.

2 Samuel 11:1 NKJV

Then David sent messengers, and took [Bathsheba]; and she came to him, and he lay with her, for she was cleansed from her impurity; and she returned to her house. And the woman conceived; so she sent and told David, and said, "I am with child."

2 Samuel 11:4–5 NKJV

But the thing that David had done displeased the Lord.

2 Samuel 11:27 NKJV

❦ 13 ❦

Bathsheba smoothed a hand over the lyre and strummed a soft chord. The day's work of weaving behind her, she held the instrument Rei had fashioned for her closer to her chest, her fingers first strumming then plucking the strings. That Uriah had allowed the introduction of such music into their home pleased her. She longed to do more, to record her words and musical notations on parchment, to include him in making music with her, but he had shown little interest.

A sigh worked its way through her, and she looked up at the sound of heated voices in the courtyard. Her hands stilled as she recognized her father's low grumble. She reached for the leather casing and quickly slipped the lyre inside, tucked it beside the couch, and grabbed the spindle and distaff from a low basket. She stood, working the wool in the spindle as she walked to the door, knowing her father would frown his displeasure if her hands were idle.

"It is foolishness, the way I see it." Uriah opened the door and moved inside, her father one step behind.

Bathsheba smiled at his glance, then nodded at Tirzah as the maid entered the room and quickly hurried off to do

Bathsheba's silent bidding. She accepted her father's kiss. "Good evening to you, Abba."

"And to you, my daughter." Eliam took a seat on the edge of the couch, hands resting on his knees. He focused on Uriah. "I agree. The king's marriages are more often than the Canaanites' calls to war. I suppose the treaties are what matter. These new wives will ensure peace with the northern tribes. But to take them now when war is upon us . . . it does not set well with the men."

Bathsheba moved to sit in a low chair in the corner, her fingers nimbly moving, fighting the sick feeling she always got when Uriah prepared to leave for battle. How was it that spring had come so quickly? Five months was not nearly long enough.

"To stay home from this battle for a wife, or in this case more than one, is an excuse, if you ask me." Bathsheba heard the sour note in Uriah's tone. His words were barbed arrows, wounding her. He would never consider shirking his duty for her, so why should he approve of the king's decision? But what had happened to the respect he'd always carried for the king? It was the king's own edicts that sent Uriah to war in the first place—the very same directives that kept him so often away from home, away from her. Twinges of envy pricked her conscience. Did the king stay home for love?

She caught Tirzah's eye as she entered the sitting room carrying a tray of cheeses and bread, sauces and dates, while another female servant followed behind carrying clay cups and a skin of wine.

"The king has always had a weakness for women, so his actions should not surprise us." Her father glanced at her, offering a benevolent smile. "Which is why I never let him see my daughter." Eliam took the wine cup from the servant and helped himself to the food Tirzah placed before him. "What woman would want to share control of her home?" He met Bathsheba's gaze again. "A woman should be a good manager of her husband's affairs, and complete the work of her hands."

His pointed look made Bathsheba wonder. Had he heard the music of the lyre as he entered the courtyard? She lowered her gaze, avoiding eye contact. Life was not made only for work. Even the law allowed for days of resting and feasting.

"The king's weakness is not what worries me so much as does his decision to let Joab lead the troops to capture Rabbah. This is the king's battle. Someone should change his mind about this war. Is Ahithophel unable to get through to him? Perhaps if we spoke to Joab." Uriah took his cup and sipped. He ripped off a piece of flat bread and dipped it in cucumber sauce.

"Joab likes leading the army, making the decisions without the king overriding his every move." Her father dipped his bread into the creamy dill and stuffed the piece into his mouth.

"But Rabbah is the last stronghold, and King Hanun humiliated David's own son! What kind of a father ignores such a slight? What king doesn't lead his troops to war in the spring?" Uriah's body grew rigid, and Bathsheba looked at him, wondering why he cared so much. So what if the king didn't go to war with his troops?

"Rabbah is also a fortress, and the city will not fall easily. David is no fool. He knows this and is sending Joab to wear them down. He'll come in time to deal the final death blow, to see the capture of the city, and to place the king's crown on his own head." Eliam swallowed the last of the wine and set the cup on the table. "If we are leaving soon, I must go. Unlike the king, I have work to do to prepare for war."

Uriah stood with him, and Bathsheba scrambled to her feet. "You're going so soon, Father? But you only just arrived." She should be used to him rushing off as he did. He had spent a lifetime running after King David to war.

He moved to kiss each of her cheeks. "I'm sorry, Daughter, but your husband and I leave in the morning for Rabbah, and I think he might like some time with you alone before we go." He smiled at her and patted Uriah on the back.

"Tomorrow? Why did you not tell me sooner?" Her emotion rose in swift, hot anger.

Uriah's hand on her shoulder made her turn. "Joab commissioned the Thirty to go on ahead of the troops to scout out the area before the rest of them leave in three days. He made the decision this morning." He glanced at her father, then wrapped his arm around her waist. "Do not fret, dear one. You knew that once we hit the month of Iyyar, war was imminent. It happens this way every year."

"Not every year." She swallowed the bitter taste of gall.

"Every year since our marriage and many years before that." His tone held a tinge of sternness, and she knew to argue would do her no good.

"We will be back before you can possibly miss us." Her father turned then and moved toward the door. He glanced back at Uriah. "I will come by at dawn."

Uriah gave a nod of acknowledgment and pulled her close. "Your father is right," he said as they watched Eliam leave the courtyard and move into the street. "This war should not take long—it's only one city."

Then why did the king wait to go, letting his men do most of the work of besieging the city for him? But she didn't voice the question, knowing that to challenge Uriah would only lead to frustration for both of them. There was nothing she could do to convince him not to go, and there was nothing he could say to convince her that his going was the right or best thing to do.

She rested her head against his chest, feeling his strength, hearing the steady cadence of his heart, desperate to memorize this moment, the feeling of her safely in his arms. Surely he would come back to her. But no war ended quickly. They all took months at a time, and even if the soldiers could get away from the battle, they would not return home until they could come as a group, with the war finally over. It was the way of things. The way it had always been.

This time would be no different.

⚜

The month of Tammuz brought a wave of summer heat, and with it a growing sense of restlessness. Two months had passed since Uriah had marched through the Eastern Gate and headed to Rabbah. Word had reached her grandfather that the Ammonites had fled inside their city, where they remained, holding out against Joab's forces. It promised to be a long siege.

Bathsheba walked with Tirzah through the marketplace to the Gihon Spring to draw water. The early morning breeze ruffled the scarf draped over her face, and she pressed a hand to her head, feeling the beads of sweat soak into the fabric.

"Perhaps another visit to your aunt's home would help," Tirzah said, shifting an empty jar from her head to her shoulder. "You know you always feel better after an afternoon with her."

"Perhaps." She had considered the thought more than once during the past weeks but had discarded the reasons to visit as quickly as they came. Chava spent more time with Aunt Talia now that she carried a third child, and Rei's wife Jarah had an infant son to care for. The sight of so many little ones should bring her joy, but it only increased her sadness.

Bathsheba readjusted the jug on her own shoulder, knowing her excuses were unfounded. Aunt Talia would welcome her visit, and once Bathsheba got past the initial sting of her barrenness, she would enjoy the children. So why did she continue to make excuses?

"We could work on some of the tunics for the poor children." Tirzah's attempt to engage her in conversation grated like iron on clay, like Uriah's sword sharpened against stone. She shivered, remembering the awful sound.

"We can talk about it later." She ignored Tirzah's lifted brow, averting her gaze to the line of women standing at the tower of Gihon. When their turn came to draw water, Tirzah took her jar and dipped it into the spring, waiting until the water bubbled at the top to fill the jar to the brim, then did the same with Bathsheba's jug.

When she finished, Bathsheba led them back along the market street, past the merchants, to their house near the king's palace. "Do you think he will leave for the war soon?" She stopped at the outer court of the palace, peering through the gates to the gleaming marble steps. The king's home shone like a jewel at the heart of the city, though with the men at war, activity coming from within had dwindled.

"Palace gossip doesn't say one way or the other. I've heard tell the king has grown bored with the new wives he took at the start of spring. They say he is moody and restless, and most of the servants prefer to stay out of his way. Some of his wives are grumpier than he is. If you ask me," Tirzah said, directing a hand toward the gates, "the king would be better off to join his men at war. Nothing good can come of a king's restlessness."

"Why is the answer to every problem a man has an invitation to go to war? Perhaps the better solution is to bring the men home and be done with this business." Bathsheba turned abruptly, splashing some of the precious water from her jug onto the hot stones beneath her feet. Irritated, she tightened her grip on the jar and moved slowly toward home, unable to stop the deep sense of longing, of missing Uriah, and thoroughly sick of the quiet city. The time had come for her purification again, and Uriah would not be here to comfort her when she had finished.

"The men need to come home." She felt her throat thicken with the admission as they entered her courtyard, knowing full well such a thing was still several months away. If only her grandfather could convince the king to bring Uriah home. But she knew even if he came, he would not abandon his loyalty to his men. He would not enjoy his wife while the men under his command were in the fields far from their own homes.

"I know you miss him." Tirzah set her jug in the hole in the courtyard's stone, then set Bathsheba's beside hers. "Perhaps he will be home sooner than you think."

"Doubtful." Bathsheba moved into the house toward the kitchens, Tirzah following. There was food to prepare and servants to feed and mending to do. She couldn't sit around pining after her husband, despite her desperate loneliness.

❦

"When do you want your bath prepared?" Tirzah asked some time later as they set the dough to bake in the oven and chopped dill and garlic for the cucumber dipping sauce. Tirzah knew Bathsheba's cycle and Uriah's strict instructions to follow the laws for every woman in the household. Once Bathsheba finished her purification, other female servants would follow, preserving water.

"After the evening meal. I will bathe in the inner courtyard as always." It wouldn't be the same without Uriah's playful banter or his welcoming arms once she was through, but she would observe the ritual just the same. Then she would retire to the room she should be sharing with him and pretend he was still with her. Perhaps by wishing it so, she would fill the void of missing him.

❧14❧

David stared at the ceiling, hands behind his head, his gaze skimming the same lines, the same jagged ruts, in the cedar beams above his bed. He yawned, his body weary yet not tired, his mind rehearsing the multiple list of grievances he'd heard that very morning. He'd passed judgment almost without forethought. The cases were different yet the same—the faces changing with the years but the pleas coming from an unbroken column of humanity begging for justice.

He was a good king. He had worked hard to judge righteously, to be fair and prudent and swift to punish the guilty. And except for the war with Ammon, the land had never known such peace.

He rose, his movements languid, the heat of the day still clinging to the inner rooms of the palace, despite the servants waving palm fronds and the cool water drawn hourly from the Gihon to refresh his thirst. The nap had revived him, but he could not shake the restlessness, the sense that he should do something—anything—to relieve his melancholy mood.

A servant entered at the snap of his fingers. "Bring me fresh wine and draw a cool bath." He moved through his bedchamber to his adjoining gardens and fingered the long, pointed leaves of the almond tree, then breathed in the scents of sage and pine. His cultivated flowers had lost their blooms in summer's heat, much as he had lost his joy. He should sort through his parchments and pen a new song, but no words played a tune in his head, and the desire to create fell away.

"Your bath is ready, my lord." The servant approached and handed him his golden chalice. He sipped the smooth red wine and waved the servant off. "I have changed my mind. Perhaps later."

"As you wish, my lord." The servant disappeared, leaving David alone. The breeze no longer carried the hot breath of midday, lifting the strands of hair from his forehead. He should have gone with the men to the battle, should leave even now to join them. Joab's disrespect and his bitter tone were preferable to this sense of aloneness. His excuse of having taken a new wife held no purpose or joy for him now. The newest group of women offered to him by the northern tribes was uninteresting and boring. And if he thought on it long enough, as he seemed consigned to do of late, most women were singularly uninteresting and boring, so why had he thought these new wives would be any different? No one matched Abigail, and no one ever would.

Irritated, he walked back to his bedchamber, but he was weary of rest. Carrying the chalice in one hand, he passed Benaiah with a nod. The guard fell in behind him, and servants bowed low and skirted out of his path as he strode down cedar-lined halls, his jeweled sandals landing on gleaming patterned tiles. He turned toward the location of the women's courtyard, slowing his gait. Bickering voices floated to him past the closed door, and the cries of small children made him pause. Soft music trilled in the background but could not override the bitter sounds of quarreling.

He whirled about, in no mood to face his wives, and took the halls in the opposite direction to the roof. "Stay here." He glanced at Benaiah, then moved up the steps, his palm skimming the rail as he ascended.

The evening breeze lifted the hairs on his arms, bringing a sense of welcome relief. He sipped again from the golden cup, the wine warming him, slowly silencing the restlessness that dogged his every step. He strolled the length of the roof, avoiding the parapet that overlooked the court of women. Even from this distance, he would not be able to escape their arguments if he stood too close to their roof. Often, when Abigail used to sit under the shade of the palm tree and stitch beautiful patterns in cloth, he would look down on her and she would catch him watching. A twinge of lingering grief accompanied the memory, and he closed his eyes, forcing it away. He could not bring her back, and the memories did him no good except to sour his mood.

He moved to the far end of the roof, away from the women's court, and edged his way to the parapet. The strumming of a lyre coming from a neighbor's house below caught his attention. He rested a hand on the rail, his gaze searching for the source of the sound. At last he spied a woman seated on a bench in the inner courtyard of her home, her head bent over a small lyre. The music, soft and haunting, made his throat thicken, and emotion filled his chest. He heaved a sigh, his knees going weak. He gripped the parapet to steady himself. Her back was to him, and he had to stand just right to see into her courtyard, whose high walls would normally keep it hidden from his view.

The music continued, its power unnerving. Who was this woman who could strum the strings with such passion, such feeling? The tune's melancholy flair matched the exact cadence of his heart. Why had he never heard her before? But the question was easily answered, as he rarely strode along this side of the roof at this time of night. Perhaps she kept the music to herself most of the time.

He stood spellbound until the chalice grew heavy in his hand, and he thought to leave her to herself, feeling like an intruder upon something private and sacred. But a moment later, she set the lyre in a leather sack and handed it to a servant, then turned and waited as another servant stripped her of her robe and tunic.

David's pulse leapt like a gazelle as she stepped into a bronze basin and the servant poured a thin stream of water over her head. The woman winced, her eyes closed, her hands lifted to the sky. Her dark hair cascaded downward to her slim waist, and he could not stop his gaze from traveling to the edge of each strand, then lingering over her glistening skin.

Heat spread through him, a fire burning and unstoppable. Who was she? Shadows spilled across her courtyard, making her body visible only in the flickering lamplight. But the darkness could not hide the perfection, the beauty, standing so innocently below him. She could not know he watched her. Not from where he stood. But when she glanced toward his roof, he took a step back, embarrassed at the thought of being caught. He had no excuse to stay here. She was obviously going through the ritual purification prescribed for women by the law. A devout woman and a musician. Did she share his lonely heart?

The possibility cheered him. Would she understand his

need, his own empty longings, that no woman seemed able to fulfill? The sound of her voice talking to a servant drew his eyes back to her again. The sight made his heart stand still. Her head was bowed as though she was praying, and the servant poured the last of the water over her head, the liquid sliding easily over her exposed skin into the basin. Every movement made his blood pump thicker, faster, until desire blocked every thought from his mind.

When she stepped from the basin and accepted a towel from the servant, David's heart quickened. He must act now before she slipped into her house. He moved unwillingly from the spot where he could see her and walked a few paces away to the stairs. At his summons, Benaiah hurried up the steps.

"Yes, my lord."

David motioned with his hand for Benaiah to follow. He peered down at the precise spot and breathed a sigh that she still stood drying herself in the courtyard. David pointed to her and met Benaiah's gaze. Benaiah backed away and David followed.

"Send someone and find out who this woman is," David whispered.

Benaiah nodded and left to do David's bidding. David stepped back to watch as the woman released the towel and allowed the servant to slip a fresh tunic over her head, his heartbeat picking up its pace again, anticipation filling him. If she were not married, he would send for her father this night and arrange a betrothal and marriage before week's end. What need would there be to wait? He could easily afford any bride price and required no waiting period. His servants might balk at putting a wedding together so quickly, but they would do his bidding whether they agreed with him or not.

He rested a hand on his beard, cupping his chin, entertaining a smile. He would set her apart from the other women. They would spend every evening he could spare making music together in her lavish apartment, the apartment he would have built for her once she belonged to him. In the meantime, he would allow her to stay in his own rooms. And why not? He had given Abigail the privilege before Chileab was born. Even if this woman conceived soon after their marriage, he would keep her close.

A throat cleared as someone approached. He stepped away once again as the woman retreated into her house, her absence leaving a void in his heart. No matter, if he could bring her into his home at week's end. How was it possible he had not seen such a beautiful woman before now? He glanced up at Benaiah, reading warning in the man's gaze.

"You have news."

Benaiah gave a nod toward the woman's house. "Is this not Bathsheba, the daughter of Eliam and wife of Uriah the Hittite?" He crossed his arms over his chest, immovable.

David looked away, feeling a sudden death blow to his plans. Bathsheba. He knew that name. They had met before, and he had dismissed her beauty because she belonged to one of his mighty men. He glanced from his roof to hers, wondering how it was possible that he didn't recognize it earlier. She was the woman who had captured his attention more than a year ago. But not so completely. Not in this way.

Irritation spiked within his breast, the earlier restlessness making his feet tread the length of the roof and back again, once, twice. But the desire to have her would not flee. He glanced toward her roof, the music of her laughter and her lyre silent now. Her husband was fighting before the gates of

Rabbah, as was her father. He could take her and they would never know of it.

His palms grew slick with sweat, his heart drumming an anxious rhythm at the thought. Would she come? But of course she would come. He was the king. She would have no choice but to obey his summons, and once she was in his private rooms . . . He let his thoughts drift, imagination making his blood pump harder again. When had a woman made him yearn for her so? Not since Abigail had stood before him in the cave the night he'd married her.

"Send for her." He walked to where his guard stood waiting and met Benaiah's gaze without flinching.

Benaiah's look held censure, reminding David of the man who had once disdained Saul's annulment of his marriage to Michal. "She is the wife of another man, my lord."

"Whatever happens, you are not responsible. Just do as I say."

Benaiah shook his head. "In good conscience, I cannot approve of this, my lord." He held David's gaze a moment longer than he would normally have done. "I will send someone else." He turned without a word and descended the steps.

15

Bathsheba rested her foot on a low bench of her bedchamber while Tirzah sat on the floor, drawing henna patterns on Bathsheba's arches and heels. The activity was useless since Uriah was not home to see their efforts, but it cheered her to do something besides keep the laws and do the chores, day after day with no one besides the servants to share them with.

"You can do my fingernails when you finish. Though I'm not sure why I bother." Bathsheba leaned back against the cushions Tirzah had propped on the bed for her comfort, sighing. "When will this war end? I am so tired, Tirzah! I want to do something, to go somewhere, to hold my husband close again."

"Hold still. You're moving too much." Tirzah dipped the reed in the dye and tsked. "Uriah could come home tomorrow, and this will have all been worth it."

Bathsheba humphed and crossed her arms. "Sabba would have said something if the end of the war was near, and you know it." She narrowed her eyes at the servant. "You haven't heard something you're not telling me, have you?"

Tirzah shook her head, then tucked a loose strand of hair behind one ear. "Nothing new. The only rumor I've heard is the one I told you about earlier, that the king might leave soon for Rabbah. The city will become quieter and even more boring once he leaves. If it's true."

"It will only give the people less to gossip over. He sits holed up in that palace and never pokes his head out. I wish he would hold a parade or invite us to another banquet or something. Maybe you are right—it is time I visit my aunt again. Chava will drool over your work, but you mustn't paint her feet even if she begs you." Bathsheba pursed her lips, enjoying the thought of seeing Chava pout over Tirzah's gifts, which Bathsheba happily employed.

"I would not even consider such a thing, mistress." She gave Bathsheba a conspiratorial look as she placed the last line along the inside edge of Bathsheba's foot, then blew on the henna and waved a hand over it to help it dry. "Your feet are fit for the king himself!"

Bathsheba giggled at Tirzah's bloated face as she puffed air over her feet. "Unfortunately, Chava will have to do." They had not seen the king since the day she and Chava had watched him return from the war, when they had stood and enjoyed the fanfare from her grandfather's roof.

A knock on her bedchamber door stopped her laughter. Tirzah slowly stood and took her time to answer. Bathsheba sat up and wiggled her feet, trying not to smudge the paint, willing them to dry faster.

Anittas stepped into the room and dipped his head in respect. "Mistress, you must dress quickly in your best robes and come at once. Messengers have come from the king. Your presence at the palace is requested immediately."

Bathsheba gripped the edge of the bed, her breath growing still. "The king? Is asking for me?" A nervous quiver worked through her. "What could he possibly want?"

"I don't know, mistress. I hope nothing is wrong. The messengers didn't say." Anittas's stricken look brought her thoughts up short. Uriah! Why hadn't she thought of him first?

"You don't think . . ." A sick feeling replaced the shudder. "He must be all right. He's strong, a mighty warrior . . ." She searched for words to convince herself her husband was not injured or worse. "But why else would he ask for me unless . . . could it be Father?" Her mother had died long ago, so if her father had been killed, she would be the first to know, except . . . no, her grandfather would be told first. It had to be Uriah.

Emotion pricked her throat while fear and excitement set her mind spinning. The king had sent for her! She must dress. She lifted one foot and touched the paint. "I think it's dry." She glanced at her hands. "But you never got a chance to stain the nails." She looked at Tirzah, beseeching.

"I will leave you two alone. I suggest you choose your best clothes, my lady. No need to wear the black sackcloth of mourning until you know why he has called for you. Perhaps it is nothing." But Anittas's words did not match the glimmer of worry on his lined face.

Tirzah was already snatching jewels from a box on a table in the corner and pulled Bathsheba's green-and-blue-striped robe from a peg along the wall. "Do you want to keep that tunic? It's fresh, but it's not your best." Tirzah moved to a basket and grabbed two pairs of sandals. "Which ones?"

Bathsheba touched the white linen tunic covering her body. "Give me the blue tunic." The pale blue matched the robe better. "And the golden leather sash for my waist, and the yellow leather sandals—they're the closest fit to complement the belt."

Tirzah nodded and had Bathsheba dressed quicker than

she expected. "What about my hair?" They had just finished combing the tangles from each strand. It hung full and thick to her waist, but she couldn't possibly wear it down to see the king.

"I'll pull it up with your jeweled ivory combs." She handed the blue scarf to Bathsheba, the same fine pale linen as in her tunic.

Bathsheba sat obediently, allowing Tirzah to dress her hair and dab a small amount of kohl on her eyes, then carefully place the head covering over her head, draping it loosely across her face. Excitement raced through Bathsheba as she walked to the door, her pulse pounding, her fear mounting.

Tirzah squeezed her hand. "You'll be fine," she whispered as the king's messengers met her in the outer courtyard.

They looked at her, their gazes assessing.

"Do you want me to accompany you, my lady?" Anittas came up beside her, giving the king's messengers a stern glance. Did he think she needed protection from the king's own guards?

"The king requested her presence alone," one guard said. He carried a torch to light Jerusalem's dim streets and turned abruptly to walk away. Bathsheba gave Anittas an apologetic look and hurried to follow while the other guard came along behind her.

They walked in silence, the sound of their marching feet barely drowning out the drumbeat of her anxious heart. At the gates to the palace, they did not pause but passed by the guards who appeared bored and uninterested.

The banquet hall came into view, and Bathsheba recognized the cedar carvings on the doors and the marble columns along the portico. The lion's head symbol of Judah greeted her on wall tapestries, and fig leaves adorned the edges of oak tables in the anterooms, where scribes sat recording something on scrolls and servants milled about cleaning and refilling oil lamps.

After several turns in the hall, they came to another carved door, where the lion's head boasted a proud look daring all who might enter to remember who guarded this place. Was this the king's private residence?

One of the guards knocked twice, and the door was opened by another guard whose stern look nearly stopped her heart. He bid her enter, then both men stepped into the hall, closing the door behind her and leaving her alone.

Nervousness made her palms moist. She took cautious steps into a walled garden. Set stones made a cobbled walkway, while a variety of trees and bushes of almond, fig, and sage sat among potted plants whose flowers were long past the bloom of spring. Water sat in pools of marble, and tall sconces held covered torches. Even in the heat of summer, the garden took her breath, its beauty unequaled to any she had seen in Jerusalem.

Music drifted to her from across the court and out of sight. She moved slowly forward toward the sound, the minor chords pulling her with unseen hands. Where was she? And then she saw him, and her knees grew so weak she searched for a place to sit. A stone bench seemed to await her, opposite him where he sat strumming his lyre, his gaze taking her in.

She reached the bench and sank down, her hands clutching the edge, her back straight. His dark eyes held her bound, his look possessive as if he knew her . . .

Her breath hitched, and her hand moved to her chest to somehow still her racing heart. He did know her. He had seen her. The realization drained her blood. She was always so careful.

Shame brought the blood rushing back, and she stood with such force she nearly lost her balance. She whirled about, her cheeks blazing. She took two steps forward, but her limbs felt leaden, useless.

"Don't go." His words were soft, like a caress.

The music ceased, and she sensed he had risen, but still she could not make her feet obey to turn and face him or run back along the cobbled path to the door, through the palace halls, and to the safety of her own house. How could she run from the king?

His touch on her arm made her middle turn to liquid. He fingered her head covering. "I heard your music. Your tunes were haunting." He turned her slowly to face him, and she was unable to stop him. "And I could not pull away."

His gaze searched hers, his dark eyes assessing, almost . . . vulnerable. Night breezes lifted the tassels of her scarf, and when his hand moved to pull the blue fabric from her face, she lowered her gaze, the action humbling her. "I share your loneliness."

Butterflies took wing inside of her. Warmth crept up the back of her neck, filling her face. Her heart thudded faster as she felt the combs coming loose from her hair and his fingers sift the strands away from her face.

"Look at me, Bathsheba."

She lifted her head, and his hands moved to her waist, expertly undoing the knot of her belt. "You know my name."

"I know more than your name, beloved." He let the belt drop to the stones and placed his hands on her arms, slowly moving them until he cupped her face and lowered his lips to hers.

His kiss was gentle, but when it deepened, images of Uriah flitted before her closed eyes. She flinched.

He pulled back, looking at her. "Do I offend you?"

Did he? She should say yes, of course he offended her. She had a husband who went to great lengths to protect her, and here she was throwing away all he had worked to do, with a man whose very look stole her breath. What was she doing here?

"Why did you call for me?" It was a foolish question, one she could already answer, but she needed to think, and she couldn't do so with him standing there looking down at her, caressing her.

He stepped back from her then, and she noticed the royal insignia on his robe, the circle of gold on his head. He had dressed as a king, not a lover. To remind her he expected to be obeyed? Would Uriah suffer if she did not do as the king was asking her to do?

"I think you already know the answer to that question."

And he would take what he wanted because he had the power to do so. This was not love. Love was at home with Uriah.

"I want you, Bathsheba." His words were a mere whisper, their meaning sinking deep, wooing her, softly stripping her resolve. "Though in truth I must sound to you like a callous fool." He moved to the bench and sat, picked up his lyre, and strummed, the music coming in soft, gentle tones, a melody tender and poignant, drawing her in.

Her heart stirred at the sound, and she sank down on the bench again, her gaze fixed on his. Shadows bathed his face, the flicker of the lamps illuminating the dark eyes and the boyish tilt to his brow. His look assessed her with familiarity and longing, and her heart skipped like a skittish gazelle, then slowed as though realizing she was caught with no way to escape.

"I don't think you are callous or a fool," she said at last. She studied her hennaed feet. "I think you are often misunderstood . . . as am I." The admission heated her face again, and she drew in a breath when the music stilled once more.

"Where did you learn to play the lyre?"

She looked up. He had not risen or sought to touch her again, but she could not escape the desire in his eyes. "My cousin taught me to play when I was a child and built a small lyre for me as a gift. My father and my husband do not care for it overmuch, so I play most often while he—while they are away." She glanced at her hands and gripped her robe, kneading the fabric between her damp palms. Why was she telling him this?

"You play beautifully. I should enjoy hearing you sing. Will you play for me?"

The question startled her, her gaze snapping to his. "I am not very good."

"On the contrary, you are quite good." The lines around his eyes softened, and he leaned against the bench, his lyre resting on his lap. He studied her for a long moment, the fire in his eyes growing to embers, and his smile melted her insides. His distance was doing strange things to her senses, his silence unnerving.

"I have made you uncomfortable calling you here." It wasn't a question, and she didn't know how to respond. "Most people do not speak easily with me, their king."

Her hands stilled from pleating the folds of her robe. "I found you quite easy to talk to that day on the roof." Did he remember?

His gaze sparked with recognition. "Ah yes, last year, when the war with Ammon first began. You were the woman I could not forget, who haunted my dreams many nights afterward." His mouth tipped at one corner, and he suddenly looked far more like a young boy than a king.

"I looked for you after that, but you stayed away." What was it about him that made her tongue so loose?

"It did not seem proper for the king to talk to a married woman across rooftops, so I did my best to forget you." His admission unsettled her even further. "But I am finding that task much harder than I expected."

She looked behind him, then down at her feet, anywhere but directly at him, but his silence only heightened the air between them until she at last met his gaze. "I have thought of you often."

His slow smile brought the flutter back to her middle, but still he did not move from where he sat. What were his intentions? But surely she knew.

"Your husband is gone quite often, is he not?"

The frankness of the question startled her. She nodded, surprised at the emotion suddenly filling her throat. "As often as my king sends the troops to war. Uriah never misses an assignment." She heard the bitterness in her tone and wondered what he thought of her now, knowing her resentment was aimed partly at him.

Tension pulsed between them until at last he stood again and took the seat beside her. Her heart quickened as he traced a line along her arm and shifted to face her. "You have reason to resent your king."

She could not speak past the knot in her throat.

He tucked her hair behind her ear and bent to kiss her

throat. "I am sorry to have caused you such pain and loneliness, Bathsheba." His kiss sent little shocks through her, making her sense of reason muddied and distant. "Will you stay and accept my love as a token of my apology?" He slipped the robe from her shoulders, his hands probing in places only Uriah had dared to go.

She should not be here. But she could not stop the longing, the desperate need to give herself to him, to know him as she was fully known.

"I will stay," she whispered beneath the gentle pressure of his lips on hers.

Emotion throbbed between them like a living, breathing thing. His kiss deepened, heating her blood, until desire won over reason.

16

Bathsheba lay perfectly still, listening to the king's even breathing. Darkness shrouded them beneath rich purple curtains hanging from the ceiling across four golden posts. The privacy should have brought her some sense of comfort, but guilt and desire warred like opposing armies within her, making sleep impossible. She should go home at once, before anyone suspected, but to move would disturb him. Did she dare? Would he even notice or miss her? What did his other women do once he had finished with them?

The questions assaulted her until her fear returned, crushing her. Why had she given in to him? She stole a glance at his face but could make out little in the dim light. Surely the night still surrounded them. She had not lain awake here long enough for dawn to come. Perhaps if she moved very quietly, she could leave unnoticed. It would be for the best. But dare she go without his dismissal?

She shifted, testing the bed's softness, and moved closer to the edge. But as she was about to swing her legs to the floor, David's arm came around her waist and pulled her to him. His breath tingled against her neck.

"Don't go. Not yet." He buried his head against her hair and drew in a slow breath.

"It isn't safe for me to stay, my lord. Someone will see me, and my household will wonder if I don't return this night." She shifted to face him and stroked a hand along his bearded jaw. "Though I do not wish to go."

He kissed her, and she responded, wishing the time did not have to end but knowing it must.

"I don't want to lose you," he said.

"Nor I you."

His arms tightened around her, and his sigh sounded strangled, as though he was powerless despite all the power that was his to wield. "You are right, of course."

She choked on a sob, unable to speak.

"There now, don't cry, beloved." He pulled her closer, rubbing circles along her back. "Everything will be fine. Am I not the king? If anyone questions you, send me word, and I will deal with them."

She nodded and sniffed against his chest, strangely comforted. He was the king. He had called for her, and she had only done her duty to obey his request. As her father and husband had done in war, so she had done in peace. She had nothing to fear.

"I only wish I could see you again." He kissed the top of her head and held her away from him, searching her gaze in the dimness.

"And I you, my lord."

"Call me David when we are alone."

"David." She smiled, though she knew it came out wobbly. "Beloved one."

He kissed her again, a gentle reminder of all they had shared, then released her. "I'm not sure we should risk this again."

Disappointment mingled with the guilt she could not shake. "No, I'm sure we should not." She touched his face once more, and bent to place a soft kiss on his lips. "Though I wish we could, David."

She slipped from his arms and snatched her tunic from the floor. Quickly dressing in the dark, she parted the curtains of his bed and stood a moment, allowing her eyes to adjust to the change of light.

She sensed his presence behind her before she felt his touch on her shoulder. "You forgot this."

He held out her blue head covering, her protection against exposure, though she was certain her guilt was evident despite any veil she might try to hide behind. The thought sent a shiver through her.

"I will send a guard to accompany you home."

Tears pricked her eyes as she turned, caught once more in his embrace.

"I will never forget you."

She nodded against his chest. "Such a thing would be impossible." Another sob worked its way to her throat, and she feared she would break down and weep in front of him. Instead, she leaned closer and kissed him one last time, then hurried to the door of his chambers.

David caught her hand as she touched the latch, brought her fingers to his lips, and gave her one last lingering look. He turned the knob and opened the door. The stern-looking guard she had seen when she arrived stood straight-backed with arms crossed.

"Take this woman to her home, Benaiah." David's command cut through her thoughts. The guard nodded and marched away, Bathsheba quickly following. He had not called her by name, probably for her own protection, though the guard surely knew who she was. She was simply a woman who had spent a night with the king. It was time she put that aside and went back to her life, knowing that the king—David—would all too soon forget her.

✄

The house sat bathed in deep darkness as she moved over the stones of the courtyard. Benaiah stood in silence, waiting for her to stop fumbling with the latch and open the door. When at last her trembling fingers managed to hold steady and slide the inside bar to the side, she turned to face Benaiah and nodded.

"Thank you for seeing me home." She attempted a smile, but his appraising look stifled the urge. He had already judged her, and would no doubt tell Uriah once he returned. How well did the king trust this man to keep his secrets? If anyone knew, if Uriah found out . . .

A sick feeling rose within her as it had since she first stepped into the king's gardens. She could be stoned. Uriah's strict adherence to the law would demand it. He would never see her pardoned, even on the king's request.

And then a new thought seized her. Would David implicate himself in this? Or would he leave her to face her father and her husband alone? She looked at Benaiah, wondering why the man had not left yet, then realized he was waiting for her to enter her house and shut the door, as any faithful guard would do.

"What happened tonight," she said, searching for the words to ask him how much he knew, how much he would say once Uriah returned. "I mean—"

"It is not mine to tell, mistress. The king's business is his alone." He nodded to her then and waved her into the house with his hand.

She dipped her head, her heart thumping hard and fast beneath the soft blue linen. Her fingers gripped the belt at her waist, while the other hand clutched the edge of the door. She stepped into the house and slowly closed the door, waiting, listening for the guard's footsteps on the stones.

"How did it go, my lady?"

Bathsheba jerked around at the sound of Tirzah's soft voice, her heart suddenly hammering like hoofbeats. "It went well. Everything is fine."

"There is no word of the master then?" Tirzah took a step closer, searching her face, but Bathsheba ducked her head and hurried down the hall to her room, needing the shelter of the quiet sanctuary, where she could crawl into bed and forget.

"My lady, are you all right?"

"I'm fine." Bathsheba moved into the room, glancing about. "Are the servants in bed?"

"They retired many hours ago. I only awoke when I heard the latch. I've been waiting on the couch in the sitting room, worrying." Tirzah steadied the clay lamp in her hand, her night tunic rumpled as though she had been trying to sleep for many hours.

"You need not have stayed up on my account." Bathsheba turned away, wincing at her cryptic tone. "I'm sorry. I'm tired. If you will help me undress, I feel as though I might stay in bed for a week."

"Yes, of course, my lady." Tirzah set the lamp in the niche in the wall and moved closer to take the scarf from Bathsheba's hands. "Where are your combs?"

Bathsheba felt her head and touched her undone hair. Heat

crept up her neck as she realized she had hurried away without her best combs, the ones her father had given her when she married Uriah. Had it not been for the king's realization that she had nearly left her scarf, she might have walked through Jerusalem's streets an uncovered, brazen woman! What must Tirzah think of her? How to explain such a thing?

"I . . ." Her tongue felt thick against the lie hovering on her lips. Tirzah looked at her with concern. Dare she tell this faithful servant the truth? "I must have forgotten them." She turned around then, her hands shaking on the golden belt, trying unsuccessfully to undo the knot as David had done so masterfully hours ago. Tears fell unbidden, and she tasted the salt as they dripped into her mouth. She quickly swiped them away, but she could not stop the need to weep.

"Leave me!" The hoarse whisper sounded more like a whimper than a command. She forced her hands to finish undoing the belt, her back turned to Tirzah until she heard the door click behind her.

She tossed the leather from her and yanked her arms out of her robe and tunic. Shivering in the dark, she fumbled for her night tunic, then tossed a day robe about her before burying her head beneath the wool covers. Uriah's faint scent still lingered on the bedcovering, bringing the events of the night into sharper focus. Memories of Uriah's passionate kisses and tender touch mingled with the king's gentle way with her, until she could no longer separate the two.

Her tears came uncontrolled now, and when she closed her eyes, Uriah's smiling face looked back at her, love evident in every feature. He did love her, didn't he? And she had thrown it all away on a whim of loneliness.

What had she done?

❧ 17 ❧

David dipped a piece of flat bread into the red lentil stew. The spicy cumin sparked his taste but did nothing to tempt his flagging appetite. The summer heat only added to the oppressive warmth of the bronze wall torches necessary to light the banquet hall. The New Moon feast marked a month since he had held Bathsheba in his arms. He should have been able to forget her by now, as he so easily did many other women. But he could not shake what would become of her if her husband ever discovered their union.

Conversation floated in and around him, and he did his best to seem attentive, but a heavy weight had taken residence in his gut, pressed down like a millstone, and sapped his strength. He wanted nothing more than to escape to his bed and hide from court life. But his counselors found him at every turn. Oh, to fly away like a bird and be at rest.

He never should have taken her. What had possessed him to call for and claim a married woman? He had become like one of the foolish ones who moved about the streets, giving in to the wayward women on the edges of town whose husbands were away at war or on business, who did not care if they dishonored them.

Bathsheba had not been that kind of woman, and he knew deep down that she mourned even now for what she had done. For what he had made her do.

The bitter taste of bile rose in his throat, and the incessant voices of his men and his wives grew louder—a thread of laughter here, the sound of bickering there. He shoved his gilded chair away from the table and rose. A bevy of servants rushed to his aid, but he waved them off and stalked out the side door, down the winding halls, to the stairs leading to the roof directly above his chambers. The roof he had avoided for a month for fear of what he might do if he saw her again.

His legs felt sluggish, and he struggled to climb despite his desperate need to do so, to get away from the constant demands on him. When at last he reached the top, he gripped the parapet and staggered along the edge of the roof, grieving. As he'd grieved for Abigail, and yet the anguish was clearly not the same.

He moved slowly, his heart picking up the rhythm of a silent drum. Would he find her going through her ritual purification as he'd done the month before? Would her music soothe the anxious lines now visible in the bronze mirror above his brow?

He paused at the spot where he'd seen her last, his eyes closed, dreading, hoping . . . but the sounds below held no music, and when he looked into the courtyard, the bath sat perched along a wall, the water jars untouched. Lights flickered inside the house—perhaps she had guests for her own New Moon feast—but no one moved on the roof or in the courtyard.

She could have already completed her purification. Or perhaps her time had yet to come. The thought turned the weight in his gut to solid stone. Surely not. In her years of marriage to Uriah she had borne no children, and he'd spent only one night with her . . .

His feet stumbled backward, his grip reaching for the railing behind him. He shook the thought aside like an unwanted messenger. But as he made his way to his bedchamber below, where her presence still lingered in every breath of his imagination, he could not shake the foreboding fear his thoughts had conjured. If by some chance he was right, his troubles were just beginning.

❦

Bathsheba sat on a bench beneath the open tent Uriah had set up for her on the roof to give her a place to weave or spin without the harsh rays of the sun scorching her. One of the many things he had done to make her life more pleasant, like the bronze basin he had acquired for her bath in her own courtyard so she could carry out her purification ritual in private. A ritual she would not practice this month, or many months hence, if her fears were proved true.

A sinking feeling swept over her, drowning her in an ever-present sense of despair, as it had every morning for the past week as she waited, counting the days, hoping against hope, silently pleading with Adonai to show her she was wrong. How could she possibly miss her time after only one night with the king, when nearly four years with Uriah had produced no heir? She could not possibly be with child. She was barren, wasn't she?

She glanced at the basket at her side, where the spindle and distaff waited for her to pick them up and continue her work, but she rested a hand on her middle instead, fighting a queasy, unsettled feeling. What should she do? If she carried a child, she must tell the king. He'd promised to protect her from anyone who would speak against her, but how could he possibly protect her from her own husband? Her fate, the punishment for adultery, was death by stoning.

A deep shudder worked through her, and her queasy feeling grew. She bent forward, holding her stomach, tears filling her eyes. Uriah was so strict when it came to the law. Would he cover her sin and claim the child as his own, or demand the truth be upheld and let her pay the penalty the law required?

She dropped to her knees on the hard roof floor, rocking back and forth, knowing in one moment that he would surely demand her death, and certain in the next that his love would conquer even this. But would it? Uriah was a man of honor, and his honor, his duty, came above all else. Oh, what should she do?

She had to tell someone. She needed to confirm her fears, to be sure. Aunt Talia's face came to mind, but she dismissed the thought out of hand. She loved her aunt, but Aunt Talia would surely tell Chava or, worse, her grandfather, and neither would keep their knowledge to themselves.

The sound of footsteps jerked her to a sitting position, and she quickly swiped her tears away. Tirzah poked her head under the tent, concern lining her plain features. Her dark hair lay tucked beneath a brown veil, and her sturdy arms held a batch of new wool ready to be carded and spun into thread. She set her burden on the ground beside the bench where Bathsheba had been sitting and knelt at Bathsheba's side.

"What is wrong, mistress?" She placed a hand on Bathsheba's shoulder, but the contact made Bathsheba stiffen. She wrapped her arms around her knees and looked at her maidservant for the briefest moment, then glanced beyond her toward the palace roof. Memories tumbled through her, and the stark realization of what she had done filled her with new dread.

Tirzah sat up but made no attempt to draw closer. She held out a hand in supplication. "Please let me help you. You have not been yourself and—" She turned, her gaze following Bathsheba's. "What happened that night?"

Bathsheba swallowed hard as the silence lingered. She had no need to explain herself to a servant, yet Tirzah was probably the only person loyal enough not to cause her more harm than she already faced by her own choosing.

But she allowed the silence to deepen, listening to the melancholy song of a dove perched along the parapet. Indecision warred within her. She rested her chin on her knees and could no longer stop the tears when she looked once more into Tirzah's assessing gaze.

"Were you with him?"

Bathsheba nodded and sniffed, squeezing her eyes tight against the stinging tears.

Tirzah shifted her sturdy bulk closer, leaning toward Bathsheba's ear. "There will be no need for purification this month, will there?" Her understanding look gave Bathsheba a sense of comfort.

"How did you know?"

"You have not been yourself since you returned home late that night."

Fear mounted inside her breast. "Do the other servants suspect?"

Tirzah gave her head a quick shake. "No. I don't think so."

"But you don't know."

Tirzah tipped her head back as though she were thinking. "No. I'm sure they don't. I haven't told anyone, and no one knows you like I do. Besides, no one else saw you come home that night or knew about the combs."

"The combs?"

Tirzah's smile was gentle and sad. "You left the ivory combs at the palace. What other reason could you possibly have to let down your hair?"

Bathsheba's eyes filmed again as she looked away, unable to accept the kindness in her servant's gaze. Tirzah would be accused if she kept such a secret from Uriah. She could be dismissed or beaten or sold into slavery.

"Will you tell my husband?" Her voice sounded small in her own ears. She was a child again in her father's house, with Tirzah caring for her as she had done since her mother had died in childbirth.

Tirzah's arms came around her then, and she pulled her into a motherly embrace, though they were closer in age to be sisters many years apart. "I would never betray your trust, Bathsheba. Your secret is safe with me."

"It will not remain a secret for long. Soon everyone will know, and my life will end." She choked on a sob, taking in Tirzah's comforting scent, burying her face in her maid's shoulder.

Tirzah patted her back and let her weep in silence until Bathsheba could no longer summon another tear. Exhaustion weighed her down. What she wouldn't give for one peaceful night's sleep where guilt did not plague her and fear did not match her guilt.

"The child is the king's then." Tirzah cupped Bathsheba's face, coaxing eye contact.

Bathsheba nodded. "It can be no other's."

Tirzah moved her hands to gently grip Bathsheba's shoulders. "Then you must inform the king. He will know what to do."

Bathsheba held Tirzah's gaze, reading her maid's insistence, knowing she spoke wisdom. She acknowledged her with a look, then turned her gaze to the palace once more, where her message would soon change whatever it was the king thought of her. If he still thought of her at all.

He had said he would not forget her. Whether he meant it then or not, now he would have no choice.

❦18❦

Bathsheba held the quill over the parchment Tirzah had secured for her in the marketplace, each letter penned with utmost care. The lessons her father had insisted on giving her now proved most helpful, though for all the wrong reasons. If she'd had to pay a scribe to scratch out her words, she would have had one more person to trust to keep her secret safe.

Her hand shook as she dipped it in the ink and tapped the end against the clay jar. Tirzah sat opposite her at the worktable in the cooking room, the only light a small oil lamp pressed up close against the parchment, but not too close to catch the expensive material on fire.

As the last word dried on the page, Bathsheba read the message through blurred vision. *I am with child.* She would not sign her name or address the message. He would know by the press of her husband's seal on the wax.

A tear dripped, leaving a soft smudge mark on the word *child.* How appropriate. Would he notice or guess the pain this had caused? Would he do anything at all to stop her death?

Tirzah moved Uriah's cylindrical seal across the table toward her. Hot wax sat in a bowl, waiting to be poured over the scroll. Bathsheba stared at the words a moment longer, fanning the ink to dry it with her hand, then at last rolled the parchment and pressed it flat. Carefully lifting the bowl, she poured a thin stream of wax as her tutor had long ago taught her to do in anticipation of one day handling her father's affairs, and rolled the cylinder over the wax, sealing her words.

"Take this to the guard Benaiah." She handed the parchment to Tirzah as she went over the instructions she had already told her several times, fearing what would happen if anyone should stop Tirzah or intercept the missive before the king's own hands held it. "Don't let anyone else have it no matter who tries to stop you. Tell Benaiah the message is for the king's eyes only."

Tirzah held the letter and tugged until Bathsheba finally released her grip. She exhaled a low, troubled sigh. "I don't want to die," she whispered.

Tirzah touched her arm. "The king will know what to do." Her imploring eyes bespoke a confidence Bathsheba wished she could believe. But as a second week had passed and her time had still not come upon her, she could not risk waiting any longer. If the king sent for Uriah, there must be time to prepare him, to fall on his mercy and allow him to cover her sin with dignity, what little there could be left of it. If she were too far along, people would know and Uriah would not so easily avoid disgrace. But if the king allowed it, if she admitted their sin to Uriah, begged his forgiveness, perhaps the king would even promote him to take Joab's place as army commander as compensation. Surely Uriah's love for her would let him be thus appeased.

Wouldn't it?

Hope surged, but as Tirzah donned her head covering and slipped into the night, Bathsheba's wishful expectations fell once more to a deep, aching despair. Her fate rested in the hands of the king, who could dismiss her as easily as he had taken her. She had no proof the child was his, no evidence she had even been with the king except for the few servants who had seen her enter the palace that long-ago night. And if the king ignored her message, by the time Uriah returned home, her shame would be evident to all. The law would not protect her then, even as it could not protect her now. She had no recourse.

Oh, Adonai, have mercy!

❧

David stood on his roof looking down on the family courtyard, where torches cast light and shadow among the trees and shrubbery, and his wives mingled, waiting for him to make an appearance. But his visits had grown little of late. He told himself their complaints wearied him, but in truth, the guilt of adultery kept him secluded from all but those closest to him.

Sometimes war sounded better than love.

Crickets hummed in the trees nearby, and the summer breeze did nothing to cool the heat that oppressed during the day. He smoothed a hand over his beard and walked away from the women's court, wondering where his desire for his family had gone. As he neared the opposite edge of the roof, footsteps came from behind. He turned to see Benaiah approach, his expression grim.

Benaiah dipped his head. "My lord." He held out a small scroll, its seal unreadable in the dark of night.

"Who is it from?" He searched the guard's face for some sign of what to expect, but Benaiah shook his head.

"A woman. I have never seen her before." Moonlight illumined his dark, bearded face, and David didn't miss the look of disapproval in his eyes. "The seal is that of Uriah the Hittite."

The familiar weight he'd carried since that night slammed into him like a fist in the gut. If he moved, he would surely stagger, giving way to his fear. He managed to hold Benaiah's gaze without flinching, his right hand circling the parchment, cautious not to crush it in his palm. "Thank you, Benaiah. You may go."

He moved to his tent pavilion, where the flames of the enclosed torches gave more light than the stars dotting the blackest night he'd ever seen. A servant approached, ready to fill his wine goblet. He allowed the gesture, then dismissed him with a wave. At last alone, he settled himself among the cushions of his couch, took a long sip from his golden cup, then carefully broke the seal, unwinding the scroll.

His eyes darted to the four lone words.

I am with child.

He stilled, his strength slowly seeping from him like water through sand. The cup shook in his hand, and he struggled to rest it on the low table without spilling it on the parchment. His suspicions had not been unfounded.

I am with child.

They had been together only one night. Hadn't she been married for years with no son? How was this possible?

The image of Bathsheba rose in his mind's eye. The penalty for adultery was death by stoning. If her condition was discovered while her husband was at war, her grandfather could exact judgment. Even as king, he could not protect her unless he came out and admitted his own guilt.

A tremor passed through him, and his skin chilled despite the warmth of the night. Such an admission could cost him the throne. The people could rise up against him and demand he step down. How could they trust a king who took another man's wife to his bed? Such a thing might happen in other nations, but not in Israel.

He reached for the chalice, wishing the intoxicating drink could banish such thoughts, but as he went to grasp it, he knocked the cup over, spilling the liquid onto the floor. Its deep red color seeped into the white lamb's-wool rug, like blood poured out.

Like a sacrifice. Or the blood of a beautiful woman stoned for a crime he had committed against her.

I am with child.

He must protect her. She had no one else. If she did, she would not have sent him this note. She knew she was at his mercy, and he knew without doubt the child was his. Sweat beaded his brow as he forced himself up on shaky limbs. He staggered to the edge of the parapet, where he could look down on her house. Darkness bathed the place in shadows, but he thought he saw the tiniest lamp flicker through the open window.

A longing so great that it took his breath shook him. If only he could go to her, could comfort her and tell her everything would be all right. He would fix this. All he had to do was call Uriah to Jerusalem and send him home. He would sleep with his wife and be none the wiser, assuming the child was his.

The plan pleased him, but he did not allow himself a smile. Too much risk was at stake, too much dependent on assumptions. Still, Uriah was faithful to a fault. Surely he would obey his king.

Taking one last look at Bathsheba's dark house, he spun around and headed to summon Benaiah. Before this night was through, he would dispatch a message to Joab to bring Uriah home.

19

The pink and gray hues of dawn crept like a spying soldier above the distant hills. Uriah blinked his stinging eyes and rubbed a hand over a well-earned yawn. He'd spent the last two nights on guard, standing watch at the south end of the camp. Fortunately for him, all had been quiet, while the Ammonites huddled behind Rabbah's walls, awaiting their fate at Israel's hands. Ammon's supplies would run out soon, and Joab had indicated he would press the attack again within the week. Uriah could hardly wait to show those arrogant malcontents exactly who they had taken to task. King David's men did not back away from a fight, and no one insulted Israel's emissaries and lived to tell of it.

He brushed a hand along the hilt of his sword and made the rounds of his commission one more time before he would hand over his post to Eliam and hit the hard ground in his tent for a few hours of sleep. He was long overdue.

The sun fully crested the eastern ridge as he turned back to his original starting point. Nothing moved on this perimeter, and that suited him well. Unsuspected enemy attacks were never Joab's first choice in war, and thankfully, due to the general's tactical wisdom, they were rarely caught off guard.

Uriah looked up as he approached the fire and raised a hand in greeting to his father-in-law. "You look rested."

"And you look worn out." Eliam straightened his helmet as if he had just now emerged from his tent and dressed as he walked, something he often did when he took an early shift. "I can't send you to your mat yet, though. The general is asking for you." He walked closer and patted Uriah's shoulder in sympathy.

"Why do I get the feeling I'm not going to like this meeting?" He met Eliam's gaze, searching for more. "What do you know?"

Eliam shrugged. "Not much. Only that the king's messenger traveled all night to get here and Joab said it's urgent." He waved a hand. "So go."

Uriah nodded once and turned, his legs infused with sudden energy. What could the king want that could possibly involve him? Had something happened at home? Was Bathsheba all right? He had learned long ago to steel his thinking away from her when he was at war. It did no good to let his mind wander to places he could not physically go. It weakened a man to have dealings with women while sitting on the front battle lines, and of course no woman was allowed in camp, but even the thought of his beautiful wife was often his undoing. So he blocked her from his thoughts. When he could. When exhaustion did not sneak in and bring her to his dreams.

His heart kicked over as he jogged faster across the compound toward the general's large tent. Joab rose from a stone seat near a fire, as did another man wearing the uniform and the lion insignia of the king. One of David's personal Cherethite guards.

Uriah halted and drew in a succession of quick breaths, telling himself his fears were unfounded. He dipped his head in respect to his commander. A servant approached and offered him a skin of water. He took it and poured a thin stream of liquid into his mouth, his silent nod thanking the man.

"You wanted to see me, my lord." He placed the cap on the water skin and held it in one hand. His parched throat wanted more, but he denied its request.

"Uriah, the king has asked for you. Gather your things and return with this man at once." Joab glanced at the king's messenger. "You don't want to keep the king waiting."

Questions darted in and out of his thoughts. "If I may be so bold, my lord, I am not a courier or a runner. Is something wrong?"

Joab lifted a shoulder in a half shrug and nodded toward the messenger, permitting him to speak.

"The king's exact words were, 'Send me Uriah the Hittite.' That is all I know." The guard shifted from foot to foot and darted a glance at the sky, sending a message Uriah could not ignore. There would be no sleep for him now. After a full night of guard watch, he would make the long trek across the hills and plains to Jerusalem, to the palace courts, for an unnamed purpose.

"Let me get my things." Uriah whirled about and jogged back to his tent.

☙❧

Bathsheba worked the distaff and spindle as she paced beneath the tent enclosure of her roof, unable to sit still for a moment since Tirzah had taken her message to the king. Tirzah sat carding the new wool nearby, and Bathsheba could feel the servant's gaze aimed her way, but she wisely said nothing, knowing there was nothing to be said. The king had gotten her message. Tirzah had assured her that Benaiah had taken it from her hand, and she had waited in the hall until he had walked away to deliver it. Surely the king's personal guard would not have failed to give the scroll to the king. Surely not.

"You're going to wear a pattern in the floor if you do not stop moving back and forth like that. You're making my head twirl about like a nervous dancer, watching you." Tirzah clucked her tongue like Aunt Talia often did, but it did nothing to lighten Bathsheba's mood.

"Then don't watch." She knew the words were clipped, harsh even, but her nerves were drawn stiff like strings on a lyre. She fingered the wool, spinning it round, at last moving out from beneath the tent's protection and gazing up at the palace roof.

Why haven't you contacted me?

Fear-wrought anger held her tongue. She wanted to shout at the man from where she stood, but her words would not penetrate his stone and marble halls, insulated as he was from her world. Did he care?

Her throat thickened as it had done every day since that night, the familiar emotion choking her. *Uriah, what have I done to you?*

The sound of footsteps made her pulse jump. Her fingers grew still on the distaff as she watched Anittas approach.

"My lady." He gave a half bow, then stood stiff and proud, as though speaking at her instead of to her. "You have a visitor. A messenger from the palace." His dark eyes skipped from her to the palace behind her. "Shall I send him up?"

Bathsheba glanced at her surroundings. Only Tirzah was

with her here. It was the most secluded place in her home. If David had a message for her, she would be safest to receive it here. "Yes, send him up." She looked at the servant, but again his gaze did not meet hers. "Thank you, Anittas."

"Yes, mistress." He bowed once more and hurried away, giving Bathsheba another reason to fear exposure. Did Anittas know? If he did, he would surely tell Uriah before she had any possible way to explain herself. While Anittas had always treated her with kindness, he was fiercely loyal to Uriah. If the spirit of jealousy came upon Uriah before she could tell him of the child, Anittas would have no reason to defend her honor. He had seen her go to the palace, and though only Tirzah had met her upon her return, Anittas slept near the outer court. He could have easily watched without her knowledge to see that she had arrived safely home.

She looked up again as a man dressed in the garments of King David's guards approached. She did not recognize the man, which meant David had not thought her situation dire enough to keep it in strictest confidence. Her spirits sank lower as she struggled to keep her emotions in check.

"My lady Bathsheba?"

"Yes." Bathsheba stepped closer. "My servant said you have a message for me?" She tried to keep her expression passive, as though whatever he might say was of no import, but feared she was failing miserably.

The guard's expression gave nothing away, no comfort and yet no censure. "The king has asked me to inform you that your husband is on his way back to Jerusalem and to expect him home by tonight or tomorrow." With that, he whirled about, strode with clipped steps to the edge of the roof, and descended the stairs.

Tirzah's hand on her arm made her jump. Her skin felt prickly and a tremor moved through her.

"Uriah is coming home," Tirzah said, as though Bathsheba had not already heard the news.

"Yes." She should be glad of it, but the fear snaking through her stole any happiness such news should bring.

"He will be with you, and everything will work out fine." Tirzah patted her shoulder. "We must take you to the mikvah, henna your feet and hands, and perfume your bed linens. He will be so taken with you, you won't have to say a word."

Bathsheba turned and faced her maid but could not return the woman's smile. "He'll know." She could not lie to him, and his one look at her would force her to give herself away.

"He won't unless you tell him."

"Anittas will tell him."

"Anittas knows nothing. He only knows you were summoned to the palace and returned after dark."

"He acts like he knows more."

"Humph! Anittas likes to pretend too much." Tirzah took the distaff from Bathsheba's clenched hands. "If you love Uriah, you will do this for his sake. For his pride. For his heir."

"His pride will not want me." The shaking grew, and she could no longer stand. Tirzah guided her inside the tent to a bench, where she managed to sit before her legs gave way.

"He loves you, Bathsheba. Once he comes, tell him the truth and fall on his mercy. When he is reminded of your great beauty, his heart will win over his head."

Bathsheba stared at her trembling hands and clenched them in her lap. She looked at Tirzah, eyes blurring with tears. "You cannot know that. No one can know what Uriah will do."

"Of course not. But soon he will be home and then you will

know. The king has sent for him to fix the problem. Perhaps the king will confess everything to him and save you the trouble." She sat beside her and patted Bathsheba's hand. "In the meantime," she said, her practical nature taking over as it always did, "let's do what we can and leave the rest to Adonai."

Bathsheba slowly nodded, but her heart could not agree. Adonai's law was what demanded her death for adultery. If the law were to be upheld, there could be no mercy.

❦20❧

Uriah stopped at the Eastern Gate near the Gihon Spring, sweat making his tunic stick to him like a second skin. He glanced at the royal guard, the man's exhaustion matching his own. He needed sleep and a good meal before he stepped into the king's presence, but he would settle for a dip in the spring to wash the sweat and grime from his body. A fresh tunic lay tucked in his pouch, and the time it would take to clean up would be worth the results of not overpowering the court with the stench of his own body's odor.

"Give me some time here. I won't be long."

The guard nodded, standing watch while Uriah quickly scrubbed and changed into his fresh tunic. Refreshed and redressed in his military garb, Uriah picked up his pace beside the king's guard and marched in silence the rest of the way to the palace. At the outer portico of the king's house, the guard who had attended him left his side, while two more flanked him, announced his presence, and escorted him into the king's audience chamber.

"Uriah, my friend, how goes the battle?" The king's earnest gaze held his, and he leaned forward, as if eager for any news Uriah had to offer.

Uriah stood straight, not used to such attention from the king, carefully choosing his words. "Things are progressing slowly. The Ammonites have holed up inside their city, but daily Joab and Abishai and some of the other commanders try new ways to draw them out. The hottest battles are near the walls, of course, where the Ammonites have a secluded spot near the citadel to shoot at us with their arrows. We have yet to breach the walls, but we have stopped all travel and commerce from reaching them and refilling their supplies. In time we will starve them out, if nothing less."

The king leaned back, his hands tented beneath his chin. "Good. The plans are all good." His gaze grew thoughtful, as though he would say something more, perhaps offer a military stratagem, but he seemed to think better of it and gave his head a slight shake. "And Joab? How does the general fare?"

Uriah drew a hand over his mouth, forcing himself not to yawn. He quickly straightened again, holding himself erect, aware even through his weariness and hunger that to be singled out in such a manner had a purpose. "The general is well, my lord. Grouchy as ever."

The king chuckled at that, and an easy smile tipped the corners of his mouth. "The man is brilliant, I'll give him that, but 'grouchy,' as you say, is putting it kindly. Joab is bullheaded and stubborn and a thorn in the side." He leaned forward again, his hands gripping the lions' heads on the arms of his gilded throne, his knuckles showing white.

"As you say, my lord." Uriah sensed sudden tension in the room and sought to dispel it but wasn't sure how. He gave the king a slight smile, but he waited to see if he would finally discover the reason he had been singled out and summoned on a courier's mission.

"And how are the men doing? Are their spirits up?"

The questions seemed normal enough, yet Uriah knew the king was given regular reports of such things. Was this truly the only reason he had been dragged here—to bring such basic news to appease the king's curiosity?

"The men grow weary with the heat, but their hopes are high that we will soon press the attack and take the city." He paused, assessing his options. To suggest that instead of sitting here asking for such reports, the king might prefer to return with Uriah and join their ranks seemed worth the risk of offending him, given that David seemed to be groping for things to say. "They miss the king's songs when they are resting under the stars. Perhaps my lord would return with me and grant their wishes." He lifted a brow, hoping to spark the king's interest. But David's gaze had drifted beyond him as though his thoughts had strayed far from his men or their wishes.

"Soon, perhaps," the king said at last. "Thank you for the report." David leaned back in his chair once more and waved a servant forward. The man approached and bowed low. "Take the gift I have prepared to the house of Uriah the Hittite." He aimed a look at Uriah and smiled while the man backed quickly away to do the king's bidding. "Go down to your house and wash your feet."

Uriah stared, taken aback by the sudden turn of conversation. At David's dismissal, he backed away from the king and left the palace, his mind churning. The king had never in his recollection suggested a man sleep with his wife while on a military mission. Long ago, before Uriah had ever joined David's band of mighty men, the soldiers had known David's policy was firm. No interaction with women during wartime. Sometimes that meant even the few days before a battle when they were still in their homes with their wives in their beds. The edict had caused Uriah to sleep on a pallet away from Bathsheba, knowing he could never keep from touching her if she was pressed so close.

Bathsheba. The thought of his wife made his insides melt. How he missed her! And now to be so close in Jerusalem, barely a stone's throw from his home, and not go to her or be with her? How could he stay away? Especially when the king had sent a gift to greet him at home, probably food of some kind for him to stave the hunger still gnawing at him.

But to do so would violate the king's own principles. Joab and his men were living in tents at war, without the privilege of a wife to warm them. How could he in good conscience return to them and deny that he had gone home, if indeed he had? To see her would make him unclean for only a day, but it would change his mind-set, muddle his thinking, make him less ready or able to return to the battle, geared to fight as he should. He could not command his men if they knew he had given in to fleshly desires while they were denied. His pride would not allow it. Besides, if his calculations were correct, she would be unclean for another week—her cycles were too precise to be any different.

As he passed under the palace roof to the portico, the late afternoon breeze feathered the hairs along his forehead. Voices filtered to him from the guardhouse. The king had barracks at the door and the rear of the palace to house the elite Thirty when the need arose, and the Cherethite and Pelethite guards under Benaiah's command, a rotation of mercenary men who kept the palace safe. The scent of fresh bread and spices made his stomach turn over in hunger once more. He needed to eat and sleep, both of which he could get—and more—if he walked through the palace gates and turned down the lane toward home. Indecision played with his weary mind, but he snuffed the desire for his wife as quickly as it came.

He moved toward the guardhouse, but the king's implied suggestion stopped him again. He glanced from the gate to the barracks, uncertainty niggling the back of his neck. What if his calculations were wrong? A groan escaped him as he closed his eyes against the image of Bathsheba's alluring form. He must not do this.

Drawing in a slow breath, clenching both hands into fists, he straightened, certain of his choice. He moved toward the sound of the men's laughter and entered their quarters. After he filled his belly, he would stretch out in a corner somewhere and sleep.

☙❧

Bathsheba stood at the small window in her bedchamber, lamplight glowing, starlight casting shadows over her home's private inner court—the court where her life had changed course forever. The bronze basin lay in a corner against the wall, where she and Tirzah had left it that afternoon. Tirzah's suggestion that she complete her purification regardless of her condition made sense, and would keep the servants from knowing the truth a while longer. If she avoided the ritual, they would have all the more reason to talk, and gossip was the last thing she needed right now.

But the lie she was continuing to perpetrate turned her heart cold. She shivered against the night breeze, the cool air stirring the myrrh wafting to her from her freshly washed bed linens, and her skin tingled with anticipation and growing dread.

The evening meal had come and gone. The roasted lamb cooked to perfection by the king's own servants had been delivered with a host of vegetables and sweets, but she had eaten the feast alone, and the taste had long ago turned to ash in her mouth. Surely Uriah should have joined her by now. The king's gift evidenced her husband's return, so where was her husband? Why had he not come home?

Her stomach tightened and another chill worked through her. Her bare, hennaed feet and the sheer tunic draping her clean, washed body mocked her. She moved from the window and sank onto the edge of the bed, tears surfacing, threatening to mar the kohl Tirzah had placed along her eyelids. Did he know? Had Anittas told him her secret? Did Anittas know the truth?

Tirzah had reassured her again and again that Uriah's servants did not suspect anything amiss. But Bathsheba's guilt told her otherwise. She had never been good at lying. Her cheeks warmed at the memory of her father's swift punishments when she had attempted such a thing. And one look from Uriah would pull the truth from her.

She stood and paced the small room. Should she don her robe and go to the palace to seek him out? No. Such a thing was unheard-of. If Uriah had chosen to spend the night somewhere else, there was nothing to be done about it on her part. If even the king could not persuade him to come home with such a gift as the lavish feast he had sent, her presence would make no difference.

If he would come to her, she would cast herself at his feet, kiss the hem of his robe, and tell him everything. She would plead for mercy and serve him however he wished the rest of her days. If he would only forgive her.

But she could not ask him, could not tell him the truth, if he did not come home. And if he did not come home, there was nothing left for her to do.

172

❦21❦

The plaintive cry of a mourning dove filled David's chambers with unwanted song. Despite a more restful night's sleep than he'd had in over a month, his mood faltered between relieved and troubled. He sat at a wide table laden with fruit and bread, sauces and cheeses, their colorful display meant to tempt his appetite. But he merely picked at the food, choosing a long, savoring drink of crimson wine instead.

Only the foolish ones got drunk in the morning, and he had no intention of drinking to such a point, but nothing else seemed able to calm his tattered nerves. He had done the right thing bringing Uriah home. By now the man had surely slept with his wife, and all would be well. Bathsheba had been wise to contact him so soon. When the child came a month early, perhaps Uriah would not notice. If he did, David would bribe the man with position and power to appease.

He broke off a piece of soft white goat cheese and popped it into his mouth. Leaning into the cushions of his couch, he sipped again from his cup. His eyes closed and he thought not for the first time how privileged Uriah was to have married such a woman. A hint of irritation tickled his neck at the realization that such a beautiful woman had been in the home of his counselor and one of his Thirty, and neither had offered her to him. Despite his promise to Abigail, they could have offered. His mind begged the question, *Why not?*

The dove's incessant funeral dirge interrupted his musings. He shoved up from the couch and strode to the open window, the liquid sloshing in the goblet. Eliam had made no secret of his disagreement with David's multiple wives. He'd seemed glad of it when David had kept his word to Abigail and not added more women to his royal family. Had he hidden Bathsheba from him for that reason?

His jaw clenched at the thought as he closed the window against the dove's irritating sound. A double knock on his door made him turn and nearly spill the wine. He steadied his hand and took a long, slow drink before striding across the long room. Benaiah always gave the door two swift raps, then waited for his summons to enter. The man was dependable, and now more than ever before David needed someone to rely on.

"Come in," he called once he had settled in his seat again. Legs stretched in front of him, he attempted to appear at ease, even if his heart and mind told him otherwise.

Benaiah stepped into the room and closed the door, then walked across the room to face David. He dipped his knee in a short bow, then straightened at the wave of David's hand.

"Tell me what has happened." He stared at the liquid almost gone from the golden cup, seeing his own fading reflection.

"My lord king, Uriah the Hittite did not go to his house last night. He slept at the door of my lord's palace in the bunkhouse with the king's servants."

David lifted his head from staring at the wine to meet Benaiah's impassive gaze. The man had an opinion on everything, but he rarely offered it, and David would not hear it now unless he asked. "Any idea why he did that?"

A muscle moved in Benaiah's bearded cheek, but his gaze did not falter. "Uriah is loyal, a soldier on active duty. He would not do something to compromise his position or authority with his men."

Heat crept up David's neck at the implied reproach in Benaiah's words, but he could hardly reprimand the man for telling him what he had asked to hear. He stood, turning back to the window, and straightened his spine. "Bring Uriah to me in my audience chamber." He would dress in full regal garb as a reminder to the man of who it was commanding Israel's troops, who it was they were to obey. Perhaps he had been too friendly and not firm enough yesterday.

David turned back into the room and saw that Benaiah had already departed to do his bidding. He summoned his servants to help him dress. He would face Uriah once more and see what he could do to persuade the man to do the right thing.

⚘

Uriah straightened the collar of his military tunic, checked the leather girdle at his waist, and pinned the striped cloak closed with the golden lion's head pendant. He looked down, making sure the clasp held secure, pride swelling within him. He had worked hard to make it into David's elite ranks and had given much to accomplish the duties that came with the captain's office. Now he could return today to the battle with confidence that he had stayed true to those duties, and infuse his men with courage to do likewise.

He checked his sword and smaller dagger and moved through the barracks, giving the place one last sweeping gaze. Raised pallets lined the walls, but each man had a small area for personal items. Not much was needed while the guards were on rotation away from home. The king supplied their food and drink while they supplied his protection. It made for a good system, and Uriah admired the king for his skill in maintaining a smooth-running government.

He ducked around a fellow guard entering the barracks as he passed through, then headed to the king's stables. He was anxious to return and would see if he could commandeer a horse or mule to make the trip faster. His sandals clicked along the tiled walkway, but he stopped as a servant approached.

"Uriah the Hittite?"

Uriah dipped his head. "Yes."

"The king has requested your appearance in his audience chambers." The servant bowed and turned to head back the way he had come.

Uriah lifted a hand and opened his mouth to object, but let the words die on his tongue. The man would not know any more than the message he had already delivered. But why would the king wish to see him again? He had already given a report on the battle, Joab, and the men. There was nothing more to tell.

But just the same, he turned on his heel and marched across the compound toward the palace. The guards opened the wide double doors at his approach and a servant announced him, as had been done yesterday. Uriah slowed his gait and walked to the throne, his gaze on the green-and-blue-patterned tiles adorning the audience chamber's floor. He came to a stop near the steps to the throne and bowed low, touching his forehead to the cool tiles.

The king's response was delayed several heartbeats, when at last Uriah heard the scepter scrape across the floor. "You may rise." The king sounded weary, as though this meeting annoyed and displeased him.

Uriah straightened, searching his mind for what he could have possibly done to cause the furrowed brow and scrutinizing look he was eliciting from the king. "May my lord King David live forever," he said, dipping his head again, not sure he wanted to keep his monarch's stern gaze. He forced his feet to hold steady, though inside he squirmed like a little boy caught disobeying his father's instructions, almost feeling the sting of the lash against his skin.

"Haven't you just come from a distance? Why didn't you go home?" The king's tone was as stern as his father's had been, his anger fleshed out in the stiff way he sat on his throne and gripped the scepter.

Uriah met the king's disapproving gaze, his thoughts shooting through him like arrows hitting their mark. Why should the king care what he did in his off-duty time? And how could he suggest such a thing when the rest of Israel lived in tents set for battle? Unless the king had some ulterior motive for this inquisition. But as he held the man's gaze, he could not fathom what that motive would be.

"The ark and Israel and Judah are staying in tents, and my master Joab and my lord's men are camped in the open fields. How could I go to my house to eat and drink and lie with my wife? As surely as you live, I will not do such a thing!" Uriah straightened his posture as he spoke, lifting his chin to show the king his devotion. Perhaps his words would have some effect, might cause the king to reconsider how foolish his suggestions were. If the king had come with them to battle, he would see for himself how important it was for the men to keep themselves in check and for the captains to set a good example. Surely the king knew this and had practiced it for years. Had he stayed home so long he had somehow forgotten?

The king's rigid posture did not lessen, but his eyes flickered with something Uriah could not define. Uncertainty, perhaps? Uriah dared to hope his words might persuade the king to act, as he should.

"Stay here one more day, and tomorrow I will send you back."

Uriah bowed, dipping forward to touch his head to his knee. He straightened again. "As you wish, my lord."

At David's dismissal, Uriah backed from the room, unable to shake the unease he felt. He should be on his way back to Rabbah. There was nothing to do in the city while he waited, and he would not go home. There was only one thing he could do, what he had devoted his life to doing. Guard the king.

❦

Bathsheba picked at the meal Tirzah had set before her, the fear in her heart swiftly replacing the hunger in her middle. Uriah's expected visit had put the household on edge, and now the tension, the whispers, and the looks cast her way over his all-too-obvious absence stole her appetite and her hope. Why did he not come?

Tirzah closed the doors to the cooking room and joined her at the table, sitting beside her on the bench. "Word has it Uriah is still in Jerusalem," she whispered close to Bathsheba's ear. "Anittas returned from the king's house after he spoke with Uriah. Apparently the king spoke with the master this morning and instructed him to remain in Jerusalem another day. The master had planned to leave for Rabbah this morning, but the king is keeping him here until tomorrow. Perhaps he will come home today before he leaves." She touched Bathsheba's arm, her look comforting. "You must not lose hope."

Bathsheba closed her eyes as she slowly shook her head and looked down. "He will not come home."

Tirzah touched a plate of ripe dates. "It's still possible. Come, you must eat something."

"If Anittas spoke to him, all is lost."

Bathsheba looked up to see Tirzah's emphatic shake of her head. "Anittas only spoke with him to settle some questions about the estate. He said nothing of you."

Bathsheba quirked a brow and leaned away, assessing her servant. "How do you know this? You could not possibly have followed him or gotten close enough to hear their conversations."

Tirzah crossed her arms over her chest. "I asked Anittas to tell me straight when he returned. He would not lie."

Bathsheba looked toward the window at the morning light streaming in through the lattices. "Everyone lies if it is to his or her advantage." She pushed away from the bench and walked to the window. Servants worked in the open courtyard, the one adjacent to their neighbor's, grinding grain and sifting wheat for the evening meal. Such normal daily tasks. She placed a hand to her middle, where the child lay helpless, defenseless. Would he or she live to see such tasks? Or would the child die within her battered body, beneath a pile of stones?

A shiver shook her, and she gripped both arms, holding herself tight against the onslaught of fear and truth and emotion. The sound of Tirzah clearing away her uneaten meal reached her consciousness, reminding her that while she lived, there was work to be done. Uriah had one more day in Jerusalem. She must prepare his favorite meal, just in case.

❦22❦

David canceled court earlier than usual and retreated to his roof, Benaiah standing watch nearby. Servants brought him bread and wine, but he left both untouched in his pavilion and began to pace from parapet to parapet. Now what? Uriah was clearly dedicated to the very rules he, David, had initiated when he had commanded his first battle. He'd modified the guidelines over the years, but essentially they stayed in place because they worked. Men fought better when they were kept from women. Their focus was single-minded, and while he could not keep a man's thoughts from straying, the practice of celibacy during wartime was a good one.

Was it any wonder that one of his best captains would confront him on such a thing? He tipped his mouth, chagrined. He was dealing with the best, and they both knew it. But did Uriah also know the secret David and Uriah's wife were so desperate to keep from him? Were his reasons to stay away from her rooted in something more than devotion?

He paused at the edge of the western parapet and ran a hand over his beard as the late afternoon shadows brought the sun ever closer to the earth's ridge. Uriah had expected to be sent back to the battle after giving his report and probably didn't expect the king to question his personal actions or motives. David's keeping him here one more day likely raised the man's suspicions. But if David had let him return so quickly without seeing Bathsheba . . .

What should he do?

His gaze lifted heavenward, but the familiar longing for Adonai had drifted from him at some point in his recent past, and his own heavy weight of guilt would not allow him to seek His face. The realization saddened him. He should never have called for Bathsheba, should never have given in to his male urges. Should he confess what he had done to Uriah and fall on the man's mercy?

He whipped around, angry with his train of thought, and strode to the opposite wall as his mind processed what such a confession could mean. At best, Uriah would forgive them both and accept the child as his own. But such an act would require great mercy. Mercy David didn't deserve, and from the way Uriah had challenged him this morning, something Uriah would not be able to give.

At worst, Uriah would demand justice, which would mean death by stoning for David and Bathsheba and the child growing within her. The kingdom he had worked so hard to gain would fall to Amnon, a son not ready or worthy of the position, or perhaps Absalom, who was too young and arrogant to command a nation. The people might even turn against David's house altogether, and then God's promise to always have a man from his house on the throne of Israel would be lost.

But if he kept silent, Bathsheba would suffer alone. She could not hide her pregnancy forever, and when Uriah returned to battle, everyone in Jerusalem would know the child was not his. Uriah's declaration and public insistence that he would not go home had sealed the truth.

David's heart pumped faster as he walked—almost raced—his pacing growing frantic until at last his legs carried him to his pavilion, where he sank onto the cushions, spent. He reached for the ever-present flask the servant had left and poured some of the dark liquid into his waiting chalice. He needed advice, wisdom on what to do, but there was no one to ask. He could not confess such a thing, and that was the truth of it. Uriah could not know, for both his and Bathsheba's sakes. He could not risk seeing her stoned on his account. An image of her perfect face, her sculpted body, bloodied and torn, made his eyes sting. No. He could not let her die.

Summoning Benaiah, he dispatched a message. "Bring Uriah to eat at my table this night." Perhaps in the eating and drinking, an idea would come to him. He stared into the rich purple liquid and drank. If the man drank enough, he might stagger to his house instead of the barracks. A discreet servant placed here or there could ensure the fact. And as long as Uriah spent the night in his own home, it would not matter what he did there. He would be too drunk to remember, and Bathsheba would be safe.

A slow smile touched David's lips as he finished the last dregs of his cup.

❧❧

Scents of garlic and cumin and the soft sounds of a lyre drifted to Uriah as he entered the king's dining hall. With Israel at war, he was surprised at the number of men eating at the king's table. But on a second look, he realized the king's sons occupied one table and his older counselors another.

King Saul's grandson Mephibosheth and his son sat with some other nobles, men whose hands had not trained for war. The room was not as filled as it would have been for a normal feast.

A servant appeared at his side as he stepped over the threshold. "This way," he said, moving ahead of Uriah, obviously expecting him to follow. The man wove past the tables and around some jugglers and led Uriah to the front of the room to the king's table. King David was already seated as though he were awaiting his arrival.

Uriah took his intended seat at the king's side, curiosity and pride mingling within him. If only Eliam—or better yet, his own father—could have witnessed this event. When Uriah returned and took his time describing this surprising night, Eliam would pester him with questions. Even among the Thirty, few men ever had the privilege of sitting at a banquet this close to the king.

"My lord, may you live forever," Uriah said, suddenly uncomfortable with the king's silent perusal. Was the man still displeased with him for keeping his vow of celibacy during war? But at the king's easy smile, he relinquished the thought.

"Uriah, my friend. Thank you for joining me. I trust you are well rested from your journey from Rabbah?" David leaned into his gilded chair as a servant walked about filling wine goblets.

"Yes, thank you, my lord. The trip was not arduous, and I am ready to return to my men." Uriah nodded to the servant, and as the king picked up his cup, he did the same, drinking as the king did, not wishing to err on the side of poor manners.

They ate a few moments in silence, Uriah attuned to the king's mood, wondering what to say to continue the conversation.

He followed the king's lead and ripped a piece of bread from the flat loaf on his plate and dipped it into the bowl of lentils. Bread and salt between them signified friendship, though Uriah still struggled to understand why the king sought his now. Why single him out? Though in honesty, he knew the privilege puffed his chest, lifted his pride, more than it should.

"Do you like music, Uriah?" The king's question refocused his attention, and he silently berated himself for not watching the king more closely.

"Yes, my lord. It has its uses. I do not admit to carrying a tune, but I appreciate the songs of worship at the tabernacle and during the feasts. The Israelites—your God derives pleasure from such a thing?" While he believed in Israel's God, he could never quite understand the various characteristics of Adonai Elohim. He appreciated order and the numerous laws laid out for men to follow, and sacrifice and the need to seek forgiveness, but he could not wrap his mind around worship that involved music and prayer and emotion.

The king glanced somewhere beyond Uriah, but Uriah did not follow his gaze. "Adonai derives pleasure from many things. He gave song to the birds, but they sing the same refrain. Only men have the ability to create something new." The king sipped from his cup again, and Uriah did the same. "Have you ever created something new, Uriah?"

Uriah set the cup beside his plate and a servant filled it again. He was not used to drinking so much wine with a meal, but he had no intention of offending the king when he was so blessed to spend time with him. He shook his head slowly. "I am not so inclined, my lord. My wife is the one with such interest, not I." He smiled and lifted his golden cup again to his lips, resting them against the smooth, cool surface, the wine tingling and warming him. "This is very good," he said after a small sip. He took a ripe fig from a platter.

"The grapes are from the best vineyards in Israel. There is plenty more, so drink up and enjoy." The king smiled, motioning to Uriah's cup. He held his own loosely in one hand, as though the goblet had become as familiar as his scepter. "You say your wife is interested in music. How so?"

Uriah studied the swirling liquid in his cup, his thoughts growing thick like wool. "She plays the lyre sometimes. Not usually when I'm around, though I don't forbid it. Her father never approved of the instrument, but I know it makes her happy, so I let her use it when her work is done." He looked at the king and tried to read his expression, but his reaction lay hidden, his gaze shadowed.

"It is good to show interest in her music," David said after a lengthy silence. "Abigail used to coax me to play for her, though she did not play an instrument herself. Her interest encouraged me, made me strive to put more tunes and words to parchment." The king studied the contents of his cup, and Uriah watched him as he listened to the muted sounds of male conversations and laughter around them.

"Abigail was a good wife to you." Uriah sensed the king's sudden melancholy and wondered again why Adonai had taken the wife the king appeared to love the most. Had the king done something to offend Adonai? Had Abigail broken one of Moses' many laws?

"Yes, she was." The king took a long drink of the wine, and Uriah did the same, though he was already struggling to keep his focus. He'd been drunk on a few occasions and managed well enough. If it pleased the king to drink until neither of them could walk straight, so be it.

"I was not as good a husband to her as she was devoted to me." The king leaned closer. "A woman needs a man to be there for her, to love her. When he is gone all of the time or she has to share him with others, she suffers." His gaze penetrated, his meaning suddenly clear.

The king was speaking as much to Uriah as he was to himself, suggesting that Bathsheba suffered because he was gone to war. But the war was one the king had commanded, calling Uriah to battle. Was he supposed to just quit before the end? He shook his head, trying to clear it, but the wine was making his head light.

"A wife of a king or of a warrior knows the expectations and risks of such a life. Your wives know they will share you, and my wife knows she will miss me. It is the nature of life." Uriah set the goblet down and pushed it away, but David motioned toward it, coaxing him to pick it up again.

"Knowing and needing are two different things." David leaned into his chair, holding the golden cup aloft. "But you are right, Uriah. Our women know their place, so why should we change? What does it matter to us? We must please ourselves most of all." He tipped his head back and tossed the liquid into his mouth.

Warmth crept up Uriah's neck, and he knew the wine had little to do with it. The king's barbed words were meant to prick his sense of guilt, to make him want to please himself or his wife above the rules and customs of wartime. Something the king himself would not have done if he had gone to war with them.

Irritation rose within him at the inference, and he sloshed the wine in his cup before taking a breath and downing the remains. He set the goblet down a little harder than he intended.

Words failed him, and a headache began along his temple. He gently rubbed the spot with two fingers.

"Have I offended you, Uriah?" The king's comment registered, raising his ire.

"As you say, my lord. If you think I am gone from my wife too much, perhaps you should join your men at war and not sit home while the rest of us fight your battles. Then the next time we go to war, I will be sure to refuse." Uriah closed his eyes, knowing he had said too much. And to the king! He should have never allowed himself to drink wine in the king's presence. His loose tongue would surely cost him the position he had achieved, or more.

"You are right again, Uriah." The king's tone was quiet, barely heard above the din of the room. "I should have gone to war with my men. But you are also wrong. If I had gone to war and had the chance to come home again, I would not spend the night with a useless monarch. I would go home to my wife and enjoy her charms." His smile dimmed as he spoke, his eyes probing. Uriah sensed the meaning despite the fog of drink, and felt his pride and honor slipping with each passing moment.

"Perhaps I should go, my lord." He knew he should wait to be dismissed, so he did not rise from his seat, but he pressed a hand to his head and blinked, trying to stop seeing double. "I'm afraid the wine has put words in my mouth, and I am not holding my own too well. Please pardon your servant and excuse me." He waited, watching. At the king's nod, he stood.

"Go home, Uriah. Get some sleep." The king turned away from him then as though their meeting held little consequence to him.

Uriah bowed low, and the room tipped as he rose. "Thank

you, my lord. Forgive me, my lord." He staggered from the king's table to the outside of the hall. Servants met him and clutched his arms, guiding him through the palace halls to the outer courtyard toward the gate.

As they stepped beneath the watchful eyes of the guards at the gate, the servants guided Uriah toward his street. They intended to take him home, and he wanted nothing more. But as the wine settled with his movement, his head cleared a little and he stopped, taking in his surroundings. This was exactly what the king had told him to do—to go home and rest. But he had vowed never to do such a thing while Joab and his men lived in tents. He could not break his vow! If he did not keep his word, who would trust him? If he lost his integrity for one night of pleasure—to please himself or his wife—what good would that bring him in the long run?

"I can't do this. I won't do this."

The servants' gentle pressure on his arm coaxed him to continue home, but he shook off the men's hands and turned around, back the way he had come. He stumbled and straightened, ignoring the imploring looks and pleas of the king's servants, and made his way back to the guardhouse at the door of the palace.

~23~

David stood and excused himself from the meal the moment Uriah left the room. Surely the man would go home this time. He had managed to get the message across well enough, if Uriah was an astute observer. The thought troubled him. If Uriah was conscious of what was going on around him, the man should have already discovered the reasons behind David's efforts, or at the very least suspected something. Had he? Had Uriah simply gone along with David's offer of friendship to cover up what he already knew? Would he stay away from his wife on purpose?

Aggravated, David stomped over tiles of inlaid stone, skimming past his halls of cedar, barely aware of his opulent surroundings. His mind played again every word that had passed between them, every gesture, look, and nuance. He reached his bedchamber, moving past Benaiah's guards. Two servants followed him inside, one lighting the lamps to dispel the moonlight, the other helping him change into more comfortable clothes. When they finished their duties, David dismissed them and walked to the window.

The view from his chambers looked out over his private gardens on one side and faced Jerusalem's Eastern Gate on the other. The height of the palace allowed him a view from every angle, but the activity in his outer courts did not interest him, and his gardens reminded him too vividly of Bathsheba. His stomach tightened at the thought of her. Had Uriah reached home yet? Would she tell him the truth or keep their shared secret? He had never asked it of her, only assumed she would keep silent.

With a woman, one should never assume.

He rubbed the back of his neck and drew in a slow breath. He just wanted this whole thing to end. To go back to that moment before he had succumbed to his own foolish impulses and change the outcome. If he had never called for her . . .

He stopped himself. He could not change the past. He could only change what would happen now.

A knock on the door pulled him away from staring at the courtyard below. "Come," he called as he strode to the door.

One of Benaiah's Cherethite guards poked his head in. "My lord, some servants are here with a message for you."

David gave the man a curt nod. "Let them in."

The guard backed away, and the two servants he'd sent to see Uriah safely home entered. David's heart skipped a beat at the look on the first man's face. "Did Uriah go home?"

The servant shook his head. "No, my lord. Uriah the Hittite sleeps at the guardhouse with my lord's servants."

Heat rushed through David's veins, his pulse throbbing in his ear. "Tell me everything." Though he already knew the answer.

"We did as you asked, my lord. We each took hold of one of Uriah's arms and coaxed him through the palace gates. We even made it onto the man's street, not far from his house, when suddenly he stops, looks around, and seems to realize

190

where he is. He mumbled something about, 'I can't do this. I won't do this,' then he turns around and heads back to the palace. We tried to talk him out of it, my lord, but he wouldn't listen." The man bowed low when he finished his speech.

"Is he telling the truth?" David asked the second man, though he had no reason to think his servants were lying to him.

"Yes, my lord, it was just as he said." The second man bowed as well.

"Go to the guardhouse and keep watch. If Uriah the Hittite goes anywhere or talks to anyone, I want to know it." He dismissed them and sank onto the cushions of his couch, defeated.

Either Uriah was a better man drunk than David had been sober, or he was playing David for a fool. Could Uriah truly be so devious that he would deny the king's request to prove a point? Or was he simply that naive? In either case, something must be done. Uriah's inaction would cost Bathsheba her life.

He shoved up from the couch, the weight of the situation pressing in on him, sapping his strength. With an effort, feeling far older than his years, he staggered to his bed and climbed beneath the curtains. If he could sleep, perhaps a solution would rise from the abyss in the morning.

He pulled the covers to his chest and stared at the dark ceiling above him. Sleep would be a long time coming.

❧❦

Overcast skies matched his mood the next morning, and David called for his parchments, quill, and ink. He stared at the tan scroll, the quill clutched in his hand, the words he'd crafted in the night repeating and reshaping themselves over and over again in his head. Surely there was another way. But no matter how many ways he had looked at it, changing his thoughts as often as he had tossed beneath the covers of his bed, he could not find one.

With a heavy sigh that did nothing to lift the millstone-sized weight in his chest, he dipped the quill into the ink and penned a letter to Joab.

Put Uriah in the front line where the fighting is fiercest. Then withdraw from him so he will be struck down and die.

He did not bother to address it or sign it. Ironically, Uriah would be faithful enough to deliver his own death warrant. If by some chance the man decided to break the seal and read the words, he would have the evidence he needed to bring David's kingdom to an end. Uriah's loyalty or treachery would soon be known, either by David's death or Uriah's.

David rolled the scroll, poured the hot wax on the edges, and pressed his royal seal in place. When it cooled, he lifted the seal and stood, then dressed in his royal robes and strode to his audience chamber.

Uriah appeared, looking more haggard than he had the previous morning. He bowed low. "My lord king, live forever."

David extended his scepter, and Uriah rose, keeping one knee bent, his gaze lowered.

"Take this to General Joab." When Uriah looked up, David passed the scroll to him, then rested both hands on the arms of his chair, his heart turning to stone. "Have a safe trip, Uriah."

"Thank you, my lord." The man tucked the scroll into the leather satchel at his waist, bowed again, and backed quickly away as though anxious to head back to his men.

David stared after him. All he could do now was wait.

₰24₰

Bathsheba stood on the roof of her grandfather's home, pulling her cloak tight against the stiff morning breeze, the gray clouds overhead blocking the full rays of dawn. She leaned against the parapet, Tirzah at her side, watching the king's gate for some sign of Uriah.

Last night, as she had lain on their bed, she had prayed, pleaded with Adonai for a chance to see Uriah, to make things right somehow. But though she had stayed awake, attuned to every eerie sound of the night, Uriah's footsteps had not been one of those sounds. His voice was absent in her home's confining walls.

Tears slipped down her cheeks before she could stop them, and she quickly swiped at them with the back of her hands. Tirzah's touch brought her shoulders up straight.

"There he is, mistress."

Bathsheba blinked, trying to see through blurred vision where Tirzah pointed. And then she saw him, walking beside a brown mule accompanied by another soldier, both men dressed in full military attire. He stood straight, his gaze on the road before him. Once through the gate, he did not pause or look in the direction of their home.

She stared after him. Should she shout down to him and force him to acknowledge her? She could take the steps two at a time and be in his arms again, could feel his strength once more before he walked out of the life she had known with him for good. After this, he would not look on her with favor, once he knew a child not his own grew in her womb. Then she would fall not into his arms, but at his feet, begging for mercy. As she could do even now if she hurried, before he moved through the city gates.

"He didn't come home." She heard herself utter the words, the disbelief still enveloping her like the murky clouds above.

"No, he didn't." Tirzah crossed her arms, her tone matching Bathsheba's despair.

Bathsheba glanced at her maid, drawing small comfort in her presence. "He has his honor, and God knows he would never do something to break that." Anger surged to the surface, but she choked it back. How could she hate him? She knew what he was like. Had always known. If not for his vow of celibacy during wartime, he might have come. If the king had told him the truth, he might have come.

She faced Tirzah, her stomach churning, unable to stop the question she had already answered. "Why didn't he come to me?"

"I don't know, my lady." Tirzah touched her arm. "As you said, he is an honorable man."

A brittle laugh escaped. "Far more honorable than the king!" She clamped a hand over her mouth to still its sudden trembling. "Or his wife."

Uriah passed farther into the distance as she continued to stare after him, her heart yearning to run to him, but her mind telling her there was nothing she could do to change things now. If she flung herself at him in public like a brazen woman, Uriah would not be pleased, and no such action would persuade him to stop his mission to return to his men. He would not come home with her. Even if she begged him.

Even if she told him the truth.

As the clouds parted, a fingertip-sized ray illumined the path toward the Eastern Gate, showing Uriah's retreating back. *I love you, Uriah.* But he would not know it now. Not unless he turned around, left the battle, and forgave her and took David's child to be his own.

Deep down, she knew it would never happen. Uriah's pride and his strict adherence to the law would not allow her or David to go unpunished. His justice would supplant any mercy he could have shown. Wouldn't it?

Doubts niggled and her heart sank with the impossible uncertainties. What would David do now? Wait until the war ended, when Uriah would return and condemn her and her child to death? She shivered again despite the warm breeze. Wrapping both arms about herself, Bathsheba waited until Uriah disappeared from view and turned aside to go home.

❧❧

Uriah arrived at the Israelite camp before dusk, left the mule in the care of the soldier who had accompanied him, and strode past rows of tents to the central fire in search of Joab. He spotted him near the commander's tent and smiled when Joab motioned him forward.

"Welcome back, Uriah. How was your visit with the king?" Joab pointed to a raised stone used as a seat a few paces from him. Joab's brother Abishai sat opposite him, and a handful of the Thirty rose to greet Uriah as he stepped closer to the group.

"How did it go? Did you get any time to wash your feet, or did the king keep you occupied the whole time?" Laughter accompanied the comment.

One of the Thirty slapped him on the back, his knowing look heating Uriah's face. "With that wife of yours, you must be feeling good right now."

Discreet guffaws followed. Uriah ignored the comments, used to the humor. Although the men might not have faulted him for sleeping with his wife, he could hold his head high knowing he hadn't.

"My wife did not have the pleasure of my company." He smiled, lifting his chin. "Though I am sure she would have liked to."

Joab snickered at that. "It takes a strong man to deny the call of such a beautiful woman. You are to be commended, Uriah."

"Indeed. Adonai knows I don't have such courage." Abishai's comment drew more laughter, but again Uriah ignored it. Though he was the brunt of their good-natured mirth now, he'd given his share of ribbing in the past.

Uriah turned to Joab. "I'm not sure the king would agree with you." He pulled the sealed scroll from his pouch. "He seems to have forgotten what it means to be at war."

Joab took the scroll from Uriah's outstretched hand. "How so?" Joab broke the seal and slowly unrolled it.

"He told me to go home and wash my feet. Seemed almost angry when I didn't." Uriah shook his head, watching Joab's brow lift slightly, his face impassive, unreadable. "The king's message—is something wrong, Commander?"

Joab's head snapped up at the address, and he quickly re-rolled the parchment. "Just some private concerns." He met

Uriah's gaze and held it, his brows drawn low over his eyes. "What else did the king say to you?"

Uriah tipped his head back, glancing at the orange radiance of the sunset beyond. The colors were bright, their glow hot, as though the sun fought to keep from resting in the west. He looked back at Joab and ran a hand over his beard. "He told me to go home and wash my feet. He sent a gift after me, a roasted lamb. I was forced to choose between obeying the king's suggestion or betraying the men in my command." He broke eye contact, doubt suddenly niggling the back of his neck. Had he done the wrong thing? "So I spent the night at the guardhouse near the palace doors. The next day the king asked me why I didn't go home. He seemed satisfied with my answer and invited me to dine with him that night." Joab didn't need to know he'd drunk too much and almost went home before the night air shook sense back into him.

Uriah watched Joab's expression, but the man's hardened look, the one that could scare most grown men, never wavered. The buzz of voices resumed around them, and Uriah wondered how much of his conversation had been overheard.

"Did you have something to say to me, my lord? Because if there is nothing further . . . it was a long journey."

Joab waited a beat, then slowly nodded. "There is nothing further. Thank you, Uriah." He cupped Uriah's shoulder as Uriah turned to leave, surprising him. "You did the right thing."

"Thank you, my lord. I wish the king had agreed with you." He hadn't realized until this moment the sense of betrayal he'd felt that the king should want him to break protocol, to in fact try so hard to get him to do so. Joab's affirmation lessened the sting of the king's misguided comments.

But as he walked toward his tent, the doubts returned. Something had flickered in Joab's eyes for the slightest moment when he first read the message, before he caught himself. Had the king given Joab a bad report of Uriah? Would he lose his position among the Thirty because he had not gone home to his wife? The whole thing made no sense!

Irritated now, he kicked a stone in his path, ignoring the pain it inflicted on his toes. Reaching his own tent, he slipped inside the dark cocoon, the darkness matching the confusion in his heart.

❧25❧

David rose from another sleepless night, his body drenched in sweat, his limbs as weak as a newborn calf. He did not argue when his servants dressed him or coaxed him to eat, but despite their best efforts, he could not rouse himself to action or free himself from this endless stupor. He swallowed a brewed tea from some plant brought in on a foreign caravan meant to give him energy, and walked with slow strides to his audience chamber. The normal fanfare accompanied his entrance, his scribes sat at their tables ready to record his every word, and his courtiers waited in the side chambers to speak with him. Men from all twelve tribes formed lines outside the palace doors, waiting to be admitted for one judgment or another. David hoped he could concentrate to give them the justice they deserved.

How had his life come to this? He had been reduced to an indecisive worrier, worse than a weak-kneed woman. He straightened his spine at the thought, willing fortitude into his emotions. By now, Joab had received his missive and within the week this whole mess should be over, and his worries forgotten.

The day wore on, the sun a sluggard in its path across the

heavens. He should welcome the day, since the nights were no friend of his, but even the light, with its work, its expectations of change, betrayed him. Every breath was labored as though a hand rested heavy on his chest.

"My lord king, a messenger from Joab has arrived."

David's spirits roused at the attendant's words. "At last, something interesting." He ignored the concerned looks of his counselors, gripped the scepter in one hand, and leaned forward as the man was admitted into his presence.

"May my lord King David live forever." The messenger bowed low, but David quickly bid him rise.

"Tell me, how goes the battle?" A question he had asked Uriah only a week ago. But he was looking for only one answer to this question now.

"The men overpowered us and came out against us in the open, but we drove them back to the entrance to the city gate. Then the archers shot arrows at your servants from the wall, and some of the king's men died. Moreover, your servant Uriah the Hittite is dead." The man did not meet David's eyes, which would not have surprised him under any other circumstance. Now he wondered if the servant knew more than he let on. He shook the thought aside. Joab would not have shared his confidence with anyone. Surely his nephew, of all people, could be trusted.

David looked at the man who was obviously waiting for his dismissal, much as Uriah had done that first day when David had all but begged him to go home.

Your servant Uriah the Hittite is dead.

It was done then. Bathsheba could now be his. The thought stirred him, awakening him, giving him more energy than he had felt in days, weeks, months even.

"Give Joab this message." He waited a moment as the man angled his head toward him, obviously listening, though kept his gaze discreetly distant. "Tell the general, 'Don't let this upset you; the sword devours one as well as another. Press the attack against the city and destroy it.' Say this to encourage Joab."

"Yes, my lord. It will be as you say." The man took a step backward but did not continue without David's dismissal.

"Has Uriah's widow been told?" To say the words aloud brought such finality.

He caught the servant's somber expression. "Yes, my lord. We traveled all night with the bodies. General Joab told us to bring them back to Jerusalem for burial. Considering Uriah's depth of service to the king and to Israel, the general said it was the least he could do."

Joab knew. David felt the blood draining away from his face even as the heat had darkened it moments before. Joab not only knew, he was sending a message that he would hold it over David, for whatever his purposes.

"Will that be all, my lord?"

The question jolted him. "Yes, thank you." David dismissed the man and leaned heavily against his gilded chair. He summoned Benaiah.

"Yes, my lord, how may I help you?"

David stiffened his back, looking over Benaiah's broad shoulder. "See to it that Uriah's widow has everything she needs to bury her husband."

Benaiah stood for a moment, and David looked at the man's stoic expression, surprised to see he had not moved quickly to follow the command. Their gazes held for a space of a heartbeat until Benaiah looked away. "Will there be anything else? Since Uriah was one of the Thirty, will my lord the king attend his funeral?"

The question brought him up short, his stomach tightening in an unexpected knot. Joab sent Uriah's body back for burial for this very purpose, and for what else? To somehow expose David? But he could hardly ignore such an event, especially if he wanted to marry the man's widow.

His breath grew slower, shallow. He closed his eyes, then met Benaiah's gaze. "Inform Ahithophel that I will attend."

"It will be as you say, my lord." He backed away and then turned to do David's bidding.

৵৲

Bathsheba wrapped both arms around herself, pulling her black cloak tight against her, but a chill settled deep within her despite the comfort of Aunt Talia's arms. Her grandfather stood stoically beside her, and her father, who had accompanied Uriah's body, kept company with a handful of warriors who had abandoned the battle to honor her husband.

The king's entourage took up a third of the valley near the burial cave whose wide mouth yawned before them, waiting to accept Uriah's broken, lifeless body. The bier rested on the shoulders of four men as the sounds of weeping mingled with the flutist's dirge, assaulting the oppressive air around her. Bathsheba's tears were thin coatings over her cheeks, long dried by the summer breeze, the taste of salt still on her tongue.

She glanced across the rocky expanse between where her family had gathered and the king stood silently in apparent grief. Her heart squeezed at the sight of him, knowing instinctively that Uriah was dead on their account. If she had

202

never given herself to the king, would Uriah be alive to love her again? She choked on a sob at the thought and turned to gaze on the bier and Uriah's wrapped body. She staggered forward, out of Aunt Talia's embrace, and closed the short distance to the men holding the bier.

They lowered it at her approach, and the flutist fell silent, the weeping softened as she placed a hand on the arm that had once held her close, now covered in white linen. She moved closer. His head and face were coated in the same strips of linen so that nothing remained for her to gaze upon. His body, once so strong, so masculine, was now prone, lifeless, his once ardent kisses no longer able to make her knees weak. The memories nearly paralyzed her, and she stumbled as she had that first time he had kissed her, had drawn the strength from her, left her breathless. She sank to the earth beside his sealed body, no longer able to keep back the convulsing sobs.

Oh, Adonai, forgive me! Uriah, my husband, my love, what have I done to you? Where have you gone? I need you!

Her knees folded beneath her robe and she rocked back and forth, the wails coming from her throat, deep and painful. She felt strong arms come around her, saw her father's tearstained face through her blurred vision, heard Aunt Talia's whispers against her wet cheek.

"Come, Bathsheba. You can't stay here." Her father's voice came to her like a gentle touch as he pulled her to her feet. She was unclean for having touched Uriah's dead body, but her father's arms around her told her he didn't care. They would purify themselves later. For now, while her father remained unaware of the child in her womb, unaware of the shame she had caused him and of the part she had played in her husband's death . . . for now, she was loved.

She clung to the thought even as she rejected it, knowing how short-lived her reprieve. The men holding her husband's bier lifted it again and carried it into the tomb.

"We have lost a great man, a great warrior, today." The king's voice floated over the valley where Uriah's tomb lay in the crevice of a hill. "Uriah was not one of us by birth, but he surely became an Israelite at heart. He obeyed the laws Moses handed down to us with utter devotion. Surely God has not abandoned his soul to the grave."

As the four men emerged from the tomb, they walked over to the heavy stone and heaved their weight against it, rolling it over the gaping mouth. Bathsheba's knees gave way again, and she drew on her father's strength to hold her up. She leaned into his chest, her vision clouded, her gaze fixed straight ahead. She could not look at David lest he read the confusion and see the fear in her heart. Even from this distance, he had to know how she felt about Uriah's loss, how she wished she had never gone to him that night. Did David hate her for what had come between them? Had his lust become a thing despised? She had cost him one of his finest warriors, one of his trusted Thirty. Surely he blamed her. Women always bore such blame.

"I am sorry for your loss, Bathsheba." She startled at the familiar voice, turning abruptly, captured by the intense look in his eyes. He offered his hand, and she looked at it uncertainly, then slowly placed hers in his. He squeezed once and released his hold. "Your husband was a good man." The king stepped back a pace, his expression somber. "He will be missed."

"Thank you, my lord." Her words, choked and throaty, pushed past her lips. She longed to search his gaze, to determine the intent behind his words, but he turned to her father, and she lowered her head appropriately, certain that any further communication between them would attract undue attention.

"Eliam, I know you held Uriah in high regard. I want you to know that anything you need to help with his loss is yours." The king's voice caught as he spoke, and Bathsheba looked up again, reading a hint of respect in her father's eyes.

"Uriah had no brother to act as kinsman redeemer." Her father's comment made her breath catch. She had not thought he would consider the need to raise a child to her husband's legacy. But to bring it up here, now . . . Was he offering her to the king?

"When her week of mourning has ended, I will be her kinsman redeemer." The king cleared his throat, then shifted to look at her. "If she will have me." His words were soft, like a comforting balm. He had done this purposely to give her hope. And with the child already on the way, he could not wait long to act.

"Thank you, my lord," she said, choking on another sob. She longed to fling herself into David's arms, but her father tightened his grip on her and she turned into his shoulder instead, weeping. The king had worked everything out, and they would be all right. She and her unborn child would not die beneath a pile of rocks, buried shamefully. Unlike the husband who did not deserve to die so young, who would never know what honor she had cost him.

❧❧

The pains came on suddenly, and Bathsheba couldn't stifle the cry that escaped with the first onslaught. She doubled over beside the bed in the chambers David had designed for her, sweat drawing a thick line across her brow.

"The midwife is coming, my lady. Here, let me help you." Tirzah, ever faithful since the day David had taken Bathsheba to his house as his wife seven months before, placed a strong arm along her back at her distended waist and helped her to stand.

"I can't."

"Yes, you can. You will be more comfortable on the cushions."

Bathsheba panted as she let Tirzah lead her, but sitting did nothing to ease the ache in her back. She pushed up with Tirzah's help and walked the length of the sitting room. Her living quarters in the palace were large, with a bedchamber that held a bed big enough for two, a table to take her morning meal, another table with all of her cosmetics, chests full of elegant robes and tunics etched with gold thread, and boxes overflowing with jewels and perfumes—costly gifts from the king. Gifts of penance, she knew, sensing the guilt in him, the guilt that throbbed between them every time his gaze met hers, every time he entered these chambers.

Though she had been his wife since the week after Uriah's burial, her new status as wife of the king had done nothing to assuage the intense loss she still felt. The weight David carried seemed to grow heavier, palpable, until the man who had wooed her seemed to disappear with the morning mist. Yet outwardly he presented a man in control, a king to be obeyed—and sometimes, when his temper snapped, to be feared. Her grandfather looked at David with questioning eyes, his weathered face lined with concern . . . and confusion. Ahithophel had looked to her for explanation, but with

Jill Eileen Smith

each passing day, the weight David carried became her own, matching the child's bulk as it grew within her. Would this birth relieve them both of the shame, of the guilt, they harbored in secret?

She moved from the sitting room to the gardens adjacent to the king's. Her placement in the palace compound had done nothing to endear her to the king's other wives, her privilege evoking bitter controversy for David not only from his wives, but from the tribes they represented as well. The stress of it all had deepened the grooves on his brow and made him moody and temperamental. And she blamed herself for all of it.

She turned from the gardens and walked back into the sitting room when another crippling pain seized her, and she fell to her knees, unable to bear it. Perhaps she would die in the birth and free David from the burden she had caused him. If only she had not bathed alone that night in the courtyard or played the music that first drew him to watch. She closed her eyes, putting the cloth Tirzah offered between her teeth to keep her cries from carrying throughout the palace.

"Please!" Her tears came as the midwife bustled into the room with Aunt Talia and Chava close behind. "Help me!" She heard her own helpless whimper and could do nothing to stop herself.

"There now, your time has come so soon! The babe must be anxious to make his way into the world." Aunt Talia coaxed her to the couch, where the midwife examined her.

"She is farther along in labor than I would have thought possible. This child will come before the night is through." The midwife lowered Bathsheba's tunic and bid her rest as she suffered the next spasms.

"Will the child live?" Chava whispered, but Bathsheba

clearly heard the words. "She can only be six or seven months along. Perhaps we should make her herbs to stop the pains."

"The child will not be stopped now." The midwife shook her head, and Bathsheba closed her eyes, pretending the pain in her middle was the only reason she had for writhing and groaning. "She's too far along."

When the babe was born, his size would silence Chava's questions. Unless, by some miracle, the child was smaller than normal. But Bathsheba could not bring herself to ask Adonai for such a favor. It was only by His grace she wasn't already buried beneath a mound of rocks for her sins.

A gush of liquid between her legs jolted her thoughts. "He's coming!" She panted against the pain as the women guided her to the birthing stool. Aunt Talia's strong hands rested on her shoulders while Chava clasped her hand. Tirzah hurried about doing whatever the midwife asked.

Agony, knife-like and sharp, bit down on her.

"Push, Bathsheba. I see the head." The midwife's calm voice coaxed her. "Again. Not too fast now. The head is coming. Again. Now!"

"Ahh!" With a shout and a massive push, she felt the child release its grip on her insides and burst into the light, the instant cry pitiful at first, then lusty and strong. So like its father.

"It's a boy. A son to carry on Uriah's name." Chava carried the swaddled infant to her to suckle, and a little cry of delight escaped Bathsheba's lips as the babe latched onto her breast. The pull of his tiny mouth drew such love from her being. How perfect, how precious he was! She traced a finger along the soft fringe of his dark hair and felt the downy smoothness of his skin. When she reached his hand, his tiny fingers drew a fist around her thumb. She laughed at the sight.

"Did you see?" She glanced at Chava, catching a look of uncertainty on her cousin's face.

"My son did the same thing when he would suckle." She smiled, but Bathsheba's middle tightened at the expression on Chava's face.

Bathsheba looked back at her son, not wanting to see the question in Chava's eyes, but unable to keep from examining the size of her son. She compared him in her mind's eye to Chava's son at his nine-month birth. The boys were nothing alike in their features, but their sizes were similar.

Chava knew.

"What will you name him?"

The right answer would be to name him Uriah. But to do so would be a living, constant reminder of all she and David longed to forget.

"I don't know yet. I will have to ask his father." Bathsheba closed her eyes, feigning sleep, not wanting to endure the silent questions, the curious looks of her cousin and aunt, or the more obvious knowing look of the midwife. She held the child close, kissing his forehead, drinking in the new scent of him, thrilling to the feel of his small, suckling mouth.

She would protect him from those who would ask such questions. She would keep him close to her and never let the world know the truth of his conception. She would let the world think he had inherited Uriah's lands and carried on his heritage. She would raise him to hold his head up, to not let the gossipers in the palace speak ill of him as she sensed they had of her. The whisperers even now could be heard through the cedar-lined halls, buzzing with jealousy and looking for a way to bring down the king.

She would not let that happen. She clutched her son's body

closer as the room cleared of all but Tirzah. She waited, hoping David would come to see the child she had borne him, the child of their passion.

But as the night deepened and the child slept beside her, her tears and Tirzah were her only companions. The king, wherever he was, had left her to rejoice and weep alone.

❧26❧

David rose before dawn and entered his private gardens, looking for some sort of respite from the tormenting dreams. He could not remember the last time he'd slept in peace or when the visions of the night had brought gladness. He raised his gaze heavenward, exhaustion and anger bubbling equally within him.

How long will You torment me?

He should have gone to Bathsheba last night after the babe had come. But he couldn't bring himself to look upon the child. Not then. His excuses were foolish. He owed it to her to comfort her, to bless the child on his knee. But the tradition seemed false, though no one would fault him. Eliam or Ahithophel should be the ones to claim the child for Uriah. Uriah, whose blood he had spilled to have the woman he could not even bring himself to visit.

How pathetic a man he was! The realization only added to his anger, this time at himself. He moved his gaze from the heavens to the hewn limestone beneath his sandaled feet. He would go to her, force himself to acknowledge the child, and somehow reassure her that life would be normal now. In time, the court gossips would forget the child's "early" birth,

211

and Bathsheba would take her place as one of his many wives. He would do his best to love her, though he knew it was his guilt that drove him. She would not be here if not for him.

He moved through the gardens to the door adjoining hers, opened it slowly, and walked among the almond trees to the door of her apartment. The sound of soft singing made him pause and listen to the sweet beauty of her voice. All anger seeped from him, and when he entered the apartment without knocking, his gaze captured hers where she sat in her sitting room, the babe nursing in her arms. Her smile drove all confusion and frustration from his heart. In two strides he stood over her, looking down on their son.

"I should have come sooner." He bent low to pull the soft linen from the babe's dark hair, careful not to touch her during her uncleanness.

"I'm glad you're here now." Her smile again took his breath. How beautiful she was, even hours after giving birth! Not fragile like Abigail had been, or disheveled as Maacah or Ahinoam or most of his other wives. "Do you want to hold your son?" Her voice, soft like a caress, drew him to her, to accept the child into his arms.

"He's beautiful, like his mother." He gazed into the baby's liquid eyes and kissed his downy head. "What will you name him?"

"I was hoping you would help me decide." Her dark eyes were luminous, and for a brief moment a flicker of sadness swept through them.

David shifted the babe against his chest, but when he rooted, looking for milk, he chuckled and handed him back to his mother. "It is not me he wants." He longed to touch her, to pull her close and restore what he had once had with her so briefly that first night. "We have until the eighth day to name him. There is no rush."

Neither of them wanted to name the child Uriah. He could sense it in her look, in the melancholy that passed between them. "Perhaps Eliam, after my father." She spoke with a certain resignation, and he sensed that pleasing her father was not as important to her as pleasing him.

"Eliam is a good name. Easier to say than Ahithophel."

She laughed and he joined her, the music of the sound lifting his soul. "Don't let my grandfather hear you say that."

"I won't." Their gazes met and held, the silence between them bittersweet, and for the first time in many months he felt a stirring in his heart, a yearning for something more in a wife—something even more than he'd known with Michal in the early years or Abigail more recently. Could Bathsheba give it to him?

"If I do not think of a better name by the time of his circumcision, we will call him after my father. It will please him." Her wistful look told him her father was not one she had easily pleased in the past. David vowed that he would never be so difficult to please in her future.

"I will give the name some thought as well." He bent closer and lowered his hand to her hair, but thought better of it and pulled back, not wanting to break yet another law and add to his guilt. "Thank you for my son," he whispered, knowing in that moment that he was more grateful for this child than any who had gone before, because of what his mother had gone through to bring him forth. "I will raise him up to sit at my right hand. I will always protect you and him, no matter what." The promise grew in strength as he spoke the words, and he knew the future would prove how hard such a promise would be to keep. But he could not, would not, let court gossip ruin his son's future or damage this woman, who was ever so slowly twining herself around the fabric of his heart.

"Thank you, David." His name on her tongue sounded like a song.

The babe whimpered, making his presence known. David chuckled. "It seems you are needed elsewhere." The aroma in the room quickly changed from sweet to acrid, a reminder of the ever-changing scents of an infant. He looked down on his new wife and son and smiled. "I must head to court. I will come again later."

He touched the top of the child's head, then turned and walked back the way he had come, feeling better than he had in a long time. Surely the pain of grief was past. Humming a tune, he entered his chambers, dressed in his royal robes, and headed to court.

❦

David dismissed the last case before the midday meal and rose from his gilded throne. He'd quickly grown weary of listening to the complaints of others and was anxious to peek in on Bathsheba and his son once more. He walked to the side table, where his counselors sat, to invite Ahithophel to join him, to bless the child on his knee, but a commotion at the door to the audience chamber drew his attention back to court. He turned and took a few steps toward his throne again.

The prophet Nathan strode with purpose, back straight, eyes dark and clear as he came to stand in the place of the accuser, to the right side of the throne. David's stomach did a wild flip at the sight of the Nazarite disciple of Samuel, the man who had brought the word of Adonai to him on more than one occasion.

Why had he come? Deep wariness swept through him as he met Nathan's solemn gaze, those dark eyes probing, assessing, seeing things David did not wish to reveal. Did he know?

A shudder, uncontrolled and unwanted, rushed through him at the thought, and he almost staggered as Nathan closed the distance and bowed before him. The action, so familiar, suddenly felt uncomfortable.

"Nathan, my friend, how do you fare this fine day?" He spoke lightly, though his thoughts were heavy and sluggish.

"My lord king, there is a matter on which I would seek your judgment."

David gave a slight nod, willing himself not to give vent to the relief such words evoked. He moved to the steps and sat back on his throne, facing Nathan. "I will hear it."

Nathan dipped his head. "Thank you, my lord." He paused, leaning heavily on his staff as though he needed the stick to give him strength, despite his vigor.

"There were two men in a certain town, one rich and the other poor."

The room grew still, every ear attuned to the tale. David's heart returned to a normal rhythm, and he relaxed against the chair.

"The rich man had a very large number of sheep and cattle, but the poor man had nothing except one little ewe lamb he had bought. He raised it, and it grew up with him and his children. It shared his food, drank from his cup, and even slept in his arms. It was like a daughter to him."

His interest piqued, David leaned slightly forward, images

of his own small flock, his favorite lambs, flicking through his thoughts.

"Now a traveler came to the rich man, but the rich man refrained from taking one of his own sheep or cattle to prepare a meal for the traveler who had come to him." Nathan paused, and David's chest tightened, dreading the next words, his anger already flaring in anticipation.

"Instead, he took the ewe lamb that belonged to the poor man and prepared it for the one who had come to him." Nathan's look never wavered, his final words piercing, heightening David's sense of justice.

"Murderer!" David leaned forward, pointing his scepter toward the place where the condemned usually stood. How dare the rich man do such a thing! Never mind that the victim was an animal, not a man. Rage exploded from a place deep within him where all of the bitterness and frustration of the past months dwelt. "As surely as Adonai lives," he said, looking squarely at Nathan, "the man who did this deserves to die! He must pay for that lamb four times over, because he did such a thing and had no pity."

Nathan stood silent as murmurs of agreement with the king's judgment filled the hall. His gaze seemed rooted to the tiles beneath his dusty feet as the sounds died away. David's anger melted to dread, his breath heavy, anxious. Why did the prophet not speak?

Nathan's chest lifted in an audible sigh, and he looked up once more, his eyes fixed solely on David, bold, unflinching, penetrating to the pit of David's soul.

He lifted a finger and pointed to David. "You are the man!"

His voice rang in the room, the words a dagger to David's heart. Bile rose in his gut, churning, nauseating him.

"This is what Adonai, El Yisrael, says."

David sank deeper into the chair.

"'I anointed you king over Israel, and I delivered you from the hand of Saul. I gave your master's house to you, and your master's wives into your arms. I gave you the house of Israel and Judah. And if all this had been too little, I would have given you even more.'"

Oh, Adonai, what have I done?

"'Why did you despise the word of Adonai by doing what is evil in His eyes? You struck down Uriah the Hittite with the sword and took his wife to be your own. You killed him with the sword of the Ammonites. Now, therefore, the sword will never depart from your house, because you despised Me and took the wife of Uriah the Hittite to be your own.'"

Every word was a stinging arrow sinking deep, rending David's heart open and laying it bare.

Adonai, forgive me!

"This is what Adonai says: 'Out of your own household I am going to bring calamity upon you. Before your very eyes I will take your wives and give them to one who is close to you, and he will lie with your wives in broad daylight. You did it in secret, but I will do this thing in broad daylight before all Israel.'"

Strength drained from him, but David forced himself up on wobbly knees. He stumbled forward, down the steps from his throne—a throne he was no longer worthy to sit upon—and moved to the place of judgment where he, as the rich man, knew he deserved to stand. He removed the crown from his head and undid the gilded belt at his waist, letting the richly ornamented royal robe fall to the tiles. Bending low, he untied the jeweled sandals—another evidence of his wealth, of the blessing God had given that he had so easily despised—and slipped them from his feet.

Guilt so deep he could not dig it out, shame so profound he could not express it, heated his blood, his face, weakening him. He sank to the tiles and spread his hands out, palms open in front of him.

"I have sinned against Adonai." He bowed his head, great sobs working through him, and he was powerless to stop them. Images of Uriah's trusting face floated before him, and Bathsheba's innocent grief. *Oh, Adonai, if it is possible, forgive Your servant's guilt.* He could no longer bear the weight of it. He knew that now. Adonai's hand had been on him from the first moment of his sin, wooing him through sleepless nights and a guilty conscience, and he had not listened.

What have I done? Please spare Bathsheba the fate Your law demands. He deserved to die. He would bear her punishment. He deserved nothing less.

He heard Nathan's footsteps and sensed the man kneeling at his side, felt a hand on his head. "Adonai has taken away your sin. You are not going to die." His voice held compassion, and he drew David up again, to his knees.

David averted his gaze, ashamed to look on the prophet, a man who had once been his friend as Samuel had been. His heart rent again at the thought of Samuel and how deeply his sin would have disappointed the man. He could not look at his sons or his counselors or the servants who had so faithfully obeyed his every word. He studied the tiles instead.

"David." Nathan's tone changed, forcing David's gaze upward. He braced himself for a blow. "Adonai has taken away your sin. You are not going to die. But because by doing this you have made the enemies of Adonai show utter contempt, the son born to you will die."

Oh, God . . . please, no! He closed his eyes, reeling with the pronouncement. Was it mercy that he lived at his son's expense? *Adonai, Adonai, take me instead!*

The room, silent in the presence of Nathan's proclamation, slowly grew to a low hum with the buzz of many voices. The secret he had worked so hard to keep, Adonai had laid bare in an instant. How could he have ever thought to keep anything from El Roi, the God Who Sees? And when had he become so proud, so arrogant, as to think he was incapable of falling from Adonai's favor? He could not recall the last time he had read the law or penned a song of worship. Not since Abigail's death. He had been walking in his own misery and self-serving pity ever since.

Nathan touched a hand to his shoulder, and David looked into the prophet's kind gaze, feeling chastened, and yet somehow . . . loved. The prophet's grief and regret were palpable, but there was no undoing what had been done.

He accepted Nathan's hand and stood, surprised when Nathan bent forward and kissed both cheeks, as if he would restore him then and there. Nathan bent to retrieve David's crown and placed it once more on his head.

Tears blurred David's vision as Nathan turned to leave. David watched him go, then moved to the side door, head bowed, and walked slowly out of the room.

❧ 27 ❧

Bathsheba stirred from a light doze at the sound of her son's soft whimper. She rose from the bed and lifted his perfect bundled body from the basket on the floor at her side. His face looked flushed in the filtered light coming through the latticed window, but his cries were not lusty enough to bring on the reddening of his skin. She placed a hand on his forehead, jerked it away, then felt his face and neck, unwrapping his swaddled body until every part of his heated skin was exposed.

Fear seized her, turning her insides cold. How was it possible that he was so feverish? He was healthy when she'd laid him down to nap. She'd only closed her eyes for a brief moment. Had she somehow neglected him? Swaddled him too tight?

Panicked, she darted quick glances about the room. "Tirzah!" She bent over the child, his pitiful chest rising and falling, his breaths coming swift, his cries weak. "Tirzah!"

"I'm here, mistress. What's wrong?" The woman dropped a bundle of fresh linens on a chest beside the bed. "These were dry, I thought we might need them soon—oh, dear one, is he ill?"

"Send for the king. No, wait. Get some tepid water. We will dip the cloths in it and cover his body with them."

"Yes, my lady." Tirzah ran from the room, returning moments later carrying a large clay jug of water and more cloths tucked under her arm. "The physician has been called," she said. She poured water into a bowl, dunked the cloth and wrung it out, and placed it over the baby's feverish head.

Bathsheba dipped a second cloth into the water and placed it on the baby's chest. But the child barely moved, and Bathsheba pulled him to her again, trying to get him to open his eyes, to persuade him to eat. Her milk came in a stream, and she coaxed his mouth open to accept the warm liquid, but only a few drops made it down his throat, the rest soaking her tunic.

Tears ran unbidden over her cheeks as servants rushed in and around her. Tirzah knelt at her side.

"What's wrong with him, Tirzah?" She was crying unashamedly now. "He was well." What had she done wrong?

The question brought her up short, stealing her breath, renewing the guilt she had carried throughout the months of her pregnancy. She looked at her maid, reading sorrow and a knowingness in the older woman's concerned gaze.

"You might as well hear the truth, as you will know the extent of it soon enough." Tirzah's sturdy hands stroked the child's gaunt cheek.

Bathsheba swallowed hard, choking back more tears. "What truth? Tell me!" Despite her best efforts, she couldn't keep the rising panic from her voice.

"The prophet Nathan came to see the king." Deep lines formed along Tirzah's brow. "He knew all about the king's . . . what the king had done. Adonai had told him, and Nathan said that because the king had killed Uriah the Hittite with the sword of the Ammonites and taken Uriah's wife to be his own, he had done evil in the Lord's eyes, and the child born to you would die." Tirzah released a rushed breath as though the words were fire to be put out.

Bathsheba felt her insides melt. She dragged in air, every breath a struggle. "No . . ." The word barely escaped past the sobs crushing her throat. "He can't do this! He wouldn't . . ." The whispered words felt like shards against her tongue. Of course He could. She and her son should have died months ago beneath a heap of stones.

She pulled her son's small body to her breast, patting his back, wanting to promise him all would be well. But he barely noticed her touch and made no indication that he was even aware of his surroundings.

Bathsheba shifted him to her lap, and Tirzah placed another cool, damp cloth over his forehead and a second over the rest of his feverish skin. Although Bathsheba stroked the fine hairs on his head, he did not move or look at her.

Please don't take my baby! But she knew God was not listening.

She closed her eyes, picturing Uriah's smiling, handsome face. If David had not sent her husband to war . . . if David had not watched her bathing and called for her . . . if David had confessed his sin to her husband . . . everything could have been different. Even if Uriah had demanded justice, at least she would have died with her child.

Please, Adonai, have mercy. But she knew there was no mercy. There had never been any mercy. David had shown the least mercy of all. Why should God be any different?

Unexpected, fierce anger rose within her, and she tasted

222

bitter tears. Months of guilt and secrecy and sleepless nights and anguish, and now she would lose the one person she loved most in the world? She choked and coughed, ragged breaths turning to sobs, her anger turning to blame.

She could have said no to the king, could have walked away. He would not have forced her. She knew it in the deepest places in her heart.

So Nathan's judgment, God's judgment, was on her as well. David had many other sons. He didn't need this one like she did. He had many other wives he could turn to when this horror had passed. He didn't need her either. She was the one who would suffer the most for this.

She wished she could die and take her son's place.

❦

The scent of almond blossoms wafted through the open windows, and David moved through his chambers to his gardens. His knees nearly buckled as he reached the spot where he had seduced Bathsheba, the hand of guilt like a blow upon his back. He forced himself to keep walking until he reached Bathsheba's adjacent gardens and let himself inside her adjoining rooms.

But the sobs he heard coming from her bedchamber chilled his blood. So soon? They'd had no time to get to know their son, to choose a name, to bless him on his father's knee. He moved on leaden feet and came to stand in the arch of the door. Bathsheba's maid stood over his wife, patting her shoulder, while Bathsheba sat on the edge of the bed, rocking their son back and forth, silent sobs shaking her.

He moved into the room, his heart constricting with her pain. He knelt at her side, placed a hand on his son. Heat from the child's skin burned to the touch despite the many wet cloths they had placed on him. He met Tirzah's gaze. "Have you sent for the physician?"

"Yes, my lord." The woman nodded. "He has come, but there is nothing more we can do."

David winced at the finality in her tone, the reproach in her gaze. He looked at his wife. "I'm so sorry, beloved." He placed a hand on her knee, but she flinched, pulling away from him.

"Get away from me!" Her words were brittle, broken, her eyes glowing as though she were the one with the fever. "I should never have let you touch me! They told me what the prophet said." She clutched the child closer to her, a great gulping cry surging from her. "He can't die! He's my only son! He cannot pay for what I have done, for what you did to me. I won't let him." She was screaming now, whether at him or at God, he couldn't tell. But the sharpness of her pain ripped his heart in two.

He looked into her crazed eyes, then backed away, gazing down on the cloth-covered body of his son, so healthy this morning but so sick now, too sick to even wail or whimper.

"Get away from me!" she screamed again, sobbing, and he did not have the strength to fight against her. In another lifetime he would have pulled her close and crushed her sobs against his chest, stroked her back, and whispered comfort into her ear. But he could offer her no comfort now. His voice, impotent against her screams, was silent as he turned and walked from the room. He ducked beneath the arch, half expecting her to throw something at him, but all he heard was the shifting of the mat with the steady rocking of her body, and the hiccuping sobs coming from her ragged throat.

He pushed past Bathsheba's aunt and cousin as they rushed

into the room, and fled into the gardens, past the divider that separated his from hers. He fell onto the smooth stones of the small court where he had wooed her, where his sin had ruined her.

Hot tears bubbled from within him, convulsing him as he found a place beside the path where he could lay in the dirt from which he was made. He longed for death. *Take me instead.* His prayers felt unnatural, no longer the sweet communion he'd once had with Adonai.

He was a child again, deserving of the rod upon his back, a punishment his oldest brother was only too happy to give for his foolishness. The loss of the lamb was costly, and his father too old to teach him the lesson Eliab willingly gave in his place. What he wouldn't give to feel the sting of that lash in full measure, in place of this loss—for once the child died, he would surely lose Bathsheba as well.

Adonai, have mercy on me! The prayer nearly choked him. He did not deserve any sort of mercy. But as the hours passed and he lay all night on the ground, he could not help but plead for that which he did not deserve. If not for mercy, who could stand before the Lord? There was none righteous, not even one.

❧

David dozed partway through the night, and when dawn came, he rose and stretched, checked on the child's status, and returned to lay prostrate once more before the Lord. He paced and knelt and wept and lay facedown again, his prayers like breath.

By the third day, contrition grew to deeper repentance. He searched his heart, appalled at the pride and rebellion he found there. How arrogant he had become! How unlike the days when he was first anointed and sought Adonai with all his heart.

Against You and You only have I sinned and done what is evil in Your sight, so that You are proved right when You speak and justified when You judge. Save me from bloodguilt, O God. You do not delight in sacrifice or burnt offerings or I would bring it. A broken spirit and a contrite heart, O God, You will not despise.

His servants came by with trays of food, but he sent them away, tasting only water, his tears his food, the earth his bed. He saw the concerned looks, the worried glances. Even Benaiah had grown more watchful, as though he wondered if David had lost his senses and was ready to take action to correct the situation.

A week passed. Bathsheba's distant wails turned to keening on the seventh day. His servants stood in his chambers, looking through the arch at him where he sat on the bench, where he had first shared Bathsheba's kiss. He caught the anxious looks, saw them bend their heads together, whispering.

And he knew the day had come of which Nathan had spoken. The son he and Bathsheba had conceived in their sin was dead.

❦28❦

Thin white clouds touched the outer recesses of the heavens, doing little to block the heat of the sun as David's entourage moved from the child's burial at the tomb of the kings back toward the palace. Had he still been living the lie he'd lived for the past ten months, he might have taken the child to the cave where they had laid Uriah's body to rest, pretending the child was conceived to honor Uriah's name.

But the truth was known now. He was not a kinsman redeemer. He was a murderer, an adulterer, and he would not try to deceive the people again. He glanced at Bathsheba, saw the way her slender body huddled forward like an aged woman, and his heart constricted. He would do anything to take the burden from her shoulders, to lift her head from its bent position, to restore her joy. But she'd made it clear she no longer wanted anything to do with him. And why not? He had ruined her life. Such thoughts of restoration were foolish—impossible dreams of an overwrought mind.

After seven days of fasting and weeping and praying, laying prostrate in the dust, he had at last washed and put on his royal robes for the burial, though food had yet to touch his lips. He would eat soon enough, after he took his leave of the

227

procession to sit before the ark of the Lord. His heart beat a normal rhythm now, despite the curious and contemptuous looks of the people gazing down on their group from the windows and roofs of their houses along Jerusalem's main thoroughfare. He deserved their scorn. Would they also reject him as their king?

The thought troubled him, and he slowed his step. He glanced behind at the women and children, the few who had agreed to join the march to the burial cave. Some surely resented that he'd laid the child in his own tomb. Others resented that Bathsheba was given such attention at all. Most of his other wives would not speak to her.

He looked her way again, longing to go to her and comfort her, but there was too much to say and no guarantee she would allow him to say it. He had almost commanded his other wives to come to support Bathsheba, to show a unified front to the inhabitants of the city, but a part of him feared they would not heed his word, making him look more foolish yet. Even Michal, who had finally accepted friendship with Abigail, walked with Abigail's children, but distant from his grieving wife. His older sons had refused to come at all, their bitterness impossible to deny.

His step slowed yet again, and he watched Bathsheba, knowing certain things would never be right again. Shame filled him as they neared the tent where the ark of the Lord rested. He knew with utter certainty that he did not deserve the forgiveness Adonai had offered.

The procession stopped when he did, and Benaiah approached.

"Send the people home, Benaiah. You can leave a guard to walk with me when I am finished."

Benaiah gave a slight nod, then stepped away to do as David had commanded. At least his men still obeyed his voice, even if his wives and children would not.

He removed his sandals and set them near the door to the courtyard in front of the Tent of Meeting, then walked barefoot toward the curtain that separated the courtyard from the Holy Place, a place where the priests and Levites kept the lamps burning and the showbread fresh on the table before the Lord. His heart yearned for Adonai, for the close relationship they'd once had. He fell to his knees and touched his forehead to the swept dirt floor.

You are proved right when You speak and justified when You judge, Adonai. You are worthy to be praised.

Tears came, pooling in his eyes, seeping into his beard, dampening the earth.

Create in me a pure heart, O God, and renew a steadfast spirit within me. Do not cast me from Your presence or take Your Holy Spirit from me. Restore to me the joy of Your salvation, and grant me a willing spirit to sustain me. Then I will teach transgressors Your ways, and sinners will turn back to You.

He sat back, arms raised to the heavens. Surrender, full and sweet, swept through him, his heart yielding every part of him, giving back to God what rightly belonged to Him. David did not deserve mercy, and he could not demand the grace of Adonai, but he could rejoice in what had been given. He could offer upon God's altar a grateful heart.

A slow and tentative peace replaced the guilt. *Worthy are You, O Adonai. Blessed is the man whose sins are forgiven!*

Could it possibly be true? He searched his heart, looking for the despair he'd known only moments before, the shame that had threatened to send him to the abyss, but the sense of forgiveness was sure, his bloodguilt gone.

Blessed are You, O Most High, and blessed is the man whose sin Adonai will not count against him.

He lowered his hands and turned them over in the dim light. They were warrior's hands but also shepherd's hands. With Adonai's help, he would lead Israel again.

Relief came like a mighty wind, his heart humbled. *Thank You, Adonai, for mercy, even in the death of this son.* He could not go where his son had gone. Not yet. And the babe would not return to him. One day he would join the child in the place of paradise where Adonai lived. Until then, he still had the work Adonai had planned for him.

David rose to his feet, his heart yearning heavenward, sensing in his spirit the relationship had been restored. Smiling, he walked back toward the curtained door at the entrance to the northern court, his stomach rumbling from his long fast.

If Adonai could forgive him such a terrible wrong, perhaps Bathsheba could welcome him again, allow him to comfort her. In time, she could conceive again and have another son to fill her empty arms. *Please, Adonai, let it be so.*

He was not in the place of God that he could control life in the womb, but he knew that soon he would need to give Bathsheba far more than physical affection. He must draw her out and let her share her grief with him, even if he risked her rejection.

❧❧

Restlessness overtook Bathsheba. If the king would allow it, she would walk the streets or else leave Jerusalem altogether, climb the Mount of Olives, fall beneath the trees, and weep for days. But she was as captive here in the palace as she had ever been in her father's house or Uriah's home. None of them had ever allowed her complete freedom to come and go without proper guards, always thinking to protect her from unscrupulous men, when the most unscrupulous of all stood watching in her own backyard.

A bitter laugh escaped her. She moved from her sitting room to the gardens David had portioned for her from his own abundance. She had slept every night—when sleep would come—on a mat in the sitting room, unable to visit her bedchamber or look upon the place where her son had so briefly lain. The very thought of him lying cold, unmoving, buried in a cave with no escape . . . She choked on a sob and lifted her gaze to the azure skies, their blue too cheery after her son's death.

How long had it been since she had stood before the tomb weeping? Two months? Three? The days blurred together in their sameness, and despite the efforts of those around her, she could not rouse herself to live again. David had tried to visit her that first week, but she had refused even to look at him, and it seemed he had given up trying.

She'd been right about one thing. He did not need her. Any day now, he would send word and have her removed from these rooms, if his guilt would allow it—probably relegate her to a small apartment in the company of his bitter wives. Fitting, as she was now one of them.

She sank to the stone bench aligning the walk, feeling the weight of her sins in the weariness of her bones. She was an outcast here, a wife of adultery. She would never be accepted among his other wives—those taken to secure treaties or appease tribes, or for love.

But in truth, had he ever loved any of them? Did he know the meaning of the word?

Confusion stirred her insides, resuming the restlessness she could not shake. Rising on unsteady feet, she trod the smooth stones, squinting as she stepped away from the shade into the sun's brightness. He didn't love her. If he did, he would have visited again and at least made a feeble attempt to woo her out of her melancholy, to comfort her in her grief.

His kisses had tempted her, drawn her in, and made her love him. Made her believe she was wanted, cared for, cherished. She kicked a small stone into the bushes with a vehemence that caused her to stumble. How false his love!

Uriah had rarely spoken his affections, but his actions had shown them, had proved his love. And she had thrown his love away that night, forgetting how often Uriah had cherished her when he was home, had loved her in ways she didn't notice until it was too late. She'd thought on it often since his death, since coming here and feeling so distant from all she'd known. Even her grandfather and Chava and Aunt Talia seldom visited now, and besides Tirzah, she had no friends here.

And still David did not come.

Oh, Adonai, why did I not die in my son's place? Even now she would join her son if God would allow it. Living was a more just punishment, perhaps a harsher punishment than death.

She took a turn in the gardens, where the shade of an almond tree beckoned, and she slowed her frantic pacing. She thought to sit on the bench beneath the tree but could not bear the weight of her heartache or the rawness of her loss. She swallowed hard and slipped to the stones on her knees, seeing again the still form of her son like a lamb sacrificed on her behalf.

"Oh, Adonai, forgive me!" Her whispered words mingled with the late afternoon breeze as the sun slipped behind a layer of quick-moving clouds. She clasped her hands in her lap and rocked back on her feet.

A touch on her shoulder made her insides grow still. David took hold of her shoulders and helped her stand, turning her to face him.

"Beloved." He lifted his thumb and drew a line through her tears across her cheek.

She looked away, unable or unwilling—she wasn't sure—to hold his tender gaze.

"Why are you here? Haven't you done enough?" She wanted to fling the words at him as she had done that first night, but her voice would not rise above the whisper of her prayer. She raised a fist to push him away, choking back her emotion, afraid it would billow from her like a raging storm if she let it.

His gentle grip on her hand warmed the frozen places in her heart. "Bathsheba, please." He spoke softly, as if to an injured child, and gently folded her into his arms. She did not stop him. "I'm sorry, beloved. I have done you great wrong, but don't send me away. I want you . . . I need you." His hushed words melted the last of her resolve. She didn't want to send him away.

He rubbed slow circles over her back as her body grew limp against his chest. He pulled her up to sit beside him on the bench, his arm draped over her shoulders, her head resting against him. Birds chirped in the trees above them, and the wind sang a faint melody in accompaniment.

"We never even named him," Bathsheba said after a lengthy silence. A soft tremor worked through her, but she would not cry. She had cried every tear she owned in the past months, and couldn't bear to give in to such emotion yet again. She had no strength left for tears.

"God named him for us." David's confident tone brought her head up. She looked into the liquid darkness of his eyes, his gaze affectionate and sad.

"Why did God take him . . . when He should have taken us?" The question had burned in her mind, but she did not expect God to answer.

"Sometimes God allows a substitute to spare a man. The sacrifices are a continual reminder of that fact."

"Our son was sacrificed on our behalf so we could live? I'd rather die."

"Our son took our punishment, that is true, but God also did him a favor to spare him the future." He stroked her cheek, his gaze filled with compassion. "He would not have fared well as a child of adultery. Everyone would have known of his beginnings, and once I am dead and could no longer protect him, men would not have been kind to him."

"Or to me." She looked away, but his hand gently drew her gaze back.

"Bathsheba, I cannot know the future. I am not in the place of God that I can say I will always live to protect you." His jaw set, and a soft glint filled his gaze, as though he spoke with authority beyond his own. "But I promise you that when you bear me another son, that son will one day sit on my throne, and he will live to protect you always."

Her breath caught. "A son born of my flesh will be king?"

He nodded and bent to kiss her, his lips carrying the salty taste of their mingled tears. "God has forgiven us, beloved. I don't understand it, but He has." He kissed her again but held back as though waiting for her to respond.

A sigh escaped and she lifted her mouth to return his kiss, a kiss born of sorrow and shared grief, a kiss to mend what was cracked and shattered.

"Let me comfort you, Bathsheba." His broken words stirred her even as she questioned how she could long for his love when he had caused her so much grief. She sat immobile, fear and anger warring with longing and forgiveness.

His fingers drew circles on her palm, his gaze unguarded, beseeching, humble. She rose, clasping his hand, and pulled him to his feet. They stood, silence and birdsong whispers between them, their breath mingling again, his deepening kiss heating her blood. She returned it in full, then let him lead her into his chambers.

❦29❦

Bathsheba paused in her stitching and placed a protective hand over her extended middle, cradling the child moving inside. The pains had begun that morning after the king sat with her for the first meal and left for court. He'd been attentive in the past nine months, spending most evenings in her company, playing music on his lyre, singing songs of Adonai to her.

The miracle of another pregnancy so soon after the death of her first son still baffled her. Perhaps she had not been barren after all. That God would smile on her again, allowing her to conceive and soon bear the king another child, seemed beyond reason and far more than she deserved. But the truth lay growing within her and would soon take his place in the world.

She glanced at her protruding middle again and rubbed a hand over the hard surface. "Be brave, little one." She struggled to stand and pace the spacious room, catching sight of her lyre resting against one edge of the couch, where she had left it after David had coaxed her to play along with him. He had given her all the privileges of first wife, requiring little of her, visiting her often. Besides a love of music and of Adonai, they shared something his other wives did not—a common failure, a common grace, and a humility born of sins forgiven.

Your son will one day sit on my throne, to protect you always. David's promised words accompanied another birth pang. She drew in a sharp breath and held it, then slowly released.

"Are they close together? How firm is the pain?" Tirzah looked up from her own stitching, making Bathsheba realize she could no longer keep the child's coming to herself.

"They grow sharper. This is the fourth since the king left." She glanced at the shadows and light trading shapes across the sheepskin rug. "You'd best send for the midwife." Bathsheba looked toward the window to the beckoning light and the scents of the almond tree beneath it. "And see if Aunt Talia and Chava will come."

Wistful longing accompanied the request. She had not seen her aunt or cousin since the babe's funeral, since the attitudes at court had changed toward her. The king had sensed it too—the accusations, some subtle, some hostile in their expressions and their words, as though she alone were to blame for David's fall. David did his best to quash the rejection, especially from his other wives and children, reminding them all that he was to blame. But his efforts did not accomplish what he had hoped.

"I will send word, mistress. If they . . . that is, if they won't come . . . is there anyone else?" Tirzah dropped her mending into a basket on the floor and lifted her stout body with an agility that Bathsheba, in her condition, did not possess. Tirzah hurried to the door of Bathsheba's chambers.

Bathsheba pressed both hands against the small of her back, counting her breaths. "If they will not come, there is no one else." At least her maidservant had remained faithful when she could have requested her leave. "Thank you, Tirzah."

The woman dipped her dark head as though the gratitude embarrassed her. She opened the door and stepped out, addressing the guard who stood watch there, barring entrance to anyone she did not wish to see. "Send word to Hannah to bring the midwife at once. Send a messenger to the house of Matthias the merchant to send his wife and mother-in-law for my mistress's comfort. And tell the king his son is on the way."

Tirzah's commands were cryptic, insistent. She never minded using the authority she'd been given and didn't mind giving her advice even to the king if he asked. Bathsheba smiled at the thought.

"Yes, mistress." The guard's words faded with his stomping feet, and Tirzah came back into the room and shut the door. She scurried to the garden and hefted the water jug brought by servants from the well that morning. Tirzah poured some into a golden cup and handed it to Bathsheba.

After taking a few short sips, Bathsheba set the cup on a low table and moved about the room, pausing at equal intervals to breathe, count, and let the breath slowly out. "This child is coming faster than the last time."

"But there is still time?" Tirzah's worried face made Bathsheba want to comfort her.

"We are in a palace with help all around us. You will not have to help me deliver him alone, my friend." She puffed out heavy breaths as she walked to her bedchamber and glanced at the small table placed under a window, where the king had sat sipping watered wine and eating dates and cheese a few hours ago. The rooms David had portioned for her were spacious for one woman, but once the child came—and if there were more children after that—she would need larger quarters.

She touched her chin, waiting for another birth pang, remembering the gleam in David's eye as he talked about building a bigger home for her. "I want to keep you close, beloved. Jerusalem has little open space as it is, and I don't want to travel the length of the city to be with you." He'd touched her hand in a fond gesture, and his smile had made her feel less like a bloated she-goat and more like the cherished woman he professed to love.

"Perhaps you can extend the palace to absorb the property that belonged to Uriah." She watched his brows draw together, his look turn contemplative.

"You would not find the memories troubling?" He searched her gaze, squeezing her hand in a gentle embrace.

"I would not have to be the one to use those rooms. Perhaps the women's quarters could be rearranged to extend my quarters here." The thought of living away from him chilled her. She did not want to lose her privileged place. "If it please you, my lord, I would live in a hut to be near you. Don't send your servant away."

He averted his gaze, as though pierced by a memory of something she could not share. His handsome face softened when he looked at her at last. "I won't send you away, beloved. Not ever." He squeezed her hand and she watched his throat move as he swallowed hard.

Another pain, much stronger this time, jolted her from the memories. Voices came from her sitting room as servants accompanied by the midwife moved about, making the place into a birthing room.

Shadows darkened the room when Aunt Talia and Chava

appeared at her door, in time for her son to burst forth from within her. His cry silenced the chattering women, the strength of it filling Bathsheba's heart with wild joy.

"He's perfect, Bathsheba. He looks like his father." Chava touched Bathsheba's shoulders, supporting her back as she expelled the afterbirth, while Aunt Talia helped the midwife clean and wrap the child.

"Thank you." She glanced back at her cousin, exhausted. "I've missed you."

Chava bit her lower lip and nodded. "As have I—missed you, I mean. Matthias thought it best that I stay away, especially after the things Grandfather said to him." She put a hand to her mouth, and Bathsheba knew her cousin had said far more than she intended.

"I'm too tired to deal with Sabba's bitterness right now." She leaned back, allowing the midwife to pull the sheets from beneath her and bathe her with cloths. The scent of rose water and mint slowly masked the heavier scents of blood and sweat. "But soon we will talk, and you must tell me what he said." She turned, catching Chava's chagrined gaze.

"It will be as you say." Her cousin seemed uncertain with her now that she was wife to the king. Whereas at first Chava had thought her somehow special to have gained the king's attention, now she seemed unsure of how to act around her, as though she were too high and Chava too low to meet as friends.

Bathsheba sighed, wondering if things would ever be the same between them. She took her son from Aunt Talia's outstretched hands.

"He's a beautiful boy, dear one," Aunt Talia said. "You have every reason to be proud. You have graced the king with a handsome son."

"Perhaps, then," a male voice said, startling her, "you could let the king bless his son on his knee." She turned to see David still dressed in his kingly robes, standing in the arch of the door to her gardens.

Aunt Talia and Chava bowed low at his entrance, and Bathsheba's heart swelled with love for him. If what Tirzah heard from the gossips was true, the king did not always visit a wife so soon after a birth or bless each child only moments after his entrance into the world. Sometimes he waited to give the blessing until the eighth day when the boy was circumcised. His presence here with her now spoke more than many words.

"I would be honored for my lord to bless his son." She released the child's grip from her breast and covered herself, then wiped the child's mewing mouth and handed him to Tirzah, who placed him in David's arms.

David sat in the chair opposite her and held the boy, looking at him with a mixture of joy and pride. "Your father loves you, little one." He planted a kiss on the boy's forehead. "More than that, Adonai loves you, and you will be blessed of Adonai." He met Bathsheba's gaze and smiled. "I had a visit from Nathan the prophet moments after Benaiah brought word that the child was safely born. Adonai sent him to tell us to name him Jedidiah, for Adonai's sake, because Adonai loves our son."

"Jedidiah is a good name, though I had planned to name him Solomon."

"And Solomon he shall be. He is Jedidiah only to the Lord." He looked at the babe and stroked the boy's cheek with his finger, then looked at her, his eyes glistening. "God's mercy is new every morning, beloved. This child is the start of a new life for us."

"Adonai has forgiven," she whispered, though by the silence in the room, she knew everyone could hear her.

"And He has sent us His love." Their gazes held then, and Bathsheba sensed that she was the only person on earth that mattered to the king at that moment. "We are blessed of Adonai, beloved," David said, handing the hungry child back to Tirzah to give to her. "And I am the most undeserving of all men to have you."

He looked at her as though he wanted to kiss her, but she knew he dare not break Adonai's laws of birth. Not after God had granted so much. She snuggled Solomon close as David left her apartment, marveling in the baby's perfect beauty and Adonai's perfect grace.

"I'll bet this boy grows up to succeed David as king," Chava said, sinking down beside Bathsheba, all previous uncertainty gone. "You'll be the most treasured woman in David's household!"

"Treasured perhaps, but only by the king." For despite the promises David had made and the blessing of Adonai through Nathan the prophet, Bathsheba still had to live in a house where David was not hers alone. And if men like her grandfather still held her sin against her, what of others?

The sword will never depart from your house.

The curse of their sin would remain. She kissed the baby's head and sighed. *But it will not touch you, my love.* By God's grace, she would see to it.

PART III

Absalom behaved in this way toward all the Israelites who came to the king asking for justice, and so he stole the hearts of the men of Israel.

2 Samuel 15:6

For David had done what was right in the eyes of the LORD and had not failed to keep any of the LORD's commands all the days of his life—except in the case of Uriah the Hittite.

1 Kings 15:5

꒰30꒱

Distant, urgent shouts woke David with a start. He jerked upright, yanking the covers, his heart pounding swift and heavy. He turned to pull the linen sheet over his wife again, but Bathsheba was already awake, holding Solomon, quieting his soft cries. A sigh escaped him with inexplicable relief. She was fine. She turned to face him.

"The babe?"

"He is well." She patted Solomon's back, whispering soft words in his ear, but her efforts did nothing to still the sounds emerging from beyond her door. Joab's voice registered in David's sleep-induced fog, with Benaiah's low growl responding in kind.

David swung his legs over the side of the bed and donned his night robe, loosely tying a knot at the waist. Whatever it was had better be good to disturb him here. His guards knew better than to interrupt his time with this wife. A privilege he allowed himself to make up for all she had lost. When he was with her, his time was hers alone.

He hugged her waist and kissed her cheek as he passed her, then walked to the door at the far end of the sitting room that led to the palace hall. His other wives lived in smaller

245

apartments throughout the spacious palace, far enough apart to keep the peace. Something he had learned the hard way in Hebron.

The arguing grew intense as he reached the door. He opened it to find Joab standing nose to nose with Benaiah. It was a wonder his nephew had not killed his favored guard yet, as he had done to so many others who had gotten in his way over the years. But Joab knew he already walked a thin line where his royal favor was concerned. The man deserved execution for what he'd done to Abner. But Joab knew David needed him. A fact David sorely despised.

"My lord king," Benaiah said, dipping his head. "We did not mean to disturb you."

Joab glared at the man, then met David's gaze. "Yes, we did." He stood straight, his shoulders flung back, chin up in his typical defiant pose.

"Has there been a death?" Nothing else could account for the distant wailing, and his stomach did a little flip at the thought of yet another loss. But if this were true, why not just wake him and tell him privately? Why argue about it and disturb the whole household?

"Worse than death, my lord." Joab's stern glance at Benaiah made his stomach dip again, then tighten into a hard knot.

"An invasion? A kidnapping? What?" Memories of Abigail's kidnapping surfaced, but he was not at war and his wives were safe in his own house.

"May I come in?" Joab, not usually one to ask, suddenly looked haggard and uneasy.

David stepped back, allowing him entrance. Joab would have suggested a meeting elsewhere if Bathsheba should be kept from the news. David glanced at Benaiah and gave a slight nod of thanks, reading wariness and something more in the man's expression. Benaiah would explain his reticence to allow Joab entrance if David asked, but at this moment David didn't care. He followed Joab into the room and took a seat on the couch nearest the window, then motioned for Joab to sit opposite him. His wiry general perched on the edge, fidgeting as if he didn't know where to place his hands, his beady eyes penetrating, accusing.

David crossed his arms, unwilling to let this upstart nephew rattle him. "Tell me quickly. Obviously this is important."

Joab nodded. "There is trouble."

"I gathered that. So tell me since you're here now."

"Amnon has forced Absalom's sister Tamar to bed with him and now refuses to marry her."

David broke out in a sweat that lifted the hairs on his skin. He leaned heavily into the couch, the blow holding him there. The words registered in painful, vivid images. In slow, deliberate motions, he uncrossed his arms and leaned forward, resting his head in his hands.

Oh, Adonai, what madness is this?

He closed his eyes, remembering the messenger Amnon had sent bringing word that he could not come to court because he was too ill to get out of bed. Concerned, David had gone to him. He had suffered enough loss, and he feared . . . always feared the curse Adonai had placed on his household.

Amnon had not seemed terribly ill, and his request for Tamar was somewhat unusual. Perhaps it was the guilt David still felt over the incident at Rabbah, when Amnon had been caught as an ambassador and humiliated before the court of the Ammonites. If he had exacted a more swift revenge for Amnon's sake . . .

But this! There was no excuse for what Amnon had done. Harming Tamar like this, the damage irreparable. David lifted his head, rubbing both temples. He leveled a measured gaze at Joab.

"Why would Amnon do this?" He could easily guess why Amnon wanted Tamar. She was the most beautiful of David's daughters, a princess worthy of a king's dowry.

"You should ask him yourself."

"I'm asking you." David stood, his simmering anger rising, bubbling like heated water. He paced to the window and stared into the night. He sensed Joab at his back.

"You allowed Tamar to bake cakes for him. Didn't the request strike you as odd?"

The sound of Bathsheba's footsteps coming into the room made him turn. Her arms no longer held Solomon, her face wide-eyed and ashen. She would blame herself for this, and he would take it from her, knowing that he alone had had the power to stop it. Amnon had asked to see a virgin sister in his own home, an unthinkable act without chaperones. David had foolishly expected the servants to be chaperone enough.

"Tell me what happened." He sank down onto the couch again and motioned for Bathsheba to join him. Joab perched on the edge opposite them once more.

"Maacah and her maids are the ones you hear weeping and wailing in her apartment." Joab motioned behind him. "Your nephew Jonadab, Shammah's son, came to me with the news."

"Get to the point."

"Tamar did as you asked and went to Amnon's house to bake cakes for her brother, who pretended to be ill."

David felt the blood drain from his face as Joab spoke.

"That's right, your son was not ill at all. It seems he and

248

Jonadab concocted the idea to get Tamar to Amnon's house so he could lie with her. Amnon got Tamar to bring the cakes into his bedchamber, sent his servants from the house, and forced her. She begged him not to do such a wicked thing. She even offered to become his wife, but after he finished with her, he hated her and put her out of the house. He refuses to marry her, despite Jonadab's pleading. She tore her robe, put ashes on her head, and walked to Absalom's house weeping."

David stood again, the anger pumping through him hot and fast. His hands clenched in and out, and he cursed the day his son was born. He strode through the room to the adjacent gardens, seething, fury making him pace back and forth, faster with every turn of the path. He kicked at loose gravel and whirled about, nearly lifting the clay pots and smashing them among the cobbled stones, but thought better of it and moved back into the house. Joab stood waiting at the window, and Bathsheba sat on the couch, hands clasped in her lap, tears drawing thin lines down her soft cheeks. His anger seeped from him like a drink offering poured out on dry ground.

Joab turned, his beady gaze expectant. "What will you do?"

It was a challenge more than a question. The act Amnon had committed was an abomination, a curse. If he counted Amnon rebellious, he would demand his son's death. If he followed the law regarding violation of a virgin, he should demand Amnon marry the girl, forfeiting any right to later divorce her. At the very least, he should cut Amnon off from the people, dismiss him from court, and never see his face again.

David rubbed a hand over his beard, seeing Amnon's ruse for what it was, hating himself for believing the lie. How could he insist on a marriage that started in such a way? This was not lust, as he knew only too well. This was hatred. He could not, would not, subject his daughter to such a thing.

"I will wait." If in time Amnon repented, and if his repentance was genuine and he sought Tamar's hand in marriage, then he would reconsider. But not now. Not like this.

"He is cursed. He should be cut off from the people." Joab's comment held no vehemence, only observation.

"He has forfeited any right to rule in my stead."

"The people may demand more."

"For now, this is all I can do."

Joab's look was grim as he walked to the door. "Absalom may not be so forgiving." He acknowledged both David and Bathsheba with a silent nod and left.

❧

"You should go to your daughter and to her mother." Bathsheba rested her head on David's shoulder after the door shut behind Joab's retreating back. "They need you."

David's chest lifted in a heavy sigh as his arms came around her. He tilted her head back and his dark eyes searched hers. She held his gaze, hoping her love was visible, that no trace of hostility or competition marred her affection.

"You are incredible," he whispered against her ear. "After all I've done—"

"Don't." She placed two fingers gently against his lips. "We cannot live in what's past."

"What is past keeps coming back. The curse haunts my every step."

Bathsheba shook her head. "No, my lord. The past does not return to haunt us. Adonai has forgiven, and as you have often told me, He does not keep a record of our wrongs. He has wiped them away from His memory. We are the ones who allow our sins to haunt our minds."

He curled his fingers over hers and kissed them. "The consequences don't go away, beloved. The sword will never depart from my house because of my sin. I have brought this upon us all." The anger he'd shown moments before had dissipated. His shoulders slumped, a man broken.

"God will give us grace to deal with the sword when it comes. Didn't He, in His grace, give us Solomon? Not everything in our future will carry the sword. Someday we will know peace again."

The distant wailing had quieted, the night sounds carrying crickets and the soft whisper of the wind in the trees. David placed both hands on her arms, his gaze steady, his look no longer hopeless. "I would ask you to come with me. I am no good with women's tears."

She touched his bearded cheek and smiled. "And I would come if it would help you, my lord. But I fear my presence would give you more than tears to handle."

Despite Nathan's acceptance of their son and Adonai's forgiveness, many in the palace, especially David's wives, considered her an adulteress and refused to acknowledge her favored status with the king, choosing to ignore her and the place she held in David's heart.

He reached for her hands, clasping them in both of his, kissing the tips of her fingers again. He pulled her close and kissed her as though he were afraid to leave, his passion eager, needing her.

"Come back to me and tell me what happens, if you can," she said when he at last broke contact, his eyes blazing.

He sifted his fingers through her hair. "I will be back before court. I don't know if Maacah will welcome me or kick me out. If she welcomes me, I may be longer."

She nodded and smiled, denying the little kick in her stomach, the one that held jealousy where she knew no jealousy could reside. To imagine him in Maacah's arms—that arrogant, beautiful woman whose children were the most honored among the palace courts, whose son was now first in line for David's throne—was hard. Too hard. But she closed her eyes for the briefest moment and insisted this was the right thing to do. Maacah and Tamar needed him.

"Go in peace, my love." She stood on tiptoe and kissed him again, a kiss he would not soon forget.

❦

David knocked on the door of Maacah's apartment, the sound a loud echo in the quiet, predawn halls. He had given her time for the tears to subside, but decided sleep would not come again to him this night, and grief could not wait. Benaiah stood a few steps back, his silent presence giving David strength.

Footsteps sounded from inside the apartment, and the door creaked open. Maacah's maidservant put a hand to her mouth, a soft gasp escaping her, and hurried to open the door and bid him enter. She bowed low, then scurried down the hall.

He stepped into the sitting room and walked to the window looking out on Maacah's private courtyard. A small altar sat in a corner of the stone court, surrounded by shrubbery. David frowned. It had been many months, years even, since he had visited Maacah's apartment. Had she taken to the worship of her father's gods in his absence? Michal had once kept teraphim in their home, a gift from her mother, but she would never keep such things here. Not now, after her restoration to Yahweh.

But Maacah had never quite embraced his God. Not as he had hoped. Tamar seemed to accept, to believe—but then what did he really know of his daughter? Absalom, whom he knew far better . . . he wasn't so sure. The young man was too confident, too arrogant, to be humble before his Maker. Though at times David thought he glimpsed a softer heart.

He turned at the sound of footsteps. Lamplight quickly illumined the darkened room, and servants swept in, plumping cushions and filling goblets with wine. Maacah stood just inside the room, arms crossed, her eyes swollen and sharp, her lips pulled into a thin, hard line.

Silence moved between them like something vivid, alive. David's stomach clenched along with his jaw, knowing anything he said to her would not make things better, could not restore what was lost.

"Where is she?" he said at last, taking a step toward Maacah. It was Tamar who needed his comfort, and the least he could do was check on her.

"In her room. She'll be staying with Absalom once she calms down. He will provide for her now." Maacah's eyes were daggers, her words dipped in poison. She lifted her chin, her defiance challenging him.

"That is not for you or her to decide. I am her father."

"Who sent her to her doom! What were you thinking to command her to visit her brother like that, without a chaperone, alone with only servants to attend? When have you ever trusted that son of Ahinoam?" She spat the words and turned her head as if she would truly spit onto the soft wool rug, but the action was only pretense for his benefit. Something Maacah had perfected in the years he had known her.

"He was ill. It seemed like a reasonable request." But did it? He'd asked himself the question over and over again and knew in a heartbeat that if he could repeat the decision, he would not make the same one again.

"Reasonable. Ach!" she spat again, only this time spittle actually fell from her mouth, and he knew if she had been standing closer, she might have purposefully landed it on him. Her hatred was palpable.

"Let me see her." He took another step toward her, his gaze steady, giving her what he hoped was a compassionate yet uncompromising look.

Maacah returned his gaze but soon looked away. She plucked a clay lamp from its niche along the wall, turned without a word, and led the way down the hall. David followed, his thoughts churning. He knew how to comfort a wife, but a daughter? He had spent his life in the company of his sons, his comrades, and his counselors, leaving his daughters to the care of the women. The few times they came to him or he visited their homes had been scattered throughout their growing-up years. What kind of a man did that make him?

The hall turned sharply to the left, and a door stood shut on the right. Maacah stopped, gave a soft knock, and opened the door without waiting for a response. David entered the room, surprised at the many lamps illuminating the spacious interior. A small sitting room held a couch and table while a bed draped in bright curtains stood like a guardian to Tamar's former purity. Her garments had been just as colorful. Garments she would no longer wear as a desolate woman.

His daughter, looking young and vulnerable, lay huddled

among the covers, buried behind the curtains, only visible because of the many lamps chasing away what was left of the night's shadows.

"Tamar!" Maacah's words snapped like quick flames. "Get up. Your father has come."

David winced at the woman's tone. Did she think he expected such a display of control? But he understood the anger was directed at him. He had aimed his own anger in the exact same location. He braced himself, knowing more was coming.

"It's all right." He stepped farther into the room, closer to Maacah, and placed a hand on her arm.

She jerked at his touch, but to his surprise did not move away from him. She needed his comfort, as Bathsheba had suggested, but he knew in an instant she would not accept it.

He held up a hand, a gesture of surrender, and walked to the bed, where Tamar had not moved despite Maacah's barked order. He sat beside her. She scooted to the far corner, pulled the covers to her neck, and stared at him with wild eyes. The girl was beautiful like her mother, and would have made some man a fine wife, ensuring a treaty of peace with a foreign nation. Perhaps even with her mother's own country, to secure that alliance for another generation. But now it would never be.

He looked at her frightened features, his heart breaking. *Amnon, how could you have done such a thing?*

He longed to pull her close, to protect her, to promise her the world, to force Amnon to do what he knew his son would not. "Tamar, my dove, I am sorry. This should never have happened to you." He extended his hand, his voice soft, trying to soothe the girl's fears. "I won't hurt you."

Tamar's tears came in silence, and when he reached for

her hand and pulled her to him, she did not resist. His arms came around her, and she buried her head against his robe and wept great sobs.

"He—he forced me . . . and then he sent me away. I begged him . . . I begged him to let me stay . . . He sent me away!"

Her wails cut deep. He had no words to comfort her, her grief mingling with his own. He held her in silence, letting her weep.

When her tears quieted, he patted her back and kissed her forehead. "What did your brother Absalom say to you?" he asked.

She hiccuped on a sob and wiped her eyes with the sleeve of her tunic. "He said, 'Has Amnon your brother been with you? But now hold your peace, my sister. He is your brother, do not take this thing to heart.' How can he say that? I cannot hold my peace!"

David touched her arm and nodded. Tamar looked at him, her expectations swimming in the pool of her tears. Absalom had not reacted in anger as David had done. Did his son think this thing was of no consequence? Or did he have other motives behind his words? But it would do no good to suggest such a thing here to Absalom's mother or his desolate sister.

"Your mother said Absalom has promised to care for you," David said at last, "so when you are ready, go and stay with him. You will be a blessing in your brother's house, my dove."

He stood then, suddenly anxious to get away, to escape from this woman, this child, who looked at him with eyes so full of pain, a pain he could not fix. If he could, he would go back and undo everything that had led to this moment, erase the bitterness, the quiet agony so expressive in those doelike eyes. If only he could . . .

He looked at Maacah, whose dark eyes, once so beguiling and lustrous, were ringed with dark circles, their expression hard, almost soulless. Her arms were crossed over her chest, her posture rigid. She did not want his comfort. So he would not give it.

"If she needs anything, send word." He nodded in Tamar's direction, then walked swiftly toward the door leading to the hall and out of Maacah's stifling apartment.

❦31❦

David took the steps up two stories, passed between two Cherethite guards, and entered his rooftop pavilion, where his wife Bathsheba and son Solomon awaited his coming. The summer heat was nearly upon them, and the tent flaps that were lifted to expose the sides afforded more comfort than the rooms below.

She was seated among the cushions, Solomon playing with blocks on the floor at her feet. She smiled, attempting to rise as he entered, but he stayed her with his hand.

"Don't get up, beloved." He moved to sit beside her as servants lifted palm fronds to move the still air away from them, while another handed them goblets of spiced wine. "How are you feeling?"

She took his hand and squeezed, a comforting gesture she often made, one he had grown to expect. "I am well." She shifted slightly, lifting the bulk of the child within. "He is active today. A healthy, strong boy."

He laughed and placed a hand on her extended middle. He was rewarded with soft blips of movement. "His kicks are strong. Surely you should lie down and rest."

She gave him a look that sent his heart beating faster. "I am resting here. There is no better place than at your side."

He squeezed her hand in response, suddenly not sure he trusted his voice. When had love become so familiar? He was used to casual closeness, even consistent caring, first with Michal, then Abigail. Surely he had loved them. But this feeling he had in Bathsheba's presence did not leave when he walked away. She crept into his thoughts, making him long for her, to sneak away to spend a moment with her even when he couldn't, when more pressing things demanded his attention.

"I love you, Bathsheba." He spoke so softly he wasn't sure she had heard him. Solomon pulled himself up off the soft rug and crawled onto David's lap.

Bathsheba leaned in to kiss David's cheek. "I know," she whispered, her eyes alight with affection. "And I you."

He turned to her and smiled, a look of acceptance, of deep understanding, passing between them. Stomping footsteps drew their attention.

"Father." A commotion showed a guard blocking a man's way. "Let me pass. I would speak a word with my father."

"The king wishes not to be disturbed. You can place your request with him another time."

"I will speak with him now!"

David leaned close to Bathsheba's ear. "Absalom."

She nodded, dipping her head toward the tent's opening. "Will you not see what he wants?"

He could tell by the sudden tensing of her jaw that she did not wish Absalom's presence near her son, and David did not blame her. Since Tamar's ruin, David trusted few of his own sons, and had doubled the guards around Bathsheba's quarters. *The sword will never depart from your house.* The prophecy haunted him at night, and he begged Adonai continually to keep the sword from Bathsheba and her children.

"I will return." He kissed Solomon's soft curls, then placed him on the floor again. Slowly rising, he brushed the wrinkles from his robe and walked to the tent's opening and addressed the guards. "It's all right. I will speak with him."

He stepped forward and walked with Absalom to the perimeter of the roof. "How does it fare with you, my son?"

"I have sheepshearers at Baal Hazor." Absalom paused, turning to David with his back against the parapet. "I would like you to come, Father. Will you and your officials please join me?"

David looked beyond Absalom to the Mount of Olives in the distance. He could not leave Bathsheba so close to her time, and the trip would be impossible for her right now, though Absalom need not know his thinking.

"No, my son." He met Absalom's gaze, then turned to walk the perimeter of the roof again. "We should not all go with you lest we be a burden to you."

"You would not be a burden at all, Father." Absalom doubled his steps to keep up with David's long strides. "My servants are fully prepared to provide for your retinue. You will find me a capable host if you will let me show you."

David stopped to watch the goings-on of the city below him. "I am sure you are a capable host, my son. But the distance is far and will be too much for the children." He glanced at Absalom, catching the slight clenching of his jaw, the twitch of a muscle in his cheek. But his son's eyes were impassive, revealing nothing.

"The children could stay behind. Leave them with their

nurses." Absalom's tone grew insistent, though his gaze remained dispassionate.

David placed a hand on Absalom's shoulder. "I appreciate your desire to include us, but it is impossible this time. May Adonai's blessing rest upon you and your men." David leaned in and kissed Absalom on each cheek. He smiled and patted Absalom's shoulder, then turned to walk back toward the pavilion.

Absalom drew next to him. "Father, wait." He reached out a hand but did not touch David.

David turned back. He told himself to appreciate this moment, as time alone with any of his children was far too infrequent.

"If you will not go with us, let Amnon come." The impassive look had left Absalom's gaze, replaced by one of urgent longing.

Prickles of concern dotted David's skin. "Why should he go with you?" Amnon was better off far away from Absalom.

"He should come as your representative, my lord. If you will not join me, then please show me your true blessing by allowing your sons to accompany me. Must I celebrate the abundance of Adonai's favor with only my servants at hand? Let my brothers join the feast and share in the bounty of the Lord your God." Absalom clasped his hands and held them out in a gesture of goodwill. Heavy locks of his dark hair hung below his shoulders, and his handsome features reminded David of the little boy who often pleaded with him to get his way. David had rarely denied the child and now found himself weakening, unable to deny the man who had replaced the boy.

"You have not exactly been on good terms with your brother. How can I know that there are no ill feelings between you?" David studied Absalom, searching his gaze for some hint of animosity, of ulterior motive behind the request. He had not protected Tamar from Amnon, and he could not fail again to protect Amnon from those who would seek his harm. But after two years, surely the danger of revenge had past.

"If I had wanted to harm my brother, would I not already have done so? Please, my lord, do not deny your servant his request." His open, earnest gaze held no apparent guile, and David felt a twinge of guilt that he had fairly accused his son of plotting repercussions.

"They may go with you," he said at last, touching Absalom's arm once more.

Absalom fell to his knees and kissed the roof's floor at David's feet. "Thank you, my lord. May the king find favor in the eyes of Adonai."

🙖🙖

The Hall of Parchments, one of David's favorite rooms in the palace, held the familiar scents of leather, ink, clay, and papyrus. It was easy to lose himself here, to let his worship of Adonai spill over from the feathered quill in his hand to the flattened parchment beneath his fingertips. The dimensions of the temple his son would one day build to Yahweh grew in depth and detail as the Spirit of Adonai came over him, filling his mind with descriptions and measurements. A thrill rushed through him as he anticipated what this new day would bring.

He stepped into the room, closing the door behind him, and sat at a table. His calloused fingers brushed the words and symbols he'd written the day before. Sinking into his seat, he spread his hands, palms open on the table, his gaze lifted heavenward, his eyes closed.

Adonai Elohai, Adonai Echad. O Lord my God, You are One. Grant Your servant ears to hear Your word and a willing spirit to sustain me.

He fingered the quill, ready to pen the words to a new song that had formed in his mind during the night.

For the director of music. A psalm of David. A song.

Praise awaits You, O God, in Zion;
    to You our vows will be fulfilled.
O You who hear prayer,
    to You all men will come.
When we were overwhelmed by sins,
    You forgave our transgressions . . .

An urgent knock on the door stopped his hand. A guard opened it and a messenger hurried in, falling prostrate near the table at his side.

"My lord king, a messenger has arrived from Absalom!" The man's breath came in spurts as though he'd run a distance.

David dropped the pen and stood, his mind whirling, processing. "Tell me what happened." He moved toward the door as the man scrambled to his feet.

"I do not know, my lord. But I fear . . . it is urgent."

David glanced at the man, read the fear in his eyes, and quickened his pace to the audience hall. The guard knew more than he let on, but David quashed his irritation, pausing only long enough for the flag bearers and trumpet players to announce his arrival. He slowed his pace, fighting an impending sense of dread, then ascended the steps and took his seat on his throne.

A new messenger approached and fell on his face at David's feet. His cry came from a strangled throat, matching the torn, dust-coated robe he wore. "Absalom has struck down all of the king's sons, not one of them is left!"

Shock rushed through David, paralyzing him. All of his sons?

He stared at the man, gave his head a slight shake. "Not one of my sons is left?"

What of Chileab? Had he gone with Absalom? He so often kept himself apart from court. And Solomon and the babe still within Bathsheba's womb were here with him . . .

"All of them?" He choked on the question, his tongue too thick.

"That is the report I received, my lord. Absalom has killed all of the princes."

David's heart kept its slow, steady beat, though he could not imagine why it bothered to do such a thing. His blood drained, growing sluggish. He forced his legs to hold his body erect and managed to walk down the three steps to the chamber's tiled floor. He looked out over the audience hall, saw the stricken looks on the faces of his comrades. Reaching for the neck of his robe, feeling the weight of his hands on the fabric, he yanked downward in one swift motion. Repeated ripping and tearing sounds moved about the room, garments ruined by grief.

He looked down at the messenger still on his knees, then met Benaiah's suffering gaze, his dazed expression matching the feeling smothering the very breath in David's lungs. Had his sin come to this? Would the consequences of his actions never end? But the thoughts only skimmed the surface of his mind, bounding away like a skittish gazelle only too happy to flee the hunter's snare.

Let me die along with them.

His knees weakened where he stood, and he moved away from the messenger and sank to the ground, the cold tiles hard beneath his limbs.

Remove Your scourge from me. I am overcome by the blow of Your hand. You rebuke and discipline men for their sin. You consume their wealth like a moth—each man is but a breath.

Hot tears scalded his throat as the face of each son passed through his thoughts. Amnon, the first show of his strength. Chileab, Abigail's maimed son. Adonijah, Shephatiah, Ithream . . . His younger sons of the concubines would have remained behind, but the thought did not comfort.

Look away from me, that I may rejoice again before I depart and am no more.

Had he misjudged Absalom so greatly? He had wondered, even questioned Absalom's motives in asking for Amnon to join his celebration, but to kill all of his brothers . . . what did he hope to gain?

Hurried footsteps crossed the tiles, and soft murmurs filled in and around the court's weeping.

"My lord king, hear the word of your nephew Jonadab, son of your brother Shammah." Benaiah bent to touch David's shoulder and offered a hand to raise him up. "Perhaps the grief is not quite so great."

David accepted Benaiah's help and stood on shaky legs. "What do you know?" he asked Jonadab. The words came out parched, like his throat.

"My lord, do not think that they have killed all of the princes. Only Amnon is dead. This has been Absalom's intention ever since the day Amnon forced his sister Tamar. My lord the king should not be concerned about the report that all the king's sons are dead. Only Amnon is dead." Jonadab stood with hands at his sides, his gaze earnest and open, though David knew from long experience of Jonadab's wily ways. The man was nothing like his father Shammah, whom David once trusted with his life.

"Why should I believe you that only Amnon is dead?"

"When the princes soon return, the evidence will bear me out." Jonadab fell to his knees and dipped his head. "I am your servant, my lord."

David looked down at his nephew for a long moment, then forced his legs to carry him across the chamber to the double doors, where common men awaited an audience with him. Guards hurried to surround him and escort him, clearing a path to the porch. He took a seat on one of the stone benches beneath the portico, the one within sight of the guard tower. Moments ticked by like mating crickets, irritating and repetitious. At last the watchman moved from his station and hurried down the stairs of the guard tower over to the king.

"I see men in the direction of Horonaim, on the side of the hill."

David nodded. "Keep watching." The direction was correct, the location close at hand.

Jonadab approached from the pillar where he'd been standing. Benaiah lowered his sword, blocking him from stepping too near. "See, the king's sons approach. It has happened just as your servant said."

David met Jonadab's gaze, acknowledging him with a brief glance, then looked beyond him. The sound of hoofbeats filled the air outside the palace gates, and as the gates swung open, the princes sitting astride white mules barged into the wide courtyard. Their voices rose in loud, guttural wails, piercing the stark quiet.

David jumped up and rushed forward. When his sons saw him, they hopped off their mules almost as one man to move toward their father. David grabbed and embraced each one, weeping, kissing their cheeks, pulling them close, drinking in the scent of them. Jonadab was right. Only Amnon was missing among those who had gone with Absalom. Amnon, who had been killed to avenge the loss of Tamar's purity.

In his private rooms an hour later, David listened to his sons recount the tale, his heart broken and humbled, grateful that Yahweh had spared the rest of them. He looked past them to the windows aligning his courtyard, hearing the whispers in the trees, the soft sounds of life stirring all around him. Absalom had fled the country, returning to the foreign land of his mother, Maacah, fearing repercussion. The young man was right to do so. It freed David from having to pass judgment on him for such an act. But it also banished him forever from David's court.

Absalom and Amnon were gone, and David grieved the loss of them both.

❦ 32 ❧

Bathsheba bent over Shammua as she changed his wet undergarments, keeping one eye on Shobab playing with wood blocks in a corner of the children's room. Her seven-year-old, Nathan, sat at a table nearby, stylus in hand, carefully forming the Hebrew letters on pieces of dried clay. Tutoring time had long since passed, and Tirzah would soon put the children to bed, but Nathan was a studious learner, determined to take after his namesake, the prophet who had both condemned his father's sin and brought hope to them again with Solomon's birth.

Bathsheba smiled at his bent head, his gaze fixed on the scraps of broken clay while battle noises came from the corner where Shobab beat one block into another. She shook her head and sighed. Shobab had listened to her father's war stories far too often and took great pleasure in reenacting them.

She tucked the last fold along Shammua's middle and placed a clean tunic over his head, tickling his feet. He cooed and laughed as she gently tossed him upward and then lifted him to her shoulder.

"There you go, little man." She kissed the baby's dimpled cheek and carried him into the sitting room where David stood at a table spread with parchments, ten-year-old Solomon studying them at his side. It was a scene she'd come upon often of late. She settled herself among the cushions of a nearby couch and positioned Shammua to nurse at her breast, draping a soft blanket over them as a covering. She met David's gaze across the room, reading the pleasure in his eyes.

Bathsheba smiled at the image they made, father and son caught up in building and planning for the future. Such times had been scarce, such peace so tentative in the past seven years since Absalom had murdered Amnon, fled to his grandfather's homeland, and returned to favor in David's court. She shivered, wishing the last thought untrue, but the people, including the king, loved Absalom, and in time Joab had convinced David to bring the young prince home.

She stroked Shammua's soft cheek as his nursing slowed, his eyes heavy with sleep. Adonai had given David success in every battle, but it was the war of wills, of revenge and desire within his own home, that worried her. Absalom was a man not to be trusted, and every thought of him made her wary, afraid. What would he do to her if he came to power, if something happened to David before Solomon was old enough to take the reins of leadership? The shiver deepened, jarring her. Shammua's hold slackened as sleep overtook him, and she used her finger to gently break his grasp.

She looked up again, catching David's profile in the early evening light. The moon was nearly full and the sky clear, illuminating the view beyond the window and bathing his face in shadow. But even the darkness could not hide the distant look or the deep lines across his brow and the slight clenching of his jaw that sometimes marred his handsome features. Too much pain had filled his life, too many failures he could not make right.

"This is the inner sanctuary that will house the ark of the testimony hidden behind the curtain. The table for the show-bread will go here, the lampstand here, and the golden altar of incense here in front of the curtain." David pointed to something on the parchment, then straightened and placed a hand on Solomon's shoulder. "Every detail must be exact. You will have at your disposal the best craftsmen in Israel, and you must use their skills, demand the best from them." David turned slightly and guided Solomon to the wide window that faced the Mount of Olives to the east. "You must not stray from anything the Lord has shown me. The building is for Him, though no building can contain Him."

"Then why do we build a temple for Him if He is bigger than the temple can hold?" Solomon's brown curls hung to his shoulders, and his dark, inquisitive eyes searched his father's face with quiet resolve.

Bathsheba stood, handing Shammua to Tirzah, and moved to join her husband and son near the window. David's arm came around her, his smile loving, possessive, for her alone. A breath passed, and he looked once more at Solomon, rubbing a hand over his son's dark curls.

"Adonai does not need a building to live in like the gods of other nations," David said, pointing skyward. "Heaven is His home and the earth is His footstool." He moved his hand back toward the table with the parchments spread over it. "He allows us to build His temple for our sakes, that we might have a place to come before Him, to learn of Him. Everything He has told me to do has a purpose in the law, patterned after what God gave to Moses on the mount. Adonai is perfect, as are all His ways. This is why you must follow the details to the exact descriptions."

"When I am king," Solomon said, looking at David, arms crossed over his chest, "I will do exactly as you say, Father."

David released his hold on Bathsheba and placed both hands on Solomon's shoulders, his gaze deeply serious. "I must remind you again, my son, you must tell no one of your coming kingdom. When we speak of the temple, we must keep it our family's secret. It is not safe to speak of such things to the others. Not yet." He released his hold and stepped back a pace.

Solomon nodded, his young face wide-eyed and somehow weary with too much knowledge. "I understand, Father. My brothers are in line for the throne ahead of me. They would not take kindly to knowing you intend to give the crown to me."

Bathsheba stepped between father and son, her thoughts troubled, wondering at the wisdom of telling Solomon so much so soon. "There will be plenty of time to discuss these things another day." She gave Solomon a look.

"Yes, Mother. Goodnight, Father."

David acknowledged Solomon with a nod, and Bathsheba kissed his cheek before he turned and left to join his brothers in their shared chambers. Soon he would have rooms of his own, but for now he still seemed to enjoy the company of the young ones.

Bathsheba watched him go, then turned to David, whose gaze once more took in the evening lights and shadows dotting Jerusalem's streets and sky. She slipped a hand in his and squeezed. "You seem troubled tonight."

Silence followed her remark, and she wished she could

lift the tension from his shoulders, the worry lines from his brow. Such burdens a king carried! And she felt powerless to ease their load.

"I wonder at my own foolishness sometimes." He stared into the distance as his thumb moved over her palm. "I'm closer to Adonai than I have ever been. Often He speaks to me, gives me visions of things I don't understand. I awaken and record them, and ask Him for insight, but I'm never told more than what is initially revealed. They are prophecies as sure as any Nathan or Gad or Samuel gave, not for now, but for some future day."

"That is good, is it not? You are wise to be close to Adonai." She stepped closer, leaning her shoulder against his chest. He seemed to welcome her nearness.

"It's the temple that worries me. Sometimes it consumes me—the details are so vast!" He turned, holding her at arm's length. "I long to see it, but the most I can do is to write the instructions and have the artisans draw them up for me, so I might at least have an image of what's to come. I have shown them to my counselors, to the priests, to Nathan—all of them tell me the plans are in line with the law. So I am confident my visions are from Adonai's hand and not my own making."

He tucked a stray strand of hair behind her ear, his gaze earnest. "I want to start the project now, but Adonai has refused me the privilege, so I gather the materials and I share the plans with the one who will build it . . . but therein lies the question. Am I putting too much on his young shoulders? The burden to build this structure is great. And he will have to be king to carry it out. Absalom and Adonijah would not allow Solomon the right to build the temple under their rule. So am I putting his life in danger by telling him now?"

Bathsheba lifted a hand to stroke his beard. "I have wondered the same thing, beloved, but I also know that you need to do this. You need to share this joy." Fear for her son warred with longing to please her husband. If she did not comfort him, someone else would gladly take her place. "We must trust Adonai to protect him. Didn't Nathan tell us God had chosen Solomon, calling him Jedidiah for his own sake? Adonai will protect him. But I agree, we must keep this quiet. As much as I know you love him, Absalom cannot be trusted."

"After what Amnon did to Tamar and Absalom did to Amnon, one could ask if any of my sons can be trusted." He bent close and kissed her. "Except for Chileab, and your sons, my love, because they have a mother who is teaching them well."

She wrapped her arms around his neck, responding to his kiss with one of her own. How she loved this man! How blessed he had made her feel, though she knew even now she did not deserve any of the goodness that had befallen her. Amnon's ruin of Absalom's sister Tamar, and Absalom's subsequent murder of Amnon, were stark reminders of how much David had suffered because of her.

Absalom could not be trusted. If he found out Solomon was the king's favored heir, what would stop him from launching an attack against her and her children, or even his own father? He had set Joab's field on fire to get the general's attention, all to set about his own selfish ends. The man was irresponsible.

And dangerous.

She shivered even as David's arms encased her. If Absalom discovered the truth of David's promises to her, could even the king protect her from the hatred of his son?

❦

His retinue behind and before, David made his way to the rear of the palace grounds, where his storehouses stood. Oxen-pulled carts ringed the area, weighted down with gold, silver, bronze, and iron taken in his most recent battle against the Edomites. Abiathar and Zadok, decked out in full priestly garb, waited nearby.

As he entered the head of the wide circle of men and women, he searched the eager crowd, releasing a breath when he saw his beloved Bathsheba with her father Eliam and her two oldest sons. Eliam's presence also spoke securely of Yahweh's forgiveness. It was Ahithophel's absence that troubled him more. Father and son never seemed to agree, and yet it had been Ahithophel's guidance David had valued the most. But he had stayed away from court six long months now, and David wondered, not for the first time, if his friend would ever return.

The thought dampened his enthusiasm, but he tamped it down and stepped forward, hands raised heavenward. "We come today to dedicate these articles of gold, silver, bronze, iron, and precious stones to Adonai. Someday, when I rest with my fathers, a great temple will be raised in worship and honor of Adonai. These few articles are among the many I have collected in battle to provide for this express purpose. May Adonai Eloheynu, the Lord our God, accept this offering." He nodded to Zadok, who stepped forward, lifted his hands, and prayed.

David bowed his head, his heart humbled as it always was when the priests offered prayers to the Lord. The many tons of gold and silver were almost immeasurable, the bronze and iron already without number. Storehouses in Jerusalem and other cities in Israel held more, including the timber and cedarwood Solomon would need—when at last David could announce to the kingdom that Solomon would sit on the throne in his place.

When the prayer ended, David looked in Bathsheba's direction. He caught a glimpse of the awe he felt in Adonai's presence as he met Solomon's dark-eyed gaze. He stood close to yet apart from his mother, a protective hand on his brother Nathan's shoulder, his posture bearing the sure marks of a royal prince. Adonai's choice of this son never ceased to surprise David, yet worry still invaded his thoughts on nights when sleep eluded him. Absalom and Adonijah stood as Solomon's greatest obstacles and would not take kindly to David's choice. Would they attempt to subvert his will?

Would the people accept a son conceived of the wife of adultery?

He shook the thought aside as he stepped back from the heavy oak storehouse doors. Brawny slaves removed the crates from creaking oxcarts, grunting beneath heavy burdens as they moved the spoils from the courtyard into the storehouse. Conversations broke out, mingling with birdsong in the palm trees lining the court.

A man cleared his throat, drawing David's attention. He turned to see Absalom flanked by two of Benaiah's men.

"My lord, may we walk together in the storehouse? Will you show your servant the riches Adonai has given to my lord the king?"

This was a privilege David had intended to show Solomon after the crowds had dispersed. He glanced beyond Absalom and caught Benaiah's slight shake of his head. The gesture, accompanied by the downward tilt of the man's mouth, gave David pause. Benaiah did not trust this son, and David did not need to glance in Bathsheba's direction to know that if she were watching, her look would be one of worry, even fear.

"It is not possible to see the whole storehouse, my son. But I can show you some of the most valuable pieces." He smiled at Absalom, extending his hand, and then moved ahead, leading the prince into the storehouse. Benaiah's swift footfalls hurried on ahead as he cleared the way for David and his son to pass.

They stepped to the side, out of the way of the workmen still carting great quantities of silver toward the rooms at the back. "We keep the silver in a sealed dark room to prevent tarnishing," David said as he moved toward a polished cedar table exquisitely carved. "This came from the king of Ammon." He lifted the lid to reveal a heavy golden crown, encrusted with a mass of jewels, sparkling on a bed of soft dark linen. His fingers brushed the gold, but he did not attempt to lift it from its case. "The crown weighs a full talent and is too heavy for daily use. I wear it on feast days."

"A masterpiece of craftsmanship." Absalom's admiration was mirrored in his gaze. He looked at David, his chin tipped slightly upward. "I will wear it with honor and pride when you name me king someday, Father. And I will build you this temple to Adonai that you speak of so often." He knelt suddenly at David's side, gripped David's hand, and kissed his signet ring. "I am your servant, my king."

David's heart skipped a beat, and he felt suddenly trapped as a bird in a cage. Sending a silent prayer for wisdom heavenward, he pulled Absalom to his feet and released a long-held breath. "Fear the Lord our God and do His will above all," he said, motioning that they walk to the next displayed item. "Then, when the time is right, you will make a wise king." The truth mixed with what would surely prove to be a lie tasted foul on his tongue.

"Thank you, Father." Absalom straightened and smiled, turning to inspect another finely crafted jewel. David patiently explained where each piece had come from, then made excuses to return to court. As they stepped once more into the late morning light, Absalom turned to David.

"Father, when I was in Geshur with my grandfather, I made a vow that if Adonai would bring me back to Jerusalem to see the king's face, I would go to Hebron and offer a sacrifice there. Do I have your permission to go, my lord?"

David searched Absalom's face, his heart softening at the earnest tone, the honest pleading in his son's eyes. Perhaps the lie was not such a lie after all. Perhaps somehow Absalom could be king and Solomon could reign with him. But the thought was ludicrous. That Absalom wanted to offer a sacrifice was good. Perhaps his heart yearned to please the Lord after all.

"Go in peace, my son," he said, kissing each of Absalom's cheeks.

Absalom bowed at David's feet once more. "Thank you, my king."

❧33❧

"Some of the men of Israel have been invited to go with Absalom to Hebron." Her father sat on one of Bathsheba's plush couches, bouncing six-month-old Shammua on his knee. Three-year-old Shobab huddled beside him, impatient to hear more of his grandfather's war stories. "I was one of them."

Bathsheba sank onto the cushions beside her father and pulled Shobab onto her lap. "Surely you won't go along with him. Would you?" She had lived to please this man from her earliest childhood, even going against her heart's desire when he asked her to marry a warrior. That he had forgiven her for choosing to please the king over her own husband, over him, still amazed her. Love swelled, and she looked at him, knowing the love she had craved from him all of her life was at last returned, mirrored in the look he gave her and in the affection he had for her sons.

"I could not follow Absalom when I don't know where he is leading. Besides, they left three days ago." Eliam stroked Shammua's soft curls, then handed him to Bathsheba, trading the baby for his toddling, warrior grandson.

Worry tightened Bathsheba's middle at her father's furrowed

brow, his look distant, distracted. "What is it, Father? You know something."

Eliam shifted Shobab from his lap to his knee, bouncing the boy and eliciting high-pitched giggles from him. He bent his head in her direction, and she leaned in, recognizing his attempt at secrecy. Shobab's laughter would mask their words.

"I do not know what Absalom is about. He is headed to Hebron—"

"To offer a sacrifice. The king told me." Somehow she could not speak David's name apart from intimacy—to anyone but him.

"Yes. So the prince has said. But I have heard talk . . ." He looked at her once more, but when he stopped bouncing Shobab on his knee, the boy leaned forward onto his grandfather's chest and grabbed his tunic.

"More, Sabba! More!"

"Shobab! Do not pester your grandfather so." Bathsheba regretted her sharp tone the moment Shammua's lip puckered, and Shobab joined his brother's strident cries. "There, there, now. Don't cry." She lifted Shammua and patted his back while her father carried Shobab to the window and pointed to something in the distance, quieting the boy.

After both boys had settled, she handed them off to Tirzah for naps. She joined her father in the courtyard off of her sitting room, where he was waiting. "Tell me what you know, Abba."

He glanced in the direction of her apartment. Servants milled about inside the rooms, but none disturbed them or was within earshot, not even the guard standing watch at the far end of the gardens, near the door to the palace halls. Guards protected her as no other wife had been before her, surrounding her as they did the king.

"I know that Absalom has been making every effort to turn the hearts of the men of Israel to love him, stealing their allegiance. Whether that allegiance will be pulled away from the king, I don't know. I think your grandfather sides with Absalom."

Bathsheba drew in a sharp breath. "Sabba! Father, how could he—" She let the words die a quick death. She knew exactly how and why her grandfather could do such a thing. "He has never forgiven me."

Eliam's arm came around her in an affectionate gesture, one she was not used to and didn't expect. Tears filled her eyes so unexpectedly she could not speak. He squeezed her shoulders awkwardly at first, then pulled her close. She rested her head against his shoulder.

"There could be trouble ahead," he said softly against her ear. "You must be prepared to protect your sons at all cost. Solomon may not pose a threat to Absalom, but that doesn't mean Absalom will see it that way. You must warn the king."

Shouts in the distance and the hurried feet of many servants stole Bathsheba's reply. She felt the loss of her father's warmth as he released his hold and hurried across the gardens to the door. He looked back and held up a hand. "Don't leave your rooms."

She nodded, fear seizing her as she fled through the door from the gardens to her apartment. Tirzah fairly ran to her side, rubbing both hands up and down her arms as she finished chewing a date, the remnants of the skins clinging to her teeth.

"What is it?" Bathsheba moved toward the children's chamber where Shobab and Shammua napped. Nathan and Solomon were in another room in the palace with Jehiel, the man in charge of their instruction. "What is happening?"

"I can't tell, my lady. The servants are rushing about. There is talk of an invasion."

Bathsheba stopped midstride and clutched Tirzah's arm. "What kind of invasion?" What foreign power would dare rise up against David? Joab, the mighty men, the army—not a man in Israel would allow an enemy to get so close to the king's capital.

"Some say Absalom is coming with clubs and swords."

Bathsheba held Tirzah's gaze, not as a master to a servant but as a trusted friend. "We must protect the children."

Tirzah ran her tongue over her teeth and nodded, hurrying to the children's chambers, and Bathsheba followed. She longed for David, for his touch of reassurance that all would be well. She would rush even now to his side to discover the truth of what was happening, but her father's words stayed her feet. She stopped, looking at Tirzah again.

"Let them sleep until my father returns. There is no sense getting them up if this is just rumor and nothing comes of it." She closed her eyes, feeling the weight of exhaustion tugging at her. Shammua still woke in the night to nurse now and then, and she had indulged him, knowing how swiftly such days would pass and he would wean.

She walked away from Tirzah to the guarded door leading into the palace halls. Her thoughts slowed with debate. Should she demand information from the guard or wait for her father to return? She whirled about when she reached the solid cedar door, her leaden steps carrying her back toward Tirzah, her fear mounting.

She missed a step, stumbled over the rug, and righted herself again. She glanced around, but Tirzah had moved into the children's chamber, her thick frame visible through the open door. Bathsheba sank onto one of the couches as the door burst open behind her. She jumped up and ran to greet her father, who stood with three guards and a bevy of servants at his back, his expression anxious and somber.

"Gather the children and come at once. We are leaving Jerusalem!" Her father's breath came hard as though he had scaled a mountain to reach her.

Servants rushed past him into the room, snatching essential items and stuffing them into linen sacks and stiff baskets. Tirzah's voice rose above the din, urging Shobab to awaken. She emerged from the room, dragging Shobab and carrying a limp Shammua in her arms.

Bathsheba took Shammua from Tirzah, patting his back and hoping he stayed asleep amidst the confusion. "Why, Abba?" she whispered. "Tell me what has happened." Her heart thumped like a galloping mule beneath her tunic, and she prayed Shammua would not feel her fear. The last thing she needed was a screaming infant.

"It is as I feared. Absalom has stolen the hearts of the men of Israel, and he is headed here. The king has commanded we leave the city lest Absalom put it to the sword." He gently tugged her wrist. "Come."

She pulled from his grasp. "My sandals. I cannot go into the wilderness barefoot."

He snapped his fingers, catching a servant's attention. "Help the king's wife into her sandals."

She sat on the bench by the door as the servant hurriedly slipped the leather straps over her feet and tied them across her arches.

"We must go," her father said as she stood. "The king is asking for you."

The admission surprised her. "Why didn't you tell me sooner?"

"I'm telling you now."

She swallowed her frustration, grateful for his protection. Of course David would need her now. No one understood as well as she did what he would be feeling, the blame he would cast on his own back for Absalom's choices.

She handed Shammua back to Tirzah, who had a sleepy Shobab by the hand, followed by a servant carrying satchels of clothing.

"Up, Sabba?" Shobab reached his hands toward Eliam.

Eliam bent down and picked up his grandson, placing him on his shoulders. "Hold on, little man."

The boy giggled as they hurried through the palace halls. "What of Solomon and Nathan?" Bathsheba asked, keeping pace with her father's strides. "We cannot leave them!"

"Jehiel will bring them with all of the king's younger sons. You can keep them with you once we are outside of the city. The king will not leave without his sons." He moved quicker, holding tight to Shobab's legs, dodging guards and frantic servants who seemed unable to decide whether they were coming or going. "Come," he said again, his voice more urgent this time.

They arrived at last at the portico where her father said David waited. She found him surrounded by armed guards, and crying women and children filled the courtyard. Soldiers had the perimeter along the gated palace grounds secured while servants swiftly tossed clothing and jewels and food in baskets and sacks onto a handful of donkeys. The scene was one of ordered chaos, and Bathsheba stood still, on the outside looking in, seeing no way to get close to the king.

"We suggested he stay and defend Jerusalem," her father said, bending low to her ear. "He has the army at his command, and Joab tried to convince him to stay. Absalom is no match for us and Jerusalem is well-fortified."

Bathsheba caught David's profile, saw the strained pull of his mouth, the slightly bent head. While he still wore the crown of Israel, his posture held the look of defeat. He had no strength to fight a battle with his son and win. And after years of making Jerusalem his city, the City of David, beautifying and building up the gates and ramparts from the stone-filled terraces of the Millo inward, he would not want to see it destroyed or see the people in it harmed. The city was at the center of his heart, his very pulse. He would not risk its ruin for his pleasure, not even for the sake of his own safety.

But what of his wives, sons, and daughters? What of Solomon? Were they safer in the wilderness than behind Jerusalem's stout walls?

Anger shot through her, surprising her that she could clench her hands at her sides—wanting to lash out, to scream with the silly women rushing about weeping and bemoaning the king's decree—yet still stand and look on her beloved, understanding him, loving him.

He turned then and caught her eye, and his look of relief drained the anger from her. He moved toward her, the guards parting to let him pass. He grasped her hand, his fingers cold to the touch. He leaned close and brushed a soft kiss on her lips, then pulled her against his chest, saying nothing. Such a public display of affection unsettled her, going against normal protocol. But these were not normal times.

Benaiah, Joab, and Abishai approached. Joab spoke for the group. "We are ready to march, my lord."

David released his grip and moved away from Bathsheba, giving quiet orders to those closest to him, his brief show of affection to her gone. The loss took the last of her strength with it, and she wavered, wondering if her legs would hold her. But she knew he would return when the timing was right, when demands on him lessened. She must be strong for him, whether she agreed with him or not.

She glanced beyond her to the cluster of women, some with young children following the king toward the palace gates, weeping as they went. She caught Maacah's eye, felt the bitter hatred in her scathing glare.

Bathsheba looked away, pulling her cloak closer to her neck. She moved through the crowd, searching for Solomon and Nathan. When she found them, she wrapped her arms around theirs and trudged after David through the palace gates, weeping with the others along the dusty streets of Jerusalem. She glanced back at the shining palace, glimpsing the ten concubines standing on the porch left to take care of the palace.

She turned away from the sight and stumbled onward, upheld by her two oldest sons, and wondered if they would ever come home again.

～34～

The sun's relentless rays licked the tears from Bathsheba's damp cheeks as they crossed the Kidron Valley and began the upward trek to the summit of the Mount of Olives. The king had waited for all of the people to cross the brook Kidron, including his foreign mercenary army of Cherethites and Pelethites in David's personal guard, and the recent Gittites, men from the Philistine city of Gath, who had come to David for refuge.

The sound of weeping floated around her, and she could not keep her own tears at bay when she saw the look of abject sorrow lining David's handsome face. He had removed his sandals at the base of the mount and now placed a cloth over his crowned head—a mark of brokenness and humility. The action pierced her, reviving a sense of guilt she thought long past.

Her own head covering already hid her hair and neck from anyone who might gape at her, but at her husband's example, she lifted the scarf higher and then removed her sandals, feeling the weight of their sin crush down upon her once more. Where was the forgiveness Adonai had granted with Solomon's birth? Had he withdrawn His favor from David and granted it to Absalom? How could it be? Adonai had promised the kingdom to her son, not the son of the foreigner Maacah! Nathan had predicted the truth, and David had assured her it was true, hadn't he?

The thoughts unsettled her as a new sense of unworthiness swept through her. She did not deserve the good God had granted. She was the least of David's wives, the wife of betrayal, of adultery, the wife the nation silently scorned. If Adonai had allowed her to die for her sin, perhaps David would not be facing this new threat to his kingdom. If she had never tempted him . . .

She glanced up, wincing at every misstep as the stones and twigs aligning the mountain path dug into her bare feet. Her tears fell anew, for David as much as for herself. He needed her . . . Did he need her? The slow climb to the summit stole the last measure of her energy, and her thoughts jumbled in her head. She leaned into Solomon, grateful for his young strength.

"Tonight when we stop to rest, you must speak to my father," Solomon said softly, his arm tucked into hers, gently tugging her higher. "I will make sure he comes to you."

She glanced down at him, his dark eyes too wise for his young face. He already sensed the power women held over the king. But what could she do? David needed time alone with Adonai to pour out his pain in music and prose. And time with his advisors to plan a strategy to thwart Absalom's efforts.

"He loves you, Ima. Play your lyre for him and let him hold you in his arms."

"Your father will spend the night making plans against your brother." She darted a quick glance around them, satisfied to realize they were far from the other wives and children of David, surrounded instead by guards and her father, who walked ahead with the Thirty.

"After that," Solomon said, his smile far less innocent than it should be for his age. How much he had seen in his tender years! How much hardship in the court of the king! "I will send him to you." He patted her arm. "He will listen to me."

She caught the hint of a smile on his face and wanted to cuff him for such a remark, but the sound of the weeping crowds stilled her hands. Shuffling sounds, like those of a runner, made her pause and turn to see who was coming. Solomon released his grip on her arm and moved ahead of her to get a better look. He crept forward, and she wanted to follow but held back. Only men surrounded the king, and the women and children stayed in their place behind him. David might overlook Solomon's presence, but not hers. Dare she risk it? Surely he would not fault her in such circumstances.

She wrapped her arms about herself to steady her shaky limbs and moved silently, careful of the prickly weeds and gravel. She slipped between the guards, surprised that they did not stop her, and came to a halt near David as the messenger fell on his face at David's feet.

"My lord king, Ahithophel is among the conspirators with Absalom!"

David stood unmoving, staring down at the messenger. Murmurs of disapproval and a string of curses filled the air around her. Bathsheba sucked in a soft breath, hoping no one heard or noticed her presence, though her heart beat fast and she suddenly felt faint. *Sabba, Sabba . . . do you hate me so much?* Her throat thickened, the tears springing once more to cloud her vision.

David lifted his gaze heavenward, and a loud moan escaped his lips. "Oh, Adonai, turn Ahithophel's counsel into foolishness." He lowered his gaze to the messenger. "If you hear any more, be swift to bring me word."

The young man nodded and hurried back down the mountain. David turned and saw Bathsheba. Their gazes held, and her heart skipped a beat. Ahithophel had betrayed him because of her. Could David see the regret in her eyes? Could he sense the remorse, the sorrow, she carried for him? *Oh, Adonai, let the blame rest on me!*

She was the first to lower her gaze, sinking to her knees, pressing her face to the dust. She knelt in the dirt, half expecting the men to continue on and leave her there. By the looks of some of the Thirty, it was no more than she deserved for the ill will she had brought down on David's house. She'd grown used to the shunning.

But as she breathed in the dirt, silently pleading for Adonai's deliverance from Absalom, echoing David's prayer to turn her grandfather's advice into foolishness, she felt his presence and saw his bare toes protruding from beneath his royal robes. He extended his hand and she took it, standing.

"I'm sorry for my grandfather's choices, my lord," she said loud enough to be heard by those standing closest to the king. "I'm sorry for all of the hurt I have caused you." She lowered her voice on the final words, meaning them for him alone.

He squeezed her fingers and intertwined them with his, turning so both of them could continue up the mountain together. He did not speak, but he also did not release her hand, giving her the comfort of his presence even here. She sighed, feeling part of her strength return.

As they reached the summit, Hushai the Archite met them,

his robe torn and dust on his head. Bathsheba moved to leave David's side, but he tightened his grip, pulling her closer. She sensed his need of her growing with each steady breath, every labored beat of his heart.

"Hushai, my friend." David let go of her hand as he embraced Hushai and kissed each cheek. "Why have you come?" He moved back to hold her hand once more, as though he was suddenly afraid she would slip from his grasp as her grandfather had done.

"I would go with you, my lord. I will stay at your side until the Lord brings you back to Jerusalem." Hushai raised plump arms toward the city, and David turned to look in the direction. Fresh tears filled Bathsheba's eyes at the beauty of the place, and when she looked once more at her husband, she caught the glint of liquid on his lashes as well.

"Jerusalem, Jerusalem . . . will I ever behold your glory again?" His whispered words cut deep. He turned back to Hushai. "If you go with me, Hushai, you will be a burden to me. But if you return to the city and say to Absalom, 'I will be your servant, O king; I was your father's servant in the past, but now I will be your servant,' then you can help me by frustrating Ahithophel's advice. Won't the priests Zadok and Abiathar be there with you? Tell them anything you hear in the palace. Ahimaaz son of Zadok and Jonathan son of Abiathar are there with them. Send them to me with anything you hear."

Hushai nodded his assent and bowed to David. "I will do as you say, my lord." He moved quickly despite his bulk, his men following in his wake as they made their way back to the city.

David watched him go for only a moment, then turned to meet her gaze. "Your grandfather has the power to do us great harm. Your sons are no longer safe. You must stay close to my guards—do not stray even to walk with the women."

"Yes, my lord." She squeezed his hand. "I'm sorry, my lord."

He bent close, his breath warm on her face, and stroked her cheek with one finger. "You are not to blame, beloved. Do not ever forget that fact." He moved quickly then, pulling her along with him up over the summit and down the mountain. "We cannot afford to rest. With your grandfather's counsel, Absalom could be on us by nightfall."

⌇⌇

Darkness fell like a heavy cloak, concealing their whereabouts in shadow, yet exposing them with the brightness of the full moon. The scratchy goat-hair blankets over the uneven ground was the life David had known before he was king—the life of exile Bathsheba had never experienced.

The day's journey had been arduous, at times treacherous. Men had met David just over the summit of the Mount of Olives, bringing provisions. She had ridden with Shammua tucked safely in a sling on her back the rest of the way, her arms wrapped around Shobab at the front, her exhaustion lifted by the donkey's capable back. For a time, the journey had felt safe, in some ways an adventure. Nathan had coaxed Solomon to race up ahead a short distance, as far as the king would allow the boys to go, then back to her side, winded. She would have paid in gold for their energy.

But the time of peace and safety had been short-lived as they skirted the town of Bahurim. The town belonged to King Saul's tribe of Benjamin, and Shimei, one of Saul's relatives, had cursed David and thrown stones at them, showering them with dirt from the opposite hillside, until they had at last passed out of his vicinity.

She flicked some of the dust from her robe now as she sat nursing Shammua, remembering the look of surprise followed by resigned acceptance on David's face as he endured the Benjamite's cursing. Abishai, David's nephew, had wanted to cut off the man's head, but David would not allow it.

Shuffling sounds rose above the mating hum of insects and the distant call of an owl. She pulled Shammua closer, comforted by his warmth, searching the darkness for the source of the noise. Solomon came into view, moonlight bathing his tired face. He glanced behind him.

"Here she is, Abba. I told you I could find her." Solomon met Bathsheba's gaze, his smile mischievous, telling her with a look that he had kept his word. "Shall I take Shammua to Tirzah for you, Ima?"

David sank down on the log next to her. "I haven't sat at a campfire in a long time." His tone held a wistful note, but when she looked up, she caught the weariness, the deep concern, lining his brow. "This is not the way I would have shown you how beautiful such nights can be." He glanced at the stars, and she followed his gaze. Blackness stretched as far as the eye could see, sprinkled with winking dots of white fire. The effect took her breath, and she warmed to David when she felt his touch on her arm. She pulled Shammua from her breast and tucked his now-sleeping body into Solomon's arms, watching him walk with steady feet the short distance to Tirzah.

David's arms came around her then, and she rested her head against his chest. They sat in silence, listening to the camp settle onto makeshift beds on the hard ground. "I spent many a night sleeping under the stars," he said at last, his voice a caress against her ear. "I learned much of Adonai, of His provision and care, during those times."

"You are blessed of Adonai, David. You are beloved of Him ... and of me." She felt his grip tighten about her shoulders, and she lifted her face to his. His kiss was warm, with a hint of salt left over from the tears that had soaked into his beard.

"Shimei's cursing today ... you understand why I had to endure it, why I couldn't allow Abishai to make him stop." His whisper held a trace of deep hurt, even agony, that the man could fling such hateful words along with stones.

She cupped his cheek, drawing a path that had marked his tears. "I understand, beloved. Who better than me? Shimei's curses were as the sting of a lash—a deserved lash." She sighed. "The stones and dirt, on the other hand ... I think the man owes me a new set of clothes." She smiled, eliciting a soft chuckle from him. He kissed her again, softly, with such tenderness that she forgot for the briefest moment where they were and why they were there.

"Adonai is great in mercy. If He so wills, we will see our home again." He lifted his gaze to the heavens once more and pulled her head against his chest. "We will rest here tonight, then cross the Jordan at daybreak."

She nodded, content to sit with him in silence, but their respite was short-lived. Voices came closer, urgent whispers behind them.

"My lord king, Jonathan and Ahimaaz are here." Benaiah stepped out of the way, and two young men bowed low at David's feet.

David released his hold on her arm, and Bathsheba quickly stood, moving into the shadows. "What have you heard?" he asked.

"My lord, you must set out and cross the river at once." Jonathan lifted one hand toward David, his gesture imploring. "Ahithophel has advised Absalom to gather twelve thousand men and set out tonight in pursuit of you. He would attack you while you are weary and weak. He would strike you with terror to cause the people to flee, then kill only you, my king, and bring all the people back to Absalom."

Pinpricks of fear coated Bathsheba's skin, running up her arms and chest, racing with her pumping blood. She held her breath, waiting for David's reply.

"Hushai the Archite has advised instead that Absalom wait and gather the entire army from Dan to Beersheba to come against you, my lord," Ahimaaz said, "and it appears that Absalom has taken Hushai's advice, but Absalom is crafty. Hushai cautioned our fathers to send word to you to cross at once, to take no chances, as Ahithophel's advice should be the course Absalom takes, if he were to do what is truly wise."

"If I were Absalom, I would do as Ahithophel says. My counselor is indeed a fierce enemy." David spoke with resignation, his words weighted with stone. "We must flee across the Jordan at once." The command came with swift movement. As David rose to his feet, his men hurried through the camp, waking the men, women, and children.

Bathsheba rushed to find Tirzah and the children, her feet stumbling over the rough ground in the dark. Torches sprang up, lit by the numerous campfires that were soon extinguished. Rippling water—pleasant background music at the campsite—now seemed like a yawning cavern as she approached the river's edge with her sons.

"Take my wives and children over first." David suddenly stood beside her, addressing the guards stationed along the bank. A makeshift raft had been thrown together before the sun had set, in anticipation of the crossing the next morning.

David turned to her, touching her back, the warmth of his hand calming her frayed nerves. "You and the children will go with Benaiah first. The water is quieter and shallow here. You could walk across it and not sink too deeply, but because of the children, the men will carry you over on the raft." He bent close to her ear. "All will be well, beloved. Do not fear."

She lifted her eyes to his, the torch showing the love in his gaze. Her heart swelled with gratitude. When she should have been last, he was seeing to her safety above all others. "Thank you, my lord. We will be waiting for you."

Benaiah came toward them and she turned to accept his help, but he did not move, his gaze on David's. "My lord, you heard yourself that Ahithophel advised Absalom to come to kill only you. While I know you, my lord, would prefer to be the last to cross to see your people safely to the other side, may I please escort you with your wife and sons over now? If you are killed, my lord, where would we be?" He stepped closer, something she had never seen him do before. "Your wife and sons would also be at great risk," he whispered.

In that moment she realized how loyal Benaiah truly had been. Even knowing what he did of their sin from the first moment until now, he had remained at David's side, protecting him, and now her and her children as well.

David gave the guard a slight nod. "Your advice exceeds that of Ahithophel, my friend." He grasped her arm and moved them down the slick bank to the water's edge. Benaiah and several other guards lifted her onto the unsteady raft as she held Shammua. Tirzah came next, carrying Shobab. Nathan and Solomon jumped on after losing a quick argument with their father about trudging beside the raft in the water. David hopped on last and slipped his arm around her waist, holding her steady.

Bathsheba's gratitude grew even as her stomach dipped when the raft rocked away from the riverbank. Four guards using long tree branches pushed the raft quickly to the river's center. The dipping and swaying of the logs strangled her breath until at last, after what seemed an eternity, they arrived safely on the other side. The guards helped them disembark and positioned them all on the opposite bank, then returned to repeat the effort all over again. Most of the men jumped into the river and swam the length, some while the women and children were being transported, and the last of the men waited until all of the weaker ones were safely on land.

Bathsheba allowed David's guards to lead her up the bank to a space of soft grass. Men built campfires to dry their clothes while the women tried to settle anxious children to go back to sleep. Exhaustion washed over Bathsheba with every lap and ripple of the river. She accepted a handful of blankets from a servant and made beds for the boys around her. In hopes that he would join her, she laid out a blanket for David at her side.

But as dawn's gray light woke her, she found the goat-hair blanket damp with dew, stretched and still as it had been when she laid it there, the camp unmoving around her. She sat up, searching for some sign of the king, fearing he had chosen to rest this night in the arms of another.

She spotted him near the campfire, surrounded by his men, his face devoid of the worry lines so visible the night before.

Relief swallowed her, draining her energy once more. Satisfied that he had not abandoned her for another wife, surprised by such a fear and her strained sense of jealousy, she lowered herself back onto the ground and begged God to get them through this.

❧35❧

David strode the halls of what had once been Ishbosheth's sprawling palatial home in Mahanaim. Joab, Abishai, Benaiah, and Ittai, his newest general, discussed—though mostly argued—military strategies as they followed him from the dining hall to the roof over his chambers. How strange to end up here at such a time as this—where the initial battle to unite the tribes of Israel against him first began. Abner had worked hard to keep Ishbosheth on the throne in this place, kept Michal from him to secure his hold of the northern tribes. Now Michal was sequestered with the rest of his wives for their own safekeeping, while he met with advisors and numbered the troops to prepare for war yet again . . . this time against his own son.

He curled both hands into fists, then released them, forcing his thoughts to calm. Would the conflict never cease? Would the consequences for his sin forever rob him of the blessings he'd so briefly known?

He stepped into the outer courtyard, where the night breezes swept beneath his soft linen robes and crept up from his feet, cooling his hot blood. Deep struggles moved within him like violent waves of the sea, betrayal and pain too strong for words. As he reached the steps to the roof, a servant approached, hurrying from the opposite direction. Benaiah stepped in front of David, hand on the hilt of his sword.

The servant fell to his knees. "My lord king, I come with news." He touched his head to the hard mosaic tiles of the court, his breath coming fast.

"Rise and speak." The men's arguments coming from behind him ceased as the servant jumped up, keeping his gaze averted to the floor.

"My lord, there has been trouble among the court of women."

"When has there *not* been trouble among the women of the king's court?" Joab's comment was accompanied by soft chuckles.

David's mouth tipped in a wry grin. Women had been his undoing from the very first, but he'd grown accustomed to their wiles, and was not so easily swayed since Bathsheba. Perhaps she alone was his true undoing.

"What have they done? Tell me quickly." He was in no mood for some petty grievance, and Hannah usually brought those to his attention. This servant was one of the palace guards. David's hackles rose.

"My lord, the men are bringing her back to the city gates now. I don't know how she managed to slip away unnoticed."

David's senses went on alert, and he straightened, giving the guard a stern look. "Speak plainly, soldier. Who slipped away?"

"The princess Maacah, my lord."

Absalom's mother. No doubt she had fed her son's rebellion against him all these years. "Which way was she headed?" Geshur, the home of her father Talmai, was farther than Jerusalem, where she could rejoin Absalom.

"Impossible to tell, my lord. She didn't get far enough to head north or south."

"Banish her back to Geshur and be done with her," Abishai said, his bitter tone matching the anger in David's heart.

David gave his nephew a look. If not for the advice of his commanders and counselors, he would never have married the woman. But that was not to be undone now.

"Double the guard at her door. She is not to leave even to eat without my approval. I will deal with her later."

He climbed the stairs to the roof, and his commanders quickly followed, taking seats along the parapet in a circle around David.

"The men have been divided, as you said, my lord," Joab said, stretching his legs out and crossing them at the ankles, the tassels of his robe brushing the dusty roof. The servants had swept, but the building was in disrepair, and needed whitewashing and new mortar where cracks had crept in. "Absalom has gathered all Israel to himself at Gilead. They are sure to head north, and it is time we set out to meet them."

David nodded. "How soon?"

"We can go tomorrow."

David lifted his gaze to the stars, his thoughts turning with a thousand regrets. "Tomorrow it will be."

❦

Surrounded by her personal guards, Bathsheba walked between Solomon and Nathan to the outer courtyard where the troops were lined up, waiting for the king's orders to move out. She caught sight of Michal and Abigail's young namesake whispering and smiling at whatever amused them. A wistful feeling swept over her that she had no daughter to share such intimacies, or a friend her equal to discuss her own female woes. Aunt Talia had passed on a few years back, and Chava rarely visited now that Bathsheba was chief wife to the king. She had all the power she could want to command a bevy of servants, but she had no friends with whom to offer good-natured complaints. Her chest lifted in a sigh, and she felt Solomon's hand on her arm.

"May I go and speak to my sister, Ima?" Solomon's gaze drifted to his half sister Abigail as the sound of the shofar blew, announcing the king's arrival at the courtyard.

Bathsheba glanced at her son. His interest in young Abigail was pure innocence at his age, but she couldn't help the niggling worry reminding her that Amnon probably once viewed Tamar thus, years before he became infatuated with her. If Solomon would be king, he would be better off keeping himself to one woman, but of course, as king, he would be expected to make marriage treaties to keep peace. She must teach him what to look for and what to avoid in a wife, and to limit his harem to as few as possible.

"Later, my son," she whispered as the crowd quieted. She moved closer and stopped near the rim of guards encircling the king.

"I myself will surely march out with you." David's commanding tone sent a pang of fear to Bathsheba's heart. If David died, all would be lost.

Joab and Abishai stepped from the head of their ranks and walked to where the king stood. Joab dipped his head and fell forward on one knee. "You must not go out with us, my lord. If we are forced to flee, they won't care about us. Even if half of us die, they won't care."

"But you are worth ten thousand of us. It would be better

now for you to give us support from the city," Abishai finished for his brother.

Bathsheba saw the lines deepen on David's brow and looked from the king to his nephews. David was not much older than Joab and Abishai, but his years as king had begun to show in the soft wrinkles of his skin. Silver now streaked his hair, and his gait held a slowness borne of sadness and defeat.

The sword will never depart from your house.

The prophet's words struck like arrows to her heart. *Oh, Adonai, how long? Will we ever know peace again?*

"I will do whatever seems best to you," David said, quenching her thoughts.

He turned, moved down the courtyard steps to the street, and walked along the road with the troops toward the city gate. Bathsheba followed with Solomon and Nathan in tow, guards before and behind her. When they reached the gate, the king stood to the side, and Bathsheba pulled her sons aside as well, staying out of the way of the guards. She glanced back to see that the other women had done the same.

The men began to march past the king in units of hundreds and thousands as Joab, Abishai, and Ittai stepped forward, awaiting David's last commission.

"Be gentle with the young man Absalom, for my sake," David said loudly, repeating the command three times. Bathsheba caught the surprised looks, the hints of frustration, on the faces of the soldiers, that the king should tie their hands this way toward the very enemy who sought their lives. But no one dared question the king. They merely nodded and moved ahead through the gates.

A tug on her sleeve made her look down into Solomon's earnest gaze. "Why does Abba give such a command to his men? Doesn't my brother seek the king's life and ours as well? Such an enemy must die!"

"Hush now! The king could hear you." She placed a hand on his shoulder and urged him to move away from the gate, out of David's earshot.

Nathan at his side, Solomon dutifully obeyed, glancing every now and then over his shoulder toward his father. "He carries a great burden," he said, halting their walk a few moments later.

Bathsheba squatted, facing her sons, meeting the gaze of first one, then the other. "It is not easy to be a king," she said, directing her words now to Solomon alone. "Your father has many sons and he loves them all, though one of them is seeking to take his life. He needs his other sons to understand and accept his judgments." She took Solomon's hands in hers and turned them over. They were the hands of a child, not those of one callused by war or hard labor. One day he would wield a scepter of peace. If he lived long enough to see such peace.

"I understand, Ima." Solomon pulled his hand from her grasp and turned. "I just think my father doesn't see that his kingdom will never be restored to him as long as my brother lives." He moved away from her and ran to David's side, taking her response with him.

꽃

Hours dragged as the sun grew large overhead. David sat between the inner and outer gates of the city, encased by the thick stone walls, fear and exhaustion twin emotions within him. Servants came and went, bringing skins of wine and baskets of bread and cheese, but he had no desire to taste their delicacies.

Solomon sat across from him on one of the stone benches, but his youthful vigor would not allow him to sit still for long. His gaze followed something moving along the ground. Squatting low, he sprawled on his belly, his gaze fixed on the object.

"What are you looking at so intently, my son?" The boy shouldn't be here. But David excused his presence with the satisfaction that Solomon's young legs could carry him far and fast if he needed to run for his life. David found him comforting, if not somewhat amusing.

"The ant." He sat back on his haunches. "Have you ever watched ants work, Abba? They are tireless. This one"—he pointed to a speck David could barely see in the enclosed room, with the windows only letting in a fraction of the afternoon light—"has carried a crumb of bread from where I brushed it off my robe all the way across the floor. Other ants have joined it there and are sharing the burden of carrying it away, probably to feed their young." He stood, brushing the dust from his robe. "They are amazing creatures, aren't they?"

Solomon gave David a boyish grin and plopped down near him again. David rubbed a hand over the boy's curls and sighed. Absalom once had such curls. If only his beauty had reached inside of him and not merely kept to the outer appearance.

"My lord king, a runner approaches," the watchman called to David from the tower above the gate. David's heart skipped a beat. He rose and stood in the arch of the door, looking out toward the road. He felt Solomon's presence beside him.

"If he is alone, he must bring good news." David rested a hand on Solomon's shoulder, tension growing along the back of his neck.

"Look, another man running alone." The call intensified an already dull headache.

"He must be bringing good news too." David guided Solomon to the road that ran between the gates.

Please, Adonai, let all be well.

Silence passed as they stood watching the road, David's breath thin, anxious.

"It seems to me that the first one runs like Ahimaaz son of Zadok," the watchman called down again.

"He's a good man. He comes with good news." But David's racing pulse did not slow, a sense of deep foreboding masking his struggle for calm.

He stood still as Ahimaaz drew near. "Shalom! Peace to you!" Ahimaaz's call carried the distance from the row of trees leading into the forest to Mahanaim's stout gates. Ahimaaz bowed low before David, touching his face to the ground. "Praise be to Adonai Elohai! He has delivered up the men who lifted their hands against my lord the king."

"Is the young man Absalom safe?" David's heart thumped hard as he tried to read Ahimaaz's expression, frustrated at the man's sudden look of confusion. Why run with news if he had no news to tell? Nothing mattered but Absalom's safety. He'd given strict orders to that fact.

"I saw great confusion just as Joab was about to send the king's servant and me, your servant, but I don't know what it was." Ahimaaz looked away, and David sensed the man knew more than he was telling, but he held his tongue. He had no desire to reprimand a good man.

"Stand aside and wait here," David said. Ahimaaz moved to stand inside the gate behind David and Solomon. David looked down at Solomon, his sense of apprehension making him realize that Solomon did not belong here now. "Go back to your mother," he said softly, patting Solomon's shoulder. "Go now."

Solomon looked up, meeting David's gaze with a perception that troubled him, and he sensed Solomon's desire to give advice to his own father. David did not need the advice of a child! But the boy turned and raced away from the gate, his last look one of understanding rather than the hurt David had expected.

The second runner approached, a man of Cush whose dark skin set him apart from the Israelite guards. "My lord the king, hear the good news!" the man said, falling to his knees before David. "Adonai has delivered you today from all who rose up against you."

Overwhelming dread rose to choke David, the sheer joy in the Cushite's eyes too telling, his words too revealing. David already sensed the answer but could not keep the question silent. "Is the young man Absalom safe?"

The man bowed, touching the dust with his forehead, then rose to meet David's gaze, his own unwavering. "May the enemies of my lord the king and all who rise up to harm you be like that young man."

The words plunged their sharp daggers into his heart, making him stumble backward. A guard's arm steadied him, but he shook it off, not caring if he fell.

"Absalom!" His voice warbled on the name, and he tore the neck of his robe. Turning, he clutched the wall, a drunken man staggering to the steps, his lips tasting the salt of his tears. "Absalom, my son! Oh, my son, Absalom!"

He reached the inner room above the gate, his strength spent from the short climb. Falling in a heap in the middle of the floor, he rocked back and forth, his arms tucked around his knees, great sobs choking him.

"Oh, Absalom, my son, my son—if only I had died instead of you!"

❦36❦

The king's cries stole through the walls of the city gate, piercing Bathsheba's heart. She made her way slowly, skirting the troops, their expressions moving from defeat to anger, raising the hair on her arms in fear. Her father had found her with the children, had warned her that what Solomon had told her was true. The king's grief over Absalom would cost him far more than the death of one son. It would bring about the disloyalty and loss of every man who had fought to save the king and his household.

The thought spurred her to move faster, and she pulled the scarf more tightly about her. Her personal guard kept pace, not letting her out of his sight. She was safe enough, but how long would it last? Would these men who protected her turn against their king? If so, none of them were safe, especially Solomon.

The weeping grew louder as she approached the gate, making her pause. The raw emotion coming from her husband was unlike any she had heard before, not even when they had lost their firstborn. She didn't even like Absalom! How could David care so much for this son that he would have preferred to die in his traitorous place?

She moved forward, but her guard reached a hand to the wall, blocking the steps to the room above. "Joab just went up there, my lady. Perhaps it would be best if you waited?"

She thought for a moment, then shook her head. "I will at least listen to what Joab would say to the king. And pray the commander is wise enough to say the right thing." She gave the man a curt nod and pushed forward, hoping he would not try to stop her again.

When she reached the roof, she walked the short distance to the room. The door stood ajar, so she hid in the shadows along the wall, listening.

"Today you have humiliated all your men, who have just saved your life, the lives of your sons and daughters, and the lives of your wives and concubines," Joab said. "You love those who hate you and hate those who love you. You have made it clear today that the commanders and their men mean nothing to you. I see that you would be pleased if Absalom were alive today and all of us were dead."

No sound or reply accompanied the remark. *Please, Adonai, let him see the truth in Joab's words.*

Joab paced to the door, caught her eye, then whirled around and stomped back into the room. "Now go out and encourage your men. I swear by the Lord that if you don't go out, not a man will be left with you by nightfall. This will be worse for you than all the calamities that have come upon you from your youth till now."

Joab waited a moment, then plodded back through the door to address her. "See that you convince him to sit in the gateway, or you and your children will soon be counted criminals—and I don't know if even I can protect you then." He brushed past her, cursing under his breath.

Or would want to? With each uncertain step, she forced herself into the small room, wondering what David's commander really thought of her. As her eyes adjusted to the dim light, she found the king sitting in the middle of the floor, head covered, tears faintly visible on his cheeks.

She walked to him and extended her hand. He looked up, and she understood at once the sorrow in his gaze. Whether he had caused it or not, he had lost so much. He took her hand and she helped him up. She pulled the frayed edges of his robe together, smoothing them.

"I know you loved him, my lord. But your men do not understand your grieving." She brushed the tears from his cheeks with her thumbs and rubbed her fingers along his brow, removing the head covering.

"So Joab has said." His voice was husky from weeping, and he looked as though the sorrow had aged him. How much longer would she have him?

She clung to his arms. "We have much left to live for, my lord. Please, don't let your grief leave me bereft!" She rested her head against his chest, and his arms came slowly around her. She listened to the steady cadence of his heart, her own racing beat slowing to match his.

"I have no wish to die, beloved. I only know that Absalom is gone from me forever. That is why I weep."

She pulled back, looked into his dark somber eyes. "When the babe died, when God took him, you said we would see our son again."

He pulled her against him again, his voice growing stronger. "Absalom was not innocent as our son was. Absalom made his choice, and his choice was to shun Adonai's teachings. When I rest with my fathers, Absalom will not be among them."

She sighed, wrapping her arms around his waist. "I'm sorry, my lord."

He kissed the top of her head. "My sin is ever before me, beloved. The sword will never depart from my house." He guided her to the door and looked up at the waning dusk. "Shalom will not reign in the land until your son is king in my place."

"God will surely give us peace now that Israel has only one king, my lord. You are the greatest king there is." She slipped her hand in his. "But come. Welcome your troops at the gate, so they will know you approve of them, and we can go home."

"Home," he said, his tone suddenly wistful. "To Jerusalem."

"Yes, to the City of David."

❦

Sounds of lutes and lyres, trumpets, and festival drums filled the night air around her, masking the heavy scent of anxiety hovering beneath the surface of David and his men. Bathsheba stood near the king, the Mount of Olives once again securely beneath her feet. She looked down on the city of Jerusalem, the golden rays of its lamps making it shine like a jewel in the king's royal crown. David's greatest glory.

But that glory could be short-lived if David couldn't bring the tribes to unite under his rule once more. After months of waiting, David had finally secured enough loyalty from Judah and Israel to bring him back to his capital, to rule as he once had. Malcontents had been among those present, and now a new threat had sent the northern tribes to abandon their king once again.

She felt her spirits sag despite the festive atmosphere, knowing David would not have peace until the army had been gathered and the man leading the rebellion destroyed.

She turned at a touch on her arm. "Tirzah, there you are. Is everything all right?"

Tirzah shook her head, glancing over her shoulder, then leaned close to Bathsheba's ear. "There is trouble. Maacah is not so well guarded as the king thinks. She is spewing rebellious words among those who will listen. With the discontent already brewing . . ." She paused and darted quick looks around her again. "I thought you should know."

Bathsheba met her maid's gaze and held it, seeing no guile in her expression. Maacah could cause David further harm, and what more did the woman have to lose? But would the king do anything about it on such a day? He had already pardoned Shimei, the man who had cursed the king the day they fled from Absalom. And with this new man, Sheba, causing the men of Israel to run after him, a woman's troublesome words were not something he would want to hear.

She nodded without speaking, then looked in David's direction. He had already started down the mountain, his mighty men and closest advisors surrounding him. Impossible to get close to him to tell him such a thing now. She would wait until he came to her tonight. Surely he would come.

The trek through Jerusalem's streets bore a happier note than the weeping that had accompanied them a few months earlier. She would be so glad to go home! She hurried closer to Tirzah and her sons as they walked, but as the group slowed nearer the palace, the sounds of the women of David's household grew closer. She glanced behind her, catching the expressions of relief and exhaustion on the faces of David's wives.

Michal sidled up next to her, offering a congenial smile. "I never went with David during his early years of exile." She touched a hand to her damp brow and brushed back loose strands of gray-tinged hair beneath her veil. "I don't know how he survived it, but if I had it to do again, I would have gone with him." She glanced up ahead where men from the city had joined David at the gates to the palace grounds. "Now I'm too old, and I must admit I am glad to be home." She turned and offered Bathsheba a smile. "You are blessed of Adonai to have so many sons."

Bathsheba looked at the woman, David's first love, feeling a sense of sorrow, imagining how hard it must have been for her, for all she had been through.

"Regrets are difficult taskmasters," Michal said, her gaze intense for the briefest moment before it skipped beyond Bathsheba toward the king again.

Bathsheba followed Michal's gaze, her heart yearning for David, longing to feel the strength of his arms around her, to allay the fears she fought daily for the welfare of her sons. To know she belonged to him above all others.

"He loves you, you know. Don't let yourself lose him like I did."

Bathsheba turned at Michal's quiet words, but before she could respond, the woman had slipped back into the crowd of David's wives and children. Bathsheba's gaze followed her to where she joined Abigail's daughter, their moment of friendship gone. Perhaps she should do more to seek the woman out. Friendships would not come if she did not do her part.

She glanced at the other women as the crowd moved forward once again, seeing the bitter Ahinoam and the angry Maacah. Haggith, Abital, and Eglah hovered near their own children, each woman living in barely tolerable companionship, always looking for a way to catch the ear of the king. An ear she had almost exclusively.

She sighed, picking her way ahead of the women, urging Solomon and Nathan to guide her forward. At last she spied Benaiah and caught his eye. He stepped aside, allowing her a better view as guards escorted ten concubines from the palace and brought them to stand before David.

"Absalom pitched a tent on the roof in the sight of all Israel," a guard said as the women knelt, lowering their faces to the dust. "On the advice of Ahithophel, Absalom took each one of them to his bed to lay claim to the throne, to secure his position as king in your place."

Bathsheba's heart twisted, and she feared the fate that awaited her grandfather after all he had done against David. He deserved death. Would she be able to keep David from commanding it after such advice? She watched the muscles clench along his jaw, his brows drawn low, his expression a scowl. But a moment later, he crossed his arms, straightening, only a hint of sorrow evident in his gaze.

"Take these women to quarters outside of the palace. Place them under guard." He paused as though weighing his next words. "They are not to leave the house nor to see my face again, but to live as widows the rest of their lives."

Soft weeping broke out among the ten women as guards stepped forward and escorted them out of David's presence. He stood in the courtyard looking up at the steps to the portico, his chest lifting in a sigh. Another guard approached and spoke something in Benaiah's ear. Benaiah glanced at Bathsheba, then motioned her forward to join David.

David turned when he saw her, his smile welcoming. "We're home, beloved."

"My lord," Benaiah said before she could respond, "there is news of Ahithophel."

David slipped his arm around her waist and drew her to him. "Walk with us, Benaiah."

The guard nodded and followed them as David led her up the steps into the gilded audience chamber. The rooms looked exactly as they had left them, all traces of Absalom and his men gone.

David let out a slow breath, then faced Benaiah. "Tell me what you know."

Benaiah bowed his head, then looked up, his expression stricken. "It appears that soon after Absalom took over the palace and slept with your concubines, Ahithophel saw that this was the only advice of his that your son would heed. When Absalom listened to Hushai and would not pursue you the night you fled, Ahithophel mounted his donkey, returned to his home, set his house in order, and hanged himself."

Bathsheba sucked in a breath as David's grip tightened at her waist. She leaned into his strength, her own failing her. He guided her toward the hall to her rooms, glancing back over his shoulder at Benaiah.

"Ahithophel betrayed my trust. His end is judgment of its own." David paused as if the whole thing were weighing him down. "Make sure Eliam knows."

"Yes, my lord." Benaiah spoke to one of his men and then continued with them down the hall at a discreet distance.

David stopped at the door to the gardens connecting their rooms. He opened the door to let her through, but she stopped him with a hand on his arm.

"My lord, there is more."

He tensed, and she wondered at the wisdom of telling him just now. "What is it?" His tone was gentle, but she sensed the strain of his patience.

"Maacah. She is angry and—".

He held up a hand and touched a finger to her lips. "I have already dealt with her, beloved. My mercenary soldiers are more loyal than half of Israel. Maacah's words did not go far. She and her daughter will be kept under strict guard until I can decide whether to keep her under my thumb or send her back to her father." He leaned forward and kissed her nose. "Do not trouble yourself over her on my account."

She nodded and moved into the gardens as he motioned for her to do so. The calming scent of almond blossoms and the sweet perfume of incense brought back the memories of the first time he had brought her here. He led her to the same bench where he had first wooed her.

"Sit with me, Bathsheba." He sank onto the bench and pulled her down beside him, his arm coming around her. "It is good to be home." He exhaled deeply, his sigh weighty yet somehow relieved.

"It is good because you're still here." She shifted to face him, touching his cheek, her fingers drawing a line in the soft curve of his jaw. "I feared I would lose you."

He smiled, his eyes closing, and she knew he enjoyed her soft caress. When he looked at her again, she couldn't pull away from the love in his eyes.

"In all the years I have walked on this earth," he said, taking her hand and pressing the tips of her fingers to his lips, "I have accomplished many things. My enemies are subdued—and we will conquer this latest threat, I assure you." She gave him a reassuring smile. "Nations I did not know submit to me and fear my name. And Adonai has promised to build a house for me. One day, long after Solomon has been laid to rest, a new king will come from my descendants and sit on my throne, and all people on earth will obey him." His look grew intense, and he squeezed her hand. "Your son Solomon will be the one to build a temple to Adonai's name, and he will rule in peace after me." He paused, looking beyond her as though seeing something in the distance.

She turned to follow his gaze, but saw nothing. She looked back and noted the sheen of tears on his lashes, but his tender smile told her that they were not tears of sorrow. "What is it, David?"

"In all of my accomplishments, I secured many wives and God has given me many children, but none of them compares to you, beloved. I took you wrongfully, and I deserved a thousand times over to lose you. God knows how I begged Him not to take you from me. Your worth is far above rubies, and none other in all of Israel compares to you."

She stroked his cheek, her own tears wetting her lashes.

"You are my most beloved, Bathsheba."

The words sang around her in the music of the night, filling her heart with joy.

"I love you, David."

His kiss silenced any lingering doubt.

~37~

Eight Years Later

Jewel-bedecked camels from Rabbah in the land of Ammon came bearing King Shobi, son of Nahash, brother of the former deposed king, Hanun. His entourage strode through the palace gates, where they sank to their knees in the courtyard of King David. Atop the gangly mounts, a tentlike covering secluded its prized passenger, Naamah, the princess of Ammon. Behind her on less adorned camels came ten maids, while fifty guards followed before and behind.

Bathsheba stood in the shelter of the portico, waiting for her servants to welcome the group, to escort the young bride to David's audience chamber, where wedding festivities would begin. By nightfall, the princess would enter the bridal tent already sparkling in the central palace courtyard, awaiting her groom, Solomon.

"Everything is in readiness for the ceremony, my lady. The tables are set, the guests are already arriving." Tirzah smiled, the lines of her face revealing the strain and the laughter of passing years. Bathsheba's children were all in the care of the palace tutors now, and Tirzah's role had once again become

317

more of confidant and friend to Bathsheba than nursemaid to the children. "I never dreamed this day would come so soon. And what a ceremony! It is as if your Solomon were already king." She lowered her voice and glanced about, but Bathsheba did not pay the comment any mind.

"I had hoped to convince the king to combine the ceremony with Solomon's coronation, but he seems to think there is no hurry." She worried her lip, then thought better of it, not wanting to undo the work of her beauty treatments or leave marks upon her lips. The treatments took longer now than they had in the days of her youth, needing more milk and honey and scented oils to smooth her skin and diminish the wrinkles along her eyes and brows.

Her chest lifted in a sigh. The king was not getting any younger, and he already was many years ahead of her. Did he think he would live forever? What happened if he grew suddenly ill, or worse?

The sword will never depart from your house.

Was David immune from an assassin's blow? And if his death came too quickly, Adonijah stood next in line for the throne. His attractiveness and charm had already won him the hearts of some of David's men—what would stop him from doing as Absalom had done? If he won the throne and David was too weak to resist him, she and Solomon would be executed as criminals. Too many in the kingdom had long memories and still viewed her as an adulteress and her children as illegitimate heirs.

"The girl appears to be beautiful, from what I can see." Tirzah glanced at Bathsheba, her look assessing. "Solomon should be pleased."

Bathsheba stepped from the shade of the portico as the

girl emerged from her enclosed pavilion. She wore multicolored robes, with sparkling rings of gold about her neck and dangling from her ears and nose, and a bright woven scarf covered all but her eyes. Her wedding attire was beautiful, but Bathsheba could not tell through the shield of her veil whether the girl was beguiling enough for her son. Her son with the wandering eyes, who had already caught the glances of too many women.

She moved into the well-lit hall and took a seat in the antechamber, waiting for David and for his guards to announce their entrance. Solomon would join his father, and then the bride would walk the length of the audience chamber to the sound of joyous melodies, her maids accompanying her. The bride's father, the acting king of Ammon, son of Nahash and vassal to David, would sign the agreement and grant her to Solomon's care.

The marriage was a good alliance, though Bathsheba hoped Solomon would not see it as an excuse to marry just any foreign princess. Naamah feared the God of Israel, as did her father Shobi. This was proven to David when Shobi came to their aid during their exile at Mahanaim, while they were on the run from Absalom.

If only Solomon would see her as wife enough. But Bathsheba knew her son too well. Once he was king, he would find reasons to build a harem of women far greater than his father had done. She could not suppress another sigh. It was the guilt she bore, despite all the warnings she'd given him.

"I have learned from your errors, Ima, as you have taught me," he had once told her. "I will not go to the house of an adulteress or tempt a woman to become one. Better to marry many women than to take one that does not belong to me."

Perhaps her teaching had not been thorough enough. But it was too late to change him now.

A commotion drew her thoughts to the present. She looked up at the sight of David following his standard-bearer and Solomon decked out in royal robes behind his father. David stopped when he saw her and extended his hand. He had never officially named her his queen, but she possessed the office in everything but the title. Somehow he never felt the need to grant her that. Perhaps when he finally crowned Solomon his coregent . . . She squelched the longing that it be this day.

"You are beautiful as always, beloved." He bent to kiss her cheek, then took her hands in his and squeezed.

"Thank you, my lord." She smiled, then looked at Solomon. "Your bride is here. Are you ready, my son?"

Solomon's mouth tipped in a crooked grin. "Ready and anxious, Ima."

"And nervous," David whispered in her ear.

They shared a knowing smile. The trumpet sounded and the standard-bearer announced their presence. David led Bathsheba to the seat beside his, then sank onto his gilded throne. Solomon stood on the step below, watching the door.

The music began, and the bride's father moved down the length of the room, followed by the ten maids, and lastly the bride. The Ammonite king placed his seal on the parchment, uniting their two kingdoms in a treaty of peace. A servant brought the treaty to David, and he stamped his signet ring in the wax and affixed his seal beside that of the Ammonite king's.

Bathsheba listened as the priest gave the blessing and watched as gifts were exchanged. Her heart swelled with pride when the ceremony was completed. Feasting would follow until Solomon led Naamah into the bridal tent to consummate their union. Then only one step remained. To place the crown on Solomon's head.

She glanced at David. And to convince the king to do so soon.

❦

Shaking woke Bathsheba from restless dreams, and at first she thought the shivers had come from her. She often woke sweating in the night, flinging the covers aside to let the night air from the open window cool her damp skin. But as she turned over in the bed, her skin brushed David's, and she startled at his visible shaking.

"Are you awake, my lord?" She couldn't tell by his closed eyes, and wondered if it was some dream that rocked him. She touched his forehead, then jerked her hand back and scooted from the bed. Wrapping a robe quickly about herself, she hurried to the door to the guard standing watch.

"Send for the physician. The king is ill." Fear snaked up her spine. If the illness were unto death, what would become of them? *Please, Adonai, do not take him yet.*

Servants sprang into action, diverting her attention from her silent prayers. The king's personal attendants brought wine, dipped cloths in tepid water, and placed them on his chest and forehead. He reached for the covers, yanking them to his neck. His eyes opened, their color glazed.

"Bathsheba?"

She rushed to him, kneeling at his side, grasping his warm fingers in her hand. "I'm here, my lord."

His chest lifted in a sigh. How was it that he could have

been so vibrant, so full of life and love the night before, and awaken so visibly ill? She stifled the anxiety urging her to panic. David would recover, and Solomon would rule in his father's place.

Please, Adonai, let it be!

"I'm cold."

She leaned forward, brushing the hair from his brow. "You are feverish. The chill is only an illusion, beloved. I've sent for the physician."

He nodded, closing his eyes again. The physician had been unable to save Abigail when her time had come. But she tamped the thoughts, shushing her fear.

Doors opened behind her, and footsteps sounded on the tiles. She stood and turned. A middle-aged man entered, his robe looking as if it had been hastily donned. His hair stood at odd angles, and he smoothed a hand over his beard, bowing low when he saw her.

"My lady," he said, rising quickly and moving to the king's side. "When did this come upon him?"

"Sometime in the night, I expect. I awoke to his shivering."

The man nodded once but said nothing as he bent to feel David's head, neck, and arms and leaned in close to listen to his breathing. At last he stood.

David opened his eyes. "What's wrong with me?" His clear gaze made Bathsheba's heart quicken. Perhaps the cool cloths had broken his fever. "Why can't I get warm?"

"The fever has made your skin too hot but your insides too cold. Let your attendants continue to bathe your skin in cool water. When the fever leaves you, you will be warm again."

David cursed softly and pushed up from the pillow. "I don't have time to be sick abed. Bring me food and wine and stop fussing over me." His voice sounded hoarse, and the barked words lacked strength.

"My lord, please. You must rest or the fever could grow worse. Then you will be unable to work at all. We don't want to carry you yet to the tomb of your fathers." The physician's sharp words did not match his gentle tone.

Bathsheba turned to a servant. "See that you do as the king requests. Bring food and wine to his chambers at once."

"Yes, my lady." The man hurried to do her bidding. She moved to the bed and the physician stepped aside.

"Do as the physician tells you, my lord." She stroked her fingers through his hair. "You must get well. We need you." She looked at him, their gazes holding in a silent caress.

He nodded, falling back against the pillows. "Every bone hurts."

The physician moved quickly to retrieve some herbs from a covered basket his servant had carried into the room. Moments later, he offered a measured dose to David.

"This will help ease the pain."

David washed down the powder with the wine offered him, shaking his head as if to dispel the remnants from his tongue. "Tastes bitter."

"It comes from the bark of the willow tree, my lord, whose taste is unfortunately not pleasant."

David closed his eyes, and his breathing grew peaceful. Bathsheba stood looking down at him, a small sense of relief rushing through her. When David recovered, she must insist he name Solomon his coregent before they risked losing him again. If he did not act, her life would be forfeit.

❦

The illness lasted a week, but the effects lingered far beyond what David expected. In the daytime, chills swept through him, and at night he could not get warm, not even in Bathsheba's arms. Months had come and gone, and this morning he lingered in his bed, the sun beckoning him, deceiving him with its promise of heat. During the winter rains the fiery orb had vanished behind a mountain of daily clouds, sinking his spirits. Did he dare trust the spring's bright rays?

How had his life come to this? He had ruled Israel for thirty-seven years. How long it seemed, and yet how short.

A knock on his door drew his attention from the dredges of his melancholy thoughts. His attendant answered while he pulled the covers farther up to his chin. Perhaps a soak in hot water would penetrate the chill. But such visits to the heated mikvah did not last, and he could not spend the rest of his days in a room of steam or huddled before an open flame. Neither flame nor water could warm his bed, and Bathsheba's changing body deceived her as well, making her too warm to get close to him. She tossed the covers, and her skin turned to sweat too often at his touch. Had all of his wives suffered such affliction? He had not spent much time with them in their later years to know.

Disturbed with the guilt that thought produced, he brushed it aside and looked up at the sound of plodding feet, surprised to see Benaiah and Hushai at the foot of his bed.

"What can I do for you, my friends?"

"We have come to offer to help you, my lord," Hushai said, loosening the neck of his robe. David kept the room as warm as he dared with hearth fires, which did not bode well for his counselors, who were always shedding their robes if they stayed too long.

"And how can you help me, Hushai? Can you give me a new body that will hold the strength and vigor I once had? I am old. I didn't think so a few months ago, but my body has betrayed me."

"We know you cannot keep warm, my lord, so we decided—" Benaiah glanced at Hushai, then back at David. "That is, we wanted to suggest that we look for a young virgin to bring to my lord king to bring back your desire, to keep you warm and attend your needs."

David smiled at Benaiah's discomfiture as a flush crept up the man's massive neck and filled his face. "Even a virgin is not likely to stir my blood, Benaiah. Some pleasures for me are past."

Was it true? But even Bathsheba no longer filled him with the desire for her he once had. His love for her went beyond physical touch. He kept her beside him now for comfort, for companionship.

"Nevertheless, perhaps a beautiful young virgin would do more good than you realize. Pardon me for saying so, my lord, but you are not sitting with a foot in the grave yet." Hushai straightened, folding his arms across his chest.

"Perhaps you are right. Go ahead then. Find a young virgin to keep me warm." He shivered beneath the woolen blankets, doubting even the most comely girl in Israel would make much difference.

❦38❦

The halls held an eerie quiet as Bathsheba took the steps from Solomon's upper floor residence to her rooms closest to the king. Her daughter-in-law Naamah was four months from giving birth to her first child, and with each passing day, Bathsheba worried. Surely Naamah would birth a healthy son—the girl was strong and capable, not delicate like the new bride Abishag who continually warmed David's bed.

Still, Naamah's health and safety did not trouble her nearly as much as David's indecision. Was she jealous of the time Abishag now spent with him? But his own health had declined sharply in the six months since Solomon took Naamah to wife. She could not deny David this one last pleasure, though he had assured her that Abishag would remain a virgin until she passed into Solomon's court.

Bathsheba brushed lint from her clothes and continued down the hall toward her chambers. Why had David continued to put off naming Solomon king in his place? The thought, once a nagging concern, had now grown to a full-blown fear.

Rumors had raged among the servants of the palace, and Tirzah was quick to keep her informed. Most of David's other sons did not seem to pose a threat to Solomon, but Adonijah, son of Haggith, next in line for the throne, avoided Solomon's company and moved about the city with chariots and horsemen and fifty men to run before him, as though he were already king in David's place. He had not gone so far as to seek the priest's anointing or to pull the men of Judah away from his father as Absalom had done, but she had no doubt his plans ran along those very lines. How would she know? His conspiracy could prove worse than Absalom's if they didn't catch it in time. And David's illness had kept him so often from court that she wasn't sure he even knew what was going on in his city.

She paused at the entrance to her apartment, glancing at the door to the gardens connecting her rooms to David's. Should she pay an unexpected visit and share her concerns? Abishag would be there. But she shouldn't have an aversion to the girl. If all went according to plan, Abishag would be her daughter-in-law one day. Solomon would surely find the girl a gift once his father no longer had need of her.

She shook her feelings aside and nodded to the guard, who opened the door to her rooms. The day of David's death seemed ever closer—something she had never considered the night she had given herself into his arms. Their age difference meant she would be a widow a good many years. A sinking feeling settled in her middle, and she rubbed her temples, trying to forestall the headache these thoughts always produced.

Oh, Adonai, I don't want to lose him! Despite the years, he was precious to her. He had given her four handsome sons, two of them already grown men to be proud of—and one a king David himself would hold in high esteem, if he would simply stop putting off the inevitable and proclaim his replacement. Adonijah surely expected David to choose him, though in recent years anyone watching could tell David favored Solomon.

She sank onto her cushioned couch and accepted a cup of wine from a servant. Tirzah had gone to the markets today and would return soon with fabric and ornaments and new trinkets from the east. Bathsheba should have taken Naamah and gone with her—the distraction would have done them both good. But the mood in the palace halls had given her pause and made her change her mind. She sipped the tepid drink and rested her head on the back of the couch, closing her eyes.

A knock at the door jolted her. She was far too jumpy and nervous today. Whatever strange malady sparked the atmosphere, the guard's entrance preceding the prophet Nathan did nothing to dispel it.

She straightened as Nathan entered the room and bowed low at her feet. He rose, refusing the seat she indicated opposite from her.

"Something troubles you, Nathan. What is it?" She set the goblet on a table beside her and rubbed her hands over her arms, her nerves making her skin tingle.

Nathan paced a short path in front of her couch, dismissing the servants from the room. Bathsheba lifted a brow, surprised at his sudden use of authority that he did not actually possess in this place. But she did not stop him or question him.

When the last servant had gone, he spoke. "Have you not heard that Adonijah the son of Haggith has become king, and David our lord does not know it?"

She sucked in a breath. The eerie stillness, the hushed words and uncomfortable glances of servants who would not look her way . . . She had, at least deep down, suspected and known it was coming, if not today.

"I had feared," she said when her breath finally released. "I had sensed trouble. I have pleaded with David to act, to name Solomon his rightful heir as he promised, but this illness . . ." She let her words trail off and looked beyond Nathan toward the open window. To complain about her husband did no good whatsoever now. They must act. "What can we do?" Helplessness overwhelmed her.

"If you will hear me, my lady, let me give you advice, that you may save your own life and the life of your son Solomon."

"We truly are in danger then."

Nathan nodded. "Yes. If these plans of Adonijah's succeed and he gains the following of all Israel, you and your son Solomon will be considered usurpers and criminals. They will not care that Adonai chose Solomon as David's rightful heir. The people will follow their own desires."

A rush of emotion added to her fear, and she could not speak.

Nathan moved closer and sat at her side. "Go immediately to King David and say to him, 'Did you not, my lord, O king, swear to your maidservant, saying, "Assuredly your son Solomon shall reign after me, and he shall sit on my throne"? Why then has Adonijah become king?' Then, while you are still talking with the king, I will come in after you and confirm your words."

"He will listen to you," she said, looking to him to assure her, knowing the relief she craved would elude her until this whole matter was settled.

"He will listen if enough of us tell him it is true. Benaiah will be there, and Zadok the priest has not followed Adonijah. But Joab is not so trustworthy, and Abiathar has offered sacrifices on Adonijah's behalf." He abruptly stood. "But all is not yet lost. Go quickly and do this."

She stood at his behest and smoothed her skirt, glancing over her attire. She had not worn her best robes to visit Naamah, but the choice was one David favored. The rest of her coiffure and makeup would have to do—there was no time to freshen it.

She hurried to the adjoining door to her gardens with Nathan following at her heels. He waited near the door while she spoke to the guard and sought her audience with the king.

❧

David huddled beneath a mound of blankets as Abishag tucked the last of the soft wool beneath his feet. The cushions of the couch were soft and gave him a chance to sit up. He grew weary of the bed. A cup of hot spiced wine rested between his hands. He sipped, smiling at Abishag.

"Are you comfortable, my lord?" She bent close to his ear, the scent of her perfume tickling his senses. Of all the women in Israel, she was one of the most charming and beautiful, with curves in all the right places. The thought of her should have heated his blood, but the best emotion he could muster was appreciation as she served him food and offered him blankets and warm drinks. Any servant in his household could easily do the same things for him, but he admitted the sight of her was more pleasing than most. Still, his love for Bathsheba could never be replaced even by youthful beauty.

"My lord?"

He started at Abishag's soft voice. "What? Oh yes, I am quite snug in all of these blankets. Thank you." The perpetual chill in his bones had only slightly lessened, but to tell her so would only make her fuss over him more.

A commotion coming from the door to his gardens made him sit straighter. Benaiah entered.

"My lord, the lady Bathsheba would speak a word with you."

Bathsheba was here? She did not normally visit without a summons. "Send her in then."

She entered in her everyday attire, minus the jewels he had bestowed on her, her smile touching the deep places in his heart. But the lines near her eyes and across her brow betrayed her true feelings. She needed something important. She would not have come otherwise. She bowed, touching her forehead to the lion's skin that covered the tile floor at his feet.

"What is your wish?"

She rose gracefully, hands stretched before her in an act of supplication. Worry lines increased along her forehead. "My lord, you swore by Adonai Eloheikhem, the Lord your God, to your maidservant, saying, 'Assuredly Solomon your son shall reign after me, and he shall sit on my throne.' But now Adonijah has become king, and my lord the king, you do not know about it."

David gave his head a slight shake, not sure he had heard correctly.

"He has sacrificed oxen and fattened cattle and sheep in abundance, and has invited all the sons of the king, Abiathar the priest, and Joab. But he has not invited Solomon your servant. My lord the king, the eyes of all Israel are on you, to learn from you who will sit on the throne after you. Otherwise, as soon as my lord the king is laid to rest with his fathers, Solomon and I will be treated as criminals."

David straightened, and one of the blankets slipped from

his shoulders. Abishag hurried to tuck it in behind him again, but he waved her away, extending a hand to Bathsheba instead. She clasped his fingers, and he jolted, almost jerking back at her icy touch. She was visibly shaking, and in that moment, he wanted nothing more than to pull her into his arms and comfort her as he once had.

But Benaiah stepped into the room again, breaking his train of thought. He released his grip on her hand and she stepped back, allowing Benaiah to approach, followed by another man. David squinted, silently cursing the slight dimness around the edges of his vision.

"My lord," Benaiah said, bending forward. David wondered how the man could seem so young when in truth he was not many years behind David's own age. "Nathan the prophet is here."

David recognized the prophet's long hair and beard and his coarse robe and tunic. Nathan stepped into the place where Bathsheba had just stood and bowed low, his face to the ground.

"Have you, my lord the king, declared that Adonijah shall be king after you, and that he will sit on your throne? Today he has gone down and sacrificed great numbers of cattle, fattened calves, and sheep. He has invited all the king's sons, the commanders of the army, and Abiathar the priest. Right now they're eating and drinking with him and saying, 'Long live King Adonijah!' But he did not invite me your servant, Zadok the priest, Benaiah son of Jehoiada, or your servant Solomon. Is this something my lord the king has done without letting his servants know who should sit on the throne after him?"

Anger flared, heating his blood, stirring him to sit straighter.

He let the blankets fall to his lap and looked at his veined hands, his gaze settling on the signet ring. The ring belonged to the one who would rule after him. Thoughts of Haggith and her son Adonijah surfaced, the young man's handsome face reminding him too much of Absalom. They had both inherited David's own apparent good looks, although where Absalom had Maacah's dark, exotic beauty, Adonijah had the attractiveness of Joseph's line, after his mother. But God had chosen Solomon, not Adonijah.

"Call Bathsheba to me," he said, folding his hands on his lap so the ringed hand rested on top.

Nathan moved away, and Bathsheba once again stood before him suddenly looking as vulnerable as she had the first night he had wooed her. Surely she knew how much he loved her.

"Beloved." He spoke softly, wanting to comfort her. She met his gaze, and he beckoned her forward. She came and knelt at his side, and he took her hand, rubbing his thumb over her still smooth skin. "I vow to you, as surely as Adonai lives, who has delivered me out of every trouble, I will surely carry out today what I swore to you by Adonai Elohei Yisrael, the Lord, the God of Israel. Solomon your son shall be king after me, and he will sit on my throne in my place."

Tears skimmed her lashes, and he smiled. He pulled her closer and brushed a stray tear from her cheek. She leaned forward and kissed him, then lowered herself with her face to the ground. "May my lord King David live forever!"

David bent toward her and touched the top of her head, the action more difficult than he expected. When had he become so weak? Had it only been a few months ago that he thought his kingdom, his rule, would last for many years to come, when he thought his life was far from over? How quickly his strength had faded, like the grass that withers.

Bathsheba rose to her feet, and David motioned for her to sit beside him. She perched on the edge of the couch and took his hand again. He smiled, holding her gaze, then looked at a servant standing near. "Call in Zadok the priest, Nathan the prophet, and Benaiah son of Jehoiada."

He looked at Bathsheba while the man went to do his bidding. "Thank you, my lord," she said, a remnant of tears still clinging to her lashes.

He nodded, but before he could speak, Benaiah, Nathan, and Zadok approached. They must have been hoping he would act and waiting in the outer chambers. Thank God for three such trusted, loyal friends.

He looked at each one in turn, hoping they could sense how much he trusted them, how grateful he was for their support. Surely his kingdom would fall into Adonijah's hands, outside of Adonai's will, without their help. And yet, nothing could fall outside of Adonai's will. Even in this He was working all things for good.

"Take your lord's servants with you," he said to Benaiah as he squeezed Bathsheba's hand, "and set Solomon my son on my own mule and take him down to Gihon. Have Zadok the priest and Nathan the prophet anoint him king over Israel. Blow the trumpet and shout, 'Long live King Solomon!' Then you're to go up with him, and he is to come and sit on my throne and reign in my place. I have appointed him ruler over Israel and Judah."

Benaiah stepped forward and fell to one knee. "Amen! May Adonai, the God of my lord the king, so declare it," he said, his approval evident in his smile. Once, this faithful guard had disapproved of David's foolish choices, and now his friend's forgiveness and acceptance were a balm and a relief. Solomon would be wise to trust Benaiah, perhaps making him commander in Joab's place.

"As Adonai was with my lord the king," Benaiah was saying, "so may He be with Solomon to make his throne even greater than the throne of my lord King David!"

"May Adonai declare it," Nathan and Zadok said in unison.

As the men filed out of his chambers to do his bidding, David shifted in his seat and looked into Bathsheba's beautiful face. "I should have done this a long time ago, beloved."

She shook her head. "You are doing it now. That's all that matters." Yet he could tell by her expression that she agreed with him but was too kind to say so.

He lifted her fingers to his mouth and kissed them. "You should go with them. Watch your son wear the crown in my place."

"I would stay with you, my lord."

He clasped both hands around hers, then released them to pull the signet ring from his finger. "Give this to your son Solomon. When he sits on my throne, send someone to tell me."

She shook her head again, and he could tell she would not leave unless he insisted. How he loved her!

"It is not every day a man becomes a king, beloved. Go, join the procession and rejoice at our son's side in my place. Then come to me and we will celebrate together."

A tentative wistfulness crossed her face. "You're sure?"

He patted her hand and released it. "I'm sure."

She smiled, and he knew he would never see anything again so beautiful, the memories between them a treasure to cherish always.

"You are my priceless jewel, Bathsheba." She stood, her eyes shining. "Now go in peace. Then come and return to me."

She bowed low once more, then kissed him and left his chambers to watch her son Solomon become king in his place.

Epilogue

Two Years Later

Bathsheba sat on a gilded chair, a circle of gold ringing her hair, the symbol that David had finally chosen his queen. In front of her, the two kings sat on royal thrones—David looking thin and frail, his body marred by age, and Solomon, his youthful frame filling out the royal robes with vigor, majesty, and splendor. Her heart surged with wistfulness and pride. Before them all stood a multitude of commanders and leaders in Israel, their numbers filling the courtyard and spilling around the sides of the palace.

A gentle breeze rustled the leaves on the trees spaced about the courtyard, a reminder that spring had come again, a time when kings went out to war, but there were no more wars for David or Solomon to fight. Adonai had indeed brought about a kingdom of peace for Solomon to rule in David's stead. And David had lived to see it.

She looked over the crowd, her gaze settling on the women

of David's court. She missed Michal most of all, whose friendship she had sought and gained in the past few years before her death. Ahinoam had joined Michal soon after, their bodies resting in David's tomb, while Maacah and her daughter Tamar had at last returned to Geshur. Only the younger wives and concubines were left for Solomon to inherit. He had vowed when his father passed on to treat them as widows.

As she would soon be.

Much too soon.

David rose slowly to his feet, the effort difficult, and she wondered what pains he suffered in doing so and how long his newfound strength would last. Sadness filtered through her, and she wished not for the first time that their lives could truly go on forever, as the blessing offered to kings proclaimed. But though the people might wish it, even loudly assert, "May my lord King David live forever," no one remained exempt from Sheol. Not even their beloved King David.

She turned her attention to catch his every word.

"Listen to me, my brothers and my people. I had it in my heart to build a house as a place of rest for the ark of the covenant of Adonai, for the footstool of our God, and I made plans to build it. But God said to me, 'You are not to build a house for My name, because you are a warrior and have shed blood.'

"Yet Adonai Elohei Yisrael chose me from my whole family to be king over Israel forever. He chose Judah as leader, and from the house of Judah He chose my family, and from my father's sons He was pleased to make me king over all Israel. Of all my sons—and Adonai has given me many—He has chosen my son Solomon to sit on the throne of the kingdom of Adonai over Israel. He said to me, 'Solomon your son is the one who will build My house and My courts, for I have chosen him to be My son, and I will be his father. I will establish his kingdom forever if he is unswerving in carrying out My commands and laws, as is being done at this time.'"

He paused, looking out over the people as though he were seeing the sheep of his pasture rather than the commanders of hundreds and thousands of his troops. He stretched his arms wide before them. "So now I charge you in the sight of all Israel and of the assembly of Adonai, and in the hearing of our God: be careful to follow all the commands of Adonai Eloheynu, that you may possess this good land and pass it on as an inheritance to your descendants forever."

He turned, facing Solomon, who knelt at David's feet. Bathsheba's tears filmed, and she blinked away the moisture, proud of the image they made, a father blessing and counseling his son.

David rested both hands on Solomon's crowned head and cleared his throat. "And you, my son Solomon, acknowledge Adonai Avinu, the God of your father, and serve Him with wholehearted devotion and with a willing mind, for Adonai searches every heart and understands every motive behind the thoughts. If you seek Him, you will find Him, but if you forsake Him, He will reject you forever. Consider now, for Adonai has chosen you to build a temple as a sanctuary. Be strong and do the work."

He lifted his hands from Solomon's head and offered Solomon his hand. Solomon took it and stood at his father's side, though Bathsheba knew by the way David swayed slightly that it was Solomon's strength now holding him up. Silence followed, and a look passed between them. Bathsheba's heart gave a soft kick at the love they shared.

Oh, Adonai, how blessed I am to see this! How good You have been to Your servant David.

David's voice pulled her thoughts back to him. She straightened, seeing that he had turned to face the crowd once more.

"My son Solomon, the one whom God has chosen, is young and inexperienced. The task is great, because this palatial structure is not for man but for Adonai, the Lord God. With all my resources, I have provided for the temple of Elohai, my God, gold, silver, bronze, iron, and wood, as well as onyx, turquoise, stones of various colors, and all kinds of fine stone and marble—all of these in large quantities. In addition, I now give my personal treasures of gold and silver—three thousand talents of gold of Ophir and seven thousand talents of refined silver—for all of the work to be done by the craftsmen." He paused, drew in a breath, and let his gaze take in the crowd. "Who is willing to consecrate himself today to the Lord?"

Bathsheba looked toward the threshing floor and the king's storehouse directly behind the palace. David was giving a staggering amount to the work. But she would expect nothing less of him. He was a man devoted, consumed, in his passion for the Lord his God. A generous man who had learned the gratitude that comes of sins forgiven.

The king took his seat again, and the people moved forward, bringing gifts presented first to David and then transferred into the care of the man in charge of the king's treasuries.

The sun rose high in the heavens, warming the pavement and the skin beneath Bathsheba's robes. Servants lifted palm fronds to cool the air around them and brought golden cups of wine to refresh them.

As the last of the gifts were placed at David's feet, he spoke.

"Who am I, and who are my people, that we should be able to give as generously as this? Adonai Eloheynu, as for all this abundance that we have provided for building You a temple for Your holy name, it comes from Your hand, and all of it belongs to You. Adonai, God of our fathers Abraham, Isaac, and Israel, keep this desire in the hearts of Your people forever, and keep their hearts loyal to You. And give my son Solomon the wholehearted devotion to keep Your commands, requirements, and decrees and to do everything to build the palatial structure for which I have provided."

David lowered his hands and bowed his head. Silence followed his prayer for the space of several heartbeats, and Bathsheba's own heart lifted with joy and gratitude and great pride in this man whom she called husband and king.

Oh, Adonai Eloheynu, hear the prayer of Your servant David. Give my son Solomon a heart to follow You with wholehearted devotion, as his father David has done.

She opened her eyes at the sound of movement in time to see Solomon standing once again at David's side. David clutched Solomon's arm, his strength ebbing with the setting sun, but his voice carried, sure and strong. "Praise Adonai Eloheynu, the Lord your God."

A shout of praise shook the earth beneath the portico. Bathsheba stood, lifting her voice to join the others, joy in Adonai's goodness to her overwhelming her once again. That He should choose to bless her when she was so unworthy . . . David's own words had said it all. All of this abundance, every blessing poured out on them, belonged to Adonai. He would grant Solomon the wisdom to build the temple David loved, and, God willing, she would live to see it.

She moved from her place behind the king and came to

341

join him, taking his arm, feeling the strength of his joy. He turned to her and smiled.

"Adonai El Yisrael has given rest to His people, beloved, that they may dwell in Jerusalem forever." He took her hand and pulled her close, kissing her lightly on the cheek. The light in his eyes reflected the love that had not diminished with the years. "I am glad I lived to see my promise to you fulfilled." He stroked her palm as his gaze shifted to Solomon. "Pray for him, beloved. He will need great wisdom to lead such a people."

The shouts and singing dwindled, and Bathsheba could see the light fading from David's eyes. "You are tired, my lord. Come inside now and rest. Tomorrow we will celebrate once more."

He nodded, slowly stepping forward, raising his hands to quiet the crowd.

"Pray for the peace of Jerusalem," David sang, the words lilting with his sweet tenor, still beautiful despite the slight warble age had brought. Bathsheba's heart stirred with the tune, knowing that peace had at last truly come, but David was right. Peace could be lost too easily. She must pray for shalom every moment of Solomon's reign.

"May they prosper who love you, O Jerusalem. Peace be within your walls, prosperity within your palaces. For the sake of my brethren and companions, I will now say, 'Peace be within you.' Because of the house of Adonai Eloheynu, I will seek your good."

The words echoed to the far reaches of the crowd, and one by one the men and women sank to the ground and bowed low before Adonai and the king.

Note from the Author

The biblical account of David and Bathsheba's story contains more details than I could flesh out in this book. How David acquired the land to build the temple, for instance, and how Absalom was killed are some of the things I chose to leave out in order to create a more solidified picture of my main characters' lives. Much research has gone into the study of these passages, but as always, any inaccuracies in historical or biblical detail are my own. I would encourage you to read 2 Samuel 7 through 1 Kings 2, along with 1 Chronicles 17–29 to get the full picture of their lives.

❧❧

To you, dear readers, a prayer:

> Lord, these really aren't my stories. You immortalized King David and his wives in the pages of Your Word. All I did was imagine how things might have been. But in the imagining, I pray that I have given hope to Your people, the men and women who will read these words.
>
> To those who have fallen far from Your grace as David

and Bathsheba once did, let them know that with You, there is forgiveness.

To those who are lonely and desperate and think that life will be better if only this or that would change, give them Your contentment.

To those who are angry or fearful or estranged from Your love, give them grace and peace to know You.

Let those who read Bathsheba's story come away changed for having known her. Let her life resonate with the theme of redemption and grace as only You can give.

🍂

To all who will read these words, thank you for giving of your time to this story. May you know the love of God, who loved David and Bathsheba in spite of what they did, and who loves you just the same.

In His grace,
Jill Eileen Smith

Acknowledgments

Though a writer may work alone getting the initial words down on paper (or computer screen), a book is never produced by one person. Without the many people who have given of their time, expertise, and prayers, my words would have never seen print. To thank them seems like an understatement, but I will do so anyway, from thc bottom of my heart.

To the team at Revell—I love working with you! You all have made my publishing experience one of great gratitude and joy. As Paul said to the Philippians, "I thank my God every time I remember you."

Special thanks to Lonnie Hull DuPont for loving *Bathsheba* as much as I do, and to Jessica Miles for helping me make this book the best it can be! To Cheryl Van Andel for another fabulous cover. If covers sell books, your designs would not need any words! To Twila, Michele, Claudia, Deonne, and the rest of the marketing/publicity team—I am in your debt. Thank you for believing in my work.

To Wendy Lawton, agent extraordinaire—I have to say it, we make a great team! I'm so grateful God put you in my life.

Jill Marie—we finished another one! I will always be grateful for the day God made us friends. Thank you for reading the first 40,000 words and telling me the truth. Starting over was tough but well worth the effort. The story rings true to me now.

A special thank-you to Dean Stengl for helping me understand Uriah's military mind-set and how he could ignore David's insistence that he go home to his wife. Your advice was most appreciated!

A special thank-you as well to Sarah Andreski for giving me insight into the heart of a military family and what it feels like to have your loved ones in danger and far from home.

To my family and friends and faithful prayer partners—I hope you know how much I appreciate and love you!

Randy—there are no heroes or kings who can compare to you. King David was an amazing man and a favorite Bible hero whom I look forward to meeting in heaven someday, but he doesn't come close to your character, your devotion, and your faithfulness. Writing this series has reminded me of just what a great man I have!

Jeff, Chris, and Ryan—my beloved sons and some great storytellers in your own right. I like to think you were doomed to love stories from birth—since Dad and I began reading to you before you could talk. Wherever life takes you, I will always treasure that we share this passion. And you know, you are always close in heart and prayer.

Adonai Yeshua, Lord Jesus, I love You. Thank You for giving us King David's story.

Jill Eileen Smith is the bestselling author of *Michal* and *Abigail*, books 1 and 2 in the Wives of King David series. When she isn't writing, she enjoys spending time with her family—in person, over the webcam, or by hopping a plane to fly across the country. She can often be found reading Christian fiction, testing new recipes, grabbing lunch with friends, or snuggling one or both of her adorable cats. She lives with her family in southeast Michigan.

To learn more about Jill or the Wives of King David series, visit http://www.jilleileensmith.com or http://www.the wivesofkingdavid.com. You can also contact Jill at jill@jill eileensmith.com. She loves hearing from her readers.

A SWEEPING BIBLICAL TALE OF PASSION AND DRAMA!

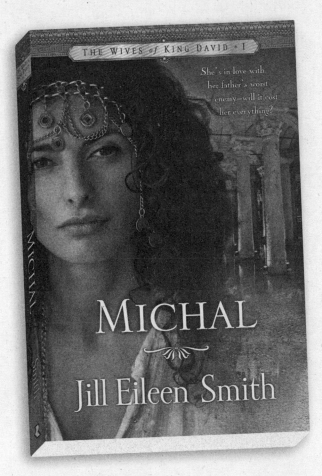

WHAT PRICE MUST SHE PAY FOR TRUE LOVE?

THE WIVES *of* KING DAVID · 2

Turmoil marked
her life—what
price must she
pay for love?

ABIGAIL

A NOVEL

Jill Eileen Smith

Her days marked by turmoil and faded dreams, Abigail has resigned herself to a life with a man she does not love. But when circumstances offer her a second chance at happiness with the handsome David, she takes a leap of faith to join his wandering tribe. Still, her struggles are far from over.

Revell
a division of Baker Publishing Group
www.RevellBooks.com

Available wherever books are sold.